The queen was not pleased. "And so you managed, in one go, to strand both my Life Mage and my general in the middle of nowhere?"

"Not to mention her husband," added Gerald.

Revi bowed. "That was certainly not my intention, Majesty. All my calculations—"

"Your calculations proved useless!" shouted the queen. "These are real people's lives you're interfering with, Master Bloom, and now you may have crippled the realm's defences by divesting us of two of our greatest resources!" Anna closed her eyes, taking a deep breath.

Gerald watched her try to control her anger. She'd planned to travel to Weldwyn with King Alric, but events here were spiralling out of control. First came the threat of an attack on Stonecastle, then word the north may also be in danger. It was too much, and the stress was beginning to take its toll on her.

Anna opened her eyes, her voice once more calm. "Have you a theory as to what went wrong?"

"I do, Majesty, though I have no way of verifying it."

"Then let's hear it."

"I suspect they were carried farther east along the ley lines. It's the only explanation that makes sense."

"How much farther?"

"That I cannot say, but the distance must be significant if Lady Aubrey cannot recall back to Wincaster."

Gerald glanced around the throne room. The queen liked to hold an open court once a week to hear the pleas of the common folk, but news of this calamity interrupted the event. She quickly dismissed those in attendance, save for her inner circle. He noted the Orc shaman watching from the side. "Master Kraloch, have you heard anything?"

"I have, indeed, Marshal. Lady Aubrey contacted me using her magic. All three travellers are well, but the gate they came through collapsed, and her power is insufficient for the return journey."

"They're a clever bunch. If I know them, they've already formulated a plan."

"They have," said Kraloch. "I suggested they travel north to find a land called Reinwick. There is a tribe of Orcs nearby who can introduce them to the duke ruling there."

# Also by Paul J Bennett

# ENEMY OF THE CROWN

Heir to the Crown: Book Twelve

PAUL J BENNETT

First Edition: August 2023

ePub ISBN: 978-1-990073-63-2
Mobi ISBN: 978-1-990073-64-9
Smashwords ISBN: 978-1-990073-65-6
Print ISBN: 978-1-990073-44-1

# Dedication

*To my niece Rebecca Polsinelli who loved to read.*

*1983 - 2023*

*Lost much too soon.*

*You will be forever in our hearts.*

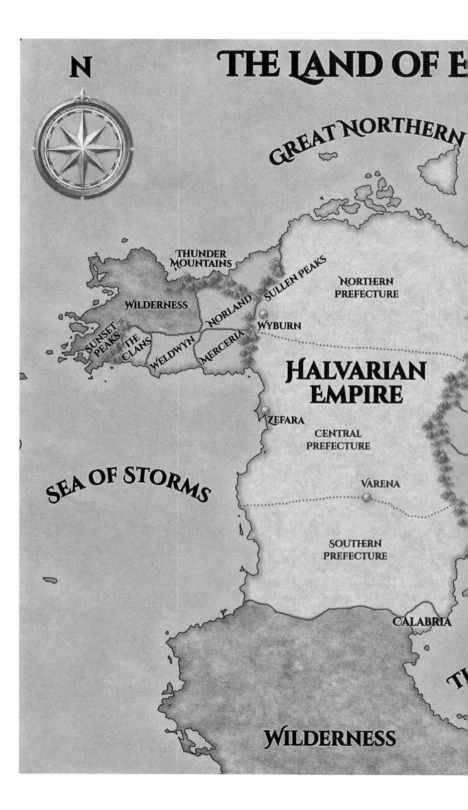

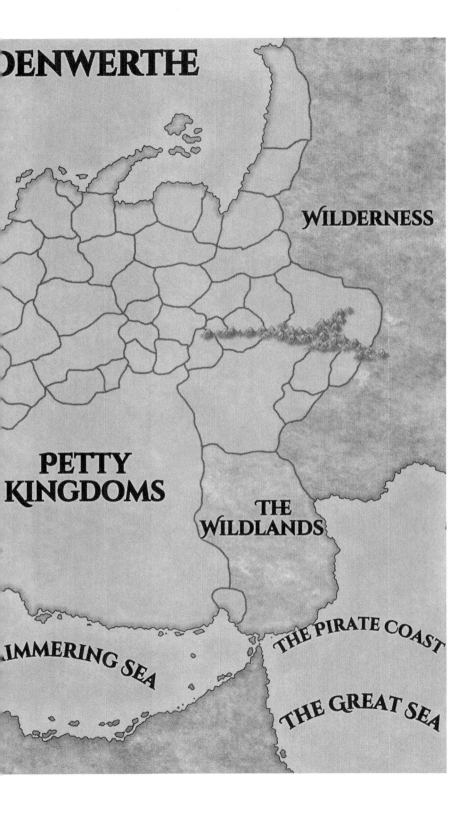

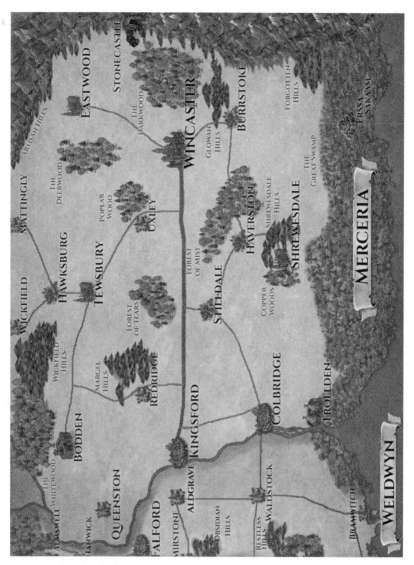

Map of Merceria

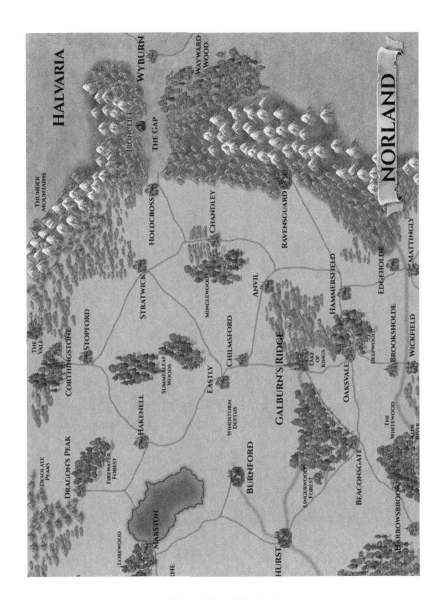

Map of East-Norland

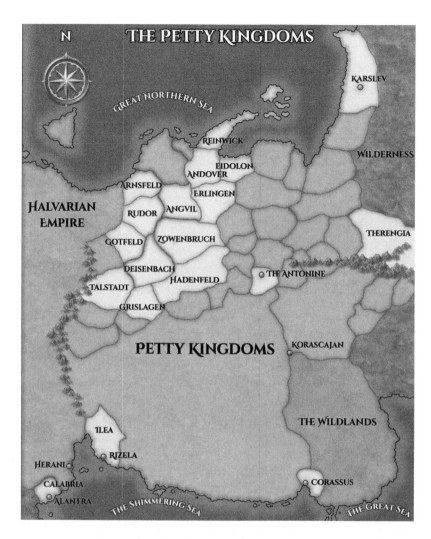

Map of Petty Kingdoms

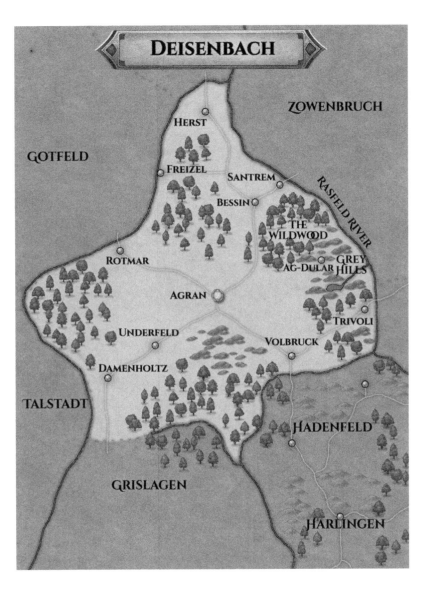

Map of Deisenbach

# ONE

## Empire

### AUTUMN 967 MC* (MERCERIAN CALENDAR)

Nevarus stood on the balcony, staring out over the vast lands of his estate as dozens of men and women toiled away in the lush gardens surrounding the Imperial Palace. The leaves had not yet begun to turn, but a chill in the air was a reminder the warmer days of summer had now passed.

The sight gave him pause. Just how many people were employed thus? He knew the Palace grounds stretched for miles, but he'd visited very little. As Emperor of Halvaria, he bore a heavy responsibility that kept him too busy to concern himself with mundane matters. Still, the question of numbers nagged at him. He turned, looking around the room at the trio of servants standing ready should he need them.

His gaze settled on the eldest one. "Janek, how many people work the fields here at the Palace?"

"I have no idea, Eminence."

"You must have some inkling."

The old fellow looked up at the ceiling, thinking. "A few hundred, perhaps? More, if you include those who work inside."

"How long have you been with us?"

Janek blinked. "Have I upset you, Eminence?"

"No. I merely wonder how long you have served the Imperial House. I seem to remember your presence under my father's rule, and here I am, decades later, and you're still hobbling around the place."

"Forty-seven years, Eminence. Give or take a few days."

"And in all that time, you never stopped to wonder at the sheer scale of it all?"

"I have little time for such frivolities, Eminence."

Nevarus laughed. "Careful now, Janek. You come close to insulting me." All colour fled the old servant's face. "Relax, man. It was said in jest. Your appointment to this court is still secure. After all, I need someone around here older than me, if only to remind myself of my own mortality."

"But you are a god amongst men, Eminence."

"As was my father, who, I will point out, died of old age. Descendants of gods we might be, but our time amongst mortal folk still has its limits."

He saw the blank look on the servant's face and sighed. No one disagreed with the emperor, for he was a living god and could do no wrong. It did, however, make for a lack of discourse. Nevarus yearned for his youth when the scholars allowed him to debate topics of interest. These days, all he ever saw was obedience and acceptance. Just once, he'd like someone to disagree with his choices, to feel alive again!

As he mulled over the possibility, the door opened.

Janek's gaze flicked to the newcomer. "The High Regent, Eminence."

Nevarus turned to his son and heir, twelve-year-old Karoulus, who'd spent less than a tenth of his years in his father's presence. Each week, the boy would be paraded out, they would exchange pleasantries, and then he would be taken away to continue his education. It had been the same for Nevarus, and doubtless, the tradition would continue with his grandson when the time came.

"I trust your studies are progressing well?"

"Indeed, Father. I am told I possess a particular affinity for mathematics."

The emperor frowned. "That is not a skill you will need when the empire bows before you. I suggest you concentrate on more useful endeavours."

"Such as?"

Nevarus ignored the boy's question. "What else have you learned?"

"Recent studies include the history of the cleansing."

"Ah. Now there's a subject I am familiar with. What have they told you?"

"It is an ongoing effort to weed out the most subversive elements of society. Great strides have been made in centuries past, so much so that today the Office of High Purifier is mostly ceremonial."

"I suppose that's true to a certain extent, but only their constant vigilance keeps us safe. Tell me, what draws a purifier's attention?"

"Acts or behaviour contrary to the natural order."

"That being?"

"Your rule, of course."

"No," said the emperor. "I mean, what sort of acts? Give me some examples?"

The youth's mouth hung open as he fought for words, but then he swallowed. "I... I'm not sure."

"Do not be ashamed. You are still young and have much to learn."

"Then what acts are considered subversive?"

"They are too numerous to warrant a full discussion, but three are considered the worst."

"And they are?"

"Worshipping a false god, obedience to a foreign ruler, and criticizing the emperor or his policies. Hold those three at bay, and we keep dissent to a minimum."

"And that's all there is to it?"

Nevarus chuckled. "It has kept the peace for centuries."

"Yet are we not almost continuously at war."

"That is our heritage, but also our destiny."

"You're talking about the great dream," said Karoulus. "The inevitable result being us ruling over the entire Continent. Tell me, Father, will that occur in my lifetime?"

"Even I don't know the answer to that. Each generation, we expand our borders a little more, our enemies growing weaker as we grow stronger. There will come a day when our legions will pour across our eastern borders one final time, conquering what remains of the Petty Kingdoms."

"And what comes afterwards?"

"Peace and tranquillity will stretch from sea to sea, allowing all to live out their lives as they should, in worshipful devotion to their God-Emperor."

"And what of those we defeat?" asked Karoulus.

"Even you, with your limited education, should be able to work that out. What has happened in the past when we conquered a land?"

"The truthseekers spread across the newly acquired area, locating areas of discontent."

"And then?"

"The purifiers move in?"

"Are you telling me or asking me?"

A knock at the door saved Karoulus from having to provide an answer.

"Who is it?" called out Nevarus.

"The High Strategos, Eminence," came the answer. "I am here to conduct you to your meeting with the High Council."

The emperor's heart sank. It appeared his time with his son was to be cut short once again. He looked back at Karoulus. "Continue with your studies but mark my words. When next we meet, I shall expect you to be able to answer my questions in greater detail."

"Yes, Father."

"Janek. Escort him back to his quarters."

"Yes, Eminence."

Nevarus waited until they left before making his way to the door. A servant opened it at his approach, revealing the countenance of Exalor, the High Strategos. The emperor walked past him without a word, and the fellow fell in behind him, his footsteps echoing on the marble floor.

"How long must we continue with this farce?" Kelson Shozarin sat back, smiling at the looks of disapproval the rest of the council sent his way. As High Sentinel, he was the most powerful Life Mage in the empire, but he didn't need his magic to tell what the others were thinking. There were six seats on the High Council, seven if you included the emperor's, yet the three lines had divided its membership into equal parts like everything else within the empire.

"You should watch that tongue of yours," warned Enelle. "Else, I might have to cut it out."

He merely laughed, which only fed her annoyance. She was the High Purifier and a Sartellian, but that didn't give her the right to order other members of the High Council about.

Footsteps grew closer, then everyone stood as the emperor entered the room. Behind him came the High Strategos himself, Exalor.

His Eminence sat in his customary seat, gazing over those assembled, stopping at the only empty chair. "Where is the High Magister?"

"In the north, Eminence," said Kelson, looking at the remaining seat. "I'm told troubles on the border delayed his departure."

"What kind of troubles?"

"Nothing you need worry about, Eminence."

"Yet bad enough that it requires my most powerful mage!"

Kelson was at a loss for words even as his fellow council members turned to him expectantly.

"Well?" snapped the emperor. "Have you an answer?"

"My understanding is he's inspecting the mages attached to the Seventh Legion, Eminence."

"And that would be where, exactly?"

"On our northwest border."

"And what about that region requires the personal attention of one of my council?"

"I can answer that," offered Exalor. "We've had disturbing news of late concerning the lands west of us, beyond the Sullen Peaks."

"And by disturbing, you mean…"

"I'm afraid there is no easy way to say this, Eminence. It has come to our attention the lands therein employ mercenaries who are not Human."

"Are you suggesting they employ the mountain folk?"

"Worse—Orcs."

Enelle snorted. "Are you trying to tell us you're afraid of greenskins, Your Grace?"

Exalor shook his head. "We are not talking about a small, wandering tribe here, but a large, organized, and might I add, a well-armoured and equipped army."

"Surely you're not suggesting they're a threat to the strength of the empire?"

"Not as long as we take them seriously, no."

The emperor steepled his fingers. "Fascinating. Have we any idea of their numbers? Is this a few companies or an entire legion's worth?"

"Nothing that the Seventh can't deal with, given sufficient resources. It might, however, be in our best interest to reinforce the area."

"We shall do a good sight more than that. What legions are nearby?"

"The Fifth is the closest, Eminence, but even that is almost a thousand miles away."

"Have we none in the central prefecture?"

"We do," said Exalor, "but it is currently employed in keeping the mountain folk at bay."

"Ah," said the emperor. "The mountain folk. Is there no end to their interference?"

"That region offers little danger to us, Eminence."

"Then why the need to maintain a legion in the vicinity?"

"To prevent them from spreading lies about us," replied Enelle. "Of course, if you wish, we could destroy their mountain stronghold. That would, no doubt, free up an abundance of men."

"That sounds like an excellent idea. See to it at once, Exalor, before they tie down any more of my warriors."

The High Strategos bowed. "Of course, Eminence."

"Good. Now tell me more about these savages?"

"Do you mean the Orcs or the Dwarves?" asked Enelle.

"Orcs, of course. Have we the location of their home?"

"We do, Eminence. In a kingdom called Merceria, which we've been monitoring for some time now."

The emperor locked eyes with his High Scholar, Karliss Stormwind. "What can you tell me about the place?"

"It is a relatively small realm," the woman replied, "akin to those found in the Petty Kingdoms to the east. In some ways, they are more primitive, having only recently acquired the knowledge of fabricating heavy armour. Their army is roughly the size of a legion but is dispersed, making it difficult to mass in one place."

"Have we a plan to absorb them?"

"Naturally," said Exalor. "Your Eminence need only give the word, and we can make the final arrangements."

"What of our plans for the east?" asked Kelson. "Surely you're not suggesting we abandon them?"

"You forget your place," said Exalor. "It is not your prerogative to question the God-Emperor's decisions."

"It is not his decisions I question, it is yours. Clearly, you have something in mind, else you wouldn't raise the subject, yet I see no indication of what this plan of yours might consist of."

"I suggest you confine your interests to the actions of your truthseekers and leave the strategy to others."

"Still," said the emperor. "He makes a good point."

"I can assure Your Eminence we have a solid plan, but coordinating it will take some time."

"How long?"

"Were you to give the order today, the legions could be crossing the border by the end of the month."

"Legions? How many are we talking about?"

"Three, Eminence. It's part of an overall strategy meant to overwhelm the Mercerian army, but as I said, it must be properly coordinated. If one moves too soon, it might upset the entire strategy."

"I would like to hear more of this plan," said the emperor.

"And I shall be delighted to inform you of the details, Eminence, but it would be best to use the map room if I am to explain it in detail." Exalor glanced around the room. "There is also the matter of who should be privy to such information. We don't want to burden the rest of the council with such matters; they have enough work keeping up with their own responsibilities."

The emperor nodded at his suggestion. "Set up the map room, and ensure the marshals provide the most up-to-date information. I expect a full report."

"Yes, Eminence."

"How long will it take you to gather what you need?"

"I can have everything ready this very evening if you wish."

"Good. Then I shall see you after dinner." The emperor rose, forcing the others to stand. "I look forward to hearing the details."

He strode from the room, and a collective sigh went up as the door closed.

"It seems some of us have work to do," said Exalor. "I suggest we reconvene tomorrow."

"I second that," said Kelson. "All in favour?"

The others in the room nodded.

"Very well," he continued. "The meeting is adjourned."

As the other High Council members exited, Exalor sat back while Kelson gathered his notes, but neither stood up.

"That went well."

"Yes, it did," said Exalor. "Though you didn't need to be so surly."

"I couldn't risk the emperor suspecting that we were working together. You did an excellent job of manipulating him, by the way. Been practicing, have we?"

"I'm not fond of playing this game, but we understand what's at risk. If that means playing along with an emperor who believes he's in command, then so be it. You and I both know the real power behind the Gilded Throne."

"Speaking of which, are they all aware of this plan?"

"Of course. You're not suggesting I'd present it to that fool if they weren't, are you? I've been planning this for months."

"Months? More like years. I remember you mentioning the idea at the emperor's ascension, and that had to be eight years ago."

"Seven and a half, actually, but I concede the point. The issue of Merceria has been on my mind for some time, but events there took on a life of their own, and it looked like their internal squabbling would be sufficient to neutralize the threat."

"A war?"

"An uprising, actually. We convinced one of their earls to make a play for the Crown. Ultimately, he failed, but it caused a lot of strife."

"Yet the Mercerians are still there."

"They are, but they were substantially weakened after that. It would've been the end of them had it not been for their pesky allies who aided in a second rebellion that put a young girl on the Throne, and she's been there ever since."

"But that's a good thing, surely?"

"It is, and it isn't," said Exalor. "On the one hand, she divested the Crown of direct leadership of the army."

"And the bad news?"

"She managed to cultivate an unexpectedly competent marshal to lead her army."

Kelson laughed. "Do you seriously expect me to believe one of those commoners rivals your knowledge of battle?"

"It is not unheard of for the enemy to possess great military minds. To think otherwise is sheer folly."

"Yes, but he's not a trained battle mage, is he? And look at your experience. Who could possibly rival that?"

"Halvaria has not been without its losses."

"You're talking about that trouble in Arnsfeld. You know that wasn't your fault."

"I am the High Strategos. I should have known the Marshal of the North was organizing that expedition. He even convinced the emperor to send some of his personal companies. It should never have happened!"

"You were busy in the south," said Kelson.

"Yes, suppressing yet more Orcs. I swear the southern continent is full of them."

"Surely that's the southern marshal's responsibility?"

"In theory, yes, but I was lured into believing my expertise was needed. I suspect it was an elaborate ruse to draw my attention away from the north."

"Who would do such a thing?"

"Who, indeed?"

They stared at each other until Kelson pointed at his own chest. "Surely you don't suspect me. What would I possibly gain by doing such a thing? I control the truthseekers, not the legions. If you want to discover who might be responsible, I suggest you look closer to home. If anyone would benefit, it would be one of your marshals. You must know all three plot to replace you. The only thing keeping them from doing so is their utter dislike for each other."

"Which makes it all the more unlikely that two of them would work together to distract me."

"Then tell me whom you suspect, and I'll set my truthseekers on them. If anyone can get to the heart of the matter, it's them."

"Come now," said Exalor. "You and I both know there's no such thing as a truthseeker. They confirm whatever you want them to. I may not be a Life Mage, but I understand how your Life Magic works. Did you forget I trained with you at the College of Mages?"

"No. Of course not, but the offer still stands. Give me the names of those you want to be removed, and I'll see to the rest."

The High Strategos sat back. "Thank you," he said. "It's nice to have someone I can trust on the High Council."

"Well," said Kelson, "much as I'd like to stay and chat, you need to gather the reports from the marshals, then get back here before the meeting with the emperor tonight. As to the other matter, I promise to look into it. It shouldn't be too hard to uncover if someone is plotting to circumvent your orders."

"You should try not to be too obvious. We don't want to scare them off."

"Oh? I should think that's exactly what we want to do. Taking flight would confirm our suspicions, but I will honour your request. I promise." He hesitated. "Anything else I can do to lend a hand?"

"No. I believe you've done enough for today."

# TWO

# Stranded

AUTUMN 967 MC

Beverly stared at the broken stones. "I don't suppose there's any chance of repairing this archway?"

"I'm afraid not," replied Aubrey. "Even if we knew how to build a new one, I can't empower it."

"And you're certain you can't contact the gate in Wincaster?"

"Absolutely. Nor any other, unfortunately."

"What kind of distance are we talking about?"

"Well, I've used recall to travel from Wincaster to Ironcliff, and that's reckoned at close to five hundred miles."

"So, we must be at least that far east?"

"I would think so," said Aubrey, "but that's only a starting point. We could be thousands of miles from where we started, but there's no way to tell."

Aldwin, who'd been picking through the stones, stood, brushing dust off his shoulders. "At least we know we went east."

"What makes you so sure?"

"The sun is in the same relative position."

Beverly smiled. "When did you start taking an interest in the sky?"

"Ever since I found that skystone back in Bodden."

"How do you figure we didn't travel west?"

"I suppose that's a possibility, but Weldwyn is said to be very open. You've been there; what do you think?"

"I agree with your husband," said Aubrey. "This does not look like any part of Weldwyn I've ever seen. What about the Clanholdings?"

"They're said to be quite bleak," replied Beverly. "Any theories about how we ended up here, wherever here is? Could Revi have made a mistake?"

"I reviewed his calculations. There were no errors I could spot."

"Then what happened?"

"My guess would be we're farther east along the same ley line we started on. As you are aware, nodes occur when the north-south ley lines intersect with the east-west ones."

"Yes. I remember Revi telling us that, but by his calculation, we should be about a hundred miles east of Stonecastle."

"And I suspect we would have, were the nodes not interfered with."

"Interfered with?" said Aldwin. "How?"

"I'm not sure. Buried, perhaps? If the other nodes were like this one, there might be stone structures atop them. That may have somehow got in the way."

"Like plugging a spring and stopping the water?"

"Exactly. Either that or someone went to a lot of trouble to purposely block them."

"Why would someone do that?"

"We know the Elves destroyed many Saurian gates back home. Perhaps something similar happened here?"

"Well," said Beverly, "we can't stand around all day debating how we got here. We should concentrate on finding a way home."

"Don't look at me," said Aldwin. "I'm a smith, not an explorer. Where would you suggest we begin?"

"Let's take stock of what we have," said Beverly. "We're all uninjured and have horses, so we're off to a good start. Does anyone have any food?" She looked at her companions, but they both shook their heads.

"How about coins?"

"I have a few," said Aldwin. "I was going to surprise you by taking you to the Queen's Arms once we were done." He dug through his purse. "Do you suppose they'd accept Mercerian coins here?"

Aubrey laughed. "We don't even know where here is. Not that it's likely to matter. Gold is gold. It's more about the coin's weight than whose picture adorns it. I have a few crowns, but I doubt they'd be enough to see us home."

"There's a few in Lightning's saddlebag," added Beverly. "I would've brought more, but I never expected to be stranded in the middle of nowhere." She looked around the area. What was left of the standing stones lay atop a small hill, giving them a nice view of the surrounding countryside.

"No sign of civilization," she said, "although the area looks quite lush, if those trees to the north are any indication. I doubt finding water will be a problem."

"What about food?" asked Aldwin.

"I wouldn't worry too much about that yet," replied Aubrey. "I've spent a fair amount of time in the Whitewood. I'm confident I'll find something to eat."

"Are you suggesting you can hunt?"

"Only for nuts and berries, but it'll be enough to sustain us in the short term. The more important question might be which direction do we travel."

"West, surely?" said Aldwin. "That's the most likely way home."

"Is it, but that would take us closer to Halvaria."

"That was our intention in coming here, wasn't it? To learn more about them?"

"That was when we assumed we could manage a safe return. We could still have hundreds of miles to traverse. Do you really want to do that through potentially hostile lands?"

"No. I suppose not. But if not west, then where?"

"I suggest north," said Beverly. "If we travel as far as the great sea there, we might be able to take a ship back to Merceria."

"Merceria has no northern coast."

"True," said Aubrey, "but all we really need to do is get me within five hundred miles of one of our circles. The most likely candidate would be the one at Ironcliff."

"Sounds like a reasonable proposition," said Aldwin. "We'll head north until we find a road, which would, in theory, lead us to a city or town. Once we're amongst civilized folk, we can get a better idea of where we are."

"Agreed," said Aubrey. "Would you like to lead, Cousin?"

"Shouldn't you contact Kraloch first, and let everyone back home know what's befallen us?"

"Yes, I suppose I should. I'll use my spell of spirit talk. You two keep an eye open. The last thing I need is a wild animal gnawing at my limbs while I'm casting a spell."


Aubrey closed her eyes, concentrating. She reached out with her magic, feeling it swell inside her, then the familiar ghostly image of Kraloch appeared before her.

"Aubrey?" said the Orc shaman. "Why are you contacting me? Have you something to report?"

"We are stranded," she replied. "Revi's spell took us farther than expected, and I cannot use my magic to recall to Wincaster."

"This is dire news. Is anyone injured?"

"No. We are well, but the trip was meant to be a short one. Thus, we have little in the way of provisions."

"Where are you?"

"That remains to be determined. I suspect we are east of our intended destination, likely along the same ley line, but I can't be certain. We've decided to travel north in hopes of reaching the Great Northern Sea. You've mentioned we have allies there?"

"Yes. A tribe called the Ashwalkers. They aided Shaluhk's friends in a place called Reinwick. They will be able to take your plight to the duke if you can reach them. Does that help you?"

"It gives us something to focus on, although I have no idea how far Reinwick would be from our present position. Aldwin says the sky is the same here, so we haven't wandered too far south or north."

"What is the land like there? Is it warmer or colder than Merceria?"

"About the same."

Kraloch nodded. "I would agree with your earlier assessment. Likely, you are merely farther east than intended. There is a good chance you may be in amongst the Petty Kingdoms, but bear in mind, we have no idea how large Halvaria is. You might just as well be in its eastern region."

"We'll know more once we reach some sort of civilization. Are there Orcs in Halvaria?"

"None that we are aware of. It is rumoured the empire took steps to eradicate our race, much as the Elves did long ago, but we have no proof of it. I shall reach out to other shamans to be on the lookout for you, but the Continent is vast, and the likelihood of them finding you is slim."

"Thank you," said Aubrey. "I'll contact you again when there's something new to report."

"I shall inform the queen of your situation." He paused a moment. "Be careful, Aubrey. The Continent is a dangerous place."

"We will be. I'll talk to you again soon." She let the magic expire, watching his image fade.

Beverly drew closer. "Well? How did it go?"

"About as well as expected. Kraloch mentioned a tribe called the Ashwalkers, who live in a place called Reinwick, which sits astride the Great Northern Sea. Are you familiar with it?"

"Can't say I am. Has it a port?"

"I assume so. Kraloch thinks we could get help from the duke who rules there."

"It's as good a place as any to start, but we'll take it slow. There's still the possibility we're in Halvarian territory."

. . .

They mounted up, then headed down the hill towards the distant woods. The sounds of birds and insects greeted them once they were beneath its boughs.

"It's peaceful here," said Aubrey.

"Yes," agreed Aldwin. "Reminds me of the Whitewood, but without all the birch trees. You don't suppose there's a Druid living here, do you?"

"I shouldn't think so. Our own experience would indicate magic is rare. You can't just pick a spot in the middle of nowhere and expect to find one, particularly an Earth Mage."

"Speaking of mages," said Beverly, "how's that new magic school of yours coming along?"

"It's had its difficulties, but we're finally making progress. Our initial batch of students have all cast their first spell and look forward to learning more."

"And what spell was that?"

"The orb of light," replied Aubrey, "which has the advantage of being a universal spell that any mage can learn."

"And what do they learn after that?"

"That depends on the individual. We have two Earth Mages, so that's easy enough with Albreda and Aldus Hearn to teach them. We also have Clara, under the tutelage of Kraloch, learning Life Magic."

"And the others?"

Aubrey frowned. "That's where things get a little difficult. Kurzak shows great promise as a Fire Mage, but we must rely on the Weldwyn mage, Osbourne Megantis, to train him."

"And why is that a problem?"

"Kurzak is an Orc, and his mastery of our language isn't strong. To add to the problem, Osbourne is... How can I put it?"

"Rude?"

"I would have said impatient, but I suppose it amounts to the same thing."

"What of Princess Edwina?"

"Kraloch has been acting as a go-between with an Orc named Rotuk, a master of air. The exchange has been quite promising, but learning a spell over such a distance through others is proving difficult."

"And they'll be able to carry on in your absence?"

"I certainly hope so," said Aubrey. "The intention was to create a place of learning that didn't require the constant presence of any one of us. In any case, I'm just another Life Mage. Both Kraloch and Revi can take my place at the drop of a hat."

"Hah," said Aldwin. "Somehow, I can't see Master Revi enjoying taking on a new student."

"I might remind you I was once his apprentice."

"Yes, but you practically taught yourself, didn't you?"

"I read everything about magic I could find, but that's a far cry from teaching myself. Revi did teach me my first spell."

"I remember," added Beverly, "although it seems to me you outgrew his tutelage quickly."

"Well, we were separated by the war."

"And now you're one of our most capable mages."

"I don't think I would go that far."

"Kraloch clearly respects you," said Aldwin. "You're the only Human mage to be taught the spell of spirit talking, aren't you?"

"As far as I'm aware, yes."

"It's strange, isn't it?" said Beverly. "We grow up under someone who trains us, but then we're equals, comrades even."

"You're referring to Gerald?"

"I am. He was like an uncle to me, yet now he's one of my peers. It's quite strange when you think about it."

"How do you imagine I feel?" said Aldwin, grinning. "I was raised as a smith. Now, here I am, hobnobbing with a couple of baronesses?"

"You are technically a baron," said Aubrey.

"I'm not the Master of Bodden—that's Beverly's birthright."

"And you're married to her. You should at least consider yourself a lord."

"I think baron suits him," said Beverly. "Besides, who's going to argue the point here? And for all we know, women might not be allowed to hold titles in these parts."

"I doubt I could act the part," said Aldwin. "I'm not exactly dressed like a noble."

"Nonsense," said Beverly. "You've spent enough time at court, and it's not as if we won't be there to watch your back."

"Assuming we are in the Petty Kingdoms, what do we know about that area?"

"Not much," replied Aubrey. "According to Kraloch, it's a large collection of realms covering most of the Continent. Apparently, they vary in size considerably, but most are run by either a king or duke. I believe there may be a principality or two in there somewhere. He also said many alliances often work against each other, so we would do well to keep our political opinions to ourselves for the time being."

"Anything else?"

"Nothing I can think of off the top of my head. Most of the information I have concerns Therengia, which lies to the east, far removed from the politics of the Petty Kingdoms." She noted Aldwin's look of confusion. "Kraloch often talks to Shaluhk, a shaman of the Red Hand, a tribe of Orcs that's part of that realm."

"Oh yes," said the smith. "I believe you've mentioned her before. Have you ever spoken to her yourself?"

"A few times, but not as often as I'd like. We both have much knowledge to exchange, particularly regarding spells, but the academy has kept me busy. I'm surprised I even found time to come on this little expedition of yours."

"Not mine," said Aldwin. "This was Beverly's idea."

"Well," added his wife, "it was actually Revi's. I just volunteered to be the one to go through the gate first. Look on the bright side. At least we're together. It could be worse—we could be stuck with Aldus Hearn?"

"He's not that bad," replied Aubrey.

"I exaggerate a little, but you must admit, the man is fond of telling his stories."

"So is Gerald."

"Yes, but Gerald's are much more interesting."

"Very well. I'll concede the point for now."

The woods grew darker as the thickening canopy of trees blocked the sun's rays. They continued in silence, alert lest danger threaten. Beverly led, Lightning easily picking his way through the sparse underbrush. There was no sign of civilization here, no footprints to follow, or signs of abandoned houses, giving the place a feeling of tranquillity.

Beverly halted, looking around, searching for something. "Do you hear it?" she called out.

"Is that a stream?" asked Aldwin.

"It is," added Aubrey. "Off to the right."

Beverly led them through the trees towards the sound, the suddenly thick underbrush forcing them to dismount and proceed on foot until they arrived at a steady stream, gurgling as it meandered north.

After a refreshing drink, they sat by the bank, letting their mounts rest. Aubrey found a blueberry bush with a few remaining berries, giving them something to quiet their empty stomachs.

"How far do you think we've gone?" asked Aldwin.

"Five miles?" offered Aubrey.

"Close to six, I'd say," added Beverly. "From here, I suggest we travel downstream. This likely drains into a larger river, and we might discover some boats on the water."

"Or possibly fish," suggested Aldwin. "I don't suppose either of you know how to coax them out of the water?"

"I hate to dash your hopes," said Aubrey, "but Beverly and I were raised as nobles. Fishing is more likely something you would have experience with."

"Don't look at me. I spent all my time in the smithy. The only food I know how to eat is the stuff presented to me on a plate. What about your magic? Could that help?"

"How? By healing the fish? I can't imagine that helping much. How about Nature's Fury?"

Beverly laughed. "What am I supposed to do, rap them on the head and stun them? Now, if we had Kasri's hammer, that would be an entirely different matter."

"Ah, yes," said Aldwin. "Stormhammer, a most remarkable weapon. It can send bolts of lightning flying through the air. Very impressive."

"So is Nature's Fury," said Beverly, "and it's even better. Do you know why?"

"Because the power of the earth resides within it?"

"No. Because you made it for me."

"Albreda empowered it, not me."

"Yes, but that wouldn't have been possible had you not crafted it in the first place." She unhooked it from her belt and held it up. Even here, in the shadow of the trees, it captured the light, reflecting it back tenfold. She smiled. "How many people can say the love of their life forged them a weapon?"

Aldwin grinned. "I'd make you another if there were any skystone left, but I used the last of it for our wedding rings."

"I don't need another weapon." She stared into his grey eyes. "You know I'd give it all up to be with you."

He chuckled. "You already ARE with me, and I'd never ask you to give up anything. You are the Rose of Bodden, Beverly, General of the Army of Merceria, Queen's Champion, and Knight Commander of the Knights of the Hound. Did I miss anything? Oh yes, the Baroness of Bodden."

"You forgot the most important honour of all, that of being your wife!" She leaned forward, their lips meeting as they came together.

After a moment, Aubrey cleared her throat. "I hate to be the one to interrupt, but we really should move on before we lose the daylight."

They broke their embrace and climbed back on their horses, following the stream once more.

"What about you, Aubrey?" asked Aldwin. "Are there any potential suitors in your near future?"

"No," said Aubrey. "Most definitely not. No offence, but the last thing I need is additional demands on my time. I intend to devote my life to improving my magic."

"Revi seems quite happy with Hayley in his life."

"Yes, and I might remind you, Master Revi sent us out here, into the middle of nowhere. I'm not saying he was distracted, but a little more study on his part would likely have served us well."

# THREE

# Home

AUTUMN 967 MC

The queen was not pleased. "And so you managed, in one go, to strand both my Life Mage and my general in the middle of nowhere?"

"Not to mention her husband," added Gerald.

Revi bowed. "That was certainly not my intention, Majesty. All my calculations—"

"Your calculations proved useless!" shouted the queen. "These are real people's lives you're interfering with, Master Bloom, and now you may have crippled the realm's defences by divesting us of two of our greatest resources!" Anna closed her eyes, taking a deep breath.

Gerald watched her try to control her anger. She'd planned to travel to Weldwyn with King Alric, but events here were spiralling out of control. First came the threat of an attack on Stonecastle, then word the north may also be in danger. It was too much, and the stress was beginning to take its toll on her.

Anna opened her eyes, her voice once more calm. "Have you a theory as to what went wrong?"

"I do, Majesty, though I have no way of verifying it."

"Then let's hear it."

"I suspect they were carried farther east along the ley lines. It's the only explanation that makes sense."

"How much farther?"

"That I cannot say, but the distance must be significant if Lady Aubrey cannot recall back to Wincaster."

Gerald glanced around the throne room. The queen liked to hold an open court once a week to hear the pleas of the common folk, but news of this calamity interrupted the event. She quickly dismissed those in atten-dance, save for her inner circle. He noted the Orc shaman watching from the side. "Master Kraloch, have you heard anything?"

"I have, indeed, Marshal. Lady Aubrey contacted me using her magic. All three travellers are well, but the gate they came through collapsed, and her power is insufficient for the return journey."

"They're a clever bunch. If I know them, they've already formulated a plan."

"They have," said Kraloch. "I suggested they travel north to find a land called Reinwick. There is a tribe of Orcs nearby who can introduce them to the duke ruling there."

"And how far must they travel?" asked the queen.

"I am afraid we do not know, Majesty. They are hoping to come across a village or town that can provide information regarding their whereabouts."

Anna glared back at Revi. "Is there any way to send them supplies, at least?"

"I could try, Majesty, but if the gate collapsed, as Master Kraloch indi-cated, then there's no guarantee they would arrive at the appropriate loca-tion. In any case, they're likely long gone by now."

"Why was I not informed of this sooner?"

"We weren't expecting them to return for some time. I had no indication that anything had gone wrong until Aubrey contacted Kraloch. I tried to reestablish the gate, but it failed, which is not surprising, considering the other end collapsed."

"I've a good mind to send you through the gate and be rid of you, Master Revi, but that would place an undue strain on Master Kraloch."

"It would take more than Master Kraloch to replace me!" The words were said in haste, and the mage immediately realized his mistake. "My apologies, Majesty. I meant no offence."

"It is not me to whom you should apologize."

"Then I ask for Master Kraloch's forgiveness."

"It is not necessary," replied the Orc. "These are trying times, and the current situation has frayed the nerves of all."

"Yes," agreed Gerald. "Now that we've finished hurling insults around and blaming others, perhaps we can work on finding a solution?"

"There is none," admitted Revi. "I'm afraid their return to Merceria is something only they can accomplish."

"Master Revi speaks the truth," said Kraloch, "although I can at least keep in touch with Lady Aubrey."

"What of her lands?" asked Gerald. "I know Beverly has someone to look after Bodden, but who will manage Hawksburg while she's trapped half a world away?"

"Orcs of the Black Arrow have been assisting her in running the barony for years. Urgon is there, too, and I am sure he is more than capable of continuing on in her absence."

Anna nodded her agreement. "Much as I dislike the idea of my subjects being stranded in a foreign land, Kraloch is right. Other things are happening here that need our attention." She turned to her marshal. "Where should we start?"

"I suggest the first order of business be Stonecastle. Beverly was placed in command of the area, but with her gone, I'll need to pick a replacement."

"Have you anyone in particular in mind?"

"Yes. Herdwin. He's already there and has a reasonably good relationship with Vard Khazad, plus the Mercerians there respect him."

"Has he anyone to assist in that capacity?"

"Kasri," replied Gerald, "but if the news from Ironcliff grows any more dire, she may wish to return home."

"Just how dire is it?" asked Revi.

"It has yet to break out into full-scale conflict, if that's what you're asking, but it won't be long before the Halvarians march through the gap."

"How much time do you think we have?" asked the queen.

"It's late in the year," said Gerald. "I doubt they'd march in winter, but as soon as the spring thaw comes, I expect they'll be on the move."

"Have we learned anything of their plans?"

"No. Everything we've looked at so far has been simple speculation on our part. We know next to nothing about their organization or the composition of their armies."

"Armies?" said Revi. "You mean to say they have more than one?"

"Most assuredly, unless you think their army is so large, they can assault Stonecastle and Ironcliff simultaneously?"

"And we know for certain it is Halvaria in both locations?"

"Herdwin and Kasri saw the enemy in the eastern passes in person, and Thalgrun's scouts have kept a close eye on the army threatening Ironcliff."

"Are we sure they are determined to attack? Perhaps they fear an attack by the Dwarves?"

"Anything is possible," said Gerald, "but it matters little. We can't simply sit here and ignore a large army that's placed itself close to an ally."

"Then we must send help," insisted Anna.

"I'd love to, but there are complications. If Halvaria intends to attack Stonecastle, we should consider what would happen if they broke through."

"They would flood into Merceria."

"Precisely, but we need a better idea of their numbers. We can't march men north if it leaves us unable to defend our home."

Kraloch took a step closer. "If I may? I might have a solution."

"Go on," urged the queen.

"Allow me to travel to the Whitewood. There, I shall seek out Albreda. With her magic, we can spy out the enemy at Stonecastle, perhaps even get an accurate account of their strength."

"Very well, Master Kraloch. Please leave as soon as you are able."

Kraloch stood in Wincaster's magic circle, gathering his thoughts. The first part of the recall spell was easy enough, but he had to visualize the circle of stone within the Whitewood to reach his desired target. He smiled at the thought, for he and Aubrey were the only mages Albreda had allowed to commit the stone circles to memory. The image came swiftly, and he began the incantation, building his magic until a ring of light emerged from the circle, creating a blinding cylinder that obscured the walls. The smell of the forest engulfed him as the light dissipated, revealing the birch trees that gave the Whitewood its name, along with the ancient circle of stones.

He took a deep breath as his eyes adjusted, enjoying his return to nature, taking delight in being away from the stale city air. When entering these woods, one waited for an escort, so he simply stood there admiring his surroundings. It didn't take long before a large wolf emerged from the trees, his grey muzzle marking his advanced years.

"Snarl," said Kraloch. "It is good to see you again, my friend." He bent over, scratching the old fellow's chin. "I am here for Mistress Albreda. Will you take me to her?"

After a good scratch, the wolf turned, leading him deeper into the trees along a twisting path. They emerged into a clearing where a pack of wolves lay strewn around an old hut, soaking up the sun as if they hadn't a care in the world. His arrival caused them no more than a casual glance, and then he was knocking at the door.

"Welcome, Kraloch," came the Druid's voice. "I've been expecting you for some time."

He entered to see her pouring tea into two cups.

"I would have been here sooner," said the Orc, "but Snarl is not as fast as he used to be."

"Yes. The poor dear is getting on in years."

"Shall I heal him?"

"It will do no good, I'm afraid. A spell of healing will not halt the ravages of time."

Kraloch sat. "What is this place?"

"My home. At least it was for many years. After Richard died, I returned here to find my inner peace."

"And did you?"

"No. Of course not, but I have come to accept that loss is inevitable. The Gods know I've had more than my fair share of it."

"You speak of your parents?"

"Yes. I lost my mother while still young, and later, Norland raiders killed my father. My search for his body led me to the Whitewood, though my first discovery of the place was farther to the east, close to the Wickfield Hills."

"And that is where you discovered your magic?"

"It was, though it took a trip to Shrewesdale for me to truly appreciate it." She picked up her cup, but the tea was still hot, so she set it back down again. "But you didn't come all this way just to talk of my past."

"No. I did not. The queen needs your help."

"Why? What has happened?"

"Have you heard about the trouble to the east?"

"At Stonecastle? I thought that was well in hand."

"It is for the moment, but we fear they may be massing for an assault."

"What makes you think that?"

"There's been sightings of additional warriors. I suggested we send you there to investigate further."

Albreda smiled. "You want me to use my ability to talk to animals to gather more information?"

"Yes."

"I'm curious as to why you didn't ask Aldus Hearn. He is a Druid, much like I."

"True," said Kraloch, "but he has a weaker connection to the animal kingdom, preferring the company of plants."

"With whom would I travel?"

"They did not tell me, though I suspect the marshal wishes to see the area for himself."

"Beverly is there, isn't she?"

Kraloch looked away for a moment. "No longer, I am afraid. She stepped through a magic portal, along with her husband and Aubrey. They are now trapped in a foreign land and unable to return."

"What's this?"

"Master Bloom theorized we could use the ley lines to get behind the Halvarian army, but things went awry."

"Did Aubrey contact you?"

"Yes, she did," said Kraloch. "They are well and are exploring the area. Unfortunately, we can do little to help, so we are concentrating on other, equally pressing matters."

"Very well. I will return with you to Wincaster, but let's finish this tea first, shall we? I'd hate to see it go to waste." She picked up her cup once more. "There. That's much better. It's such a nice day today. Why don't we move outside."

Kraloch lifted his own cup, and they stepped outside. "Is it my imagination," he said, "or has your pack grown even larger?"

"It is the gathering," she replied. "I thought it would be nice to have all the packs together for once. Well, all those that inhabit the Whitewood. They are my family, and it also serves to encourage mating."

"We have wolves back home, but they usually don't breed until the new year."

"As they do here, but in some ways, they're much like us—they like to get to know their prospective mates. Is it not so in Orc society?"

"It is," replied Kraloch, "but my magical studies have kept me far too busy to enjoy such things."

"That is a very sensible approach. Had I followed that advice, it would have saved me a lot of grief."

"You speak of Lord Richard?"

"I don't regret our relationship, but his death was like a knife to my heart."

"Grief is a natural part of life."

"You've grown wise in your later years."

"I am a shaman. That is my stock in trade."

Albreda laughed. "You've picked up a lot more Human expressions of late, although I'm hesitant to say whether that's a good thing."


Anna collapsed in a chair, and Storm padded over, placing his head on her lap. She stroked it absently, staring at the fire. "We have a problem," she said.

"Only one?" replied Gerald, looking up from a pile of papers he'd scattered all over the floor.

She leaned forward. "What in the name of Saxnor are you doing?"

"I'm looking over my notes."

"Don't you have staff to handle all that?"

"I do, but I still need to make decisions."

"And what has that to do with all those papers?"

"These are reports. I have to make a few changes with Beverly temporarily out of command."

"What sort of changes?"

"During the war, I had lots of people who could assume command of detachments. However, now I find myself coming up short. Beverly replaced Fitz, but if our army is to remain effective, I need more commanders or generals. I'm not sure which."

"What you really need is something between a commander and a general. Perhaps you need a new position? You could call it a commander-general?"

"No," said Gerald. "That's too confusing. It makes it sound like they would outrank a general."

"The purpose of these people would be to command in battle, correct?"

"Yes."

"Then how about a battle commander?"

"That's not bad."

"Actually, I've got an even better name. Do you remember the campaign against the Earl of Eastwood?"

"Of course. I may be old, but I haven't completely lost my memory. Why? What is it you're getting at?"

"Fitz created a name for how to break the army up."

"Yes. Brigades. We used the same idea when we liberated Weldwyn."

"Correct," said Anna. "So, what if we made them brigade commanders? You could make it an appointment rather than a rank."

"I like that. That also lets me appoint people without worrying about seniority or title."

Anna laughed. "When have you ever worried about any of that?"

"If you must know, ever since I became the Duke of Wincaster. People have such high expectations. Why couldn't you have just left me as marshal?"

"Because I chose you as my father, and it's only fitting you have a title."

"I'm a commoner."

"Not anymore, you're not." She paused to look at him. "Does it really bother you that much?"

"No. Sorry. It's just that I have a lot on my mind lately."

"You mean our troubles with Halvaria, or something a little closer to home?" There was no mistaking his blush. "It's Jane, isn't it? You want to marry her."

"Would that be so bad?"

"No. Of course not. Have you spoken to her about it?"

"I haven't proposed, if that's what you mean. I suppose I felt too much guilt."

"Because you lost your first wife?"

He nodded, too upset to speak.

Anna pushed aside Storm's head and rose from her seat. She moved closer, crouching down and hugging Gerald. "It's all right to feel sad. She was a big part of your life."

"Look at me," he replied. "Blathering like a child."

"Jane loves you, you know. And if you examine it from a certain point of view, you're already married. You've certainly spent enough time in each other's company."

"That we have."

"Well, whatever you decide, you have my full support."

"But we can't just live together. It's not right."

"Not right? If I followed that advice, I never would have become queen. It wasn't right that gave me the Throne, nor was it what made you my marshal, not to mention my closest friend. If you had done what was right all those years ago, you'd still be trimming the maze back in Uxley. Instead, you're here in the Palace with a new family and a grandchild. We might not be blood relatives, but we love you just the same."

Gerald stood, stretching his back. "Thank you. I needed to hear that."

"Good. Now, where are we concerning these new... What did we decide to call them?"

"Brigade commanders," replied Gerald. "And don't try playing games with me; you have a perfect memory."

"So I do, though I sometimes wonder if that's a curse rather than a blessing." She smiled at the grin that broke out on his face. "Who do you have in mind?"

"My first thought was Sir Heward. Sorry, I should say Lord Heward, but he's still at the Norland court."

"What about Hayley?"

"She'd be a good candidate, but her duties as High Ranger keep her busy. Lord Lanaka is a fine commander of horse, but he's training up our replacement cavalry."

"Lord Preston?"

"He'd be a fine choice," replied Gerald. "Anyone else come to mind?"

"As a brigade commander?"

Gerald snapped his fingers. "Of course. Tog. I can appoint him and give him command of our coastal region. That would provide him with authority to pull troops from Colbridge if needed. What about Alric?"

"I'm afraid he's far too busy with his duties as King of Weldwyn. How about Carlson?"

"Too inexperienced. He's only just been made commander. Have we any news of Arnim?"

"I'm afraid not. Hayley has people looking into it, but he and Nikki appear to have vanished. I hope nothing has happened to them."

"Knowing them, they're probably deep behind Halvarian lines, spying out the enemy."

"Let's hope so. Where does that leave us in terms of appointments?"

"I've got Herdwin taking over command of our troops in Stonecastle, Tog will look after our efforts along the coast, and Preston to oversee the rest of Merceria. That allows me to concentrate on overall strategy."

"It seems you have things well in hand."

"Perhaps, but it wouldn't hurt to encourage more people in terms of leadership. Saxnor knows it served us well in the Norland campaign, and when it comes time to fight Halvaria, we'll need every advantage we can get."

# FOUR

## Strategy

AUTUMN 967 MC

E xalor settled into his seat, waiting for the emperor to join him in the map room. Inlaid into the floor in front of him sat a mosaic depicting nearly the entire Continent, or at least it purported to. The lands adjacent to the empire had been updated over the years, but the farther east you go, the more inaccuracies inevitably crept in. Around this depiction were chairs for each High Council member, although he was the only one present today.

His gaze wandered over to the small, coloured blocks littering the floor, placed there using the information provided by his marshals to reflect the current location of their legions.

He looked up as the door opened, admitting the emperor. Exalor stood, bowing deeply. "Your Eminence. I took the liberty of laying out what we know of the enemy dispositions."

Nevarus wandered over to the depiction of the Sullen Peaks. "Is this what they call 'the gap'?"

"It is. You'll notice it sits just west of Wyburn."

"And these grey blocks? Do they represent Orcs?"

"No, Eminence. Those are the Dwarves, who've holed up in a place called Ironcliff. We estimate their numbers to be somewhere in the vicinity of eight hundred, but an exact count has proved elusive."

"Why is that?"

"The bulk of their army sits within their mountain fortress, and while our scouts are good at what they do, they can't masquerade as Dwarves."

"Nor would I expect them to. Tell me, have you a plan for prying them out of their hole?"

"We have, Eminence. The Seventh Legion has been reorganized to include additional footmen, and we've gone to the trouble of building some siege engines. In addition, several Earth Mages will assist."

"And the Seventh is otherwise at full strength?"

"It's slightly over strength at twenty-seven hundred men. We felt it was a prudent precaution, considering what they're up against. If you recall, the last time we encountered the Dwarves, it cost us dearly."

"Ah yes, in the east. What was the name of that place again?"

"Dun-Galdrim, though that was what they called it."

"I recall my father speaking of it. How long did it take us to eradicate them?"

"Two years, Eminence, though admittedly, we knew little of their defensive works before the assault. In the fifty years since, we've learned much from the remains of their civilization."

"Such as?"

"Their use of traps and false tunnels effectively delayed our progress. Their tactics also lured us deeper into the mountain, where they crawled through secret tunnels to get behind us. We won't make that mistake again."

The emperor wandered farther west. "I note you've made some recent changes to the map. I don't recall seeing all these towns before."

"It's called Norland—not the most original of names. Our scouts have been observing them for some years now in preparation for this campaign."

"And this Norland, I assume it's a kingdom?"

"It is."

"And how many warriors does it possess?"

"Not many. It has a relatively new queen who's been unable to unite the earls."

"Ah. I assume there is some discord?"

"There is. Some years back, they went to war with Merceria and came out on the losing side."

"So they're weak?"

"Very. And their few remaining warriors are scattered over a large expanse. We don't anticipate them being a problem, but we must first force the gap. I won't lie to you, Eminence. The assault on Ironcliff may carry a high cost."

"Yet I sense you have a contingency plan."

Exalor smiled. "Indeed, I have, Eminence. The attack on the mountain folk is but one part of three." He picked up a staff from beside his seat and made his way to his emperor. "Here lies another stronghold," he said, pointing. "A place called Stonecastle."

"Another Dwarven stronghold?"

The High Strategos nodded. "There is a legion in the area, ready to commence the assault when we deem it prudent. They will force their way through the mountain passes and flood into Merceria."

"I'll admit I'm not a strategist," said the emperor, "but it seems to me there are several points at which the enemy could stall us."

"You are correct, Eminence, but that is all part of my master plan. We intend to draw the bulk of their army eastward to counter the threat. Now, this is where timing becomes important. While we tie their men up in the east, we land a third legion in the south."

"According to this map, that's a swamp."

"It is, but they've recently begun efforts to clear the mouth of the river to encourage trade. We will seize this"—he pointed at a place labelled Trollden —"and then advance up the road to Colbridge while our fleet sails up the river to support them."

"What do the Mercerians have in the area?"

"Not much, according to our latest reports. The toughest opposition will be a group of Trolls, but they lack the numbers to hold us up for long."

"Trolls? It was bad enough to hear they had Orcs. What other denizens of darkness have they at their disposal?"

"Some small lizard-like creatures, but in our estimation, they are only useful as skirmishing troops. The bulk of the Mercerian army consists of footmen and archers."

"Have they cavalry?"

"They do, but not in numbers akin to ours. Our typical legion at full strength has six hundred horsemen, and we will attack them with three legions. The Mercerians, however, can barely scrape together five hundred."

"And what is this area west of Merceria?"

"Weldwyn. They are allied with Merceria but recently suffered a catastrophic war."

"You say they are allies?"

"Yes, but we have agents at work to keep them busy farther west, in a land called the Twelve Clans, where we've been fomenting unrest."

"How does that affect Weldwyn?"

"A Princess of Weldwyn married a clan chief. Her very presence will draw them into a protracted war, thus draining them of resources to help the Mercerians."

"You have given this much thought."

"I've created contingency plans for all the neighbouring realms, Eminence, although this one has been the most challenging."

"What is your estimation of how long it will take to subdue them?"

"A year, perhaps two. Much depends on the delay rooting out these Dwarves will cause."

"And you're confident three legions are enough?"

"It gives us a combined strength of almost eight thousand men. They had their largest army ever at the siege of Summersgate, yet it numbered less than three thousand. I believe three-to-one odds are more than sufficient."

"Two and a half, actually," said the emperor, "but I concede the point. When do you plan to start?"

"I'll travel to each of the involved legions to brief their respective commander-generals, but I don't expect that will take more than a few weeks."

"Surely you don't intend to march with winter approaching?"

"No, Eminence. Several things must be taken care of before the campaign can begin. My visits will ensure each officer understands what's expected of them and reveal each legion's part in the grand scheme. In addition, we must organize supplies, for the enemy territory is notoriously sparse compared to the rest of the Continent."

"Ah, yes. We'll need wagons, along with pack mules."

"Precisely."

Nevarus nodded. "You may consider the matter approved. Begin operations in whatever time frame you deem best. I only ask that you keep me informed of the campaign's progress."

"Most certainly, Eminence."

The emperor turned his attention eastward. "While I've got you here, let's talk a little about the Petty Kingdoms, shall we?"

"What, in particular, would you like to know?"

"We possess twelve legions, correct?"

"Thirteen if you include the men here in the capital."

"If three are busy in the west, that should leave nine."

"Assuming you want to keep the garrison here, yes, Eminence. Why?"

"In your opinion, would nine legions be enough to conquer the Petty Kingdoms?"

"That would depend on our strategy."

"And how would you conduct the campaign?" The emperor waited, sensing the man's reluctance. "I know you've been planning this for years."

"I've considered several scenarios," said Exalor, "but in my opinion, the best choice would be a two-pronged attack."

"Go on."

"I would place two legions on the border with Ilea, the rest massing in the north."

"Surely you don't mean to sweep through Arnsfeld again?"

"No, Eminence. I would send two legions to hug the mountains and march deep into Talstadt. They would then turn east, threatening Grislagen and Hadenfeld. At the same time, another three legions would march through Rudor and into Angvil and beyond. Recent reports indicate a Northern Alliance has formed, and we'd want to force them to engage us."

"By my count, that still leaves two legions unaccounted for."

"They would be my reserve to be used depending on how the enemy reacts."

"And what is your assessment of the enemy?"

"Arnsfeld proved itself remarkably resilient, so much so that we had to rethink our plans. I assure you, however, we won't be taken by surprise again. If there's one thing I can say for certain, the Imperial army has learned from its mistakes."

"Who would be the biggest threats to this enterprise?"

"That's difficult to say. We've taken steps to neutralize the Temple Knights of Saint Cunar, but in their absence, it seems those of Saint Agnes stepped forward, although not in numbers akin to what their brothers used to field."

"And this Northern Alliance?"

"A recent development, Eminence, formed this past year. They have yet to field an army, but based on the numbers they gathered for their last war, I expect they can manage close to five thousand men."

"That many?"

"Indeed," said Exalor. "Which is why my challenge will be to draw them into battle sooner rather than later."

"I'm not sure I follow your reasoning."

"The longer we wait to engage them, the more time they have to gather allies. My strategy will be to lure them with an opportunity to destroy one of our legions."

"You intend to sacrifice a legion?"

"No, Eminence. I mean to trick them. They shall march to battle only to discover themselves facing not just one but three. Of course, this is mere conjecture at this point unless you're suggesting we initiate our offensive now?"

"No. I am merely contemplating our future. Having said that, it would be nice to accomplish the great dream at some point in my lifetime."

"I assure Your Eminence, such a thing is within the realm of possibility."

"You mentioned earlier the Seventh Legion went through some changes. Have any of the others undergone such a process?"

"Not as yet, but the idea has merit."

"And if you were to make such changes, what would be their nature?"

"I would spend the time to increase the quality of some of our footmen. Most of the provincials are little more than a peasant levy."

The emperor drew in a sharp breath. "That would be a bit dangerous, wouldn't it? I'd hate to see them turn on us."

"We could mitigate the risk by arming them only when they reach the border regions."

"And the nature of this increased quality?"

"As you are aware, half of a legion, two full cohorts, consists of provincial troops. The footmen presently number three hundred per cohort but wear light armour. I would give them all more weapons training and mail hauberks."

"That would be expensive, wouldn't it?"

"It would," replied Exalor, "but the investment is worth it to speed up the great dream. After all, what is a few thousand coins when compared to the dream of a united Continent?"

"Well, it makes perfect sense when you put it that way. I assume the Imperial Coffers are sufficient to handle such an expense?"

"I'm afraid I wouldn't know, Eminence. That would be the domain of the Imperial Treasurer."

"Then I shall send word that you are to be informed. Can you prepare an analysis for the costs involved?"

"Most certainly."

"Then do so, and have them delivered to the treasurer. I shall tell him to be expecting it."

"As you wish, Eminence."

"What about the marshals?"

"What is it you'd like to know?"

"Which ones would be involved with executing the great dream?"

"The Marshal of the North would oversee the campaign against the northern Petty Kingdoms, while his counterpart, the Marshal of the South, would handle the invasion of Ilea."

"And the Marshal of the Empire?"

"His legions are not involved with the overall campaign. Instead, he would be in charge of finding replacements for those warriors lost in battle."

"I doubt he'd like that."

"He is a loyal subject and will do his duty. He's also participating in the attack against Merceria, so he'll already have had an opportunity to impress people."

The emperor chuckled. "And by people, you mean me?"

Exalor bowed. "Of course, Eminence. There is no greater glory than to serve the Gilded Throne."

"I look forward to hearing from you when you commence your campaign against Merceria." A servant scrambled to open the door as the emperor strode from the room.

The High Strategos took a deep breath, releasing his pent-up tension. The present ruler of Halvaria could be argumentative at times, even stubborn, but today he followed the path Exalor guided him down. His gaze swept to the floor. The wooden blocks had done an excellent job of convincing the emperor victory was assured. Now, it was his duty to ensure they reached the desired outcome.

"Your Grace?"

He looked up to spot his aide, Wingate. "What is it? Can't you see I'm busy?"

"My apologies, Your Grace, but this report just arrived from the north."

"Let me guess, the Marshal of the North?"

"Yes, Your Grace. It's marked urgent."

"When is it not?"

"I beg your pardon, my lord?"

"Never mind. Well, don't stand there like a fool. Give it to me!"

The aide stepped forward, taking care not to dislodge any of the carefully placed blocks.

Exalor ripped the message from Wingate's hands, tearing open the seal. He scanned its contents, looking for anything that might indicate trouble, but all was well for a change. "What is so important about this?" he asked.

"I cannot say, Your Grace."

"I wasn't talking to you."

Wingate fell silent.

Once more, the High Strategos scanned the letter. Was there some kind of code? It was written clearly enough but relayed nothing of import. Had the Marshal of the North completely lost his mind? Then he spotted a vague reference to scouts, and the marshal obviously didn't mean his own. Did this indicate the enemy was preparing for the empire's attack?

He turned to his aide. "I must travel north to Wyburn."

"You have a meeting with the Inner Council, Your Grace."

"When?"

"Tomorrow morning. You could use your magic to return first thing?"

"No. I'll need more than a few hours to investigate this. I'll have to delay my trip until after the meeting. Clear my schedule."

"Yes, Your Grace. Might I ask for how long?"

"Two weeks for now. I'll let you know if I'll need more time."

"Will you be taking any of your staff with you, Lord? You should at least travel with some guards?"

"Of course I shall bring guards. What do you take me for, a fool? Honestly, Wingate, I sometimes wonder why I keep you on as an aide."

"I wouldn't know, Your Grace. Perhaps I serve to remind you of what it was like when you were starting out?"

"Don't be ridiculous, man. I graduated from the finest magical academy on the Continent. Can you lay claim to such an accomplishment?"

"I am not a mage, Lord."

"Clearly, and yet you have your uses." Exalor closed his eyes and took a deep breath. "I sometimes forget others do not see the grand scheme of things. You must take no offence."

"If you insist, Lord."

His eyes snapped open. "How large is the marshal's entourage?"

"Do you mean the Marshal of the North?"

"Of course. Who else would I be talking about?"

"At last count, his staff numbered twelve, Your Grace, although that does not include any other mages assigned to the prefecture as auxiliaries."

"And how many of those are bodyguards?"

"Only four, assuming he's following Imperial Regulations."

"Then I shall take five, along with yourself."

His aide paled. "Me, Your Grace? Surely someone else would be more appropriate. I am but a humble clerk."

"A clerk who knows his business. Your memory is excellent, Wingate. I count on you to observe all you can when we travel north. In the meantime, I suggest you get some sleep. Tomorrow's going to be a long day."

"Understood, Your Grace." Wingate turned to leave but then halted, twisting around to face his master once more. "Shall I send a reply north, Lord?"

Exalor thought it over. It was common courtesy to reply to messages, particularly those marked urgent, if only to confirm they'd arrived. However, the marshal had been overstepping the bounds of his authority of late.

"My Lord?" repeated Wingate.

"Leave it until morning."

"That will worry them up north, Your Grace."

"Good. It will serve to remind them who's in charge."

# FIVE

## Travelling

AUTUMN 967 MC

Beverly halted Lightning. Before her, the swiftly running river stretched to the northwest. "It looks like we may have to adjust our plans."

Aubrey trotted over beside her cousin. "I don't suppose there's a ford anywhere nearby?"

"Not that I can see."

"Can we swim?" called out Aldwin.

"I wouldn't suggest it. The current here looks strong, likely too much for the horses or us."

"It occurs to me this river must eventually lead to the sea. Perhaps we'd be better off to continue following it."

"I don't suppose we could wait here in the hopes of seeing a boat?"

"No," said Aubrey. "If we're in the middle of the wilderness, I doubt there'd be any river traffic. Aldwin has the right idea; follow the river downstream. Sooner or later, we're bound to encounter some signs of civilization." She looked up at the sky, judging the time of day. "We've got a few hours yet before it gets dark."

"It's too bad Albreda isn't with us," said Aldwin. "She could send a bird to find a nearby town. I don't suppose you could conjure a familiar, Aubrey?"

"There are risks to having a familiar."

"Such as?"

"The bond between a mage and their animal companion is strong. Should the familiar die, the mage would be permanently injured."

"Injured? In what way?"

"I suppose you could say they would lose part of their life essence. Consider it a form of enfeeblement, like one might have were they old."

"Albreda is old, and nobody would call her feeble."

"Her connection with nature is from her mastery of Earth Magic rather than through a familiar."

"What about Snarl? Isn't he a familiar?"

"No, he's not. He just happens to be one of her friends, although I suppose you could say the same thing about any animal living in the White-wood. She has the ability to communicate with almost any creature there. That doesn't guarantee they're all friendly, however."

"It doesn't?"

"No. Nature is still nature. Meat eaters kill their prey; even magic can't overcome that limitation."

"So you're saying the wolves are dangerous? I have a hard time believing that. I've seen Snarl plenty of times, and he's never tried to take a bite out of me."

Aubrey chuckled. "You eat meat, yet you don't bite your wife. At least, I assume you don't." She held up her hand. "What goes on behind closed doors is none of my business."

Aldwin's jaw dropped, but Beverly merely chuckled. "Come now, Cousin. You're embarrassing him."

"Sorry. I couldn't resist. Let's move along, shall we? We won't make any progress standing around gawking at the water."


They camped beside the river that night, setting out early the next day. The weather was pleasant, and Beverly estimated they'd covered thirty miles or more by late afternoon. The woods had thinned a little, making their journey even easier. It would have made for a nice ride had Revi not stranded them in the middle of nowhere.

The sound of running water ahead came as a bit of a surprise. Thinking the river simply bent, Beverly rode on only to discover a point where two tributaries joined. They were now forced to make a decision: either to turn west and follow the newly discovered river or attempt to swim across.

As luck would have it, their side of the river opened into grassy fields, so they headed west, hoping for a place to cross. It wasn't until late in the evening that the river narrowed, and they splashed across to build a camp in the woods.

Aubrey was soon asleep, but Aldwin remained by the fire, poking the wood every now and again to send sparks flying up into the night sky. "It's rather nice here, though I'd enjoy it more if I had a full belly."

"As would I," replied Beverly, "but I doubt there's a tavern within fifty miles of us." She cast her gaze around. "Then again, there could be one only a couple of hundred paces from here. It's hard to see anything through all these trees."

"At least we can continue north now. Do you really think we'll find signs of civilization? We know so little about the rest of the Continent."

"I've been thinking about that. Aubrey is very powerful. She can recall from Wincaster to Summersgate, which is a substantial distance."

"And?"

"Well, it only follows if she can't take us home, we must be farther away than that distance. Now, I'm no expert at navigation, but I have the feeling we're well beyond Halvaria."

Up early the next day, they were soon back in amongst the trees. Their mood was glum as they rode north, for Aubrey found nothing to eat. The sun sat high in the sky when they finally ran across a trail that broke through the trees. They halted, examining the area.

"Cart tracks," said Beverly, "and recent ones, if I'm not mistaken."

"Finally," said Aubrey. "Some good news. Which way do we go?"

"Either way should work. If someone's hauling cargo, they must be going somewhere. Conversely, they must be coming from somewhere. The only question is, which is closer?"

"I'll go east, just to the bend in the path. I suggest you do the same west. With a bit of luck, we'll see something that will decide for us."

"And what do I do?" asked Aldwin.

"Remain here," replied Aubrey. "We need you as a reference point so we don't stray too far."

"Well, as long as I'm doing that, I'll dismount. No sense in making my backside any sorer." He climbed down from the saddle as the two women rode off in either direction.

Aldwin's stomach growled loudly, and he looked around, hoping for something—anything—that might fill it. Spotting what he believed to be a wild blueberry bush, he tied his horse to a nearby tree and went into the foliage.

There, he found several plants and gathered what he could, intending to share his bounty. When he stepped back onto the trail, he spotted Aubrey approaching, followed by four riders. He was about to give a cheer when he noticed the grim look on the Life Mage's face.

"You, there," called out one of the men. "Stand away from your horse."

Aldwin dropped the berries and put up his hands to show he meant no harm. As the riders came closer, he noted one had a crossbow trained on Aubrey. Their leader dismounted, as did two others, leaving the last to watch over Aubrey. They all drew their swords, and the leader advanced on Aldwin. "We don't want any trouble now."

"Nor do I."

"Unbuckle your sword and toss it aside."

Aldwin did as he was told.

"Now, hand over your coins, if you please."

"I beg your pardon?"

"You heard me. Hand over your coins!"

"Are you trying to rob us?"

"Shut up!" the fellow shouted. "Hand over all your coins before I order your companion killed."

Aldwin had spent almost his entire life in the relatively safe confines of Bodden and Wincaster. Being accosted by bandits, especially here in the middle of Saxnor knew where, took him completely by surprise.

Hearing galloping coming up from behind him, he jumped to the side as Lightning ran past, saddle empty. The leader of the bandits tried to halt the mighty beast, only to be trampled underfoot. Fearful of harm, the other two moved out of the creature's range.

Distracted by the commotion, the crossbowman failed to notice Aubrey as she turned in the saddle and pointed at him. He let out a tremendous yawn, then fell forward, his horse shifting beneath him, dumping him unceremoniously to the ground, where he lay snoring.

Beverly burst from the woods, smashing her hammer into one, knocking him from his feet, blood splattering the ground. The last villain vaulted back into the saddle and rode off.

"Good timing," said Aldwin. "You had me worried for a moment. It's not every day I see Lightning rushing down a road without you in the saddle."

"I needed to distract them," replied Beverly. "If I rode back, they might have killed Aubrey."

"Well, I, for one, am thankful."

"As am I," added Aubrey. She climbed out of the saddle to examine the fellow she'd put to sleep. "This one's alive."

"This one isn't," replied Beverly. "What about the fellow Lightning trampled?"

"I may be wrong, but I think the crushed skull finished him off. At least we have a prisoner."

"Yes, and he can likely tell us where we are."

"This one has some coins." Beverly produced a small purse and emptied it into her palm. "They look very similar to ours in size. This side depicts a face and says King of Deisenbach. Does that name mean anything to you, Aubrey?"

"No. Though I imagine it's one of the Petty Kingdoms. How much is there?"

"Hard to say. I'm not sure what these coins are worth. If they're anything like ours, it totals no more than two sovereigns."

"This fellow has a few, too, but they're assorted. Some say Zowenbruch. There's also one that has Hadenfeld on it. Either these men travel quite a bit, or we're close to the borders of all three. We could even be in one of them."

"At least we know we're not in Halvaria."

"What about this prisoner?"

"I'll bind his hands," offered Aldwin. "When he comes round, we can ask him some questions."

"I can wake him whenever you like," said Aubrey.

The smith was tying the last knot as Aubrey cast her spell.

The man's eyes fluttered open, and he looked around, startled to find himself in such company. "What happened?"

"You attacked us," said Beverly. "Two of your companions are dead, while the third fled. The choice you now face is whether you want to join them?" She nodded at the two bodies.

"I'm sorry," he said, "but these are desperate times. We would never have attacked if we knew your companions travelled with a Temple Knight."

"I am no Temple Knight."

"Of course you are. Why else would a woman wear armour?"

"I am Lady Beverly Fitzwilliam, Baroness of Bodden."

He turned ghostly white. "For Saint's sake, that only makes matters worse."

"Saints?" said Aldwin. "That's who Lanaka worships, isn't it?"

"Yes," added Aubrey. "And I know from speaking with Shaluhk that the Temple Knights of Saint Agnes are women. That must be who he thinks you are."

Beverly turned back to the prisoner. "Why are you attacking people on the road?"

"To survive. I used to be a farmer, but then the king's taxes drove me to ruin."

"We are heading to Reinwick. Do you know it?"

"Never heard of the place, but if you're looking for directions, someone in the capital could help you."

"The capital of…?"

"Deisenbach, of course. Where else would I be talking of?"

"And what is the name of this capital?"

"Agran. It's where the king lives." He nodded to the west. "It lies in that direction, though it's several days away."

"Are there any villages hereabouts?"

"Lumly. About half a day's travel from here."

"In the same direction?"

"Yes. Of course, you could go east. That would take you to Trivoli, but then you're on the border with Zowenbruch."

"And why would that be of any concern to us?"

"Let's just say there's bad blood between our two kingdoms. In any event, Agran is the better destination, particularly if you want to find this Reinwick place you're talking about."

"How do we know you're telling the truth?"

"Promise not to kill me, and I'll lead you there."

"Why should I trust you not to lead us into another trap?"

"You're obviously an experienced warrior," the fellow said. "And I'm not one to lie to a noble; it would be the death of me."

Beverly looked at Aubrey. "What do you think? Can we trust him?"

"It appears we have little choice."

"Very well. Untie him."

"Are you sure?" said Aldwin. "The man's a common bandit."

"This is not the first time I've dealt with this type of thing. You remember Samantha?"

"The ranger? Of course. Why? Are you suggesting she was a criminal?"

"I first met her while in the service of the Countess of Shrewesdale."

"Well, I, for one, will be keeping a close eye on him."

"We all will. What is your name, rogue?"

"Keon, my lady."

Aldwin untied him. "No trouble now, or it'll be the end of you."

Keon massaged his wrists. "I give you my word. I'll behave."

"Let's get moving," said Aubrey. "I don't know about you, but I'm starving."

"One moment," said Aldwin. He ran over to where he dropped the blueberries and gathered what he could. "These should tide us over."

According to Keon, the Rusty Axe was typical of travelling inns that dotted the roads of the Petty Kingdoms, offering modest food and rooms for weary travellers.

The Axe was little more than a rectangular building, with four rooms upstairs that the proprietors rented out to guests. Downstairs was the common area, along with a kitchen and, presumably, the owner's rooms, though these were not visible from where the group took their seats.

They'd put their horses in a covered paddock, little more than a fenced-in area with a canopy in one corner to ward off any possible rain. Beverly had balked at leaving their mounts so exposed but was assured nothing would threaten them. She sat with the others and waved over a man wearing a stained apron.

"What will you have?" he asked.

Beverly placed a Mercerian sovereign on the table. "What does this buy us?"

"A bowl of stew and a room for the night."

"For all of us?"

The fellow looked at each in turn, settling on Keon slightly longer than the others. "There are only four rooms, and one is taken."

"Three will do."

He nodded and scooped up the coin. "I'll go get you some bowls."

"Have you been here before?" Beverly asked Keon.

"I was here last night, along with my companions. I imagine he's wondering where the others went."

"What's next?"

"We continue on this road to Volbruck, then head north to Agran. If we get an early start tomorrow, we'll be in Volbruck by midnight, provided you don't mind riding in the dark."

"And the distance we must then travel to the capital?"

"About three days."

The owner returned, carrying a tray, which he set down, placing the four bowls onto the table, along with spoons. After that, he reached into a pocket and removed three keys. "For the rooms," he said, tossing them down.

Aldwin, wasting no time, slid over a bowl, dug out a spoonful and shoved it in his mouth. Almost immediately, his eyes bulged.

"Problem?" asked Beverly.

He swallowed, then gasped for air, fanning his mouth with his hand. "It's hot."

"Of course it's hot," said Keon. "It just came from the pot. What did you expect?"

"No. I don't refer to the temperature, but the spices." He was about to say more when a young woman placed four tankards on the table. Aldwin grabbed one and took a mouthful. "That's better."

"Too hot?" asked Aubrey.

"No. It's quite tasty, just not what I expected."

"Is this food typical of the area?"

"Aye," said Keon. "Folks around these parts like a little kick to their food."

"Kick?"

"I think he means hot," said Beverly.

"What a strange expression. Anything else we should be aware of?"

"Such as?" said Keon.

"What are the sleeping conditions like?"

The fellow shrugged. "Fairly typical, if you ask me."

"Meaning?"

"Each room has a bed that fits two."

"Aldwin and I will take one," said Beverly.

Keon looked at Aubrey, raising his eyebrows.

"No," the mage replied. "You and I are not sharing a room. We have three keys, remember? You get one all to yourself."

Keon shrugged. "Have it your way."

"I would, however, like to thank you for leading us here and telling us where we are. Are you interested in long-term employment?"

"Meaning?"

"I think I speak for all of us when I say it would be beneficial to have you with us while we travel around Deisenbach. We haven't much in the way of funds at the moment, but I'm sure our fortunes will change, eventually."

"I'll make a deal with you," said Keon. "Keep me fed, and I'll be your guide."

"Agreed."

# SIX

## Stonecastle

AUTUMN 967 MC

Gerald halted his mount. "There it is, the Fortress of Stonecastle."

"Fortress?" said Albreda. "Isn't it a city?"

"It's both, actually, and what you see of it now is only about a quarter. The rest lies beneath the mountain."

"Remarkable."

"You like it?"

"Yes, particularly the walls. Note how they appear to be made of one large rock. Clearly the mark of Earth Magic."

"I've heard they can meld stone, although I suspect it took years, if not decades, to work it on such a scale."

"I would agree," replied the Druid. "The mountain folk are far-sighted to take such measures. Has it ever been attacked?"

"Not as far as I'm aware, although I don't claim to be an expert in such things." He saw the gate open, and then five warriors came out. "Looks like we've garnered some attention."

"Then we'd best go and introduce ourselves."

They edged their horses closer.

"Halt," called out the tallest of the group. "Identify yourselves."

"I am Lord Gerald Matheson, Duke of Wincaster and Marshal of Merceria. With me is Albreda, the Mistress of the Whitewood."

The guard moved closer. "Are you expected?"

"I did not send word ahead, if that's what you're asking. I'm here to check up on the frontier. I've received reports that the enemy has been active of late."

"That's putting it mildly." The Dwarf bowed. "My name is Captain

Galman Boldhammer. I assume you'll wish to pay your respects to the vard?"

"Yes, of course. Then we aim to ride to the frontier."

"Such terrain is best traversed on foot," replied Galman. "Your horses will be perfectly safe here." He led them through the gate.

"This is most interesting," said Albreda. "I've never seen a Dwarven city before. Their use of stone is quite masterful."

"We pride ourselves on our craftsmanship." The Dwarf looked up at her. "Is it true you can talk to animals?"

"Of course. I am a Druid, after all. Can your own masters of stone not do so?"

"We have no masters of stone. Then again, there aren't a lot of animals in the mountains… at least not ones that aren't trying to kill us." He paused, fearful he might have caused some distress. "Don't worry. There's none around these parts."

The main road of Stonecastle was straight as an arrow, leading from the gate to the mountain. They'd gone about two hundred paces when a voice called out. "You, there!"

They slowed, craning their necks to spot a Dwarven female hurrying towards them from one of the buildings. "Are you Gerald Matheson?"

"I am. And you are?"

She halted, then wiped her hand on her leather apron. "Pardon my manners. My name is Margel, and my forge mate is Captain Gelion, cousin of Herdwin Steelarm."

Gerald halted. "Pleased to make your acquaintance." He dismounted before extending his hand, shaking hers.

"I knew it had to be you," she continued. "Herdwin's description was spot on."

"Allow me to introduce Albreda, Mistress of the Whitewood."

"THE Albreda?"

"None other," replied the Druid. "It appears my reputation precedes me, although I'm surprised they've heard of me this far east."

"Your power is said to be the greatest in all of Merceria."

"It likely is, not that I tend to worry about it. Is there something we can do for you?"

"My lord, Lady Albreda, would you consider allowing me the privilege of hosting you during your time here in Stonecastle?"

Galman cleared his throat. "They're on their way to see the vard, Margel. They don't have time for pleasantries."

"Actually, we do," said Albreda. "After all, we can't just barge in on the king. He's likely a busy man. Or are you insinuating all he does is sit on his throne?"

"Uh, no. Not at all."

"Then we shall allow you to carry word to His Majesty's court, so arrangements for a visit can be made. You can contact us here once everything is ready. I assume that will be acceptable?"

"Of course, Mistress."

She dismounted, then turned to Margel. "We would be delighted to take you up on your offer. Captain Galman can take care of stabling our horses." She glanced at their guide. "I assume you have such facilities here?"

"Yes, Mistress. Of course." He moved closer to her mount, looking ill at ease.

Noticing his hesitation, Albreda walked to the beast's head, rubbed its ears, and whispered something unintelligible. "There. I've told her to behave. She won't be any trouble."

The escort moved off, horses in tow.

"If you'll come this way," said Margel. "I've got a nice new barrel of ale that wants tapping."

They followed her in, and much to Gerald's surprise, what they assumed to be a one-storey building was actually two. The structure reminded him of Herdwin's home back in Wincaster, with the second floor dug into the ground, or in this case, the rock.

Margel noted his interest. "Downstairs are the sleeping quarters, including the guest rooms, not that we have many these days. No. I take that back. We didn't use to have visitors, but then Kasri and Herdwin came last year."

"Yes," said Gerald. "On their way to Kharzun's Folly, if I recall. He told me all about it."

"That's one of the reasons we're here," added Albreda. "We hear there's been some activity of late."

"So there has," said Margel. "The last I heard from Gelion, he said there were more Humans on the other side of the gorge. Do you think they're getting ready to mount an attack?"

"It's certainly a possibility. I've come here at Gerald's invitation to use my magic to spy out the enemy encampment."

"I doubt that would work. From what I've heard, there's no clear view of it."

"Ah, but that's where my magic comes in. I shall summon an eagle to fly over it, allowing me to ascertain their strength, assuming you have eagles in these mountains?"

"We do, but not so many that they're easy to find."

"Don't worry yourself over such trivialities. My magic will take care of that."

"I couldn't help but notice your apron," said Gerald. "Might I enquire as to your profession?"

"I am a senior member of the stone guild."

"You mean stonemasons?"

"I believe that is the Human term, but our guild does more than build stone structures. We also include skilled artists who shape stone, giving it greater beauty."

"Like a sculptor?"

"Some are, but the vast majority are specialists in finishing stone. You might think of them as experts in decorative stonework. People like me build things, then they come in to put on the finishing flourishes. Have you nothing similar in Merceria?"

"Not that I'm aware of, and from what I've seen so far, it's our loss."

Their host smiled, then poured them all a tankard of ale. "Come and sit," she said. "You must be weary after the trek to get here."

"Is Gelion in town?"

"He was. His company was on reserve status but has marched back to Kharzun's Folly."

"Reserve status?" said Albreda. "I'm afraid I'm not familiar with the concept."

"Those standing guard in the city have regular duties, while the conditions at the frontier are harsh. The custom here is to rotate different companies through such places, allowing them time to rest and recuperate."

"And how much rest do they get?"

"Typically, two weeks at a stretch, but with what's happening to the east, they've shortened that."

"For everyone?"

"Gelion is one of the senior captains and has direct experience with the situation."

"Yes," said Gerald. "He accompanied Kasri and Herdwin when the bridge fell, didn't he?"

"Indeed."

"We shall be sure to mention his valour when we see the king—excuse me, I meant the vard."

"King will suffice," said Margel. "We don't expect outsiders to know all our customs. I should warn you, though; the court of Stonecastle can be a little…"

"Treacherous?" offered Albreda.

"Confusing is what I was about to say, but I suppose it amounts to the same thing. I'm unsure how much you know about us mountain folk, but the guilds hold the real power here. There's also the matter of Herdwin's official, or rather unofficial, status with the vard."

"I know he's had his differences with the smiths guild," said Gerald. "Does that still trouble him?"

"I should say so. The guild masters dislike that he has a close friendship with the vard. They fear he will usurp their influence."

Albreda scoffed. "That appears to be something you Dwarves have in common with Humans."

"Treachery?"

"No, egos."

"Surely you don't think all Humans are that bad?" said Gerald.

"I'll admit there are exceptions, but not everyone is as sensible as the queen."

The door flew open as a young Dwarf barged into the room. "Margel! The Marshal of Merceria is here!" He halted when he noticed the visitors.

"So I've heard," she replied. "This is Lord Gerald Matheson, Duke of Wincaster and Marshal of Merceria. With him is Albreda, Mistress of the Whitewood." She smiled warmly at the younger Dwarf. "This is my cousin Tindal. He's undergoing his quest for knowledge."

"Which is?" asked Albreda.

"When a Dwarf comes of age, they don't always know what they want to do as a profession. Thus, they undertake a year of service with a guild, testing their aptitude and desires to see if they're a good fit."

"And after that?"

"If it's not for them, they move on to another guild. Otherwise, they begin an actual apprenticeship."

"And what is Tindal apprenticing in?" asked Gerald.

"Warriors guild," replied the youth, though calling him such might stretch the truth a little, for he sported a beard; although, admittedly, it was on the shorter side.

"And how long have you been a warrior?"

"Only five months," replied Tindal. He stuck out his hand. "Pleased to meet you, Marshal. My cousins speak highly of you."

"Your cousins, being?"

"Why, Gelion and Herdwin, of course."

"Is every Dwarf related?" asked Albreda.

"In a sense, yes," replied Margel. "Since we're such long-lived folk, we tend to have multiple generations alive. You Humans might be blessed to see three generations alive at once, but we often have nine or even ten."

"That must get very confusing."

"Oh, it is, but we manage. We still count mothers, fathers, sisters, and brothers, but we refer to everyone else as a cousin. It's much simpler that way."

"Yes," added Tindal, "but each Dwarf is expected to know all their relatives by name, if not by sight."

"So," said Gerald, "are you still considered to be in training?"

"Not at all. I passed my axe training two months ago."

"And now?"

"I form part of the reserves. We supplement the regular companies on occasion as well as man the walls, thus freeing up more experienced warriors for other duties."

"And are you enjoying it?"

"It's exhausting," said Tindal. "We just returned from marching to Kharzun's Folly. Mark my words. They'll be fighting there by the spring thaw."

"How do you come by this opinion?" said Margel. "You've yet to have any formal training in tactics. What makes you an expert all of a sudden?"

"I'm not. I'm just repeating what I heard. All the warriors think war is coming"—the young Dwarf nodded towards Gerald—"and so does the marshal."

"What makes you say that?"

"He sent Mercerian warriors here to bolster our defences."

"He's right," said Gerald. "We have six companies here in Stonecastle. You've probably seen them around the city. It's hard to miss that many Humans amongst your own folk."

"I'll admit I noticed them," said Margel. "I'd just hoped it was only a precaution. I can't say I much like the idea of war coming to us. It was bad enough when Merceria fought and we sent our warriors to help. However, this is something else entirely."

"How?" said Tindal.

"Every warrior expects to fight; they train for it, live for it. It's as natural as drawing breath. Other folk like me dread the very idea."

"I agree," said Gerald. "War is to be avoided wherever and whenever possible, but there comes a time when we're forced to make a stand."

"Are you saying you don't want to fight?" asked the young Dwarf.

"Nobody wants a fight. Well, nobody in their right mind does."

Tindal shook his head. "But Herdwin talks as if you're the bravest person he knows."

"Don't confuse bravery with foolhardiness. Let me ask you this; would you fight in a burning house?"

"Our houses can't burn. They're made of stone."

Albreda laughed. "He's got you there, Gerald."

"So he does, but perhaps I can put it another way. Would you fight in a tunnel that was collapsing?"

"Of course not. I'd be crushed." Tindal waited for a response, but then it was as if a light went on behind his eyes. "Ah. I see what you're trying to say. That's very profound. I understand why you were made Marshal of Merceria."

"Gerald has been a warrior almost all his life," explained Albreda. "He began as a youth, much like yourself, and it took him a very long time to reach his current rank."

"How long?" asked Tindal. "Centuries?"

"For Saxnor's sake. How long do you think Humans live?"

The young Dwarf shrugged. "I have no idea. Your elders are not as ancient as ours, but I presume he still has many years left. Why, his beard is still short!"

Gerald chuckled. "That's because the Human custom is to keep it trimmed."

"Why would you do that?"

"Long beards tend to get in the way, especially when riding horses."

"Ah, yes. I see now. We have no horses."

"None at all?"

"Well, workhorses, but none we can ride into battle. That would be ridiculous in the mountains."

"Tell us your impressions of Kharzun's Folly," said Albreda.

Tindal sat, accepting a tankard from Margel. "Before Herdwin destroyed the bridge last year, it spanned the gorge. Vard Kharzun built it many years ago."

"For what purpose?"

"He hoped a road east would encourage trade, and it's said he spent a considerable sum on its construction. It took the architects guild's best minds to come up with the design, but in the end, it proved fruitless. The trade never materialized, and the bridge became synonymous with a waste of coins."

"And that's why they now call it Kharzun's Folly?"

"Precisely." Tindal chugged back a good portion of his ale. "There were other repercussions as well."

"Such as?"

"The other guilds were dismayed by the expense, which led to them taking over the realm's finances. Gelion says that marks the turning point."

"I'm sorry," said Gerald. "Turning point?"

"Yes. The guilds have always been influential here in Stonecastle, but taking over the responsibility of the treasury pushed them to their current heights of power."

"So they control the king?"

"I suppose that's one way of looking at it." The young Dwarf grinned. "Not that it stopped him from doing what he wanted."

"You've lost me on that one. Care to explain?"

"Vard Khazad and Herdwin worked together before he ruled. His Majesty was a supervisor in the mining guild while Herdwin underwent his quest for knowledge. The two formed a fast friendship that still exists to this day, which is why Herdwin was allowed to oversee the expedition to Kharzun's Folly last year, despite having no status."

"He's a commander in the Mercerian army," said Gerald, "not to mention a master smith."

"And I'm sure he's well-respected back in Wincaster, but that does nothing for him here."

"That makes my trip here a little more difficult. I had intended on putting him in charge of the Mercerian companies stationed here."

"But he already commands at Kharzun's Folly, though it doesn't sit well with the warriors guild."

"If the guilds are so influential, how is that possible?"

"I can answer that," said Margel. "Herdwin has more experience in battle than any warrior of Stonecastle, and Khazad used our alliance with Merceria to justify his command."

"So you're suggesting his appointment is purely political?"

"I doubt the vard sees it that way, but it allowed him to assign the person he felt most suitable to the task."

"And how does your husband feel about all of this?"

"Why would it matter?"

"Well," said Gerald. "I assume he's a member of the warriors guild. Does the thought of being under Herdwin's command irritate him?"

"Not in the least. And before you ask, I imagine the other Dwarves feel the same. He's a rare breed, Herdwin. It can't be easy carving out a new life for himself, and the folk of Stonecastle respect that."

Tindal chuckled. "That's one way of looking at it."

Albreda glared at him. "You have something to add?"

"What my cousin said is true, but she's unaware of the full ramifications."

"Which are?"

"Herdwin is more than an accomplished warrior. Yes, his prowess on the battlefield is respected, but it's more than that. Younger Dwarves like me see him as an example of what we could do were we not oppressed by the guilds."

"Hardly oppressed," said Margel. "And you should be the last person complaining."

"But we are, don't you see? Our society is stagnant."

"How can you say that? Do you not all have hopes of advancing in your respective guilds?"

"Only after centuries of toil. The Mercerians have the right of it; a person should be able to make their own way in life without the interference of a group of guild masters addled by old age."

"You paint a rosy picture of us," said Gerald, "but Merceria is not without its problems. Yes, people can chart their own path if they have the means, but many live in poverty, their choices limited by their lack of funds. Your way of life may be carved in stone, but it has stood the test of time. How old is Stonecastle?"

"I'm not certain," said Tindal, "but it existed during the war of the Elves and Orcs, which was nigh on two thousand years ago."

"Merceria is only nine hundred and sixty-seven years old, barely half the age of Stonecastle."

"Your point?"

"You should concentrate on evolving your way of life instead of overthrowing it. You're more likely to see an improvement."

"Why, Gerald," said Albreda, "you've become quite the diplomat."

"It comes from spending so much time in the queen's presence."

# SEVEN

# The Inner Council

## AUTUMN 967 MC

E xalor Shozarin looked over his notes as the others entered. The Inner Council was the true power of Halvaria, yet it wasn't without its problems. The three lines who controlled the empire were constantly at each other's throats, vying for position.

In the past, this animosity had boiled over on numerous occasions, even resulting in the deaths of three of its members, but they had come to a consensus after that. Each of the three lines of the family held four seats on the Inner Council; if some members were absent, the other two would match the depleted numbers. It kept the council from erupting into violence, but it could still get heated on occasion.

Exalor noted the arrival of Kelson, one of the other Shozarins on the council. They'd known each other for years, and he was amongst the few people the High Strategos could trust to speak the truth. The same could not be said of the other arrivals.

The Stormwinds entered next. Murias, typically the more outspoken of the two, sometimes let her temper get the best of her. Fadra, on the other hand, was more scholarly, with a bald head and a tendency to squint a lot, no doubt due to his failing eyesight. Unlike the Shozarins, who generally remained within the empire, both Murias and Fadra had spent years in the courts of the Petty Kingdoms. As such, they could be counted on to keep the council updated on what happened outside the empire's eastern borders.

As usual, Edora and Agalix Sartellian, the Fire Mages of the group, were late. Agalix bore strong opinions about a variety of topics, while Edora seldom spoke, though when she did, it exposed a remarkably keen mind.

"Welcome, everyone," said Exalor. "I thought we might proceed by asking if there's anything noteworthy to report?"

Murias Stormwind responded first. "Perhaps it is to you we should direct the question. I understand you met with the emperor?"

"I did, but that's hardly news."

"Yet you spoke to him in the map room, which is a little more interesting. I assume that means the Western advance is about to commence?"

"You're a little premature. As you might suspect, I finally briefed His Eminence on our plans, but they won't commence for a few months yet."

"Why ever not?" demanded Murias.

"It takes time to coordinate a strategy of this complexity."

She clenched her jaw, readying for an argument. "It's been in the planning stages for years!"

"In which case, a few more months won't matter," replied Exalor. "The plan has always been and will continue to be a spring offensive."

Agalix Sartellian cleared his throat. "And does it still include the participation of three full legions?"

"You know it does. Why do you ask?"

"I'm curious as to which ones will be used. You've said the Seventh is to be employed in the north, while the Third is massing in the western provinces of the Central Prefecture, but I have yet to hear which will bear the brunt of the seaborne invasion?"

"What does it matter?" replied Exalor. "Are not all of our legions capable of bringing glory to the empire?"

Agalix smiled. "Of course, but you know as well as I, some are more experienced than others. I'd hate to see this little escapade of yours endanger our plans for the great dream."

Exalor guessed what the man hinted at. Each of the three marshals represented a different line, and Agalix wanted a Sartellian overseeing the naval campaign, quite a stretch, considering the Stormwinds, being Water Mages, were best suited to handle such an assignment. This happened every time a military operation was proposed, with each line vying to take control of the reins.

These thoughts flashed through his mind, as they always did at times like this. "As I informed our emperor, we have twelve legions at our disposal. More than enough to finish off the Petty Kingdoms, even without my three."

"Your three?" accused Murias. "Do you now claim them as your own? Careful. You are treading on thin ice here."

"My apologies. I meant mine only in the sense I will oversee the campaign to the west. In any case, even our most pessimistic predictions indicate we need only muster seven legions to conquer the Petty Kingdoms."

"By my reckoning, that still leaves two unaccounted for."

"We thought part of them might be used to form the core of two additional legions."

"We?" said Fadra. "I don't recall this council approving any of this?"

"Because I am only now bringing the idea forward. It's actually Kelson's suggestion."

Everyone's gaze swivelled to the High Sentinel.

"Well?" said Murias, her tone leaving no doubt it was a command.

Kelson cleared his throat. "We've all been working towards the great dream. Generations of our forebearers planned out how that was to be accomplished in exquisite detail, but we will be the first generation to witness it."

"And?" pressed Murias.

"As you are all aware, their plans were to come to fruition on the one-thousandth-year anniversary of the founding of Halvaria."

"Yes," replied Agalix, "but that was more than two hundred years ago."

"That is precisely my point. How much longer must we wait?"

"The great dream can't be rushed," cautioned Murias.

"And I'm not suggesting we do," said Kelson. "I'm merely ensuring we have sufficient numbers to counter any unexpected circumstances when the time comes."

"By forming new legions? This sounds like a power grab to me."

There it was again, thought Exalor, the claim that he and Kelson were trying to place the Shozarins' needs above that of the others. He hoped Kelson might offer a rebuke, but the man only attempted to placate Murias. "I assure you this is no such thing. We would spread command of the newly formed legions amongst the three marshals as it always has been."

Exalor coughed. "Well," he said, "that might not be entirely true."

Murias glared back. "Meaning?"

"It might be worth our while to consider creating a fourth marshal, one who would be responsible for carrying out the campaign against the Petty Kingdoms."

"That won't sit well with the Marshal of the North. He's expecting to lead the attack!"

Edora, who'd remained silent until this time, leaned forward, resting her arms on the table while clasping her hands together. She was not one to speak at length, but her words carried significant influence. "I could care less about the Marshal of the North. Tell me again why we don't consolidate all our forces under the High Strategos?"

"Here we go again," said Agalix.

"If you recall," said Kelson, "we tried that centuries ago. It led to the breakup of Therengia. It also put too much power in the hands of one individual, nearly breaking the family pact."

"Yes, but the lessons we learned have served us well ever since."

"Dispersing command of the legions to three marshals prevents any one line from taking the Throne for themselves."

"Agreed," said Exalor, "yet there are still problems controlling them. Just look at the fiasco of Arnsfeld! That would never have happened had I full control of all our armies."

"Yes," said Agalix, "but then you might be tempted to put yourself on the Throne, undoing centuries of work."

"With all due respect," said Exalor, "my proposal is to add a marshal, not give any one of us greater power. If anything, it would undermine the influence of the others."

"I doubt that would work. We have three lines, not four. How would we decide which one would supply the marshal?"

"Agalix makes a good point," said Edora. "The last thing we want is an imbalance of power."

"Then we stick with three," said Exalor. "Now, can we get back to the business at hand?"

"Which is?"

"The great dream. I understand there's been some developments of late?"

"There have," said Fadra, "and none of them good. Where would you like me to start?"

"You're a Stormwind. How about we start there?"

"As you wish. As you are likely aware, our part of the family has suffered some... reverses of late."

"And by that, you mean defeats?"

"That's one way to look at it."

"One way?" said Agalix. "They lost Reinwick, then Andover, and now they can't even gain a toehold in Hadenfeld. There's no way you can claim a victory after that."

"I might remind you," said Fadra, "they killed a Sartellian in Andover, not a Stormwind."

"Yet Gregori Stormwind organized the entire thing, did he not?"

Fadra withdrew a handkerchief and wiped his forehead. He was about to say something when Murias stepped in. "Our recent class of graduates show tremendous potential."

"Hardly something to brag about," bit back Agalix.

"All this is fascinating," said Exalor, "but in the end, meaningless. We are on the verge of the great dream; such political losses mean little against the strength of our legions. I'm more interested in the armies we have to face."

"So am I," added Edora. "Let's start with Reinwick, shall we? I'm told they're a part of some sort of alliance now?"

"Yes," replied Fadra, "with Andover, although there are rumours Eidolon may soon be joining them."

"And if that becomes a reality, what numbers could they field?"

"Nearly three thousand men were on each side when Andover and Reinwick last fought."

"And you didn't see fit to inform this council of that development? Why, that's more than a legion."

"It is, but our assessment of their quality is that it pales compared to our forces."

"What of Hadenfeld?" asked Edora.

Fadra shook his head. "I'm afraid we're looking at similar numbers since its reunification."

"This is all very perplexing," said Murias. "In the face of such numbers, we might need to postpone the great dream."

"No," said Fadra. "In my opinion, it must be now or never."

"Meaning?"

"The longer we wait, the stronger the influence of these new powers grows. In another five years, we might find ourselves outnumbered."

"But the Petty Kingdoms are a constantly shifting political landscape. What happened to all those old alliances that threatened each other?"

"I'm afraid there's an increased feeling of solidarity lately."

"Why is that?" asked Murias.

"While I hate to admit it, our very success has become our worst enemy. Our experts feel the threat of invasion has now grown to the point where there is no other option but to oppose us. Of course, that debacle in Arnsfeld didn't help. Thanks to our Sartellian marshal, everyone believes us capable of defeat."

"That was six years ago," said Agalix. "and the Marshal of the North was cleared of any wrongdoing."

"Yet the damage was done."

"I don't understand," said Edora. "I thought the Cunars were the unifying force. With them out of the way, things should have improved."

"And so they would have, were it not for the Temple Knights of Saint Agnes. A member of their order defeated us."

"I heard it was two," added Exalor. "One on land, the other at sea, if I recall. I might add, none of this would have happened had I been there to oversee the campaign."

"I've heard enough," said Edora. "We are wasting our energies discussing the past and laying blame. Let us concentrate instead on the here and now." She turned to Fadra. "What about this new power in the east?"

"You mean Therengia? They've been trouble for the Volstrum but are considered too far removed from the empire's borders to be of any consequence in a longer campaign."

"They could march west and assist. What sort of numbers are we talking about? Don't tell me there are another six thousand warriors, or I'm likely to strangle someone!"

Fadra chuckled, a rare show of emotion on the part of the scholar. "The last reliable numbers we have on them are from when they suppressed a rebellion in Novarsk. According to witnesses, they fielded only about eight hundred warriors."

"Yet they conquered Novarsk," said Agalix. "There are also reports of them using those massive beasts of theirs."

"Beasts?" said Edora. "I've heard nothing of this?"

"It's only a rumour at present," replied Fadra, "designed, no doubt, to explain the loss of the Temple army some years ago."

"And what do these rumours suggest?"

"The creatures are said to be twice the size of a horse. Clearly, a lie meant to excuse the cowardice of the Cunars."

"No," said Exalor. "The Temple Knights of Saint Cunar might have been trouble for us, but they were never cowards. If they report large beasts, we can assume the statement is the truth."

"Ah, but that's just it," said Fadra. "None survived."

"Then how do we even find out about these creatures?"

Murias placed her hand on Fadra's shoulder. "Actually, the Duke of Erlingen commanded part of the expedition, and the survivors of his army brought reports of the beasts to our attention. Then, Graxion Stormwind confirmed their existence when he went to Therengia on a diplomatic mission."

Edora leaned back in her chair. "So, we have a presence in their court? Why didn't you say so earlier?"

"I'm afraid they rebuffed our efforts. We have since learned that the country is under the control of someone named Athgar. I believe you've heard of his wife, Natalia Stormwind?"

Kelson sighed. "Not this again. Didn't the Volstrum sort this out ages ago?"

"Wait," said Exalor. "Tell me more of this woman. She was a battle mage, was she not?"

"She was," said Fadra, "and one of our more accomplished graduates, possibly the strongest we've ever produced."

"How is it you lost her?" asked Edora. "Surely you're not suggesting you parted ways amicably?"

"Not at all. She fled the Volstrum shortly after graduation. There is some speculation she objected to our breeding program."

"Correct me if I'm wrong," said Kelson, "but didn't you report she was in custody some time ago?"

"And so she was, but she escaped and fled to Reinwick."

"Reinwick?" said Edora. "Do you mean to suggest she was responsible for this so-called Northern Alliance?"

Fadra remained silent while his eyes betrayed the truth.

"This is not good news," said Exalor. "We sit on the threshold of completing the great dream only to discover not one, not two, but three potential enemies with large armies."

"Therengia is not large," insisted Fadra.

"Yet they've carved an empire out of the east. We can't simply ignore that!"

Everyone in the room fell silent. They all understood the risks. If they attacked now and failed, they would jeopardize the work laid down by generations.

"There is a solution," said Edora. "I propose we do as Kelson suggests. Take a portion of our reserve legions and use their strength to form a core for two new ones."

"Six would be better," said Agalix. He turned to Exalor. "Is that possible, given the time frame?"

"Yes, provided you don't want the campaign to start next year. But it still doesn't solve the problem of who would command them."

Agalix dismissed the notion with a wave of his hand. "We simply give two legions to each of the marshals, thus maintaining the balance. What if we wait another year to embark on the great dream?"

"Now, that, I can work with," said Exalor. "It will also give me time to finish off the Mercerians, freeing up a further three legions."

"Not so fast," said Kelson. "They'd still be needed to garrison the defeated lands."

Exalor shrugged. "I can make do with two for that purpose if necessary. I've been sowing the seeds of discontent for some time now."

"Discontent?" said Edora. "Perhaps you'd care to explain?"

"Certainly. The Mercerians took it upon themselves to arm the Orcs.

Not only do they serve in their army, but they are employed as road wardens."

"Rangers, they call them," added Kelson. "They often billet them in taverns across their territory."

"Yes," continued Exalor, "and we've used that against them."

"In what way?" asked Murias.

"By appealing to the basic Human distrust of other races. It worked so well for us amongst the Petty Kingdoms. All we did was emphasize their more savage qualities."

Kelson chuckled. "Yes, and pour coins into spreading the word amongst the cities of Merceria. The results proved most successful."

"And this helps us, how?" pressed Agalix.

"I'll let the High Strategos explain, as it was his idea." Kelson bowed to Exalor.

"We fomented unrest in several locations. They are admittedly small affairs, hardly the type of thing to threaten the Mercerian Crown directly, but it forced them to dispatch warriors to the far reaches of the kingdom to maintain the peace. The idea is to divest them of the ability to mass their army once our attacks commence."

"Yes," added Kelson, "and the impact has been much more extensive than we envisioned. It appears others within their realm feel as we do."

"Not quite," said Exalor. "A number of their nobles were taking advantage of the situation to further their own ambitions against the queen's rule."

"Interesting," said Agalix. "Is there something there? Could we engineer a rebellion? It would save us a lot of trouble."

"That tactic has worked well in the Petty Kingdoms, though not so much in recent years, admittedly."

"But would it work in Merceria?"

"I'm afraid not," said Kelson. "Since taking the Crown, their queen has allowed her marshal to reform their army considerably, resulting in a strong sense of loyalty amongst their warriors."

"Yes, but to the queen or her marshal? Perhaps we could set them at odds with one another?"

"I doubt that would work," said Exalor. "The two share a close bond, one that cannot be broken, at least not without years of investment."

"Then perhaps something more drastic?"

"What are you suggesting?"

"What if their marshal were to meet with an accident?"

"It wouldn't work," said Kelson.

Edora leaned forward. "Why ever not?"

"He's cultivated an experienced and loyal command structure. Were we to eliminate him, we would find ourselves facing his replacement."

"And that is bad, how, exactly?"

"The Marshal of Merceria is a known quantity," said Exalor. "I've studied his tactics and understand his strategies. Were he to be replaced, we would lose that advantage."

"Your agents have been busy," said Fadra.

"I have been planning this campaign for years."

"Where did this marshal come from? A military academy?"

"Not at all," replied Exalor. "He appears to be a man of low birth taken under the wing of one of their barons. He also spent many years on the border with their northern neighbour, a place of almost constant fighting."

"Are you suggesting he's competent?" asked Agalix.

"Very much so, I'm afraid."

"Come now. You are the preeminent battle mage in all the Continent, and you think he's a danger?"

"Only a fool discounts the capacity of an enemy. He is clever, I'll give him that, but I may have found his weakness."

"Which is?" asked Fadra.

"He takes great care to avoid losing men."

"So he's cautious, then?"

Exalor shook his head. "He's not timid, if that's what you're implying, but he won't sacrifice men if he can avoid it. The result is, he has a very loyal following amongst his men. Well, I use the term men, but there's all manner of creatures in their numbers."

"And all of them are loyal?" asked Murias.

"Almost fanatically so."

"How is that even possible?"

"To understand that," replied Exalor, "you must examine the fellow's record. He spent most of his adult life as a sergeant, if you can believe it, but then injury forced him out."

"Then how did he become marshal?" asked Fadra.

"He met the woman who now sits on the Throne, though she was only a young girl at the time. They somehow scraped together enough warriors to put down a rebellion."

"The same one we backed?"

"Precisely," replied Exalor. "They also convinced Dwarves and Elves to help them."

"And the Orcs?" asked Edora.

"They didn't come along until later," offered Kelson. "If you recall, we urged their earl to recruit the brutes to help in his insurrection, not that it did any good."

"You still haven't explained how he came to be the marshal?"

Exalor sighed. "It's a very long story, so I'll try to give you the short version. During this initial campaign, he got his first taste of command. Later, when they rebelled—"

"Rebelled?" said Agalix. "Are you suggesting there was a second rebellion?"

"There was. One that put the young girl on the Throne, but I digress. He later honed his skills fighting in the Weldwyn invasion."

"Which is?"

"Weldwyn is the land lying west of Merceria. The two realms were bitter enemies in the past, but some years ago, a loose coalition known as the Twelve Clans invaded from even farther west."

"You make it sound as if they've had nothing but war."

"In a sense, it's true," offered Kelson, "and it's provided the Mercerians with a very experienced army."

Fadra shifted in his chair. "And here I thought my news was bad. It appears I am in good company this day."

"Unlike your situation," said Exalor, "we've studied these people for years. Can the same be said of this Northern Alliance? Or Hadenfeld? And what about Therengia?"

"You can't compare Merceria to the Petty Kingdoms."

"Can't I? Why ever not?"

"I'll grant you the Army of Merceria is well-trained," said Fadra, "but by your own reckoning, it is no larger than any in the Petty Kingdoms. How could that possibly compare to the dozens of kingdoms we've dealt with in the east?"

"Admittedly, it might not sound like much, but my study of history has shown time and again that a small army, when well led, can often overcome a larger adversary."

"Then it's a good thing you've made a study of this fellow. What did you say his name was?"

"Gerald Matheson, the Marshal of Merceria."

# EIGHT

# Deisenbach

AUTUMN 967 MC

Volbruck was not much to look at, but it reminded them of Hawksburg in size, with the vast majority of buildings single-storey structures. The keep, however, was visible from several miles away, and as they grew nearer, they halted, taking in the sight.

"Remind you of Bodden?" asked Aubrey.

"Yes," said Beverly. "It's similar in design, but there's not much you can do with a square keep."

"There is one big difference," added Aldwin. "No outer courtyard. They don't appear to suffer from raids in these parts."

"Raids?" said Keon. "Who in the name of the Saints would raid a baron's keep?"

"Have you no enemies?"

"None bold enough to attack something like that. Where is this Bodden place you speak of?"

"It's my home," said Beverly. "A barony back in Merceria."

"Merceria? Never heard of it."

"That comes as no surprise," said Aubrey. "It's hundreds of miles from here to the west."

"West? You mean in Talstadt?"

"No. I mean west of Halvaria. I trust you've heard of that?"

"Ah, yes. The evil empire. Around here, we mostly use it to frighten children. We had a good scare a few years back, but nothing came of it."

"A scare?"

"Yes. Rumours were, the empire crossed into a place called Arnsfeld, wherever that is."

"And when was this?"

"Back in oh-three."

"Oh-three?" said Aldwin. "I don't understand. Have we travelled through time as well as space?"

"I doubt it," said Aubrey. "I suspect they use a different calendar here. What year is it currently, Keon?"

"Eleven-oh-nine," the fellow replied.

"We use the Mercerian calendar. To us, it's nine-sixty-seven. That makes a difference of"—she paused as she thought it through—"one hundred and forty-two years, if I'm not mistaken."

"You don't calculate the date based on the Saints?"

"Saints?"

"Yes. Saints Reckoning, the Holy Father calls it. I'm told it's numbered after the founding of the Church."

"We Mercerians base our date on the founding of our kingdom."

"Who's your king?"

"Queen Anna," said Beverly.

"You don't have a king?"

"We do, and we don't."

Keon screwed up his face. "That makes no sense."

"Our laws allow the queen to rule regardless of whether or not she's married."

"And is she? Married, I mean?"

"Yes," replied Aubrey, "to King Alric."

"So he's a king, then? I thought you said SHE rules Merceria?"

"She does. He's the King of Weldwyn."

Keon shook his head. "This is much too complicated for me."

They continued on, making their way through the streets of Volbruck. They'd stocked up on extra food at the roadside inn, intending to head straight through town, for Keon indicated the road led to the capital. What they hadn't expected were the strange stares that greeted them.

"Have they not seen a knight before?" asked Beverly.

"Most assuredly," replied Keon, "just not a female one who's not wearing a scarlet tabard."

"And what is the significance of scarlet?"

"It marks a woman as a Temple Knight of Saint Agnes."

"Ah, yes," said Beverly. "The female fighting order. I should quite like to meet one. I'm curious how they go about their duties."

"It's not you they're staring at," noted Aubrey. "It's Aldwin."

"That's to be expected," said Keon.

"Why?"

"On account of his eyes. You don't usually see his type riding horses."

"His type?" said Beverly. "Whatever do you mean?"

"He's clearly a descendant of the Old Kingdom. That makes people nervous."

"What in Saxnor's name are you talking about?"

"I'm no scholar," replied Keon, "but everyone knows the story. Centuries ago, there was a great kingdom—Therengia, they called it. A brutal empire occupying much of the central Continent. The other kingdoms created an alliance and crushed them."

"And these people all had grey eyes?"

"Yes. It's what sets them apart from everyone else."

"Therengia," mused Aubrey. "That's Shaluhk's home."

"That's likely the new one," said Keon. "They don't use that term around here. It's said to be bad luck, hence the name 'Old Kingdom'. Not that the common folk care about a person's eyes. It's the higher-ups you need worry about."

"I assume you mean nobles?"

"Nobles, reeves, anyone of import. They all fear an uprising at the hands of the grey-eyes. I suggest we pass through town quickly if you want to avoid any trouble."

"Then we shall continue on our way."

Once they cleared the town, the area opened into lush, green pastures. They were well out of sight of Volbruck when they spotted a wagon off the road in a field. A man had unhooked the horses and led them to a nearby stream while a woman tended a fire over which a haunch of meat sizzled, its smell tantalizing the travellers. She waved as they drew closer.

"Greetings," called out Aubrey. "May we join you?"

"Most certainly," the woman replied. "It's not often we see a knight on the road, particularly one in their armour. On your way to the tournament, are you?"

"Tournament?" asked Beverly.

"You're a woman?"

"You can't tell?"

"My pardon, Sister. I assumed someone armoured thus would be a knight. Shouldn't you be wearing the colours of your order?"

"I'm not a Temple Knight; I'm a baroness. My name is Beverly Fitzwilliam, and this is my husband, Aldwin, and my cousin, Aubrey Brandon, Baroness of Hawksburg."

The woman stood, then did a clumsy curtsy. "My apologies, my lady. I didn't realize I was in such august company." She eyed Keon. "Is that your only servant?"

"Servant?" he replied. "I'm more of a guide. These folks are foreigners."

"What's this about a tournament?" asked Beverly.

"That's why we're heading to Agran," replied the woman.

Having noticed the interaction, her husband returned, leading the two horses. "What have we here?"

"They're on their way to Agran," replied his wife.

"For the tournament?"

"Apparently not."

"We're not from these parts," offered Aubrey.

"Clearly," replied the fellow. He took in her attire and that of her companions and, realizing what they were, quickly bowed. "Pardon my manners, my lady. I am Viden, a smith by trade, and this is my wife, Nymin."

"A smith," said Beverly. "So is my husband."

Viden's gaze wandered to the grey-eyed Aldwin. "He is your husband?"

"Yes. Does that surprise you?"

"I told you," whispered Keon.

"Sorry," said Viden. "It's rare to see one of his kind with a trade."

"I'm right here," said Aldwin. "You can speak to me directly."

"He means no harm," said Nymin. "You just took him by surprise."

"You say you're smiths?"

"Yes. That's right. On our way to the tournament." Nymin nodded at the wagon. "We carry a portable forge in there."

"Is this something you often do?" asked Beverly.

"A few times a year. Smiths are in demand at such things, particularly someone who can fix armour."

"Speaking of which," said Viden, "might I ask who made yours?"

"Why?" said Beverly. "Is there something wrong with it?"

"Not in the least, although it's a little archaic. The workmanship, however, is exquisite."

She smiled. "My husband made it."

He nodded at Aldwin. "You're quite skilled."

"If you think that's something," said Beverly, "look at this." She retrieved Nature's Fury from where it hung on Lightning's saddle. The weapon caught the sun, making it appear to glow with an inner light.

Viden took the weapon, examining its craftsmanship. "It's remarkably light for a hammer. What's it made of?"

"Sky metal," said Aldwin.

"Never heard of it."

"Some call it godstone."

The smith's eyes bored into him. "Truly? And you managed to work it?"

"Yes, although it took a special forge to smelt it."

"Special, how?"

"One of Dwarven design."

"Now you're pulling my leg." Viden handed the weapon back to Beverly.

"I assure you he's not," she added. "This weapon is called Nature's Fury."

"Funny name for a hammer. I should think a better name would be soul-stealer or sword-breaker—something to that effect."

"It's imbued with Earth Magic."

"We should probably be on our way," said Aubrey. "We've still miles to travel before we reach Agran."

"You won't get there today," said Nymin, "or tomorrow. Why don't you stay the night here? It's much safer that way for all of us."

"I have an idea," said Beverly.

"Which is?" asked Aubrey.

"I could supplement our few coins if I enter the tournament."

"You used to hate the idea of tournaments. Don't tell me Jack Marlowe convinced you otherwise?"

"No, but by the sounds of it, we've got a long way to go to get to Reinwick, and some extra funds would make it a lot easier."

Viden took an interest. "Have you ever competed in a tournament before?"

"I have not, though I witnessed a few in Weldwyn. I am, however, very experienced in battle. Does that count?"

He looked over at Lightning. "That's a fine horse you have there. He would fetch a high price, more than enough to cover your entrance fee."

"He's not for sale."

"Entrance fee?" said Aubrey. "You have to pay to enter the tournament?"

"Naturally," replied Viden. "Of course, the winnings more than compensate for the expense, providing you are successful."

"What's the prize?"

"A paltry sum by the standards of nobles, but the real treasure is in the ransom."

"I'm afraid I don't understand."

"When you defeat an opponent, they pay you the cost of their armour and weapons; at least they do in the joust."

"And you know this, how?"

"Easy," said Nymin. "He's a smith, remember? All that armour can take a beating in the tourney, and someone has to repair it."

"So they pay if they lose?" asked Beverly. "That seems a way to quickly empty a person's purse."

Viden waved off the remark. "They're nobles, like yourself. Coins mean little compared to their reputation, and even a defeat can increase one's fame."

"I'm not sure I like this idea," said Aubrey. "The last thing we can afford to lose is your armour."

"If you're interested, I might have a proposition for you."

"Go on," said Beverly.

"You say you're low on funds. What if I fronted you the fee to enter the joust?"

"Why would you do that?"

"For a percentage of the winnings. Five hundred sovereigns might not be much to a noble, but to people like us, it's a fortune."

"And if I lose?"

He shrugged. "Then I'll have wasted my meagre savings. Of course, if you felt guilty about it, you could always give me your horse?"

"That's a huge gamble," said Aubrey. "And Lightning is a Mercerian Charger, easily worth double that."

"A Mercerian Charger? Can't say as I've ever heard of such a thing, but he's larger than anything we have around here."

"Beverly is our greatest champion. You'll earn your investment back and then some."

"I thought you were opposed to the idea," said Beverly.

"That was before I realized how much we could make. Perhaps even enough to take a boat north. Do they have riverboats here?"

"Yes, they do," said Nymin. "Though you wouldn't find them in Agran. Only the great rivers have those."

"Great rivers?"

"Agran has smaller waterways but nothing to rival those forming the borders of Deisenbach."

"And this place is how far away, precisely?"

"Three days, maybe four?"

"What do you say?" asked Viden. "Do we have a deal?"

Beverly thought it over. It was a risk, to be sure, but there was no way she would chance losing Lightning. "I'll wait until we arrive in the capital before making my final decision. I need to see what this tournament is about to determine if I'd be any good at it."

"Perhaps you'd like to travel there with us? There's safety in numbers."

"Thank you," said Aubrey. "We shall be happy to take you up on that offer."

. . .

Three days later, they topped a rise, and the City of Agran stood off in the distance, almost all its buildings white.

"There she is," said Keon. "The Pale Lady."

"Strange name for a city," said Aldwin.

"It's a strange city."

"What makes you say that?"

"You'll see once we're amongst its streets. Are there cities like that back where you're from?"

"Yes," replied Aldwin. "Our capital, Wincaster, is easily twice the size and is surrounded by a wall."

"Agran has never been attacked," replied Keon. "Though we've seen our fair share of wars."

"Does that mean you've never been invaded?"

"No. Far from it, but most conflicts are little more than border skirmishes. I doubt an enemy blade has ever been within fifty miles of the capital."

Beverly nodded. "We, too, have had our fair share of border clashes over the years. It would be interesting to compare notes."

"Is that where you learned to fight?"

"It was."

"Did she tell you she's a general?" asked Aubrey.

Keon looked at the mage. "I can never quite tell when you're being serious."

"In this case, she is," said Beverly.

"And a Knight Commander of the Order of the Hound," added Aldwin.

"All right, you two. That's enough of the ego-stroking. Any more, and my helmet won't fit."

The wagon slowed, causing the rest to follow suit.

"Problem?" asked Beverly.

"Not so much a problem as a slight difficulty," explained Viden. "I may have neglected to point out one teeny item regarding the joust."

"Which is?"

"You're a woman."

"And you just noticed that now?"

"That was clear from the moment you first spoke. No, I'm referring to the fact that only men compete in competitions of this nature."

"Why is that?"

"It's considered unladylike."

"But there are women knights, aren't there? What about the Temple Knights of Saint Agnes?"

"They don't compete in such things. It's against their vows. You'll see them all over the tourney grounds, though. They often act as officials, ensuring people don't break the rules."

"And there are no other lady knights?"

"None I've ever heard of." Viden turned to his wife. "You?"

"Don't look at me. You've been doing this longer."

"There must be a way around this," said Beverly.

"There likely is," replied Viden, "but you'd have to check with whoever's in charge."

"Doesn't the king oversee such things?"

"His Majesty is far too busy. Don't worry. He'll be watching once the competition gets underway, but he's not about to take on the actual work of preparing things. He's more than happy to delegate that to others. Good thing, too. It gives folks like me a chance to get involved."

"So, where do we go from here?"

Viden stood up and gazed westward. "Do you see that field over yonder? The one with all the tents?"

"Yes."

"That's the tourney field. Nymin and I will set up the forge in the south where the knights assemble before their events. I suggest the rest of you head into town. I'm told there's an inn there called the Sword and Scabbard that's not too bad. Tell them I sent you, and they might give you a better price."

He sat back down. "Hang on a moment." He dug down behind his seat and pulled forth a purse. "Here. You might need it." He handed some coins to Aldwin. "Take my advice," Viden continued. "You do all the talking. They expect you to be a servant, which is safer than revealing your true identity. And for Saint's sake, don't carry a sword. We get visitors from other realms, and many don't look too kindly on arming a grey-eye. No offence."

"None taken," replied Aldwin. "And thank you for your aid. We'll see you again come morning. Any idea when things start?"

"I'd leave the inn just after sunrise if I were you. Registration begins at first light, and though it won't close till noon, you don't want to spend all day waiting on the herald to write your name down."

"When does the jousting begin?" asked Beverly.

"I haven't seen the schedule, but generally, these things don't start until the day after registration. However, you will see many preparing for it."

"And how does one do that?"

"Oh, they joust with targets or sometimes with each other, though only at lower speeds. They don't want to injure anyone before the tourney begins. Are you familiar with how the jousting works?"

"I am aware of how they do it in Weldwyn. I believe there are three passes, are there not? The object is to break a lance on a shield or unhorse one's opponent."

"It's the same here, though they use a points system. Any hit is worth a point. If you break your lance on a shield, that's two, but the highest score is three for dismounting your opponent. Be warned, however, hitting anyone in the head is an automatic suspension and forfeiture of your entrance fee."

"That doesn't sound too bad. Any idea where I could find some lances?"

"Plenty of folk around the tourney field can supply them for a few coins."

"In that case, we will bid you good afternoon and see you tomorrow morning."

The Mercerians had only gone a few dozen paces when Aldwin pulled up beside his wife. "You better take this," he said, offering his scabbard.

"I don't think I fancy the idea of leaving you unarmed."

"Nonsense. I'll be fine. It just so happens I have the Champion of Merceria here to keep an eye on me."

"That's not all I'll keep on you," she replied, a smile curling her lips.

"Oh, come on, you two," said Aubrey. "Can't you at least wait until you've found a room!"

# NINE

# Ironcliff

AUTUMN 967 MC

(In the language of the Dwarves)

Thalgrun Stormhammer, Vard of Ironcliff, sat on his throne while the guild masters argued. The warriors guild had been pushing for increased funds for years, and now that an enemy massed on the border, it was approaching a crisis in funding. On the other hand, the bankers guild accused them of exaggerating the threat and refused to budge. All the while, the other guilds stood watching, eager to make their own claims for increased budgets. Thalgrun sighed. Would there be no end to this?

A herald arrived, making his way through the crowded throne room to bow before his lord and master. "Majesty." He'd lowered his voice to avoid the guild masters hearing what he had to say. "A visitor from the Wayward Wood is at the gate."

Thalgrun leaned in close, speaking quietly. "The Wayward Wood, you say? Why in the name of Gundar would they send an envoy here?"

"He would not say, Majesty. Shall I have him escorted into the throne room?"

"No. Such things are better done in private. Take him to my study, and I'll speak to them there."

The herald nodded, leaving the room as unobtrusively as possible.

Thalgrun turned to the guild masters. "I've heard enough."

All within fell silent.

"Lord Garnik. You claim you need more to arm us. Is that correct?"

"Indeed, Majesty."

"Explain to me, if you would, how such funds would be spent were they to be made available."

The Master of the Warriors Guild puffed up his chest, then scratched his beard. "The primary cost is armour. If we are to suffer a siege, it's imperative everyone is properly defended—"

"Yes," interrupted Lord Strodar, "but our stores of armour are sufficient for such things. Are you trying to tell us we have somehow emptied our armouries?"

Thalgrun held up his hand. "You shall have a chance to make a case for the bankers guild," he said. "Right now, I'm more interested in what Garnik has to report."

"Thank you, Majesty. Now, as I was saying, we need more armour. Currently, we have enough to equip all our regular companies, as well as the Mountain Guard."

"Mountain Guard?" sneered Strodar. "Why don't you call it what it is—a militia!"

"Quiet!" snapped Thalgrun. "If I have to speak to you again, you will be escorted from the room."

"You wouldn't dare!"

Thalgrun rose from his throne and descended to the floor. Even so, he still towered a good half a head over the banker. They locked eyes, each waiting for the other to falter.

"My Lord," interrupted a voice.

Both turned as Agramath, the master of rock and stone, entered the room. The new arrival gave Strodar a withering glare, strong enough to force the fellow to look down at his feet. The mage then bowed to his vard and smiled. "I've received news from the south, Majesty."

"Which is?"

"The Mercerians fear an attack on Stonecastle."

"Are they asking for help?"

"No. Merely informing us of developments. Their marshal suspects it might be part of a larger strategy by the Halvarians."

"To launch a simultaneous attack on us?"

"Precisely."

Thalgrun turned back to the banker. "What think you now, Master Strodar? Still unwilling to release the funds?"

"Are we to now release funds at the merest hint of a rumour? Where is the proof?"

Agramath smiled. "I think you'll agree the source of this particular bit of information is beyond reproach."

"I shall be the judge of that!"

"With your permission, Majesty, I should like to summon the bearer of this news."

"By all means," said Thalgrun.

It took only a wave, and then great doors were thrown open to a Dwarf in golden plate armour. It didn't take a genius to realize who it was.

"Kasri Ironheart," called out the Master of Revels. "Designated Successor to the Throne of Ironcliff, Commander of the Hearth Guard, and Dragonrider!" He said the last word with particular pride.

The guild masters moved aside, bowing in acknowledgement of her accomplishments.

"Thank you, Master Malrun," said the new arrival. "So nice to see you in such good spirits."

"Kasri!" called out the vard. "It's so good to see you."

"And you, Father, although I wish it were under better circumstances."

Strodar stared at the ceiling, looking decidedly uncomfortable.

Thalgrun didn't even try to hide his smile. "Did you come from Stonecastle?"

"I did, Father. By way of Wincaster. I arranged transportation with Master Revi Bloom in case you had questions." She quickly glanced at Strodar before turning back to the vard. "I assume the bankers are once more withholding funding. Even a pending threat does nothing to release the purse strings?"

"Are you certain they mean to attack Stonecastle?"

"It's difficult to be absolutely sure when we can't see their entire army, but they've become particularly active across the gorge."

"Gorge?" said Strodar, finally finding his voice.

"In the mountains east of Stonecastle, there was a bridge called Kharzun's Folly that Herdwin destroyed, but the enemy remained on the far side. Of late, they've been up to something. We're just not sure what."

"How can you be certain?"

"They built a tower similar to what you might expect at a siege. We think they may be hiding something behind it."

"How large is this tower?"

"Not high enough to drop a ramp, if that's what you're asking. However, it gives them a good view of our side."

"Interesting," said Agramath.

"I fail to see how," said Garnik. "They must still build a bridge."

"True, but that may answer the question of what they're up to. It seems to me a good view of the surrounding area is just what they need to cross, or rather, a view of the opposite side."

"What are you suggesting?" pressed the Master of the Warriors Guild.

"That they possess their own masters of rock and stone or, as Humans call them, Earth Mages. I believe they intend to create a new bridge by shaping the stone."

"But that would require them to manipulate the stone by hand, would it not?"

"You might think so," said Agramath, "but any spell can be employed at a distance if the caster is of sufficient strength."

"Could you do such a thing?" asked Thalgrun.

"I don't know. I've never tried. It's possible in theory, but it would take a great deal of practice."

"How does that help us?" asked Garnik. "We are facing a massive army poised to march through the gap. That's nothing like their struggle in Stonecastle. Of course, with Kasri back here to command the Hearth Guard, we have a much better chance of inflicting heavy losses."

"I am not staying," she replied.

Her statement shocked everyone save for her father. The guild masters stared at her, eagerly awaiting an explanation.

"You refuse to return in our time of need?" said Garnik. "Is that what we can expect from our future vard?"

"I respect Kasri's decision," said Thalgrun, "as should you all. When the Halvarians attack, we will not meet them in the gap. They would easily outmanoeuvre us, potentially preventing our warriors from retreating to Ironcliff. Would you so readily sacrifice our own people?" He stared at each guild master in turn, none meeting his gaze.

"I will return to break the siege," Kasri assured them, "but until then, my place is by Herdwin's side."

"Herdwin?" sneered Strodar. "He's still guildless. Hardly a fitting forge mate for a named successor."

She wheeled on him, her hand instinctively reaching for her hammer. "Speak ill of him again, and I will create an opening in your guild."

Strodar blanched, looking at his vard. "Are you going to let her talk to a guild master this way?"

"You insulted her intended forge mate. It is within her rights to seek recompense. I suggest you apologize before blood is spilled." The vard lowered his voice ever so slightly, making him sound even more threatening. "I would also learn to bite my tongue if I were you. One day, Kasri will be Vard of Ironcliff, and you and I both know how long a Dwarf can hold a grudge."

The fellow's eyes betrayed his inner struggle as they flipped back and forth between the vard and his daughter. He finally settled on Kasri and made a sweeping bow. "My apologies, Kasri Ironheart."

"Is that all you have to say?"

"What else would you have of me?"

"It was not me whom you insulted, but Herdwin Steelarm. I insist you acknowledge his right to forge with me."

"Now, now," said Thalgrun. "Let's not push this too far."

It was too late, for Kasri and Strodar were locked in a battle of wills, neither willing to back down. The vard shook his head. It was bad enough having to deal with the guilds, but this situation with his daughter could quickly spiral out of control.

"I might remind you," said Garnik, "that Kasri is a member in good standing of the Guild of Warriors. Will you now insult us by shaming part of our extended family?"

"They are not yet forged," said Strodar. "So the claim of family is over-reaching."

"You and I both know that when one of our female folk makes up her mind about forging, there is nothing she'll let stand in her way."

There was a long pause as Strodar silently stood there, an internal struggle warring within him, then he sighed. "I apologize for besmirching the good character of Herdwin Steelarm."

The entire room let out a collective sigh of relief.

"There," said Agramath. "That wasn't so hard, now, was it?"

"On that note, I must leave," said Thalgrun. "I trust you'll remain in Ironcliff for a while, Kasri? You and I have much to discuss."

"Of course, Father."

"Good. I hereby dismiss the court. I have things to attend to."

"Anything I can help you with?"

He looked at her, deep in thought. She'd grown much in recent years, not in body but in spirit, and was now a strong leader and an accomplished tactician. "Yes," he finally said. "I believe there is. Come with me, and I'll tell you who's come to visit."


Flan had never seen the home of the mountain folk before, let alone their king. He wandered around, examining the oversized chairs. The room lacked the warmth of wood, but that was to be expected. After all, Dwarves were masters of stone.

From what little Flan knew, the mountain folk were said to be much the same height as his own people, yet the furniture here seemed to indicate they were larger in both height and width. Like his brethren, Flan was thin of frame, his arms and legs gangly when compared to these dwellers of stone. He'd noticed they had a preference for facial hair, something that was a new experience for him.

The door opened to admit two Dwarves, at least a head taller than he himself but nowhere near as thin. The elder of the two's facial hair fell almost to the floor.

"*I bring you greetings from the Aralani,*" said Flan, in the ancient tongue common to all Elder races. "*My name is Flan Delving.*" He made an awkward bow.

"*Good day to you,*" replied the vard, using the language of his ancestors. "*I am Thalgrun Stormhammer, and this is my daughter, Kasri Ironheart. Please. Have a seat, won't you?*"

The visitor stared at a chair. At first, he took the words as a gift, but then the full meaning became apparent. He climbed into a chair, marvelling at its soft seat. The other two followed suit, then a servant entered, bearing drinks.

"*Do you partake?*" asked Thalgrun. "*It's wine. I'm led to believe it's a favourite of your people.*"

"*Thank you. That would be delightful.*" He accepted a proffered cup, then took a sip. "*It's nice.*"

"*Well, Flan. Do I call you Flan, or have you a title?*"

"*Flan will do nicely. My folk don't believe in such things.*"

"*But you have someone in charge, surely?*"

"*There is our elder, but she's just like us, only older.*"

"*Might I ask the purpose of your visit?*"

"*I was sent to bring news of our plight.*"

"*That sounds serious,*" said Kasri.

"*And it is. The large folk came to the Wayward Wood, cutting down our trees and slaying any of us they find.*"

"*Large folk? You mean Humans?*"

"*Yes.*"

"*Likely Halvarians,*" said Thalgrun. "*Tell me, how many trees did they take?*"

"*Three hundred and forty-two at last count.*"

"*You are very specific,*" said Kasri.

"*They were our friends.*"

"*Any idea why?*"

"*Mostly for fire, but they also use the wood to build the big wagons.*"

"*Big wagons?*"

"*Yes. Strange-looking things with four wheels and a long spoon.*"

"*Long spoon?*" said Thalgrun. "*What's this nonsense?*"

*"I believe he refers to catapults,"* said Kasri. *"The arms of which resemble a spoon."*

*"Oh? I suppose they do, now that I think of it."*

*"This would seem to prove they're intent on a siege."*

*"It does,"* said Thalgrun, *"though it still doesn't tell us when."*

*"What of your own people, Flan?"*

*"They fled deeper into the woods, but the Humans were relentless. I did not come to ask for help but to warn you these vile creatures will not stop."*

*"Is there nothing we can do?"* asked Kasri. *"What if we evacuated your people back to here?"*

Flan let his gaze wander around the room. *"Your way is not ours. My people would suffer without the comfort of the woods."*

*"Have you no army? No warriors?"*

*"Only hunters and those in small numbers. The Humans greatly outnumber us. The only way of escape would be through the gap, and they would quickly overwhelm us with the beasts they ride."*

"Horses," said Thalgrun in the Dwarven tongue. "The one thing we can't counter."

"Perhaps," said Kasri, "but the Mercerians can."

"Could we convince them to send some to our aid?"

"Possibly. They're certainly no use at Stonecastle."

"And how long would that take?"

"It depends on how many we need. They could use our magic circle to transport a company, but even that would take several days. Anything bigger would have to come overland."

Thalgrun grunted. "Which would require marching through Norland. You don't need to explain the politics of that." He drained his tankard before looking back at his guest, switching back to the elder tongue. *"I assume this intrusion is on the eastern side of the Wayward Wood?"*

*"North and east,"* replied Flan. *"The first trees cut down were those closest to the great city."*

*"Can you not retreat to the south?"*

*"That would place us even closer to their lands."*

*"Are you suggesting your entire eastern border is Halvaria?"*

*"Our entire land, save for the western mountains and the small portion that lies astride the gap borders theirs."*

*"We have no forests,"* said Kasri, *"but farther west, in the land called Norland, I'm told there are some that might suffice, if only temporarily. Would you consider going there if it meant the survival of your people?"*

*"If we could make it there, yes, although the journey would prove difficult."*

"*What can you tell me of your people's ability to fight, should it prove necessary?*"

"*We are a peaceful folk, not ones to engage in battles. Our weapons are likely considered crude by your standards, while our small stature forces us to remain concealed rather than fight.*" He withdrew a dagger and held it out, hilt first. "*See for yourself.*"

Kasri took it, then held it up for a good look. "*Exquisite workmanship. It appears to be made of shadowbark.*"

"*It is. It takes great skill to hone it to such a sharpness, but the wood seldom wears.*"

She passed it to her father. "*Remarkable. Have you a lot of this wood?*"

"*We do, though we only harvest what falls naturally.*"

"*A pity,*" said the vard. "*It would be worth a fortune elsewhere.*" He returned it to Flan, noting the faraway look in Kasri's eyes. "*You have a plan. I can tell.*"

"*Well, the beginnings of one.*"

"*Care to share?*"

She stood without warning. "*I need to get to Wincaster. The sooner, the better.*"

"*Wincaster?*" said Flan. "*Where is that?*"

"*Far to the south, but we have a mage who can traverse that distance in the blink of an eye, maybe two.*"

"*How does that help us?*"

"*There is a skilled horseman there named Lanaka. If anyone can lead your people out of danger, it would be him.*"

"But that would be the queen's decision," Thalgrun warned her in the tongue of their people. "She agreed to an alliance with us, but helping Flan's people puts her men in direct danger."

"I've not spent much time in the queen's company," said Kasri, "but Herdwin speaks highly of her. I don't think she would refuse aid when the Aralani's very way of life is in danger." She grinned. "She also likes learning about other cultures and people, and it's not every day she learns about a new race."

"They're not new," said Thalgrun. "They've been around for thousands of years."

"Yes, but the Mercerians have never encountered them."

"Then go find Revi Bloom. Tell him you need to return to Wincaster immediately."

"I can't," she replied. "He needs time to recover his energy."

"Then take Agramath. He committed the Wincaster circle to memory, did he not?"

"You know he has."

"Then tell him I approved this transport. Revi can follow tomorrow once he's had a chance to rest. If I learn anything else, I'll send along a note. And no dawdling while you're down there. I need Agramath back here as soon as possible. He's one of the few advisors I trust."

"Yes, Father."

He hesitated. "And what of you, Kasri?"

"Me?"

"Will you return with him?"

The guilt on her face was easy to recognize, even for Flan.

"No. Until the siege is to be broken, I'm needed elsewhere. Once the counteroffensive starts, however, you can expect me to play my part."

"Good. Now be off with you. I have things to discuss with Flan here."

# TEN

## The Frontier

AUTUMN 967 MC

E xalor Shozarin stood in the circle, closing his eyes in concentration. The teleportation spell was not the easiest of enchantments, and a lapse of attention could easily send him miles off course. He pictured the magic circle in Wyburn within his mind before letting the power flow through him.

The floor runes glowing beneath his feet added to his power, and then there was a sudden jarring sensation as his body was flung across hundreds of miles. He felt stretched beyond breaking, but mere moments later, the sensation abated, and he opened his eyes to the familiar granite floors residing in the College of Mages.

"Home, at last, I see," came a voice.

He smiled, turning to Mistress Anexil, his old tutor.

"To what do I owe the pleasure of this visit?" she asked.

"I'm afraid I'm here on the council's business rather than a personal note."

"One doesn't preclude the other."

Exalor paused for a moment. He'd intended on heading straight for the legion's camp, but Anexil's presence here presented him with an opportunity rather than an interruption. "I shall take you up on that invitation."

She chuckled. "I thought you would. You were never one to refuse a drink and a chat."

"I assume you're familiar with my coming campaign?"

"Naturally. It's the talk of the family." She waved her hand to indicate the door. "Shall we find somewhere private to speak?"

"Of course."

They stepped through the doorway, then continued down the hall.

"It's been years since you graduated, and look at you now. Without a doubt, you are our most accomplished graduate."

"I had a good teacher."

"And your power grows still." She was silent for a moment, then continued. "Go ahead. Ask your question."

"Who says I have a question?"

"You always sought answers. Why should now be any different?"

"You know me too well. The upcoming campaign is a complex one."

"And?"

"To have it succeed, I need people I can trust to carry out their part."

"And you think the Marshal of the North isn't up to it?"

"He made mistakes in Arnsfeld."

"For which you should have removed him."

"I couldn't," replied Exalor. "He has too much influence."

"I bet you're regretting that now."

He grinned. "You know me all too well."

"I'm sensing your next question will be my opinion of the fellow."

"It is. I value your counsel."

"If it were up to me," said Anexil, "I'd have him meet with an unexpected accident. Such things can be arranged if necessary."

"And his Sartellian successor? You know as well as I that we must replace like with like."

"Not necessarily. A replacement of this importance would take months to push through the council. You would be within your rights to install an interim marshal while we wait for the Sartellians to put forward their candidate."

"A valid point. Who do you have in mind?"

"A much more capable soul. Idraxa—you remember her?"

"If I recall, she was two years behind me at this very institution."

"She was indeed. While she lacks actual war experience, she scored very high in strategy and tactics."

"And her magic?"

"She's rated a Master of Enchantment. You needn't worry on that account. She also has the advantage of being a fellow Shozarin, which means you can trust her."

"Still, it's late in the planning stages to make such a change."

"Why don't you meet her in person? That will give you a much better idea of her capabilities."

"You've recommended her. That tells me she's more than merely competent."

"And the accident? Shall I make the necessary arrangements?"

"Plan, but don't execute until I give the word. I must ensure my alibi is undeniable."

She paused beside a door. "Understood. Now, let's have that drink, shall we?"


The Seventh Legion was one of the most decorated in service to the emperor, with many of its men having served for over twenty years. First formed over two centuries ago, it made a name for itself during the more recent Calabrian campaign. With that conflict some forty years past, few veterans remained, yet the tales of their accomplishments had not diminished. If anything, they'd grown, giving the entire legion a pride few others could boast of.

Commander-General Bastien Lambert was not typical of a legion commander, for he hailed from one of the conquered territories, though if you were to ask, he would prefer the term 'liberated'. He'd begun as a provincial officer, but his brilliance had him advancing quickly in rank.

By the age of twenty-two, he was a captain and two years later given command of an imperial company rather than a provincial one. From there, he advanced to captain-general after another five years. Still, getting promoted to commander-general had taken considerably longer, but he was now at the height of his profession.

He could advance no further, for to reach the exalted position of marshal, he must be a trained battle mage. Instead, he resolved to leave his mark by improving the organization of the Imperial legions, a task for which he was particularly well-suited.

He wandered through the camp, surveying his troops. They were in good spirits, as expected under the circumstances. The offensive would not begin for some time, yet they were eager to play their part. He imagined the Seventh Legion marching through the gap, pushing aside any opposition with ease. His path soon brought him to the field to the south, where men laboured at building the mighty engines of war. The sight of the things reminded him of the siege in his future.

He had studied the Dun-Galdrim campaign and was sure he could defeat the mountain folk entrenched at Ironcliff, yet he had a nagging feeling it would be difficult.

"Ah, there you are!"

He wheeled around at the call to see Stalgrun Sartellian, the Marshal of the North. "My pardon, Your Grace. I didn't notice you there."

"The legion looks in fine shape this morning."

Bastien wanted to tell him it was always in fine shape, but that would only irritate the fellow. The man possessed a prickly temper, and his attempt at civility this morning could only mean one thing. "I assume we're to expect visitors today?"

"We are indeed. How did you know?"

"Just a hunch, Your Grace. Might I enquire as to whom we're expecting?"

"The High Strategos, Exalor Shozarin. You can guess what that means."

"That the campaign will soon commence?"

"That would be my guess." The marshal looked around nervously. "Are we sure everything is in order? I'd hate for any deficiencies to show up now."

"I assure you everything is prepared, Your Grace."

"Good, good. I thought we might begin by showing him the changes you've made to the imperial cohorts."

"Wouldn't assembling them for a parade be more appropriate?"

Stalgrun paused as the idea sank in. "Yes. Good point. Have them assemble to the west."

"By cohort?"

"What kind of a question is that?" the marshal snapped. "Of course they are to assemble by cohort. Surely you're not suggesting we mix the imperials in with the provincials? It's simply not done."

Bastien fought to remain calm. Did the fool think so little of provincials? But to avoid further arguments, he simply nodded. "I'll see to it immediately, Your Grace." The commander-general returned to his command tent, his mood soured by the exchange.

Exalor was not an enthusiastic rider, preferring to walk, but there were times when it was necessary to be in the saddle, and this was one of them.

He trotted down the long line of warriors, the Marshal of the North at his side. Behind them rode the legion's commander-general, along with several of his staff. Enjoying the unseasonably warm weather, Exalor was grateful the chill of the north had not yet descended. When they reached the end of the line, he brought his horse to a halt.

"Well?" said Stalgrun. "What do you think?"

"A fine body of men," replied Exalor. "Though I note you've made a few changes. Your idea?"

"No. I'm afraid that was done without my permission."

"Then whose?"

"You would have to ask Commander-General Lambert."

Exalor swivelled in the saddle, looking directly at the legion commander. "Was this your idea?"

"It was, Your Grace." The fellow's eyes held no apology.

"The legion's formation has served us well for centuries. Perhaps you'd
care to explain why you made these changes?"

"We are to assault a Dwarven stronghold, Your Grace. Under such
conditions, having footmen rather than archers is more beneficial. I, therefore, reduced our complement of crossbowmen, replacing them with an
additional company of foot."

"I cannot argue with your reasoning," replied Exalor. "Though I am
curious why the same was not done with your provincials?"

"It would require greater funds to equip them, Your Grace."

"And if I made such funds available, how long would you need to adapt?"

"A month, perhaps two."

"Very well," said Exalor. "You may begin taking the necessary steps to
reorganize your provincial cohorts. I will send word for the funds to be
released this very day."

"Thank you, Your Grace."

"Tell me about these siege engines you've been working on, Marshal."

"Yes, of course, Your Grace," replied Stalgrun. "As you are no doubt
aware, the Imperial Archives have extensive records on the assault on Dun-
Galdrim."

"I am well aware. Many were written in the hand of my predecessor."

"Indeed. Then you no doubt recall the initial attack stalled due to an
inability to break the fortress's gates."

"They were made of shadowbark, and our rams proved ineffective."

"They did. Eventually, however, they came up with the idea of using a
trebuchet to reduce it."

"Yes," agreed Exalor. "It was named *Colossus*. Still, I did not see one
amongst those engines of war to the south. Or have you hidden it away
somewhere?"

"Not at all. The problem with such a siege engine is they are largely
immobile. Catapults and ballistae, on the other hand, can be transported
much easier."

"And you think them sufficient to bring down the gates of Ironcliff?"

"I believe so, Your Grace."

Exalor glanced at Lambert. "You don't agree, Commander?"

"Ironcliff has two gates that we must breach, Your Grace. The outer,
which allows access to the city, and the mountain gate, leading into what
they call the under-mountain."

"Go on."

"The outer gate will fall relatively easily, and the marshal's siege weapons will prove useful there."

"But you doubt they can breach the mountain gate. Is that it?"

"It is, Your Grace," replied the commander-general. "I've also studied the layout of the place, at least as far as we've been able to observe."

"And?"

"A siege engine, even a trebuchet such as the *Colossus*, could not strike the mountain gate. The city's buildings block the line of sight."

"It's a trebuchet," said Stalgrun, bristling. "It launches stones at an angle."

"Yes, but the mountain gate is recessed, making it impossible to hit except by a straight-on attack."

Exalor smiled. The commander-general had gone to great lengths to prepare for the coming campaign, while the Marshal of the North did little to demonstrate his own competence.

"Would you like some refreshments?" interrupted Stalgrun.

"Yes," replied Exalor. "Very much so."

"Then, if you'll follow me, I have a tent for just that purpose."


As the afternoon wore on, Exalor made the necessary small talk, congratulating the captain-generals on how impressive their cohorts were and assuring them they all had the full support of the empire behind them.

After the meal was finished, he stepped outside for some fresh air only to find the commander-general staring off to the west.

"Taking a break?" asked Exalor. "I can't say I blame you. If I weren't the High Strategos, I'd probably be doing the same."

"My apologies, Your Grace. I shall leave you to your privacy."

"Wait. I interrupted you, not the other way around. Stay. I would have words with you."

"By all means, Your Grace."

Exalor followed the man's gaze. From their present position, the two mountain ranges defining the gap were visible, and though they couldn't see any sign of their enemy, he knew they were there, waiting. "We have it on good authority Ironcliff will call on the Mercerians for help."

"I'm well aware. I've read your briefing."

"Then you are also aware there is a possibility you may find yourself fighting Orcs or even Trolls."

"My men are prepared to face whatever they throw our way."

"I'm glad to hear it." Exalor lowered his voice. "Do you still have the crossbows from those disbanded companies?"

"I do. Why?"

"I suggest you give them to your provincials. I realize it would require further training, but it's worthwhile, especially should you be forced to face off against Trolls. I might also remind you Dwarven mail is considerably stronger than our own, so they would prove doubly useful."

Bastien stared back, hesitating for a moment. "That would contravene Imperial policy."

"I decide what breaks policy. Still, if it will make things easier, I will issue an edict allowing it for the Seventh."

"Then I shall see to it first thing tomorrow morning, Your Grace."

"I'm sure it won't be easy. In my experience, archers are often loath to part with their weapons, even if it is for the good of the empire. Whatever you do, though, don't throw away their old bows. Once the campaign is over, they must be returned."

"Of course, Your Grace."

"I've followed your career with a great deal of interest, Commander."

"You flatter me, Lord."

"Perhaps, but now I'm about to put you in a difficult situation."

"Which is?"

Exalor smiled. "Give me your true opinion of the Marshal of the North, and don't hold back. I shall not hold a single word against you."

Bastien didn't answer right away, instead thinking it over. Finally, he nodded. "But I fear you won't like what I am about to say."

"Say it anyway. I admire honesty."

"He is a man who lacks patience."

"I did not expect you to say that. Would you care to clarify?"

"He is more interested in political gain than military success. I fear he would throw the entire campaign beneath the horses' hooves if it elevated his own interests."

Exalor chuckled. "Don't hold back on my account."

"Is it true he was behind the debacle in Arnsfeld?"

"You heard of that?"

"I did, Your Grace. News travels amongst the armies of the empire."

"Yes. It's true."

"And he was forgiven?"

"Forgiven is a strong word," said Exalor. "Stalgrun has some powerful friends, and he's a Sartellian. As such, he wields considerable influence."

"Then I shall do what I can to ensure the success of the coming campaign."

"There. That's the spirit. Now, you must excuse me. It's time to return to the others." He took a step, then paused, looking at Lambert once again. "I assume you are a man who can adapt to change?"

"Yes, Your Grace. Why?"

"Nothing that need concern you at this particular moment, but in the following weeks, you may find some... unexpected changes." Exalor said no more, disappearing into the tent.

Anexil Shozarin looked up from where she worked. "Exalor! Back so soon?"

"You knew full well I intended to return. I have more work to do in the capital."

"Yet you could have teleported directly from the camp."

"And miss the pleasure of your company? I think not."

"Did all go as expected?"

Exalor frowned. "Unfortunately, yes. Is your offer still on the table?"

"Of course. Have you a timeline in mind?"

"Anytime in the next week or so, but give me time to be free of this place."

"And Idraxa?"

"Have her remain here in Wyburn, but don't tell her why. I have some work to do with the council before I can get her confirmed as the interim marshal. I'll send word when she should officially begin her duties."

"Are you particular about what type of accident should befall the Marshal of the North?"

"No. I leave that in your capable hands." He paused a moment. "Though I suppose if it were something lascivious, it might help reduce the influence of his line."

"I shall bear that in mind. Anything else I can do for you while you're here?"

"Yes. Keep an eye on Commander-General Lambert. I'd hate to see Stalgrun's people blaming him for the death."

"He shall be as safe as a newborn child."

# ELEVEN

# Problems

AUTUMN 967 MC

Beverly stood waiting. Ahead of her, the line moved at a desperately slow pace. The herald performing the duty asked the same questions of each entrant, then, after accepting the admittance fee, he added their name to the list of those competing.

She looked around, hoping to spot Aubrey or Aldwin, but they were with Viden and Nymin, helping to set up their smithy. Even Keon had abandoned her, claiming he needed to scout out her opposition.

"Next," called out a voice. Beverly stepped forward to find herself finally before the table where the herald sat, conducting the registration with quill in hand, ready to write her information into a large tome. "Name?" he demanded.

"Dame Beverly Fitzwilliam," she said, thinking it better to enter as a knight.

He looked up in surprise. "You're a woman."

"Thank you. I hadn't noticed. Why? Is that a problem?"

"Of course it's a problem. Sister knights are not permitted to participate in games of this nature. You should know that by now."

"I am no sister knight."

He stared back, unsure what to say, then shook his head. "It matters little. You must be a member of an order of chivalry to compete."

"I am Knight Commander of the Order of the Hound."

"Never heard of it."

"Nor have I heard of half the orders here," scolded a nearby knight, "yet you let them compete."

"She is a woman and thus is prevented from partaking in such manly pursuits."

"Says who?" the knight pressed. "Show me where it says women can't compete?"

"With all due respect, Sir Hendrick, you should confine your interest to the competition rather than the administrative side."

"My apologies." He walked past the line, slowing as he passed Beverly.

"He's a fool. Ignore him."

The herald turned back to Beverly, forcing a smile. "I'm afraid I cannot register you at this time."

"Because I'm a woman?"

"Because there are irregularities in your registration."

"Such as?"

"I have no record of this chivalric order. What did you call it?"

"The Order of the Hound. It's Mercerian."

"It's what?"

"Mercerian. That is to say, it resides in the Kingdom of Merceria."

"There is no such place."

"I assure you there is."

"Prove it."

Beverly looked around, not quite believing her ears. "Do you suppose I am just some commoner who saved up and purchased all this armour so I could participate in a tournament?"

"Stranger things have happened."

"Have they? Like what?"

"I can't think of anything in particular now, but I've heard it all."

"Then answer me this, Master Herald. What would it take to allow me to compete?"

He sat back, hemming and hawing. "Well, I suppose a letter from the king would suffice, not that he'll see you. His Majesty can be quite selective, especially at times like this."

"Like what? Are you at war?"

"Saints, no. I merely meant he is busy socializing before the tourney gets underway."

"And where do I find this king of yours?"

"How would I know?" the herald barked back. "Do I look like I associate with royalty?"

"Isn't that precisely the role of a herald?"

"Begone, before I call the guards!"

A woman's voice interrupted. "Is there a problem here?"

"This woman is holding up the line. Please escort her from here."

Beverly noted the woman's scarlet tabard. "You're a Temple Knight."

She grinned back. "Is it that obvious?"

"My pardon. I'm not used to such sights."

"And you are?"

"Lady Beverly Fitzwilliam, Baroness of Bodden."

"You said you were a Knight Commander," said the herald.

"I am, along with the Queen's Champion and General of the Mercerian army. Would you like to know my marital status as well?"

He visibly shrank.

"My apologies," said Beverly, then turned to the Temple Knight. "It's been a trying week." She stepped from the line, allowing others to proceed. "This fellow tells me I can't register for the tournament."

"Did he say why?"

"First, he said it was because I'm a woman. Then he told me he didn't recognize my order. Tell me, do your people compete?"

"No, but not through lack of ability; it's because of our vows. Instead, we oversee the competitions, stepping in when needed to enforce the rules."

"And is there a rule banning me from competing?"

"Not that I'm aware of, but there's no precedent for it either. Tell me, from where do you hail?"

"Merceria. A land which lies to the west, past Halvaria."

"You're a long way from home."

"Believe me, I know."

"Surely you're not suggesting you came all this way just to compete?"

"No, but we're stranded here, and I need to win some funds to get back home."

"You must think very highly of yourself to believe you can take on the knights of the Petty Kingdoms."

"I spent my entire adult life and a good portion of my childhood training to be a knight. I don't know much about these knights of yours, but where I come from, we're in an almost endless cycle of war. I've seen more battles than I care to count. Does that qualify me to compete?"

"Can you use a lance?"

"Lance, sword, axe, mace—I've trained in them all. Even a bow if needed, although I don't claim to be an expert."

"Remarkable."

"The herald indicated a letter from the king might allow me to compete. Do you know where I could find him?"

"I do. If you'd like to follow me, I'll introduce you. I'm Sister Rowan, by the way. Have you been in Agran long?"

"We only arrived last night," replied Beverly. "Yourself?"

"I'm part of the garrison here."

"And what's that like?"

"It's all right. Not as exciting as my last posting, but I don't mind."

"Why? Where were you?"

"Down on the coast, in a place called Ilea. Ever heard of it?"

"I'm afraid not."

"I get that a lot," said Rowan. "Not that it matters." She slowed as they neared a group of tents. "My captain should be right over there, and she'll know how to find the king."

They went in amongst the tents, emerging into a small clearing where a sister knight sat at a table, poring over reports. She looked up when she noted their approach.

"What's this now, Rowan? Bringing us new recruits?"

"I'm afraid not, Captain. This is Lady Beverly Fitzwilliam, Baroness of Bodden."

"My lady," replied the knight, giving a brief nod. "That's quite the armour you have there, though I fear it's a little archaic."

"Where I come from, we are only now adopting armour like yours. I assure you, however, it's more than capable of protecting me."

"I'm sure it is. How can I help?"

"I seek an audience with the king."

"So do half the people here. I'm afraid you'll have to do better than that if you want his attention."

"I wish to enter the tournament, but I'm told I need the king's permission."

"And when you say the tournament, you mean the joust?"

"I do."

"You'd need quite the horse for that."

Beverly smiled. "I lack only the king's permission."

The Temple Captain rose. "Then come with me, and we'll see if we can find him."

"You know him?"

"Of course. I'm the senior Temple Knight in these parts and spend a lot of time at his court. I'm Temple Captain Giselle, by the way. Where did you say you were from?"

"Bodden. It's in Merceria."

"I'm afraid I'm not familiar with it. Is it one of the Petty Kingdoms?"

"No. It lies far to the west, beyond Halvaria."

"Past the empire? How in the name of the Saints did you find yourself here?"

"It's a long story."

"Have you a short version?"

"Yes—magic."

"You need say no more."


King Justinian leaned on the railing as two knights charged straight at each other, their lances striking with a tremendous crash, and a cheer of approval went up from those watching the joust. A bead of sweat rolled down his forehead, and he wondered if the competitors might be just as uncomfortable as him. The heat could become unbearable within the constricting confines of their armour, so he'd ordered large barrels of water made available to slake their thirst.

"Sire?" said Sir Langmar. "The Temple Captain approaches."

"Oh?" He turned. "To what do I owe the pleasure, Giselle?"

"This is Lady Beverly Fitzwilliam, sire, the Baroness of Bodden."

"Pleased to meet you, my lady, although I usually greet visitors of your calibre at court."

"I came seeking your help, Your Majesty."

"My help? What could I possibly do for you?"

"I've been told I require your written permission to enter the tournament."

"I assume from your armour you know how to joust?"

"The lance is just one of many weapons I am proficient with."

The king shook his head. "No, I can't. My queen would never condone violence against a woman."

"With all due respect," said Giselle, "I very much doubt that would be the queen's response."

"Let us go and ask her, shall we? Come along now, else we'll miss our chance."

"Chance?" said Beverly.

"Oh yes," replied Giselle. "The queen is not one to spend much time at the tourney, and the last thing we want to do is ride all the way over to the Palace."

Sir Langmar led them, setting a fast pace, and they were soon outside a large, decorative pavilion. A regally attired woman sat outside, sipping from a chalice, but stood at the king's arrival, bowing reverently.

"Ah, there you are," said the king. "Thank the Saints I caught you in time." He turned to Beverly. "My wife, Queen Helisant. My dear, this is Lady Beverly Fitzwilliam. Baroness of... What did you say it was?"

"Bodden, sire," replied the Temple Captain.

"Yes, of course. The baroness wants to compete in the joust, if you can believe it. What do you think? Do we allow her to risk injury?"

"Is she skilled?" asked the queen.

"I assume so, else why would she ask?" The king sneezed. "Saints alive. That's the last thing I need."

"Come, husband. Sit while I ponder this puzzle you have given me." Her gaze wandered over Beverly. "There's something about your manner that suggests you're not afraid. Have you dealt with kings before?"

"Indeed, Your Majesty. Where I'm from, I'm the Queen's Champion."

Helisant's eyebrows raised. "How interesting."

The king withdrew a handkerchief and blew his nose. "Well? What do you think? I can't send her into the slaughter, can I?"

"She's a champion, my dear. Did you not hear her say as much?"

"We only have her word for that, and what does it say for the quality of her warriors if the Queen's Champion is a woman?"

"Test me," said Beverly.

Both royals turned to stare at her.

"Let me face someone of your choosing in a contest of skills," she continued. "If I can beat them, would it not prove my competency?"

"I don't know," said the king.

"What is there to lose?" soothed his queen. "It will add an air of the unexpected to the tournament, if nothing else."

"You have convinced me. Sir Langmar?"

The knight stepped forward. "You wish me to fight this woman, sire?"

"Saints, no. I want you to choose someone else for her to fight. A knight who is here for the tournament, perhaps."

"I shall see whom I can find, Majesty." The knight bowed, then went off in search of a worthy opponent.

"Are you travelling alone?" asked the queen.

Beverly was about to name all the members of her party, then remembered the warning concerning Aldwin's eyes. "No. My cousin, Lady Aubrey, and two others accompany me."

The king looked skyward, judging the time of day. "I am tired," he said. "I need to go lie down for a while. Let my people know where they can find you, Lady Beverly. I'll send word when we have found a suitable opponent."

"And if I defeat him, you'll permit me to compete?"

"Most assuredly. Now, off you go. I need my rest."


Aubrey shook her head. "He said what?"

"That I'd have to prove myself against a knight before he allows me entry to the competition."

"Unbelievable."

"Why do you find this surprising?" asked Keon.

"She's the Queen's Champion," said Aldwin. "Have you any idea how many battles she's seen? Or the number of foes she's defeated?"

"Not a clue, but her armour looks like it's never been damaged."

"That's because I spend a lot of time repairing it."

"Well then, perhaps you should leave it a little dented and scratched next time."

"What is the calibre of knights here in Deisenbach?" asked Beverly.

"I wouldn't know. I'm a farmer, remember? And a failed one at that."

"You talked as if you were familiar with tourneys."

"And I am," replied Keon, "but only from the point of view of a spectator."

"Then tell me what you've observed."

"I've only seen a few jousts, but it seems to me the trick is in having a steady horse. I suppose it also takes strength to hold the lance aloft and steady as you approach your competitor. I remember one I saw down in Volbruck. The competitors there weren't of the same quality as what you see here, but it was still impressive."

"And what was so interesting about that particular joust?"

"The lance punctured a knight's breastplate, killing him. Of course, it wasn't intentional. At least, I don't think it was. That sort of thing does happen on occasion."

"Likely a flaw in the fellow's armour," said Aldwin. "Did they not have healers standing by?"

"They did, but what can herbs do for such a wound?"

"He didn't die immediately?"

"No. Did I not say? After several days, the wound became inflamed, and he died of a raging fever."

"So let me get this straight," said Aubrey. "He didn't die from the lance, but an infection?"

"Infection? What's that?"

"It occurs when…" She noticed the look of confusion on Keon's face. "Let's just say something got in the wound and leave it at that, shall we?"

"Aren't you afraid the same thing could happen to your cousin here?"

"No. Beverly has survived her fair share of wounds over the years. In any case, I'm a Life Mage. As long as she's still breathing, there's a good chance I can heal her."

"I'm sorry," said Keon. "Did you say you were a Life Mage? As in a wielder of magic?"

"Yes. I put you to sleep when we first met, remember?"

"So that's what magic feels like."

"Have you no other Life Mages in this land of yours?"

"We do, but they're rare."

"How rare?"

"I doubt you'd find more than one in ten kingdoms have them."

"I'm surprised. With the Continent's long history of magic, I would think it would have more."

"I can't speak to history," replied Keon, "but magical healers are the stuff of legend. If what you say is true, you could command a king's ransom."

"Then perhaps that's better," said Aubrey, looking at Beverly. "That way, you wouldn't have to risk life and limb."

"On second thought, perhaps not," added Keon. "Forget I mentioned it."

"Why?"

"I just recalled the story of King Kayson."

"Who is?"

"He was the King of Rudor, wherever that is. He's been dead for decades now, but the story goes he came across a Life Mage who could use her magic to keep him young."

"Your point?"

"He imprisoned her, forcing her to cast spells to prevent him from aging."

"So, what you're suggesting," said Beverly, "is that a king might hold a Life Mage as a prisoner?"

"That would be the point of it, yes."

"This Life Mage," said Aldwin. "What happened to her?"

"No one knows, but it's said she outlived the king by casting a spell that aged him prematurely."

"That's utter nonsense," piped in Aubrey. "You're describing a Hex Mage —a purveyor of curses."

"Hex Mage?" said Keon. "I don't think I've ever heard that expression."

"The term witch would apply, but that label is often used for Earth Mages as well."

"And you know this, how?"

"From the other mages back in Merceria, of course."

"Other mages? How common are spellcasters in your land?"

"Well, let's see," said Aubrey. She began counting off fingers. "There's Albreda and Aldus Hearn, the Earth Mages; Revi Bloom, my old mentor;

Kiren-Jool, the Enchanter; not to mention Kraloch, and that's only in Merceria."

"Saints alive, that's a lot. Most Petty Kingdoms would be happy to have just one."

"I'm surprised. I assumed magic was far more common here in the Continent."

"Why would you say that?"

"I'm told they have many in Therengia."

"I wouldn't use that name if I were you, especially around here. It's likely to draw an undue amount of attention."

"Well," said Beverly. "The last thing we can afford is for Aubrey to be made a prisoner, so we'll stick with me entering the tournament. If what Viden tells me is true, I don't need to win the whole thing, only a couple of rounds, then I can bow out gracefully."

"And will that give us the funds we require?" asked Aubrey.

"As long as I defeat two knights, yes. The value of their armour and weapons should be more than enough to get us to Reinwick."

"And after that?"

"That largely depends on what we discover once we arrive."

# TWELVE

# Lord of Stone

AUTUMN 967 MC

All eyes turned to Gerald and Albreda as they entered the throne room of Stonecastle. Vard Khazad sat there, absently rubbing beneath his eyepatch, while the masters of each guild, and their deputies, clamoured for the vard's attention. Today, however, they would have to wait, for the visit of such distinguished guests took precedence. The Mercerians halted ten paces from the throne.

"Your Majesty," said Gerald. "I bring greetings from Queen Anna of Merceria."

"And this is?" said Khazad, nodding at the Druid.

"Albreda, Mistress of the Whitewood," she replied. "I come to offer my expertise."

"You are a long way from the forest, Druid. We would have been better blessed with a visit from a master of rock and stone."

Albreda straightened to her full height. "Have you any idea to whom you are talking?"

A hush fell over the room, but she wasn't done.

"How dare you sit on that slab of granite and insult me. I've a good mind to collapse these halls around you!"

Guards moved forward, weapons at the ready.

Gerald held up his hand. "My apologies, Majesty. I should have explained, Albreda is the most powerful mage in all of Merceria."

"And that gives her the right to threaten me?" shouted the vard.

"You are the one who questioned my power," she replied. "I might remind you I came here at the behest of Queen Anna. King or not, I suggest you mind your manners."

A knot formed in Gerald's stomach. Albreda could be difficult at times, but this was completely unexpected. He glanced around at the guards, ready to pounce. One word from the Vard of Stonecastle, and they would be locked up in a dungeon for the rest of their lives.

Unexpectedly, Khazad laughed, breaking the tension. "You are right, of course, Mistress Albreda. My pardon for the jest, but I had to test your resolve."

The Druid smiled. "As I suspected."

"You knew?" whispered Gerald.

"Of course I knew. Herdwin warned me what to expect."

"When? He's been at Kharzun's Folly for the last few months."

"I was at Lord Richard's estate in Wincaster when he returned from his adventures last year."

"You could have warned me," he replied. "I almost died of fright."

"I knew they wouldn't kill us."

"No, but they might lock us up."

"And start a war with their ally? I very much doubt they'd go that far. Besides, I'm told Dwarves like to argue."

Khazad waved them forward. "I am pleased by your visit. I feared the court of Wincaster had not taken our plight seriously, especially after General Fitzwilliam failed to return."

"I can assure you we have," replied Gerald. "Unfortunately, Lady Beverly was lost to us, which threw our plans into chaos."

"Lost? Do you mean to say she died?"

"No. Transported elsewhere by magic, unintentionally, I should add."

"And who do you plan to replace her with?"

"I shall assess the situation for myself, but as to replacements, my first choice would be Herdwin Steelarm."

"Outrageous!" came a call from behind them.

Gerald turned around to see an elderly Dwarf pushing through the crowd. "You cannot assign such an important task to a lowly, guildless smith!"

"And you are?"

The Dwarf puffed himself up to his tallest height. "I am Lord Thyrim Broadaxe, Guild Master of the Warriors Guild, and if anyone is to command the defence of Kharzun's Folly, it should be me!"

"With all due respect," said Gerald, "the defence of what remains of that bridge is a joint venture between your realm and ours. Your king agreed to a Mercerian being placed in command."

Thyrim looked at his vard. "What is the meaning of this?"

Khazad stared him down. "I'll not deny it. While you have served us faithfully for years, Thyrim, you lack experience in war. The Mercerians, as you well know, have seen many battles."

"It still doesn't excuse appointing Herdwin Steelarm as commander."

"Yes, it does," said Gerald. "He's an experienced warrior and ranked commander in the Mercerian army. I don't choose to appoint him because he's a Dwarf but because he's the best one to assess the threat to the security of both our realms." He noticed the look of distaste not only on Thyrim's face but the other guild masters as well.

"I should also point out he sits on the Royal Council of Merceria, where he is ranked as an earl." He didn't mention it was a ceremonial position or that Herdwin had only been given it because he represented Khazad, the Vard of Stonecastle.

"This is unconscionable!" insisted Thyrim.

Khazad stood, demanding the attention of all in the room. "This is not the time for petty squabbles. We must put our differences aside in the interest of preserving our way of life. Merceria has come to our aid, and in so doing, brought warriors to help in our defence. Even as we speak, over three hundred Humans are in our streets, willing to give their lives, if necessary, to defend our realm."

"We owe your people a debt," said Gerald. "You aided us in our time of need, and now we return the favour. Merceria stands shoulder to shoulder with the Dwarves of Stonecastle and will continue to do so, regardless of what may befall us."

"Now, that," said Thyrim, "is something I can agree to." He turned, moving through the crowd, the other guild masters patting him on the back to recognize his change of opinion.

Gerald turned to the vard. "Perhaps, Your Majesty, this meeting would be more productive in private? Over an ale or two?"

Khazad grinned. "A man after my own heart. I shall have the heralds dismiss the court, then we can sit down and have a little chat."

A short while later, they sat before a roaring fire. Khazad, insisting he was the host, had poured them an ale, then settled into his chair.

"I assume you're here to see the situation for yourself?"

"I am," replied Gerald. "Our thought was that Albreda would use her magic to get a better idea of how many men we're facing."

"You possess the ability to scry?"

"Not scry," replied Albreda, "but I can call on an eagle to spy out their camp."

"Is there a range limitation to this spell?"

"There is if I wish to see it for myself. Having said that, I can still have the bird fly farther afield, but then I'll have a little more difficulty interpreting what they've seen."

"I'm afraid I don't understand."

"Animals don't always see things the same way we do. To them, the concept of companies or command tents is foreign. Thus, it would fall to me to ask the right questions."

"And when they're closer?"

"That," said Albreda, "is a little different. Within range of my magic, I can see through their eyes."

"So they become a familiar?"

"No, not in the normal sense. My connection would not be as strong as that between Revi Bloom and Shellbreaker, for example."

"Who?"

"A mage of Merceria, one with a familiar like you've just referenced."

"Then how do you see through their eyes? I'm no mage, but wouldn't such a spell be more appropriate for a master of air?"

"And so it would be were it not for my connection to the Whitewood."

"She's a wild mage," explained Gerald. "Thus, her powers sometimes defy our normal method of classification."

"A wild mage? How interesting. I've heard all such folk are self-taught."

"As I was," said Albreda.

"The prevailing thought," added Gerald, "is that she owes much of her power to that very fact. Mages, I'm told, are taught strict rules concerning the harnessing of their power. Having none to follow allowed her to attempt things others would never dream possible." He turned to the Druid in a moment of inspiration. "Is what Khazad said true? Is your ability more akin to Air Magic?"

"I suppose it might be considered so. Why?"

"It occurs to me that Princess Edwina requires an Air Mage to teach her spells."

"I hadn't considered that. I shall give it some further thought once we return to Wincaster."

"As to your army," said Khazad, "will you be sending any additional men?"

"That's difficult to say," replied Gerald. "We're currently stretched to the limit, and there are disturbing rumours coming out of Ironcliff."

"What kinds of rumours?"

"The same people threatening you are preparing to march on Ironcliff."

"Will you send them help?"

"If we can, but to get there, we must pass through another realm's lands. We could send some via magic, but that would be draining on our mages."

"Yes," agreed Albreda. "But I'm sure we could get a company or two up there if we had sufficient warning."

"We could do with one of those circles here," said Khazad. "It would make it much easier to communicate with your queen."

"That is a marvellous idea, Majesty, though I must warn you it can be expensive."

"Why is that?"

"Large amounts of gold are used to harness the magic a circle needs to operate. It also requires a mage to sacrifice a portion of their own magic to empower it, though we are blessed in that, at least."

"I shall consult with my advisors. Have you someone knowledgeable about such things?"

"We do," said Gerald. "Unfortunately, Aldwin's in the same predicament as Beverly and Aubrey."

"You only have one who knows how to construct a circle?"

"We have many who understand what's needed, but only one with the skill to actually do the work, although I imagine Herdwin would be up to it if given a chance."

"Ah, yes. Herdwin."

"You don't seem surprised."

"If I'm being honest, I'm not. I've always known him to be an exceptional smith. If it were within my power, I'd order the guild to make him a master, but membership in such an august organization is beyond my control." He paused, taking a swig of his ale. "Say, could a member of our smiths guild construct a circle?"

"Possibly," said Albreda. "Can they take precise instructions?"

"I'm not sure what you mean by that. Are you asking if they possess the ability to craft detailed products?"

"No. I'm asking if they can subvert their individual tendencies to make the structure their own? The gold and inlaid runes of power need to be made to exact measurements. To deviate, even a little, would throw off the balance of power when casting. Aubrey and I discussed the technique at length before completing our first circle."

"But Aldwin built the Wincaster circle," said Gerald.

"Yes, he did, but to my specifications. I doubt another smith would be so meticulous."

"I shall forward my extensive notes to you, Majesty, once I return to Wincaster," continued Albreda. "If you arrange for its construction, I will find a mage to empower it for you. In fact, I'll go one better. We'll find a Dwarf who can learn magic so you can use it."

"You can't," said Gerald. "We need Aubrey for that, and she's stuck out in the middle of nowhere."

"Oh yes. I keep forgetting. Well, the building of it will take some time. I'm sure she'll be back amongst us by then."

"We can certainly hope so. As for Stonecastle, do you require more men to safeguard its walls?"

Khazad frowned. "That largely depends on how many of the enemy are coming. We have enough to watch the walls, but should they breach them, we can't be everywhere at once."

"How many men did we send?" asked Albreda.

"Two hundred foot," replied Gerald, "along with two companies of archers. And when I say archers, I'm referring to longbows, not the shorter type the rest of our companies employ."

"I thought only the rangers used those?"

"You would have been correct in the past, but with the Orcs now comprising a good portion of the Queen's Rangers, it's freed up archers to create a more permanent company."

"Or, in this case, two? Or are you hiding others?"

"Just the two at this point. It takes many years to master a bow of that power. Some of our Orcs employ warbows, but I'm more likely to need them in the north. Besides which, Dwarven arbalests are still the superior weapon."

"I'm curious," said Khazad. "We're not forcing you to overextend yourselves, are we? I'd hate to think you're stripping away your own defences to help us here."

"The queen feels, as do I, that the defence of Stonecastle is the preferred method of protecting Merceria. If we hold the enemy here, we stop them from pouring into our lands. It also has the advantage of forcing them through a very narrow opening, the pass to the east. I haven't seen them myself, but I would think that much easier than trying to stop them on the eastern plains of Merceria."

"When will you leave for Kharzun's Folly?"

"Tomorrow morning, weather permitting."

"Then I shall find someone to show you the way. You're staying at Captain Gelion's house, yes?"

"We are," replied Gerald.

"Good. I believe there's a young apprentice there. What was his name?"

"Tindal?"

"That's the one. He is, if I'm not mistaken, familiar with the route. I shall dispatch orders for him to be your guide."

"He'll like that," said Albreda, "especially considering he's only an apprentice."

"Any advice?" asked Gerald.

The vard stared back, deep in thought. "None that I can think of. Give my regards to Herdwin when you see him, and tell him I won't let the guild usurp his position. Do you need supplies?"

"We have some travelling rations."

"I'll arrange to top you up before you leave. Should you require more, the last tower before the bridge is well-stocked."

"And the bridge itself?"

"Gelion fortified our side of it, though I can't tell you how extensive those defences are. You'll need to make that observation yourself."

"In that case, we will bid you farewell, Majesty."

"Farewell, and may Gundar watch over you."

They set out the next day before the sun was up. Khazad, true to his word, supplied them with extra rations, though admittedly, they were stonecakes. Tindal led them on foot, the terrain to the east too precarious for horses.

"How far is it?" asked Gerald.

"That largely depends on the weather," replied Tindal. "There are three towers along the way, each spaced a day apart, but that assumes clear weather." He looked up, noting the sky. "If it stays like this, we'll be there in no time."

"And if it turns bad?"

"Then we shall seek shelter wherever we can."

"Tell me," said Albreda. "Do you like the life of a warrior?"

Tindal shrugged. "It has its moments."

"Do you think you'll join the warriors guild once your quest for knowledge is over?"

"I'm not sure. I might move on to the miners or even the stone masons guild. Margel seems to think I possess a gift for it."

"A gift, you say?"

"Yes. While I was still a youth, I used to assist her from time to time. She said I showed great promise."

"I wonder," said Albreda, "if it might be more than that? Tell me, have you ever shown an affinity for animals?"

"No, but then again, what animals am I likely to see in these parts?"

"That is a valid point." They walked on in silence a while, and then Albreda spoke again. "Just out of curiosity, why the miners guild?"

"I don't know. I suppose I always liked the idea of being surrounded by stone. It gives me a sense of peace. Why? What difference does that make?"

"Who said anything about making a difference?"

"What is it you're getting at?" asked Gerald.

"Those with a capacity for magic often exhibit an unusual interest in the element in question."

"He's a Dwarf. His entire life revolves around stone. Is it so hard to believe it's only a part of his culture?"

"I once thought as you," said Albreda, "but experience has taught me not to ignore coincidences. Tell me, Tindal, why did you choose to spend time in the warriors guild and not go into stonework immediately?"

"My home was threatened from the east," the Dwarf replied. "I couldn't just stand by and do nothing."

"So you had no desire to follow in your cousin's footsteps?"

"I have hundreds of cousins," said Tindal, "and they cover off most of the guilds between them. If I were to emulate them all, I'd be over a hundred by the time I finished."

"Still, you must admit, it's a curious coincidence that you came into our lives when Stonecastle requires a master of rock and stone."

"Are you suggesting it was fate?"

"No. I don't believe in such things."

"Really?" said Gerald. "Wasn't it fate that brought you to the Whitewood?"

"It was not. Had I not succumbed to the call of magic, someone else undoubtedly would have."

"Yet you found your family."

"I did," replied Albreda. "But once again, it wasn't fate that brought them to me; it was their caring nature and maternal instincts."

"The Whitewood taught you magic."

"No. On that, you are also wrong. It led me to the stone circle, that much is true, but it took me travelling to Shrewesdale to unlock its secrets. I suppose some may claim that to be the work of fate, but I prefer to think of it as the result of a lot of hard work."

"Yes, but had you not found that stone circle, you would never have been tempted to make the trip."

"Fang accompanied me, and he didn't end up using magic. How does your fate account for that?"

"It doesn't," said Gerald. "But perhaps his purpose was to keep you safe?"

"Hmmm. I hadn't considered that. You may be onto something there. I will, just this once, concede the point. It was my fate to become a Druid."

Tindal pondered her words. "Does that mean I could become a wielder of magic like you if I studied hard enough?"

"Don't be ridiculous," she snapped back. "You can't just choose to become a mage. It must be in your blood!"

# THIRTEEN

## Into the Mountains

### AUTUMN 967 MC

The rain drummed incessantly on the carriage roof, making conversation difficult. Exalor looked out the window and frowned, the downpour obstructing his view.

"How much farther?" he snapped.

"Some way yet, Your Grace," replied Wingate. "Were we able to fly, we would be there in no time, but the roads in these parts meander back and forth to overcome the steep incline."

"This is a miserable place. I can see why we avoided it in the past. Tell me again the history of this area."

His aide cleared his throat. "There is but a single path leading up into the mountains, Your Grace. Some years ago, our scouts discovered a series of towers at higher altitudes. Further investigation revealed Dwarves had built them. Unfortunately, we were unable to ascertain anything else until our agents in Merceria reported the presence of a Dwarven fortress, or city, depending on your point of view."

"Yes. I read the reports about Stonecastle. They were sparse on details but hinted it was similar in size to Dun-Galdrim."

"Indeed. Yet, as you say, there was little in the way of substance. Our legion took some prisoners when we moved into place last year, but they proved unable to speak our language."

"Unable or unwilling?"

"Either way, we got nothing out of them."

"Which leads to our present situation," said Exalor.

"There was that part about the bridge collapsing, Your Grace."

"Trust me. I'm familiar with the details. It kept me up for weeks trying to devise a way to overcome that particular obstacle."

His aide raised his eyebrows. "You found a solution? You never informed me."

"This may come as a shock, Wingate, but sometimes I like to keep things to myself. As it happens, I've had mages practicing something new."

"That sounds exciting, Your Grace. Any chance you might be willing to reveal what they're up to?"

"Not yet, but you'll be the first to know when the time comes. Suffice it to say, when the offensive begins, that gorge will no longer be a problem."

"And the troops on the other side?"

"We shall brush them aside as we have every other enemy of the empire."

The carriage slowed as the ground levelled off. Although the rain still came down in torrents, he could see the tents marking the edge of the legion's camp.

"Not to state the obvious, Your Grace, but we have arrived. Shall I go and fetch the commander-general?"

"Give him a moment. I'm sure word of my arrival will not have escaped the notice of his guards. I shall be interested to see how long it takes him to react, considering I gave him no advance warning."

"It would be nice if this rain would cease."

"On the contrary. It gives us the chance to see how a legion operates in adverse weather. An offensive campaign like ours will need stalwart warriors. I wonder if the Third is up to the task?"

Figures advanced, shrouded in cloaks to ward off the rain. One knocked on the carriage door while another called the rest to attention.

Exalor smiled at his aide. "You may proceed." He waited until Wingate opened the door, then stepped from the carriage, ignoring the torrential downpour.

"Welcome, Your Grace," a voice called out. "I'm sorry we didn't prepare a more fitting welcome for you, but we received no word you were coming."

"Clearly an administrative oversight. I shall be sure to look into the matter upon my return." Exalor glanced at the guards, who looked miserable and thoroughly soaked, but they remained at attention, displaying their discipline despite their discomfort. He returned his gaze to his greeter. "And you are?"

"Captain Francesco Cardosa, Your Grace. Captain of the Second Company, First Imperial Cohort."

"Cardosa, you say? Is that Calabrian?"

"Yes, Your Grace."

"I am here in my capacity as High Strategos, Captain. Sir or Lord will suffice."

"Yes, sir. Shall I take you to see the commander-general?"

"Actually, I'd prefer it if you showed me the camp."

The captain stared back, struggling to balance his loyalty to his commander against his duty to the empire. "Of course, sir."

They walked towards the tents, their boots picking up mud as they went.

"Tell me," said Exalor, "how is the morale of late?"

"Discipline is still intact, Your Grace."

"That wasn't what I asked, Captain. Now speak the truth. You shan't shoulder any blame."

"The men are restless, sir. We expected to see some fighting when we moved up into the mountains, but nothing came of it other than a small skirmish, and we've been here for over a year. Does your visit portend a change in our fortunes?"

"I can neither confirm nor deny that until I've spoken with your commander-general." Exalor halted, taking in the view. Only a smattering of tents were visible through the downpour, but what he could see made him hopeful. "The sentries appear alert."

"They are, sir. To be otherwise would lead to disciplinary action."

"You speak as though there has been some trouble."

"A few fights, sir. Not unusual when a legion gets bored."

"You mentioned you were in the First Imperial Cohort. How would you rate the provincials?"

"They appear to be in good spirits. Surprising, considering our current circumstances."

"Would you care to explain?"

"Provincial troops are typically uncomfortable with the harsh realities of camp life."

"Yet they make up half the empire's armies."

"They do, sir, but most of those legions are in cities, where they live in buildings rather than tents."

"And you think that preferable?"

"On the contrary. Experiencing life in camp only serves to harden them."

"On that, we are in agreement." The High Strategos looked skyward, but the rain gave no indication of letting up. "I've seen enough, Captain. Take me to your commander-general."


Like all legion camps, the higher-ranking officers' tents were located in the centre, which made issuing orders easier while allowing some protection for these individuals should the place be attacked.

Commander-General Esteve Solinak, noting the unexpected approach of the High Strategos, put down his drink. The visit had been unannounced, not the sort of thing that usually brought good news, and he had to wonder if his career was in jeopardy. It wasn't unheard of for people in his position to be relieved of command before an offensive. The thought sent a chill down his spine.

"Your Grace," he said in greeting. "You honour us with your presence."

"I've been inspecting your legion, Commander. I must say what I've seen of it impressed me."

Relief flooded through the commander-general. "I'm glad we were up to your standards, Your Grace. Would you care for a drink? Something to warm you on this chilly rain-swept day?"

Exalor moved under the canopy. "Yes. That would be nice." He waited until a servant fetched him a cup. As was the custom, it was first passed to Wingate, who took a small sip, pronouncing it safe.

"I'm interested in the organization of your legion," continued the High Strategos.

"I modelled it on the standard establishment, Your Grace, that which has served the empire well for centuries."

"Yet I can't help but feel some alterations are long overdue."

"Alterations? With all due respect, sir, the legions have proven their effectiveness again and again. Why risk making changes?"

"Ah," replied Exalor, "but the legions we have today are not the same as those from two hundred years ago. As the art of warfare evolves, so do the legions, unless you're suggesting heavily armoured horsemen have been here forever?"

"You make an excellent point, as always. Was there something in particular you had in mind?"

"I shall respond to that with a question of my own. What weaknesses does a legion possess?"

"None that I'm aware of. It's the perfect blend of footmen, archers, and cavalry."

"Is it, though?"

"Our history would certainly seem to indicate it is."

"On the surface, I would agree," said Exalor, "but your men will soon face a far more savage enemy than we've ever dealt with before. An enemy, moreover, that's had years to perfect its tactics. To ensure success, it behooves us to adapt the structure of the legions to deal with this new threat."

"I understand your concern," said Esteve, "but I'm curious to hear what changes you're suggesting."

"I want the provincial foot to be better equipped. Specifically, I want them trained up to the level of the imperial footmen."

"We haven't the armourers to upgrade all that mail, Your Grace."

"But you could update their weapons and training?"

"I suppose it would depend largely on how much time we have. When is the offensive due to commence?"

"Not until early spring," replied Exalor. "Will that give you enough time?"

"It's doable."

"Good. Then I expect you to get working on it right away. Any questions?"

"About the upgrades, no, but I have several concerns about some of the finer points of the campaign."

"Let's hear them."

"It primarily concerns the issue of supply. This campaign will take us deep into the mountains, and we're all aware of how scarce food is there. A typical offensive of this nature would use wagons to haul supplies, but the narrow paths prevent such things."

"Yes, that might be an issue. I suggest you use pack horses."

"I'd thought of that, Your Grace, but there are few available, thanks to the remoteness of our camp."

Exalor turned to his aide. "When we return, send word to have some shipped here. Actually, let's change that. Instead of horses, arrange for donkeys or, better yet, mules. They're likely to be far more suitable to this terrain." He turned back to the commander-general. "I'll need some numbers before this can be arranged."

"I shall have our estimates to you before the day is out, Your Grace."

"Excellent. Anything else you'd care to bring up? You mentioned you had several concerns. That turn of phrase would suggest there was more than one."

"The timing is worrisome. Spring spreads throughout the empire in a consistent manner, but up here in the mountains, it can often prove troublesome."

"Of that, I am fully aware. You must bear in mind, however, your part in this campaign, though crucial, is not the offensive that will break the enemy's back."

"It's not?"

"No. Your responsibility is to tie down as many enemy soldiers as you can. Of course, if you do happen to break through, then so much the better, but my plans only call on you to get as far as the Dwarven stronghold."

"Stonecastle?"

"That's the one."

"That is also my third point of concern, Your Grace. We lack proper siege engines."

"Your task is not so much to breach their defences as it is to tie them up."

"Understood, yet if we are to eventually march into Merceria, the city must fall."

"Let me reassure you," said Exalor. "Before your part of the campaign launches, several Earth Mages will arrive to breach the walls of Stonecastle. All you need do is have the men ready to take advantage of their magic."

"And the gorge?"

"They will look after that as well."

"You have addressed all my concerns, Your Grace."

"I understand it's unusual to hear of such things directly from the High Strategos in person, but I believe the fewer people who know, the better."

"You fear someone might try to undermine you?"

"We all realize how much politics infuses the ranks of the army. Now, let's see about getting me to that captured tower, shall we? I'm eager to visit the site."


The next morning, Captain Cardosa and a company of imperial footmen escorted them to the gap. Exalor sat silently in his carriage throughout the tedious trip, leaving the commander-general no choice but to do the same. It wasn't until the captured Dwarf tower came into view that the High Strategos took an interest in his surroundings.

"Fascinating," he said, ignoring the massive wooden tower constructed to block their end of the broken span. "It looks quite old."

"From what we could tell, the Dwarves fused the stone to make it," replied the commander-general. "Are our own mages capable of such things?"

"Not to my knowledge. Then again, perhaps, with some study, they might learn to adapt." He shifted his gaze. "And you built the tower to my specifications?"

"Yes, Your Grace, although I struggle to understand its design."

"It serves two purposes: on the one hand, it provides the enemy with what they think is our strategy, namely dropping a platform through which our men will proceed."

"And the second?"

"It gives our mages a clear view of the opposing side, which is critical if we are to succeed here."

"You harbour doubts?"

"In my plan, no, but it depends on the legion's bravery to carry it to fruition."

"My men will not shirk their duty, Your Grace."

"Good. Then when the time comes, I will await word of your success. I should warn you, however, the rest of the way is likely to be a bitter struggle. The mountain folk are notorious for fighting in such terrain. You can expect heavy losses."

"Have we a better idea of their strength?"

"My estimates place their numbers at close to four hundred warriors," replied Exalor, "but I expect the Mercerians to have reinforced that with some of their own men."

"Even were it double, we still have numerical superiority."

"I am fully acquainted with the strength of a legion, but conventional wisdom calls for two to three times the number of defenders when dealing with a siege. I should also point out that your horsemen will be useless in this terrain."

"Agreed," said Solinak, "but they'll prove decisive once we break through to Merceria."

"You're more optimistic than I." Exalor exited the carriage and strode towards the remains of the bridge, moving to one side to allow an unobstructed view of the gorge and the Dwarven defences. "How curious. They've erected a wall, not that it'll stop us."

"Careful, Your Grace. Their bows are particularly effective against our armour."

"They are not bows—they are arbalests."

"Isn't that the same as a crossbow?"

"Our studies indicate they have a greater range as well as the armour penetration you mentioned."

"Might I ask why we have not adopted them ourselves?"

"Their construction is complex, and superior strength is required to reload them. It is far more cost-effective to arm our archers with more conventional weapons." He met the gaze of a distant Dwarf. Was this the enemy commander sizing up his opponent? The thought struck him as interesting, and he raised his hand in greeting. His opponent replied with the same gesture.

"How curious," said Exalor. "I wonder if that fellow realizes to whom he waves?"

"Likely not, Your Grace. The mountain folk are not known as great thinkers."

"Do not mistake obstinacy for lack of understanding. If we underestimate our opponents, it will only lead to ruin."

"Are you suggesting their warriors are as good as ours?"

"In their own way, yes. Remember, they will be defending their homes in terrain with which they are intimately familiar. Only a fool would discount the threat." He glanced over his shoulder. "How many of those towers have they?"

"Aside from that which we captured, only one, as far as we can see."

"There are likely more," said Exalor. "Unless I miss my guess, they'll be one day's march apart. Of course, that's by Dwarven reckoning."

"How could you possibly know that, Your Grace?"

"They are similar to those they had in Dun-Galdrim. They are, in essence, rest towers, allowing warriors to seek shelter while travelling to the farthest frontiers of their kingdom. I read we had quite the trouble with them on that campaign. I don't intend to let them get in the way this time."

"Surely you're not suggesting we start bombarding it now?"

"No, of course not. We'd be well out of range. Besides which, our Earth Mages will make short work of them."

"And when are they to arrive?"

"Some time yet, but rest assured, they'll be here when needed." He looked around at the warriors present. "Are these Captain Cardosa's men?"

"No, Your Grace. This is the First Company, Second Imperial Cohort."

"Is their captain around?"

"No," replied the commander-general. "He's back at the main encampment."

"Why is he not here?"

"It's not common practice for officers to camp within range of the enemy, Your Grace."

"If his men are to suffer these uncomfortable conditions, then I want him here sharing the ordeal. Is that clear?"

"Yes, sir. I shall issue orders to that effect as soon as we return."

"You mean as soon as YOU return. I'll not be going with you."

"You intend to remain here?"

"No. I have pressing business elsewhere. I shall be using my magic to depart momentarily."

"Is there anything else I can do for you, Your Grace?"

Exalor looked around the location, lingering on what remained of the bridge. "No. You've been most helpful, Commander-General Solinak. I look forward to reading reports of your further adventures."

"Thank you, Your Grace."

"Oh, don't thank me; thank the emperor for making this entire thing possible!"

## FOURTEEN

## Tournament

AUTUMN 967 MC

A ldwin tightened the straps on Beverly's breastplate. "If we'd only waited another few weeks before stepping through that gate, you'd be wearing your new armour."

"It's not as if we knew we'd be stranded in the middle of nowhere."

"I don't understand," said Aubrey. "Didn't you master plate armour some time ago?"

"I learned how to make it," replied Aldwin, "but then the Dwarf smith returned to Ironcliff, along with his tools, so I've spent the last few months creating my own set."

"Tools?"

"Yes. Forms, for the most part, which I use to shape the armour." He tapped Beverly's pauldron. "Take this, for example. It's not easy getting the right shape."

Keon, watching the exchange, shook his head. "I still don't understand how a grey-eye learned a trade. Have they not heard of the Old Kingdom where you're from?"

"No," said Beverly. "And even if we had, we wouldn't judge people solely on the colour of their eyes. What a barbaric practice."

"You say that now, but you don't know our history."

"Then why don't you enlighten me?"

"I'm no scholar, but everyone knows how the Old Kingdom conquered half the Continent, holding us in thrall, lording their power over all."

"Strange," said Aubrey. "That's not the version I've heard."

"It's true. I swear it."

"I understand that's what you believe, but history is usually far more complicated."

"Has your own home not suffered from war?"

"Most certainly, but we learned to adapt. The realms which used to be our enemies are now our allies. Peace offers far more benefits than war."

Aldwin grunted as he tightened the last strap. "Remind me to replace this buckle. It's looking a little worn." He moved around, stepping a few paces back to stand before his wife, casting his gaze over her.

Beverly placed her hand on her hips and swayed slightly. "Like what you see?"

He grinned. "Of course I do, but you're about to fight. I need to ensure everything is where it should be."

She squatted twice before stretching her arms to either side, loosening up her muscles. "Feels fine to me."

"Will you use Nature's Fury?"

"No. That would feel like I was showing off. My sword will suffice, although I'll carry my shield." Aubrey handed it to her, and she stared at the coat of arms painted upon it—her father's crest, with the addition of a rose to signify her mother. Aldwin had made it for her some years ago, and though battered and bent many times over, he always managed to restore it.

After her father's death, she'd become the Baroness of Bodden, adopting the crest as her own, yet the sight of it still reminded her of him.

"Are we ready?" called out the herald.

Beverly shifted her gaze to the area in the practice field, which had been cleared for her to fight the king's champion. All the tourney's entrants gathered to watch this woman who'd demanded the right to prove herself. Keon revealed that significant amounts of coins had been bet on the outcome, but it was not the custom of Mercerians to place bets where people's lives were concerned.

Aldwin handed over her sword, and she stepped out onto the field. The knight who awaited her was somehow familiar. His visor was up, his blade held in a relaxed manner, but it was when he spoke that she realized he was the one who'd advocated for her as she tried to register.

"Are you ready, my lady?" he asked.

"Most certainly."

"I shall try not to be too aggressive."

"You should do no such thing," said Beverly. "I am a veteran of many battles, Sir... what was your name again?"

"Sir Hendrick, my lady."

"And where do you hail from, Sir Hendrick?"

"Most recently, the Duchy of Erlingen, but I travel around. Is this your first attempt at a tourney?"

She considered bluffing but decided against it. Her father believed she should always be honest, which was now part of the Order of the Hounds' vows. She settled on a compromise. "In these lands, yes, it is."

They waited in the sun for the king to arrive. Several knights made disparaging remarks at Beverly's expense, but her opponent wheeled around, stomping over to the group in question. "You are being brutish. Need I remind you we are all knights here and are sworn to be courteous to those of the fairer sex."

The speech quieted them, at least for the moment. The king's arrival got them talking again, although Beverly's gender was not their topic so much as her prowess, or lack thereof, in battle.

A pale King Justinian halted, looking over the two combatants, squinting slightly when the sun caught his eye. A servant produced a small stool for him to sit on, but he waved it away.

"You may proceed," he announced.

The king's man, Sir Langmar, stepped out from the crowd to stand between Beverly and her opponent. "This fight will continue until one of you yields. It is not an affair of honour; thus, blood is not required to be drawn. Is this clear?" He looked at each in turn.

Beverly nodded, as did Sir Hendrick, then Sir Langmar drew his weapon and held it up. She watched, expecting her opponent to rush, but Sir Hendrick simply stood there after the king's man sliced his sword between them.

Beverly shifted slightly to her left, anticipating a countermove, but the fellow only raised his blade into a guard position.

"Come now," she said. "Don't be timid."

Still, he refused to budge, so she took the initiative, advancing with a flurry of vicious cuts that put him on the defensive, driving him back several feet, then she retreated.

The attack had taken him by surprise. As a more or less friendly duel, he'd elected to keep his visor up, but now he flipped it down, signifying he was serious about the fight. Beverly lowered her own visor, settling in for an extended battle.

~

Aubrey watched as Beverly struck again. She'd seen her cousin in combat before and knew she was probing her opponent's defences.

"It won't be long now," she said.

"For what?" asked Keon.

Beverly moved in closer to Sir Hendrick. From their angle, they could see little save for her back, but then the man's sword went flying.

"That," said Aubrey.

"For Saint's sake!" shouted Keon. "Not again! My luck is terrible when it comes to things like this."

"What are you talking about?"

"I might have placed a few coins on Sir Hendrick."

"What coins?"

"The ones you gave me."

"That was to buy food," said Aubrey.

Aldwin shook his head. "Idiot. I could have told you she'd win."

"How was I supposed to know? Sir Hendrick is a three-time tourney champion!"

"Truly?"

"Well, not for some years now, but he was renowned in his younger days."

"Hush," said Aubrey. "It appears Keon's champion has yielded." She watched as Beverly and Hendrick approached the king. They exchanged words with His Majesty, and then the two combatants wandered over to the other Mercerians.

"Your speed surprised me," said Sir Hendrick. "Your fighting master taught you well. Might I ask who tutored you?"

"The Marshal of Merceria," replied Beverly. "Though, at the time, he was only a Sergeant-at-Arms."

"A sergeant who became a marshal. I've never heard of such a thing. Sounds like your home is a most curious place."

"You took your defeat remarkably well."

"I can acknowledge one's skill without resorting to name-calling. You show great promise, my lady. By the end of this tournament, your name will be the talk of the town."

"May I ask if you are going to compete in the joust, Sir Hendrick?"

"No. I'm afraid my jousting days are behind me. You're not competing in the foot combat, are you?"

"I hadn't planned on it. Why?"

He grinned. "I'd hate to face off against you again."

"What does the foot combat consist of? Is it like a giant melee?"

"No, you're thinking of the Grand Melee for commoners. The foot combat is a series of one-on-one fights between knights. After what you just did, I imagine you'd do well at it."

"Why is that?"

"Your technique is brutal, if you'll pardon the expression."

"Meaning?"

"It's clear you've seen actual battle. Knights who frequent these tournaments often consider themselves... Well, I suppose the word 'refined' comes to mind."

"I'm only jousting to win some coins. I understand ransom is the order of the day?"

"It is. In my youth, I accumulated quite the purse, but my back will no longer permit it. In any case, I wish you well."

"Thank you," said Beverly. "I wish you the same."

He wandered off, removing his helmet and ignoring the jibes of the other knights.

"He seems nice enough," said Aubrey. She nodded towards the king. "What did His Majesty have to say for himself? Did he hold up his end of the bargain?"

Beverly chuckled. "He did, although I think it's more the queen's doing."

"So you're in?"

"I am. Now, if you'll excuse me, I must see a man about registration."

That evening, they sat around a fire beside Viden's wagon. The smith was in a good mood, buoyed by Beverly's defeat of Sir Hendrick. "Everyone's talking about you."

"Oh? And what are they saying?"

"Many things, though not all were flattering. There's some speculation the king arranged everything to make you look good."

"Are you suggesting Hendrick lost on purpose?"

Viden held up his hands. "Don't blame me. I'm only passing on what I heard."

"Ignore him," said Nymin. "It'll make your victory all the more rewarding."

"Do we have an idea of who you're facing?"

"Yes," replied Beverly. "Someone named Sir Owen. Do you know him?"

"Can't say as I do."

They all looked at Keon, who shrugged. "What?"

"You were looking into the contestants," said Aubrey. "Have you heard nothing?"

"Had I a few more coins, I could have discovered a lot more."

"Then you shouldn't have gambled them away."

"Let him speak," said Beverly. "He clearly knows something."

"She's right. I do," replied Keon. "Sir Owen is new to the circuit."

"Circuit?" said Aldwin.

"Yes. Knights like these travel from town to town, participating in whatever tournaments they find."

"And they make a living doing that?"

"The more successful ones can. Take Sir Hendrick, for example. He's been doing this for years."

"Have they no master to serve?"

"Some do. There are two types of knights amongst the Petty Kingdoms, three if you include Temple Knights."

"And they are?"

"Those who serve a specific chivalric order and then the knight errants who travel the Continent in search of fame and glory, or, more realistically, wealth."

"But aren't all knights sworn to a lord's service?" asked Aubrey. "That's how we do things back in Merceria."

Keon shrugged. "I'm only passing on what I've heard over the years. I have no way of verifying whether it's true."

"All that aside," said Beverly, "can you tell me nothing further about this Sir Owen?"

"I'm afraid not. He's too new to all of this. I suppose, in that sense, he's just like you."

"Who does she joust with after Owen?" asked Aldwin.

"Either Sir Leonid or Sir Alfonce, whichever one wins their round. Both are well-known amongst the people of Deisenbach."

"Why is that?"

"They serve the king."

"So the king has his own knights compete?"

"Of course," replied Keon. "After all, what better way to impress people than to have champions in his service?"

"Champions?" said Beverly.

"Yes, though, come to think of it, almost all the competitors here have won at least one tournament. It would hardly be called the Tournament of Champions, otherwise."

"Tournament of Champions?" said Aubrey. "You didn't think to mention this earlier?"

"I thought you knew?"

"How would we know? We're from a different land!"

"It doesn't matter," said Beverly. "My intent here is only to win enough to get us to Reinwick, not take the full prize. With any luck, I can do that with only a single joust."

"Will that be enough?" asked Aubrey.

"It should be," replied Keon. "Saints know, armour costs a fortune. Why, I'd wager even one knight's ransom would be enough to set me up for life."

They rose early the following day, eager to be there well before the jousting began. Beverly walked Lightning onto the field, garnering plenty of looks from the other knights.

"That's a fine beast," called out Sir Hendrick. "Where did you get him?"

"He was a present from my father," she replied.

"He's massive. I don't think I've ever seen his like. What breed is he?"

"A Mercerian Charger. My cousin raises them."

"I daresay you could fetch a good price for him. Would you be willing to sell?"

"No. He and I have gone through too much together."

"Yet you risk him in the joust?"

"I'll part with my armour before my horse."

Hendrick laughed. "Spoken like a true knight. Good luck, Lady Beverly, and may the Saints look out for you this day."

"And to you!"

She fell in behind the other knights. The trumpets blared once King Justinian took his place in the Royal Box, indicating the parade would soon begin. Beverly climbed into her saddle, waiting as the other contestants straightened their line. The herald announced a name, and the appropriate knight would ride past the king, offering a salute. The crowds loved it, as did His Majesty, who turned around three times, encouraging his subjects to cheer louder.

At the calling of her name, Beverly urged Lightning forward at an easy gait. While other mounts appeared nervous, her mighty charger remained calm beneath her. She passed by the king, holding her sword up in salute. The crowd stilled, unsure how to respond to the concept of a woman competing, then the blaring trumpets announcing the start of the tournament broke the awkward silence.

Beverly rode over to Aldwin, who waited with her lance. Sir Owen stood at the other end of the field, his armour gleaming atop his dun-coloured horse. Theirs was the first joust of the day, and judging from their cheers, the crowd was eager for it to begin.

"Take your places," called out the herald.

Beverly took her helmet from Aubrey, then turned Lightning, guiding him with her knees. She stopped at the end of the lists, placed her helmet atop her head, then flipped down the visor. The lance she kept upright, ready to lower once the joust was underway.

The herald moved to the railing separating the contestants from the crowd, then raised a flag on high. Down it swept, and Lightning exploded into action, thundering towards their opponent. Beverly focused on Sir Owen, lowering her lance as her target grew closer. She braced, ready for the hit, and then her own lance struck home, the tip shattering as it smashed into his shield.

She cast the remains aside, and the crowd roared as Sir Owen thundered past, his own lance having failed to score a hit.

"Two points," said Beverly. "Not bad for a first pass. What do you think, Lightning?" She reached down and stroked the horse's neck, slowing her pace as she trotted back to the other end, where Aldwin waited with another lance.

"Do that two more times," he said, "and the first round is yours."

"Is that all?"

"As long as you remain in the saddle, yes."

"I shall bear that in mind." She grabbed the new lance and trotted to the starting place.

Sir Owen stared at her, his visor up to take the measure of his competition. His horse shifted nervously beneath him, hardly surprising, considering the size of Lightning.

With the swing of the flag, her opponent flipped down his visor and came rushing for her, his horse kicking up dust as they picked up speed. She remained calm as Lightning responded in kind, and soon they charged towards each other, lances reaching out, hoping to pluck one another from the saddle.

Beverly leaned into it, her lance once more striking Owen's shield, but as it hit, his own struck her shield. While she had the wherewithal to remain in the saddle, Owen, less experienced, fell backwards, his feet coming loose from the stirrups. He flailed around, dropping his lance, his efforts only frightening his horse even more. It reared up, throwing the young knight to the ground, where he landed with a loud thump, but Beverly was well past him by then.

She slowed, craning her neck over her shoulder, watching him as he turned over to lie for a moment on his stomach before he got to his feet, waving as the crowd cheered him on.

Beverly sought the herald. "Three points to Lady Beverly," he called out. "One point to Sir Owen."

She rode over to where the knight limped back towards his horse. "Are you all right?" she asked.

"I'm fine," he replied, although the grimace on his face indicated otherwise. "I just need to catch my breath."

Aldwin cheered her on as she returned to the starting line. "Five points," he said, "and he has only one. One more hit like that, and it's yours."

"One more like that, and that knight might be dead," she replied. "You'd best have Aubrey stand by. Something tells me she may be needed."

He passed up another lance. "This is it. All you need to do is finish him off, and his ransom should be enough to get us to Reinwick."

She shook her head. "I'm not sure I can do this."

"Nonsense. You could make a career out of this if you wanted."

"No, thank you. If we weren't pressed for coins in the first place, I wouldn't be here. Fighting for someone's entertainment goes against everything I believe in."

He reached up and took her hand in his. "You're almost done. You can do this."

Beverly breathed deeply. "You're right. I'm being foolish." She looked over at Sir Owen, who'd finally calmed his horse enough to climb back on and return to his starting position.

Even though the herald signalled the start of the final pass, she gave her opponent time to gather himself, waiting until he nodded before urging Lightning into a run. Beverly lowered her lance, using her strength to keep it lined up with Owen's shield. She struck dead centre, the impact travelling up her arm as her lance splintered while his glanced off her shield, failing to break. She slowed Lightning before turning in the saddle, waiting for the herald to speak.

"Two points for Lady Beverly," he called out, "one for Sir Owen. The winner is… Lady Beverly."

The crowd cheered, including the queen, though her husband only clapped a couple of times before he turned to speak with Sir Langmar. Beverly rode off the field to find Aubrey waiting for her.

"You did it," called out the mage. "Now we can collect the ransom and continue on our way!"

# FIFTEEN

# Kharzun's Folly

AUTUMN 967 MC

K harzun's Folly was once an ingenious display of Dwarven engineering spanning a large gorge. However, Herdwin Steelarm destroyed the bridge one year ago to halt the enemy's attack. Now, all that remained were several feet of stone on either side, jutting out into the air as silent witnesses to the destruction he'd wrought.

Gerald peeked over the wall protecting Gelion's arbalesters. "I see what you mean when you say it's a strange structure."

"Yes," added Herdwin. "Just look at the size of that monstrosity!"

"It's tall, I'll grant you that, but I can't see how it would help them get across. Even if it has a boarding ramp, it couldn't possibly be long enough to reach our side."

"Could they be hiding something behind it?"

"Like what?" asked Gerald.

"I have no idea. This is about the strangest thing I've ever seen."

"Aye," agreed Gelion. "They just sit there, day after day, staring back at us as if it were the most normal thing in all of Eiddenwerthe."

"Is this wall a recent addition?"

"It is. We built it to protect our arbalesters. So far, it's proven effective."

"And will likely continue to do so," said Gerald. "But it would be nice to see what's coming from behind that tower of theirs."

"Let's find out what Albreda can do," said Herdwin. They moved away from the wall to where Gelion's company had dug out a cave. Albreda sat within, chatting with some Dwarves, but she stood as they entered.

"Well?" she called out. "Spot anything interesting?"

"It's all quite mysterious," said Gerald. "Have you ever come across something like that before?"

"In the Whitewood? Not likely!"

"But you've travelled around, haven't you?"

"I don't make a habit of visiting the mountains," the Druid replied. "Even if I did, I doubt I'd be out amongst the enemy."

"Can your magic help us?"

"Yes, but give me a chance to gather my wits, then I'll call upon an eagle to assist me."

"An eagle?" said Herdwin. "Will no other bird suffice?"

"Eagles have the sharpest eyes, Master Smith, although I suspect any creature of the air would prove sufficient to see the enemy here."

"Creature of the air? Are you suggesting you could conjure something else? A gryphon? Now, that would be a sight to see!"

"I am not conjuring. I am summoning."

"What's the difference?"

"Conjuring creates a creature out of thin air, whereas summoning calls on a creature in the area to come to my aid."

"Is that really much of a difference?"

"Of course there's a difference. What kind of question is that? A conjured creature has no intellect—it is nothing more than a manifestation of the caster. A summoned animal, however, is a living, breathing creature, free to make its own decisions."

"And you've done this before? Summoned birds, I mean?"

"Naturally. It's how I keep an eye on the Whitewood."

"Don't your wolves do that?"

"They do, but they cannot be everywhere."

"When would you like to begin?" asked Gerald.

Albreda peeked outside the cave. "In the morning would be better. There's not much light left."

"Couldn't you summon an owl?" asked Tindal.

"And how would that be of use?"

"They can see in the dark, can't they?"

"That they can, but I've yet to find one that can see into a tent. How, then, would you expect me to count the enemy warriors?"

The young Dwarf stared at his feet. "Sorry. I hadn't considered that."

"As I suspected," replied Albreda.

"How long does it take to summon an eagle?"

"Ordinarily, not long at all, but it all depends on what's in the area. Back home, I could have one here in mere moments, but these mountains are likely sparsely populated."

"Is there a limit to your range?"

"Naturally. The spell's power also lessens with distance."

"Which means?"

"If you were standing two hundred paces away from me, could you hear my voice?"

"I think so," replied Tindal.

"As well as you can now?"

"No, of course not. Your voice would grow weaker the farther away I was."

"It is the same thing with summoning."

"Magic sounds very complicated."

"Of course it's complicated. That's why people spend decades studying to become mages."

"How long did it take for you to master magic?"

"That was different," replied Albreda. "I'm self-taught."

"Could I teach myself magic?"

She took a deep breath, letting it out slowly. "It is not beyond the realm of possibility, but in my experience, very few are capable of it."

"Now you have me interested," said Gerald. "Who else is self-taught?"

"Lady Aubrey, though she happened upon her grandmother's notes, which aided her studies."

"I thought Revi taught her?"

"He covered the rudiments of Life Magic, yes, but her own research made her the mage she is today."

"Who's Aubrey?" asked Tindal.

"One of our Life Mages," replied Gerald.

"You have more than one?"

"We do—three, to be exact."

"Astounding! We have none."

"I'm beginning to realize just how rare they are. When I was younger, we only had one, a fellow named Andronicus. Weldwyn had one as well, whereas Norland had none at all."

"And now you have three," said Tindal. "How did that come about?"

"Let's see if I can get this right. Revi Bloom learned from Andronicus, Aubrey learned from Revi, and Kraloch, well, he's an Orc shaman, so I don't know if we can really call him one of ours."

"I don't suppose you could loan us one?"

Gerald chuckled. "No. I'm afraid there's no one to spare. Though, come to think of it, I believe one or two are undergoing training. Albreda would know more."

"There are five students," said the Druid, "but only one shows any aptitude for Life Magic, a young woman named Clara. I doubt she would be of much use right now. The last I heard, she was yet to master the orb of light."

"The what?" asked Tindal.

"The orb of light. A rudimentary spell that provides a magical source of illumination."

"And that's a spell usable by Life Mages?"

"It is a universal spell, able to be employed by any mage. Try to keep up, will you? It's getting tiresome having to explain everything twice."

Gerald cleared his throat. "At the risk of dragging this out, is there anything else we should be aware of?"

"Like what?" asked Albreda.

"Could enemy mages discover that you're casting?"

"There is no way to detect it, if that's what you're asking. However, there is the possibility they might notice an eagle flying overhead."

"Why is that?" asked Tindal. "We see birds all the time."

"Aren't eagles rare in these parts?"

"They are. What I meant to say is it's not unusual, on occasion, to see a bird flying overhead."

"Yes, I understand that," said Albreda, "but would such a creature naturally circle above an enemy camp?"

"Er... no. I suppose not."

"Now do you understand what I'm getting at?"

"I do," replied Tindal. "But even if they saw your eagle, what could they do about it?"

"A myriad of things. If they have Earth Mages of their own, they might summon an eagle or something worse."

"Worse? Like what?"

"Use your imagination."

"I'm told I don't have one."

Albreda looked at Gerald. "This entire conversation is proving most tiresome. I'm going to go get some sleep." She wandered off deeper into the cave.

"Did I say something wrong?" asked Tindal.

Gerald laughed a moment before the earnest look on the Dwarf's face quickly sobered him. "I wouldn't worry too much if I were you. A lot is happening here, and she must conserve her strength."


The next day began with a cold wind from the north, reminding all that winter would soon come to the high mountain passes.

Gerald stepped outside, immediately regretting his decision as a gust threatened to tear the cape from his shoulders. He noticed Gelion Brightaxe crouched next to the wall overlooking the gorge. "Trouble?"

The Dwarf shook his head. "Nothing we haven't seen before. They've moved some archers up into that tower of theirs."

"You think they mean to attack?"

"I doubt it. More likely, they're trying to estimate our numbers. They'll loose off a volley or two any moment now, and we'll sound the alarm."

"And then they count your warriors as everyone takes up their positions?"

"Precisely. How did you know?"

"It's what I would have done in their shoes. Of course, I wouldn't have attacked in the first place."

"Even if your queen ordered it?"

"My queen would never do such a thing."

Gelion peered over the wall, drawing the attention of an enemy archer before he ducked down, chuckling as an arrow flew overhead. "They're lively today. Must be the cold weather putting a little spring in their step." He popped his head up again, then ducked, drawing the same response.

"That's a dangerous game you're playing," said Gerald.

"I agree, but it has its purpose."

"Which is?"

"Watch and see!" Once more, he raised his head, although he only exposed his eyes this time. Sure enough, an enemy archer drew back his bowstring. Gerald heard the click of an arbalest as a bolt flew across the gorge, striking the Halvarian in the chest, knocking him back out of sight.

"There," said Gelion. "Did you see that?"

"How often have you done that?"

"Only about half a dozen times. They get wise to it fairly quickly, and then we take a break for a few weeks, hoping to fool them again later."

Gerald nodded. "I imagine that would keep them on their toes."

"It does."

"How would you rate your chances of stopping an assault?"

"That largely depends on the number of warriors they send," replied the Dwarf. "If they somehow created a bridge, we could withstand hundreds. Why? How many have they got?"

"We won't know until we get a better look."

Albreda appeared at the entrance to the cave, the wind whipping her hair around, but she took no notice of it as she focused on the sky.

"What's she doing?" whispered Gelion.

"Getting ready to cast, I imagine. Have you never seen a mage use magic before?"

"Can't say that I have. What does it look like?"

"You're about to find out."

The Druid closed her eyes and lifted her face skyward as words of power tumbled from her lips, then she raised her hands, palms upward. The wind calmed, and it was easy to forget they were in the mountain passes. She continued her litany, all the while her voice quieting to a whisper.

Gerald felt a desire to move closer and wondered if it might be the wolf within him but quickly dismissed the idea. He was his own man and made his own decisions. He looked at Gelion, staring at the mage, intrigued by the scene.

"Is this what all magic looks like?" asked the Dwarf.

"No. I've seen more than my fair share of healing magic, which looks nothing like that."

"And how long will this spell continue?"

"I imagine until something answers her call."

At Gerald's words, a high-pitched whistle bounced off the mountains.

"Unless I'm mistaken," said Gelion, "she's got her answer." He looked up, scanning the sky for the source of the sound. "There."

Gerald looked to where he pointed at a smudge in the distance. "My eyesight's not what it used to be. What is it?"

"An eagle, and an impressive one too."

It flew closer, finally coming into focus, its wingspan almost as long as Albreda's outstretched arms, but its grey colouring was the more remarkable feature.

"It's a Cairn Eagle," said Gelion. "Also called a Mountain Coaster; they're rare in these parts."

"Coaster? Revi's familiar is a Black Coaster, but he looks nothing like that."

The Dwarf chuckled. "They're called coasters because they can stay airborne for long periods, coasting on air currents. I doubt they're the only birds to do so."

"What do they eat?"

"Anything they like."

The creature circled before it dove, heading straight for Albreda. It flapped its wings and slowed at the last possible moment, landing gently on her arm.

"Astounding," said Gelion. "I've never seen its like."

The Druid placed her forehead against the bird's. It was an odd sight, yet somehow Gerald knew something had passed between them because the eagle let out a screech and flew off, climbing rapidly.

Albreda lowered her arms, noticing the stares of those around her for the first time. "What are you looking at?" she snapped. "Have you never seen a Druid at work before?"

"No," replied Tindal.

"Then it's time some of you travelled more." She noted Gerald and walked over. "It seems I was drawing a crowd."

"You can't blame them, can you? Stonecastle has no mages."

"That's hardly my fault." She kept watching the eagle as it flew eastward.

"Do you think this will work?"

"Of course," said Albreda. "He's already looking down on their side of the gorge."

"And what does he see?"

"Not much, unfortunately. Certainly not an army waiting to attack. I doubt more than fifty men are within striking range."

"Then what are they doing?"

"We shall find out shortly. I'm sending Swiftwing farther east."

"Swiftwing?" said Gelion.

Albreda spared the Dwarf a quick look of condescension. "You have a name, Captain. Is it so hard to believe a creature should have one too?"

"Not when you put it that way."

"What do you know about the area to the east, Captain?"

"Not much. Our patrols rarely went any farther than that tower over yonder."

"There is a path that descends, looping back on itself to make the journey less steep. I'm following it now."

Gerald tried to picture it in his mind. "I imagine you'll find more men at the end of it, although it's anybody's guess how far away that would be."

"I see it," said Albreda. "There's a plateau where a large group of tents sit." She quieted; her eyes darted around as if she were looking down on it.

"How many?" asked Gerald.

"It's a sizeable army. I estimate at least two thousand. They're also arranged in perfect symmetry, which indicates they're disciplined." She broke contact, then let her eyes focus as she turned to the marshal. "I'm afraid there can be little doubt they are preparing for war."

"Any indication as to when they'll begin?"

"I can see a camp, not read minds."

"How do you know they're preparing for war?" asked Gelion.

"Men marched around in the open spaces, practicing with their weapons."

"They still need some way of crossing the gorge," said Gerald.

"I saw no sign of siege equipment of any type, but that doesn't preclude the possibility there are mages present."

"Still, winter will soon be upon us. I doubt they'd try an assault when the snow is about to come."

Gelion grunted. "So, there's good news for a change. What about the makeup of their army?"

"The bulk is foot," replied Albreda, "but there was a substantial number of horsemen, not that they'd be of much use in the mountain passes."

"Interesting," said Gerald. "That tells me they intend to break through to Merceria. What kind of numbers of horse are we talking about?"

"Five or six hundred, at least, possibly more. Archers, too, though what I could see of them appeared unarmoured."

Gelion stared back, trying to understand what it all meant. He finally gave up, turning instead to Gerald. "What do you make of all this, Marshal?"

"I think I understand their objectives, although I still have no idea how they intend to get across that gorge."

"Could you be a little clearer?"

"The army's composition, and the fact there were no siege engines, suggests they're not interested in taking Stonecastle, at least not immediately. Instead, they mean to block you off and march the bulk of their troops directly into Merceria."

"But they'd have to go through the Darkwood. I doubt Lord Greycloak would allow that."

"Nor do I," said Gerald.

"Perhaps they don't know about the Elves?"

"It's possible, but I suspect otherwise."

"Might I ask why?"

"Call it a gut instinct, if you like," replied Gerald, "but I can't help but feel this is part of something bigger."

"Such as?"

"The same enemy is threatening Ironcliff in the north. Could this be an attempt to divide our forces?"

"If so, it's a brilliant strategy. We Dwarves don't have the large numbers of warriors you Mercerians can field, but we know how to defend our homes. If what you're suggesting is correct, it likely means both Ironcliff and Stonecastle would be surrounded for the sole purpose of letting the rest of their forces flood into Merceria."

"Except that in the north, it would be Norland."

"I'm no expert in politics," said Gelion, "but even I know Norland has no real army anymore."

"They know," said Albreda.

"Know what?"

"Of Merceria's ties to both these Dwarven strongholds. They intend to bleed you dry."

"Or," suggested Gerald, "they plan to tie down our troops and hit us elsewhere."

"Where else could they strike? The Clanholdings?"

"No. I doubt they'd try that again. I discussed this very matter with the queen only a few weeks ago. I believe they intend to attack from the sea."

"Like the Kurathians did in Weldwyn?"

"You saw the Halvarian camp. I imagine these people are far more organized than those who attacked Weldwyn. If they intend to take on Merceria, they'll have to land at Trollden."

"Or sail up the river to Colbridge," suggested Albreda.

"No," said Gerald. "Trollden guards the river. If they do come from the sea, that's where they'll land."

# SIXTEEN

## The Coast

AUTUMN 967 MC

The city of Zefara sat on the western coast of Halvaria, serving as the empire's largest port, nestled within a natural harbour that protected shipping from the ravages of the Sea of Storms.

Exalor Shozarin appeared in the magic circle, his spell having carried him over five hundred miles. The effects of this form of travel no longer exhausted him, but his aide, Wingate, often found it disturbed the contents of his stomach. As he staggered from the casting circle, the poor fellow looked pale as snow.

"Wait here and recover," said the High Strategos. "I'll not require your services until later."

"Yes, Your Grace."

Their arrival garnered some interest, as evidenced by the guards who entered the room with their swords drawn. At the sight of Exalor, they sheathed their weapons.

"Your Grace," said their sergeant. "We weren't expecting any visitors."

"I prefer to arrive unannounced; it prevents people from covering up their misdeeds." He smiled as the fellow's face fell. "I trust all is well here in Zefara?"

The guard brightened considerably. "It is, Your Grace. Shall I inform the Marshal of the Empire you're here?"

"Not yet. I'd like to look around before I get tied down in meetings. Is the admiral here?"

"He's down with the fleet, Your Grace. Overseeing some repairs."

"Of what? I wasn't aware any of our ships had damage?"

"I'm afraid I don't know the details."

"That's unfortunate," said Exalor. "You may carry on with your duties."

"And if the Marshal of the Empire asks after you?"

"Then inform him of my arrival. Of course, he won't like that, but you can tell him it was my decision not to reveal my presence."

"Yes, Your Grace." The sergeant bowed, then ordered his men from the room. He looked back at the High Strategos once more before exiting.

"That's better," said Exalor. "Now I can think." He wandered around the room, ordering his thoughts. The teleportation spell could be disorienting when he travelled so far, and he often found mental exercise a good remedy. "Now," he muttered to himself, "what was it I came here for?"

"To see the fleet," offered Wingate weakly. "You wanted a full accounting of the ships."

"Ah, yes. That's right, and now I've learned some require repairs. I suppose I'll have to see what that's all about." Exalor looked at his aide. "Take care of yourself, Wingate.." He left the room, following the scent of the sea.


Admiral Kozarsky Stormwind stood on the dock, looking over the fine lines of the ship before him. *Resplendent*, the newest ship to come off the slips, was far and away the fleet's grandest. Having finished its maiden voyage, it was ready to take on the flagship role it was designed for.

He smiled. In theory, the empire had three fleets, the Northern, the Shimmering, and the Storm, each named after the seas they commanded. Halvaria had not put much effort into replacing its losses since its defeat at Alantra, but with the great dream nearing completion, every slip within the empire was suddenly busy.

"I hope I'm not interrupting?"

The admiral turned to see Exalor Shozarin. "I wasn't expecting you, Your Grace. Then again, that's your way, isn't it—to appear unannounced?"

"It is, though I can hardly fault you for disliking such visits."

"On the contrary. My command is an open book."

Exalor moved up beside him. "Is that your newest?"

"It is. The *Resplendent*. What do you make of her?"

"I'm no expert in such things, but she looks ready to sail."

"And she is. All we need is permission to board her fighting complement."

"It would be premature to load them just yet, but be patient. It won't be long now." Exalor shifted slightly, turning to survey the rest of the harbour. "How many ships have you?"

"Over two hundred of varying sizes, although you won't see them all in

Zefara, for the bay is not big enough. Instead, they're scattered along the coast ten miles in either direction."

"And how would you rate the morale of your people?"

"Good."

"But not exceptional?"

Kozarsky grimaced. "The empire's fleets have not exactly distinguished themselves these last few years."

"You refer to Alantra?"

"I do. We commanded the Shimmering Sea until that Holy Fleet showed up."

"That was not your fault," said Exalor. "If you recall, a Sartellian was in command."

"Aye, it was, and a Shozarin in the north. With all due respect, neither of those two should have been made an admiral."

"You know as well as I that the fleets, like the marshals, must be spread out amongst the three lines."

"I do, but I don't have to like it. Doesn't having a Water Mage commanding ships make more sense?"

"I'm not disagreeing with you, Admiral, but rules are rules. In any case, it now falls to you to demonstrate the correct way to employ a fleet."

"That's one way of looking at it."

"Is there another?"

"We both know my appointment was political. I wouldn't put it past the Sartellians to try to sabotage this campaign or your own line."

Exalor straightened his back. "I have taken pains to limit possible political influence. This campaign is based on a complex strategy requiring the cooperation of all three lines."

"You'll get no argument from me. Does that mean I can expect the Marshal of the Empire checking on my every move?"

"He'll be far too busy dealing with our central thrust against Merceria."

"So I'm free to operate on my own?"

"As alone as any of us can truly ever be." Exalor took a deep breath, enjoying the fresh air. "I heard we have damaged ships?"

"Yes, the result of a collision. It comes from having new vessels and under-trained crews. Don't get me wrong, increasing the fleet size was overdue, but it's outpacing our ability to crew them all."

"How long does it take to whip a crew into shape?"

"Usually a few months, but it depends on who's in command. Unfortunately, experienced captains are hard to find these days."

"Will the coming winter hamper your training efforts?"

"A little," said Kozarsky. "Why?"

"I'd like the fleet fully prepared before the assault begins."

"I thought we were only landing the warriors?"

"You are," said Exalor, "but we cannot discount the possibility you may encounter some opposition at sea."

"But the Mercerians have no ships."

"None we know of, but news comes slowly from that part of the Continent, and we must also consider their ally, Weldwyn, who has ships."

"So I've been told, but I doubt in such numbers as to cause us any trouble."

Exalor looked around the dock, ensuring no one else stood within earshot. Then he reached into his belt and pulled out a scroll case.

"Here," he said. "Take this."

"My orders?"

"Precisely. You may peruse them at your leisure, but I doubt you'll find any surprises."

"When is the campaign to commence?"

"I shall send word when we're ready, but until then, you're not to get ahead of yourself. Arrive too soon, and you'll throw all our plans into disarray."

"Understood."

"I have complete trust in you, Admiral, but there's always the chance the Marshal of the Empire might take a direct interest in the affair, despite his other duties."

"And if he does?"

"Then you may rely on the contents of that scroll to keep you out of trouble. Remember, I outrank the Marshal of the Empire, despite what he claims."

"He is the senior marshal," noted Kozarsky.

"Yes, and I am the High Strategos. My rank supersedes all."

The admiral bowed. "Of course, Your Grace. Might I ask a question?"

"Yes. I encourage it."

"Am I allowed to send my ships out on training exercises?"

"Yes, but not within sight of the Mercerian coast or that of Weldwyn."

"And the Clanholdings?"

"They are of little consequence. Why?"

"A voyage there would require a good knowledge of navigation, particularly as the ships wouldn't be able to hug the coast."

"As long as you take into consideration my earlier restriction."

"Most assuredly, Your Grace."

"I would also urge you to stay the course, regardless of what you may hear."

"I'm not sure I follow," said Kozarsky.

"As I stated earlier, this is a complex campaign that depends on timing. You may hear rumours that might cause you some concern."

"What types of rumours?"

"Ones of a political nature."

"And if I do?"

Exalor chuckled. "It's not a case of IF, it's a case of WHEN."

"My question still stands."

"I would advise you to ignore it, but a man in your position can only do so much. Instead, I suggest you consider the source." He gazed out over the fleet once more. "This is your destiny, Admiral. These ships, your future. Embrace that, and you'll win everlasting fame."

"And if the politics get in the way?"

"Remember, I have complete trust in you, despite what others may insinuate. Need I say more?"

"No, Your Grace."

"Good. Now, let's get aboard the *Resplendent*, shall we? I'm eager to see what all the fuss is about."


That evening, Exalor sat in a borrowed room, sifting through written reports.

"Here's another one," said Wingate, recovered from his earlier ordeal. "It states their general has gone missing."

"Missing?" replied the High Strategos. "Let me see that." He took the page, scanning its contents. "Where did this come from?"

"Our agent in Wincaster, Your Grace. According to the attached note, he thought it important enough to contact Lord Kelson directly."

"This concerns General Fitzwilliam."

"I wasn't sure if it referred to the elder or younger."

"Then you haven't kept up on things. The elder Fitzwilliam died last year. This clearly refers to his daughter, the knight."

"Does that make it of less import, Your Grace?"

"No. Her loss could well work in our favour, for she was one of the marshal's top people." He scanned the letter again. "This does not mention what happened to her, merely that she has disappeared. Have we any further information?"

"Not that I've seen so far," replied Wingate, "but there are still several reports to wade through."

"Was she ill?"

"I've read no evidence of that, Your Grace. Could she be in disgrace? It's not unknown for people in the Petty Kingdoms to disappear when accused of something."

"Were this coming from the east rather than the west, I might be inclined to agree with you, but that is not the Mercerian custom."

"It isn't?"

"No," said Exalor. "Their own marshal was accused of murder some years ago, then imprisoned for it, yet he still commands their army."

"Have these people no morals?"

"They are a warrior race, the descendants of mercenaries. They take a much more pragmatic approach to such things. It's something my plans for conquest had to account for."

"You make them sound like the Dwarves. They're both so stubborn."

"Tenacious might be a better word for it. In the Dwarves' case, it's due to their short stature. One can't retreat very well when their legs are so short."

"And the Mercerians?"

"They'll retreat if needed, but from what I've learned, they do so carefully. We shan't see any disordered flight on their part during the coming campaign."

"If you don't mind me asking, Your Grace, what can we expect to see?"

Exalor put down the letter and leaned back in his chair. "The Mercerians are disciplined, rivalling even the Temple Knights of Saint Cunar."

"But that could give us an advantage, surely?"

"If they fought as stubbornly as the Cunars, then yes, but the Marshal of Merceria is not above giving up ground to gain a tactical advantage."

"You make him sound incapable of defeat."

"Do I?" said Exalor. "I certainly didn't intend to. Any enemy can be beaten if proper care is taken to study their tactics. Losses will likely be high, but we can afford it. Even if we traded lives at a two-to-one ratio, we still have plenty of men to spare." His gaze drifted back to the letter, and he wondered how much more it left unsaid. "Are there any other reports of missing people?"

"Not that I've seen, Your Grace. Why? What is it you're thinking?"

"It occurred to me that she might have set out on a scouting mission."

"Against us?"

"Naturally. Who else threatens their borders?"

"No one, so far as we know, but if she were spying on us, where would it be?"

"In the north," said Exalor. "The so-called 'gap' is the only place I can think of where she could do it without our knowledge. They certainly couldn't do so opposite the Dwarven stronghold of Stonecastle."

"Perhaps we should send word north for the Seventh Legion to watch out for her?"

"That's not a bad idea. I knew I kept you around here for something."

Wingate beamed. "Shall I send word on your behalf, or would you like to report in person?"

"A letter will do. I'm not going to teleport back up to Wyburn only to ask the acting Marshal of the North to keep her eyes open. It would sound like I was begging. You write it, but let me read it over before you send it."

"Yes, Your Grace."

They returned to the process of reading through the reports. Sometime later, Exalor noticed his aide acting strangely.

"Is something wrong?" he asked. "You've picked up that letter and put it back down again three times."

"Sorry, Your Grace. It's just that I'm not sure what to make of this."

"That being?"

"Some time ago, there were reports of a pair of Mercerians apprehended trying to uncover our agents."

"Yes, I remember. What of it?"

"They were taken aboard one of our ships, the *Fantine*."

"How is that of concern to us?"

"It's in port, Your Grace."

"You mean here? In Zefara?"

"I do. According to this, they've been here for some time."

"And by some time, you're referring to…"

"I don't have the dates, but it wouldn't be unreasonable to conclude at least a month, perhaps even two."

"And they've done nothing with them?"

"I'm afraid not. If I recall, their capture was a spur-of-the-moment decision. I doubt they had any plans for long-term imprisonment. They're here, along with the usual assortment of miscreants and ne'er-do-wells. When the local governor heard you'd arrived, he sent a letter asking what is to be done with them."

"Have we names, at least?"

"Yes, Arnim and Nicole Caster. Do you know about them?"

"I do indeed," said Exalor. "Lord Arnim is, if I recall, a minor noble, and his wife, a close confidante of the Queen of Merceria."

"Might they know something valuable?"

"Quite possibly."

"Could they provide some insight into their missing general?"

"I doubt it. They were captured long before we received word about her disappearance. Still, they might be able to tell us if there were any rumours at court concerning an illness on her part."

"Aren't we assuming she was scouting our legions?"

"Yes," said Exalor, "but if Lady Beverly Fitzwilliam will be missing for an extended period, wouldn't they go to the trouble of concocting a cover story?"

"I fail to see how that would be of benefit to us, Your Grace."

"You must look at all the pieces, Wingate. If we learn what that story is, we can actively seek to discredit it, thus proving our suspicions."

He watched his aide trying to work things out. "So what you're suggesting is, if they claim she was ill, we can prove she's not? But they have Life Mages, do they not?"

"They do; thus, their cover story would need to be a little more original than an illness."

"A pregnancy?"

"You know, I hadn't considered that. I'm not used to thinking of our enemies as women."

"If she were with child, where would she go?"

"To Bodden, obviously, which makes it easy to disprove. We have someone in Bodden, don't we?"

"Yes, Your Grace. If you recall, he was looking after Sir Randolf."

Exalor scowled. "Now you mention it, that entire thing ended up being a complete waste of time. I never should have listened to Kelson."

"Our man is still in place. Shall I send word for him to check in on the baroness?"

"You might as well. If she's in residence, it won't take too much to prove it."

"And if she's not?"

"Then we should go with our original supposition that she's out on a scouting mission."

"I'll arrange for the message to be sent, Your Grace. What do you want to do about the Casters?"

"All things considered, I think I should pay them a visit, don't you?"

"And then?"

"I'll make that decision after I've spoken to them."

# SEVENTEEN

# Champion

## AUTUMN 967 MC

Viden rubbed his hands together, savouring the moment. "Here comes Sir Owen. I can already feel the gold flowing through my fingers."

The knight, his head downcast, slowly led his horse towards them.

"It can't be easy accepting defeat," said Aubrey. "And you eliminated him in the first round, Cousin."

"I did, yet it still took three passes to do so. I sense Sir Owen has a bright future ahead of him, but I doubt jousting is one of his strengths. He needs to find a lord who will take him under his wing."

The knight halted before them. "Lady Beverly, I am here to pay my ransom." He took a step forward, offering the reins of his horse.

"I don't understand," replied Beverly.

"I lack the funds to pay the value of my armour and weapons. I, therefore, offer my mount in payment."

"That's generous of you, but I already have a horse."

"Then you must sell Morningstar. He will fetch a handsome price."

"I am not a vendor of horses. That's more my cousin's territory."

"Don't look at me," said Aubrey. "I'm a breeder, not a merchant."

"But you sell Mercerian Chargers!"

"I do, but there's a waiting list for those, and they're not the sort of horses to be sold at auction."

Sir Owen shook his head. "If you do not accept my horse, then I must forfeit my armour and weapons."

"Have you no coins at all?" asked Beverly.

"Only enough to eat, and even then, I do so sparingly."

"How did you become a knight?"

"I was a farrier by trade in service to Lord Deiter Heinrich, the Duke of Erlingen. Some years ago, I was travelling in his retinue when we were set upon by a band of ruffians."

"And you saved him?"

"No, I saved his wife."

"How? Did the duke not travel with an escort?"

"He did, but he was lured away by a ruse. You see, the bandits struck, then withdrew, the knights following. Shortly thereafter, a second group attacked. The duke had ridden off with most of his knights, so it fell to me and the other remaining members of his retinue to keep his wife safe. He rewarded me with a knighthood and a small purse."

"So you belong to an order?"

"Sadly, no. Entry into the Knights of the Sceptre is restricted to those of noble birth. Instead, I became a knight errant, trying to make a name for myself through service to a worthy noble. Unfortunately, such things are hard to accomplish, and there's been little opportunity to distinguish myself."

"You must have done something right. That armour of yours looks to have cost a fair amount."

"It was a gift from the duchess. Her reward for my efforts."

"I see," said Beverly. "And how many tournaments have you competed in?"

Sir Owen looked down at his feet. "I'm afraid this is my first."

"Just our luck," said Viden. "A brilliant victory by Lady Beverly, and all we get is broken promises. Where are the coins we're due?"

"As I said," continued the knight, "I haven't enough."

"Then give us what you have and be on your way!"

"No," said Beverly. "I will not force a man into starvation." She turned back to Sir Owen. "You say you are from Erlingen?"

"Yes, my lady."

"Do you know Sir Hendrick?"

"I know of his reputation. He is said to be an honourable and fair knight."

"And where is Erlingen, relative to our current location?"

"North and East. The quickest route would be through Zowenbruch. Erlingen is on its northern border."

"Are you familiar with a place called Reinwick?"

"Indeed, though I've not been there myself. It lies astride the Great Northern Sea."

"Could you guide us there?"

"Are you offering to take me into your service?"

Beverly wasn't sure what to make of the man's suggestion. She turned to Aldwin. "Well? What do you think?"

"I'd wager he's a better choice than Keon."

"I resent that," said their erstwhile guide.

"You'd not even heard of Reinwick when we found you."

"True, but I helped you get to Agran."

"I rest my case," said Aldwin. "Far better to put our trust in someone familiar with the route we'll be taking."

"That makes sense," agreed Beverly. "What do you think, Aubrey?"

"While I'm not opposed to the idea, it does give us another mouth to feed."

"I can help in other ways," insisted Sir Owen. "I've studied the knights in the competition and can tell you their weaknesses."

"That would be helpful," replied Beverly. "You may now consider yourself part of our retinue."

"Great," said Viden. "Another fool with which to split the winnings. Will there be no end to this travesty?"

"Hush. You'll get your coins. I promise you. Now, who am I to fight next?"

"Let's see," replied Keon. "According to the herald, someone named Sir Gadron."

"Are you certain?" said Owen.

"Yes. Why?"

"He is known to cheat, my lady."

"How does one cheat in a joust?" asked Beverly.

"The rules state a lance must strike squarely in the chest or shield, yet Sir Gadron often aims for the shoulder, leading to grievous wounds."

"Has no one called him out on this?" asked Aubrey.

"Who would dare? He's said to have the ear of the king."

"Which king?" asked Beverly.

"Justinian, the King of Deisenbach. He's also the favourite to win the competition."

"How is it that I'm to face him? If I recall, it should be either Sir Leonid or Sir Alfonce."

"He was added at the last moment. Such is often the case where he's concerned, for it allows him to pick his opponent."

"So you're suggesting he picked me on purpose?"

"Indeed, my lady. Likely because he believed you to be weak."

"You should withdraw from the competition," said Aubrey. "We can't risk you getting injured."

"And yet nothing has changed; we still need funds to get us to Reinwick."

This is our only chance, and if I must risk taking on Sir Gadron, then so be it."

Aldwin chuckled. "You should know better than to try to dissuade my wife. Once she makes up her mind, there's no turning back."

"Your wife?" said Sir Owen.

"Yes," said Beverly. "Do you have a problem with that?"

"He has the grey eyes of the Old Kingdom."

"A fact of which I'm well aware."

"But if he's married to you, wouldn't that make him a baron?"

"It would." She watched the younger knight as he grasped the concept. "Our customs are different back in Merceria."

"Clearly."

"Does this mean you no longer wish to serve me?"

Sir Owen straightened. "It matters not," he replied. "I shall serve you faithfully until you discharge me from my duties." He looked at Aldwin. "I apologize if I offered offence, Lord."

"I like him," replied the smith. "He reminds me of a younger version of Sir Preston."


With the second round of jousts about to begin, an increased air of excitement filled the crowd, so much so that they pressed against the railing, forcing the Temple Knights to intervene. This, in turn, caused a delay in the proceedings.

Up in the Royal Box, the king tapped his foot in frustration. "Perhaps, in future, we should avoid allowing the commoners to observe."

"We can't do that," said the queen. "Else, they'd soon be rioting."

He looked at her in surprise. "Surely you jest?"

"I would never joke about such things. The people want blood; better it is on the lists than in the streets."

The king was about to say more when an overwhelming need to sneeze came over him. He withdrew his kerchief, covering his nose just in time to avoid spraying his wife.

"My pardon," he said, quickly tucking away the bloody cloth. "Who's next?" He looked at Sir Langmar.

"Sir Gadron," replied the knight. "I believe he's set to face off against Lady Beverly."

The king chuckled. "That ought to put her in her place."

The queen did not join in his laughter. "I fail to see why you take such delight in the thought of her imminent defeat."

"She is a woman and therefore doesn't belong in the lists. To make matters worse, she's a foreigner."

"So are half the knights present this day, yet I don't see you complaining about them."

"Sir Gadron will soon unseat her. Just you wait."

"You are confident."

"And why wouldn't I be?" said the king. "I have yet to see Sir Gadron allow anyone to get the better of him."

"Perhaps she will be the exception."

The king relaxed back into his chair, his gaze wandering to the field. Sir Gadron trotted into position and adjusted a strap while at the other end, the Mercerian woman sat on her massive charger, looking calm and collected as if this were the most normal thing in the entire Continent.

The herald raised the flag, and everyone leaned forward in anticipation. Down it swept, then hundreds of pounds of horseflesh bolted forward, hooves thundering across the field. Lances dropped, and King Justinian held his breath as the combatants collided with a crash. The aim of both riders was true, striking shields and bringing a cheer from the crowd.

"Very nice," muttered the king. "A classic example of fine horsemanship and a steady hand."

"That's quite the horse Lady Beverly has," noted Helisant. "Are you familiar with the breed?"

"Can't say I am, although it would fetch a high price in these parts."

"I wonder if she'd consider parting with it?"

"I doubt it. You know how knights are when it comes to their mounts."

The two knights replaced their lances and lined up for another pass. The flag swept down, then once more, hooves dug in. The king leaned forward, engrossed in the moment, willing Sir Gadron to win the round.

This time, Lady Beverly's lance struck the centre of Sir Gadron's shield, sending splinters flying. Her opponent, however, missed his mark, driving the lance into the woman's shoulder and twisting her around in the saddle. She bent over backwards, and it looked like she was about to topple from her seat, but somehow regained her balance.

"She's wounded," said the queen.

"Yes. It appears Sir Gadron's lance slipped beneath the pauldron. That never would have happened if she had proper plate armour. It's her own fault for wearing such an archaic form of protection."

"She won't be able to continue with a wound like that."

"Then she must withdraw." Justinian sat back, a smile creeping across his face, then one of Lady Beverly's retinue, a woman, moved up to intervene. "What's this, now?"

Lady Beverly dismounted, and the woman placed her hands over her shoulder.

"She appears to be a healer of some sort," said the queen.

"What in the name of the Saints is she doing?"

"Perhaps her shoulder has popped out of its joint. I hear that's a common issue in jousting."

"Am I seeing things," said the king, "or are that woman's hands glowing?"

Moments later, Lady Beverly rotated her arm, acting as if she were uninjured.

"Astounding!" said Justinian. "Was that magic or a trick of the light?"

"We shall soon see."

The crowd watched expectantly as another member of the lady knight's retinue ran over to the herald. They exchanged words, then the herald turned to those watching and announced the competition would continue.

"Saints alive," said the king. "She's getting back on her horse. She has determination. I'll give her that."

Sir Gadron took up his starting position for the final time, staring down the lists at his opponent. He'd raised his visor to see the results of his handiwork, but now, with Beverly preparing to ride again, he made a show of hoisting up a lance and testing its weight. Not satisfied with it, he insisted another be fetched.

King Justinian felt a familiar sweat beginning to build and cursed. He wanted to wipe his brow but knew the sight of blood on his kerchief would only lead to further worry on his wife's behalf. He tried to ignore it, focusing instead on the drama about to unfold before him.

The two knights took their positions for the third and final pass. The flag dropped, and then the fight was on, their steeds thundering towards each other.

Sir Gadron's lance struck first, ripping into Lady Beverly's damaged pauldron, blood flying out even as her own lance hit her opponent dead centre. To the crowd's astonishment, the blow's force knocked Sir Gadron from the saddle, and he landed in a loud crash, his horse careening off to one side.

Lady Beverly slumped forward, blood running freely down her arm. She had, once more, remained in the saddle, but her limb hung uselessly by her side, her shield having fallen to the ground. Then her servant was there, taking the reins of her horse and guiding her from the field.

The herald turned to face the crowd. "Sir Gadron is disqualified. I declare Lady Beverly the winner."

Those watching called out in dismay, for the king's favourite knight was a popular contestant.

"So much for your champion," said Helisant. "I suppose that's what comes from cheating."

"I would hardly call it that."

"Then what would you call it?"

"An unfortunate error on the part of Sir Gadron. It's not easy to aim a lance when your horse is in full gallop."

"That didn't affect his aim on the first pass."

Justinian shrugged. "I would have to disagree. Not that there's anything we can do about it now. It's a pity, really. He was the favourite to take the prize." He felt another sneeze coming and dug out his kerchief. He barely got it into place before his nose expelled its contents. He looked up to see Helisant staring at him.

"Still bleeding?" she asked.

"Yes," he replied. "I fear it's getting worse."

"Then it's time we did something about it."

"I've seen physicians by the score. What else is there?"

The queen looked over to the field. "You mentioned a mage?"

"The one who helped Lady Beverly? To be honest, I'm still not certain if it was magic or not."

"She fought Sir Gadron after being wounded. You're not suggesting one can shrug off such a wound?"

"Yes, but a Life Mage? Here in Deisenbach? What are the chances?"

"Quite good, apparently," said the queen.

"Do you think we could engage her services?"

"Let's not rush things. First, we need to determine if she is, indeed, a purveyor of Life Magic."

"And assuming she is?"

"Then we take measures to ensure her cooperation."

"How much will that cost, do you suppose?"

"Unfortunately, we are not in a position to barter. There might be another way, though."

"You intrigue me," said Justinian. "What is it you have in mind?"

"Did you notice the servant who spoke to the herald?"

"Yes. Why do you ask?"

"Then you weren't paying enough attention. Did you not notice the fellow's eyes?"

The king sat back in shock. "Are you suggesting what I think you are?"

She smiled. "Let's just call it a little insurance, shall we?"

"But he's only a servant. How would we use that against her?"

"I think you'll find he's much more than a servant."

"Whatever do you mean?"

"Did you not notice the looks they exchanged before the joust?"

"You're imagining things."

"Am I?" replied Helisant. "I would beg to argue."

"But you said he's a grey-eye."

"Indeed, but there's no guarantee they are held in the same low regard back in their own lands. What was it called again?"

"Merceria," interjected Sir Langmar. "I have it on good authority, it lies far to the west."

"There. You see?" continued the queen. "Their land is beyond the borders of the Old Kingdom."

"What is it you're proposing?"

"Isn't it obvious?" She turned to search the seats behind her. "Ludmilla? Where are you?"

"I'm here." A woman rose from her seat and came closer, bending over to speak softly. "What can I do for you, Majesty?"

"We need more information about Lady Beverly's companions."

"I shall see what I can arrange, Your Majesty. Is there anything, in particular, you'd care to know?"

"Yes, a couple of things. First, I'd like you to learn more about the woman accompanying them."

"And second?"

"Find out all you can about the grey-eyed individual, and determine the nature of his relationship with Lady Beverly."

"And if I find something, do I take more direct action?"

"Saint's, no, at least not yet. For now, I'm more interested in learning what we can about these visitors. We know a lot about Lady Beverly, but the rest of her retinue is still a mystery."

"I assume you don't want them to know you're taking an interest?"

"Naturally. Will that be a problem?"

"Not at all, Majesty, though it may take a bit of time."

"Take all the time you need, but be thorough. We have important decisions to make."

Ludmilla nodded, straightened her back, and looked over at the lists to where Lady Beverly was leading her horse away from the tournament. The grey-eyed man walked beside her, with the rest of her entourage following. Ludmilla waited only long enough to determine their destination before leaving the stands.

King Justinian noted her departure. "She left in a hurry."

"Of course," replied the queen. "She is on the business of the Crown!"

# EIGHTEEN

# Wincaster

AUTUMN 967 MC

A cleansing light bathed the room as a white cylinder filled the magic circle, then vanished, leaving Albreda, Gerald, and their horses.

"I don't know if I'll ever get used to that," the marshal noted.

"Don't be silly. You've travelled by way of that spell on numerous occasions."

"I have, but it still makes the hairs on the back of my neck stand up."

"That's the magic coursing through you," replied the Druid.

A queen's guardsman, Evard Brenton, opened the door with his weapon drawn, as was required of all who stood watch over the Wincaster circle.

He relaxed when he recognized their familiar faces. "Sorry, Your Grace. We weren't expecting you."

"Hardly surprising," snapped Albreda. "We ourselves didn't know we were coming till a few moments ago."

"Good job on such a quick response, Evard," said Gerald. "You can return to your post now."

The guard nodded his head. "Shall I call for someone to take your horses?"

"Yes, thank you."

Gerald waited as another member of Anna's guard entered, then he handed over the reins and turned to Albreda. "I suppose we should report directly to the queen."

"Yes. It seems we have much to share, although none of it is good."

They made their way through the Palace, their presence raising little interest amongst the guards stationed there.

"Where would Her Majesty be this time of day?" asked Albreda.

"Likely in her study," replied Gerald. "It's her favourite haunt of late."

"Because of all her maps?"

"Yes. Hardly surprising when you think of it."

"I would have thought she'd have commissioned a map room for that express purpose by now. Saxnor knows there are enough spare rooms in the Palace for such a thing."

"That's a marvellous idea. I daresay she would have eventually come up with that herself, but she's been run off her feet since the birth of Prince Braedon."

The guards snapped to attention as they approached the queen's study.

"Is she in?" asked Gerald.

"Yes, Your Grace."

"Is that you, Gerald?" Anna called out. "Come in."

He opened the door to see her sitting at her oversized desk, papers strewn across it.

"What are you doing?" he asked.

"Going over reports. Things have been getting troublesome of late."

"Meaning?"

"More complaints concerning Orcs."

"Weren't Arnim and Nikki looking into that? Have we still not heard anything?"

"Nothing at all. It's as if they simply vanished." She stopped, noticing the Druid's presence. "Oh, hello, Albreda. I trust things went well in Stonecastle?"

"That depends on your definition of well. I spied out the enemy encampment, but I wouldn't say it was good news."

"Let me guess—they have an army massing?"

"They do. I estimate their strength to be about two thousand souls."

"Yet they still haven't attacked. What are they waiting for?"

"That remains to be seen. Gerald thinks they're waiting for spring, but I'm not so certain."

"What makes you say that?"

"Their camp is still relatively high in the mountains, hardly the best place to wait out the winter months. Wouldn't moving them down into the plains be a wiser decision?"

"I disagree," said Gerald. "Winter would be the toughest time to attack, not to mention the difficulties it would present to their supply lines. One can hardly live off the land in the mountain passes."

"You make a good point," replied Anna. "Were there any signs of mages present?"

"We saw no one in pointed hats, if that's what you mean."

The queen chuckled. "Perhaps we should equip some of our own warriors with such things to confuse our enemies."

"I saw no signs of magic," continued Albreda, "but I suspect that's what they'll use to cross Kharzun's Folly."

Anna immediately sobered. "What makes you think so?"

"The Dwarves took years to build the old bridge, and they likely had Earth Mages to help. If the enemy is to build their own, they can hardly do it while within range of the Dwarven arbalests."

"Then tell me how they'll cross."

"I've given it some thought, and while I'm more familiar with the living world of the forest than I am of mountains, I believe I know how they might proceed."

"Go on."

"If you recall, Aldus and I used animated trees to gain entry to Wincaster during the siege. I suspect they could do something similar in the mountains using stone."

"I'm not sure I follow," said Gerald. "You made the trees walk to the walls. Are you suggesting stone could be made to do the same?"

"Possibly, but you miss my meaning in this case. Conjuring a golem of stone would do nothing to cross the gap, but it's within the realm of possibility that a well-trained Earth Mage could cause stone spikes to erupt from the ground."

"I've never heard of such a thing?"

"Nor I, but if I can cause vines to erupt from the ground, why not stone? In the end, it's basically the same."

"Is it?" said the queen. "Vines are living things, but can we say the same for rock?"

"Magic is about the manipulation of things. Elementalists each have their favoured element, but all spells are related. Take me, for example. I am an Earth Mage by the common term, yet I specialize in the world of living, breathing creatures. Aldus, on the other hand, prefers plants."

"I'm no expert in magic," said Gerald, "but that's a far cry from using something like Fire Magic, isn't it?"

"Is it? In the end, we both manipulate things. A Fire Mage produces flames, but she can still conjure creatures, albeit of fire. Such a spell is not so different from my own summoning."

"Now, wait a moment. You yourself said there was a difference between summoning and conjuring. By your own words, conjured creatures possess no mind of their own."

"Yes, which is why the magic of the earth is superior. When I summon a wolf, or an eagle, for that matter, I don't need to worry about what they're getting up to unless I'm trying to see through their eyes. Something like a phoenix, however, requires the caster to split their concentration."

"I'll not debate the merits of magic," replied Anna, "but I'd like to get back to this theory of yours. You say they could grow stone?"

"It's a possibility, but I cannot know for certain. Magic is a complex concept, and much is subject to interpretation."

"Let's assume they could grow stone. How would they employ that to cross the gorge?"

"There are several methods that spring to mind. They could create a massive vertical spike and then drop it across the gorge, but stone can be unforgiving. There's no guarantee it wouldn't shatter when it hits the other side. On the other hand, they could use their magic to extend the stone along the gorge wall, forcing it to flatten out and spread to the other side."

She closed her eyes for a moment. "On second thought, that likely wouldn't work."

"Why not?" asked Gerald.

"For that to work, their side of the gorge would need to be lowered by the amount of stone they manipulated. Thus, it would end up being too low on the other side."

"I thought you said they could create their own stone. Couldn't they create large spikes that jutted across the gorge?"

"Likely they could, but spikes would be hard to traverse. I suppose they could then flatten them using an additional spell. I really need to talk to Agramath to know more."

"The master of rock and stone from Ironcliff?"

"Yes, unless you know another capable of such things?"

"Don't look at me," said Gerald. "I'm a warrior, not a mage."

Anna's frown said volumes about the situation they found themselves in. "Could shaping stone be used to widen the mountain passes?"

"Most certainly," replied Albreda. "Though if our trip from Stonecastle to Kharzun's Folly is any indication, they'd have a tough time doing so."

"Would you care to expand on that?"

"That type of magic is all about volume. The longer the path, the greater the amount of stone they need to manipulate. I am considered a powerful mage, but even I would have difficulty with something of that length."

"We're assuming they don't have a lot of mages," said Gerald. "What if they have plenty?"

"Plenty being?" asked Albreda.

"Who knows? Ten, twenty? Perhaps even hundreds? We can't assume they experience the same problems we do when identifying magic wielders."

"Yes," said the queen. "You make a good point. The question now is how we prepare to counter that possibility."

"We can't," replied Gerald. "What I mean to say is we've done all we can to prepare for this attack, but until we have a better idea of how many mages they have, what can we do? We barely have enough to operate our magic circles."

A knock on the door drew their attention.

"What is it?" Anna called out.

"Lady Kasri and Lord Agramath, Your Majesty."

"That's good timing. Send them in."

The door opened to the two Dwarves.

"Greetings, Your Majesty," said Kasri. "We come from Ironcliff."

"And?"

"It's not good, I'm afraid. The enemy appears to be massing. We received news that they attacked the Wayward Wood."

"Which is?" said Gerald.

"A forest lying near the eastern entrance to the gap."

"I assume someone lives there?" asked Anna.

"They do, Majesty. The Aralani, but you may know them as Wood Elves."

"Wood Elves?" said Gerald. "I don't believe I've ever heard of such a thing, have you?" He looked at Anna.

"Only in books. They are said to be small folk, similar in size to Dwarves, but thinner of frame."

"True," said Kasri, "but that leaves out the most important thing; their connection to nature."

"Tell me more."

"They are primitive by our standards, using little more than wooden tools and having no warriors to speak of."

"When you say Halvaria attacked the woods, can you be more specific?"

"They are chopping down trees in great numbers," said Agramath. "We suspect they're using the wood to make siege engines."

"That seems to indicate they mean to attack Ironcliff directly."

"Precisely my vard's fear."

"What can we do?" asked the queen.

"My father would like to help the Aralani," said Kasri, "but we lack the necessary manoeuvrability and would soon be surrounded if we attempted any relief."

"You need cavalry," said Gerald. "We can send you some, but we'd need permission to ride through Norland."

"Not necessarily," offered Albreda. "Given sufficient time, we could transport some through the recall spell."

"That would require a lot of power," said Agramath.

"True, but it would be much faster than sending them overland."

"How long would that take?" asked Queen Anna.

The Druid thought about it before answering. "That largely depends on the mages at our disposal. The more accomplished mages could likely manage three trips a day before we used up our magic reserves."

"How many could you take with you on each trip?"

"That is a far more complex calculation. My estimate is three men along with their horses."

"I've seen you take more."

"True, but that was for a single spell. We must conserve our strength if we are to make multiple trips. Now, let's see. How large is a typical cavalry company?"

"Fifty men," replied Gerald. "Assuming it's at full strength."

"Then, with four mages… two days."

"Is that all?" said Agramath. "I had no idea your mages were so powerful. Perhaps we could bring more than one company?"

"Not so fast," said Anna. "We'd still need to supply them, unless you're suggesting you have food suitable for horses up in Ironcliff?"

"We do, though I fear it would soon be depleted if we tried to feed all those mounts."

"We'll send fodder, along with the Wincaster Light," said Gerald. "They're well-trained in scouting out the enemy. I'd also like to add a second company, perhaps some Kurathians?"

"Good idea," said the queen. "And a third, if we can manage it. I suggest we give Lanaka command of the expedition, but that's your call." She glanced over at her closest friend. "It looks like it's time to appoint one of those brigade commanders we discussed."

"I agree. I'll send word to Lord Lanaka right away. As to the Wincaster Light, they're in Tewsbury. I'll issue orders for them to ride to Hawksburg. The mages can take them from there."

"You mentioned four mages, Albreda," said Anna. "Have you specific people in mind?"

"I do. Apart from myself, I should like Aldus Hearn, Revi Bloom, and Lord Agramath."

"Could we speed things up by using more?"

"While more are at our disposal, I fear the drain of such a prolonged use of magic is beyond anyone else. Were Aubrey here, I would include her, but we don't have that luxury."

"Still," said Gerald, "only two days to move an entire company is impressive."

"What do you think, Agramath?" asked the queen. "Will three companies of horse be sufficient to help the Aralani?"

"It's certainly a good start."

"What of you, Kasri? Will you return to Ironcliff?"

"No. My place is in Stonecastle, beside Herdwin."

"Then we'll send you there with some supply wagons for our warriors. At least that way, you're not travelling alone."

"Thank you, Majesty."

"Well," said Gerald. "It appears we've some work ahead of us. I hate to even suggest the idea, but do you suppose Bronwyn might see fit to send aid to Ironcliff? It would certainly ease pressure on us."

"I hadn't considered that," said Anna. "I know she's been raising her own troops, but I've yet to hear whether or not she's been successful."

"According to Heward, she was hoping for ten companies, but his recent reports indicate she's stagnated at only six. Which is probably better in the long run. The last time she had her own men, she betrayed us."

"I remember," said the queen, "but I feel having her own warriors is to be encouraged this time. The earls of Norland are a fractious bunch, and if she is to truly rule, she'll need to stand on her own two feet."

"Haven't things calmed down since the war?"

"They should have, but the earls are still at each other's throats. They see every crisis as an opportunity to advance their own influence. If they had their way, they'd be broken up into six different kingdoms and constantly fighting border wars."

"Sorry," said Gerald, remembering the two Dwarves. "This is hardly the sort of thing you likely want to hear."

"On the contrary," replied Agramath. "Norland sits on our western border, so it's good to know where they stand regarding a war. You don't think they'd support Halvaria in their invasion, do you?"

"I hope not," replied Anna. "Bronwyn knows her present position only came about because our army supported her claim. Were it not for us, the earls would still be arguing over who should rule."

"And yet," said Kasri, "she was not your choice, was she? To be Queen of Norland, I mean."

"She was not, but we honoured their wishes in the end."

"Yes," added Gerald. "She was the only candidate they could all agree on. Even then, some wanted to see her married off, the idea being whoever became her husband would rule the kingdom."

"I trust Lord Heward is in no danger of falling under her charms?"

"Not in the least," said the queen. "Sir Heward is well aware of her past and has taken steps to ensure he doesn't fall under her spell."

"Is she an enchanter?" asked Kasri.

"No, merely a woman with the natural charms the Gods gave her."

"You Humans amaze me. Sometimes, I think all you think about is having children."

"Do they not do so back in Ironcliff?"

"Some do, but it's not something that's discussed out in the open. In our society, the female chooses who she'll forge with, not the male."

"A sensible way of doing things," agreed Anna. "We Humans would doubtless be better served if we adopted such a practice, but I fear such is not in our future."

"You did all right by our ways," said Gerald. "You married Alric."

"I did, but that wouldn't have happened had I not shown him my true feelings."

"Ah," said Kasri. "So you chose him. I see we're not so different after all."

Agramath grimaced. "All this is no doubt of interest to Your Majesty, but could we return to the topic at hand?"

"Yes, of course," said Anna, quickly sobering.

"We were talking about Norland and its army. Perhaps you might be better served to get their queen to allow you to march a larger force through their territory?"

"I will send word to Heward this very day. I should also contact the Orcs at Ravensguard and see if they would be willing to provide some hunters to aid you, Master Agramath."

"That would be most acceptable, thank you. Now, you must excuse me, for I need to return to Ironcliff to make arrangements. If we are to be receiving companies of your cavalry, we need to find a place to house them."

# NINETEEN

# Prisoners

AUTUMN 967 MC

Nikki sat against the cell wall while Arnim paced through puddles of putrid, stagnant water. They'd spent weeks at sea only to be hauled ashore in some distant town and locked away in the deepest recesses of a fortress, with only the dim glow of a distant lantern.

"Pacing will do you no good," she said.

"It helps me think."

"About?"

"Why they kept us alive. Surely it would be more pragmatic to execute us."

She stifled a laugh. "You're complaining because we're still alive?"

"Not at all. I'm just trying to figure out the why of it."

"Perhaps they want to parade us in front of people as an example of their superiority?"

"Then why keep us locked up for months on end?" He turned around, ready to walk to the other side of the cell. "Sorry. I'm not in the best of moods."

"Understandable, considering the situation we find ourselves in."

"How long do you reckon we've been here?"

"Long enough that the guards are now wearing warmer jackets, which indicates winter is here or on the way."

Arnim moved closer, sitting down beside her. "How much longer must we endure this indifference?"

"At least we're together."

"Thank Saxnor for small blessings."

"I wonder how they knew our identities?"

"We've gone over this before," he said. "They must have spies in Merceria."

"Yes, but who? And does that mean the queen is in danger?"

"I doubt that very much. She's surrounded by people she's known for years; they'll keep her safe."

"And what of us?"

"I've been thinking about that."

Nikki laughed. "You've thought of little else for months now, but go ahead, I'll humour you. What's your newest theory?"

"They've gone to great lengths to keep us alive. Yes, we're in a stinking cell, but they've fed us much better fare than gruel. Hardly the typical meal given to a prisoner."

"Perhaps their customs are different here?"

"I thought of that," replied Arnim, "but something doesn't sit right. The guards mention other prisoners, and they're clearly in much worse shape than us."

"As you said earlier, they know who we are. Perhaps, as nobles, they treat us differently?"

"There's more to it than that. I think they're getting us ready for something."

"What makes you say that?"

"Have you noticed our food quantity increasing in the last few days?"

"I have, as a matter of fact. Why? What do you think that means?"

"That they're fattening us up for something."

"Are you suggesting they're going to sacrifice us?"

Now it was Arnim's turn to chuckle. "No, but unless I miss my guess, we'll soon find ourselves with a fresh change of clothes and a chance to clean up."

"You think we're about to meet someone important?"

"I do, though I can't imagine who."

"We know they serve an emperor; the guards indicated as much. Could he be coming here to see us?"

"Wouldn't it make more sense for us to be taken to him?"

"Why would you say that?" asked Nikki.

"Do you think Queen Anna would go to the dungeons of Wincaster to visit with a prisoner or have one brought before her?"

"I believe she'd do exactly what she felt like regardless of court etiquette."

"Yes, well, I doubt the Emperor of Halvaria would be so inclined. From all accounts, this realm is massive, and their capital could be hundreds of miles away."

"That's likely still closer than Merceria." Nikki fell silent, and he placed his hand atop hers.

"The twins will be fine. There are plenty of people to look after them."

"I know that, but what's to become of us? Will we ever see them again, or simply languish in a cell for the rest of our lives?"

"That remains to be seen, but we mustn't give up hope. We've survived worse things."

"Such as?"

He grinned, although it was hard to see in the gloom. "We reconciled after years apart."

She took his hand. "Yes, we did. Thank you, Arnim, for being you."


Their endless days were finally broken by the appearance of a well-dressed visitor carrying two bundles. "You are Lord and Lady Caster?" he asked, standing on the other side of the cell door.

"No," retorted Arnim. "We're replacement prisoners sent to take their place. Of course we're Lord and Lady Caster. Who else would we be?"

"My name is Wingate. The High Strategos sent me to prepare you for a visit."

"Oh yes? And who in the name of Saxnor is the High Strategos?"

"His Grace, Lord Exalor Shozarin. The greatest battle mage of this era."

Arnim frowned. "And who came up with that one—himself?"

"Obviously, the customs in Merceria are different from ours." Wingate sniffed. "I should think you two might be more amenable to a change of clothing and a chance to clean up after months of incarceration?"

"And we are," said Nikki, rising to her feet. "Are we to change here, or will you take us somewhere more inviting?"

"We shall take you to separate rooms where you may wash."

"We go together or refuse to cooperate."

Wingate sighed. "It matters little to me." He turned to his escort. "Unlock the cell."

The guard moved closer, producing a ring of keys. "Don't try anything," he warned. "There are more guards just outside the door."

"We won't attempt to escape," said Arnim. "After all, where would we go?"

The door swung open with a groan, and their new visitor stepped inside, handing over the bundles of clothes. "They are rather plain," he said. "I'm afraid we don't have nobility here in Halvaria."

"But there's a ruling class, surely?"

"Yes, but not based on bloodline; rather, it's based on the ability to cast magic."

"Does that mean you're a mage?" asked Nikki, taking her new clothes.

"I am merely a clerk, madam."

"But your master is a battle mage, whatever that is."

"A battle mage is a wielder of magic who specializes in the study of war."

"What kind of magic does he wield?"

"Enchantments," replied Wingate. "Not that I expect you to understand."

"I know precisely what that means," said Nikki. "We have mages in Merceria."

"That's right. I'd forgotten about Kiren-Jool, though he is, technically, not Mercerian; he's Kurathian."

"You are remarkably well-informed," said Arnim. "But you fail to appreciate he's a Mercerian now and has been for some time."

"Ah, yes. I'd forgotten how you people do things. Very well, I shall concede the point. Now, follow me, and I'll conduct you to a room where you can clean up."

They were escorted up a steep set of stairs and through a labyrinthine collection of corridors to eventually arrive at a surprisingly well-decorated room, outside of which a pair of guards stood watch.

"You may change here," announced Wingate. "You will find wash basins and cloths within. I shall come and fetch you once His Grace deems it convenient."

They entered, the door being slammed shut behind them.

"At least they gave us some privacy," said Nikki. She pulled off what remained of her dress. Arnim moved to the window, gazing out at the courtyard below.

"What do you see?" asked his wife.

"Soldiers drilling."

"And?"

"They appear very disciplined. I'm disappointed. I expected more of a rabble."

"Is there an escape route?"

"No. There are far too many out there. I'm afraid we have little choice but to remain the guests of these people." He walked over to the table and peeled off his shirt. "Whew. I didn't realize how much I stink!"

"That's what you get when you stay in the lesser inns of the Halvarian Empire."

. . .

Sometime later, a guard brought them a plate with generous portions of freshly cooked meat and two bottles of wine. Arnim dug in, but Nikki ate sparingly, preferring water over the wine.

They'd barely finished their meal when Wingate reappeared at their door. "I trust the meal was acceptable?"

"It was," replied Nikki. "Thank you."

Their host bowed. "My pleasure. Now, if you'll follow me, His Grace is ready to see you."

They travelled through more corridors to arrive at a thick, ornately carved door guarded by two men. One was a warrior, but the other wore no distinguishing marks other than an odd medallion around his neck depicting a bird engulfed in flames. It meant nothing to Arnim, but he resolved to commit it to memory as he stepped through the doorway. Shelves lined the walls of the room, each holding bronze statues depicting warriors armed with various weapons.

"This is Lord Arnim and Lady Nicole," Wingate announced to the room's sole occupant.

"Ah, yes," said their host. "The notorious Viscount and Viscountess of Haverston. I presume I'm pronouncing that correctly?"

"You are," replied Arnim.

"I am, as I'm sure my aide told you, Exalor Shozarin, the High Strategos. You might consider me the empire's counterpart to your marshal."

"We refuse to reveal anything about the Army of Merceria."

"I don't expect you to. Besides, I already know everything I need, for we've been studying your little kingdom for some time now."

"And what is it you think you learned?"

"That you are a very resilient kingdom. I must admit I was a little surprised you defeated Kythelia's army, but to counter the Norland invasion and then turn around and defeat them? That was a masterful stroke. People like yours would thrive under the empire."

"Sorry. We're not interested."

"I would have been disappointed if you were," said Exalor. "Your people are descended from mercenaries, are they not?"

"Apparently you don't need me to tell you our history."

"No, I don't. Still, it's interesting to consider, isn't it? Despite your relative isolation from the rest of the Continent, you still developed your own nobility. I wonder if that's due to long-lasting social constructs from your original homeland or because it's a logical part of Human culture?"

"I wouldn't know."

Exalor sighed. "No, I don't suppose you would. Then again, history was never your strength, was it?"

"Is there a point to this discussion?"

"I am merely trying to ascertain your ability to converse. You'll need it where you're going." He smiled as Arnim frowned. "Don't worry. We won't separate you; that would detract from the entire experience."

"What are you getting at?" asked Nikki. "Where are you sending us?"

"Even farther from the borders of your precious kingdom to our capital, Varena."

"To what end?"

"Why, to meet the emperor. As it turns out, he has a fascination for your people."

"What is it you hope to achieve?"

"His Eminence wishes to learn more about the mortals who will grow to worship him."

"We worship Saxnor," said Arnim, "the God of Strength."

"A fact of which I'm well aware. Let me reassure you, I'm not saying we expect you to change your beliefs, merely that you face the inevitability that the God-Emperor will soon reign over all the civilized lands, yours included."

"The Marshal of Merceria won't allow that to happen."

"I know all about your precious marshal. I've studied him for years now. In fact, I'm looking forward to matching my skills against his. I'm told he is a master at adapting to new threats."

"You have no idea what you're up against."

"On the contrary, I know exactly what I'm up against. Not that I'd expect you to understand. Your battle experience is substantial, yet you've never commanded an army. On the other hand, I have many campaigns under my belt, all ending successfully." He went silent for a moment. "Now look at what you made me do. The last thing I wanted to do was to brag."

"It won't help you," insisted Arnim. "You'll still lose."

"You have no idea the numbers at my disposal. Not only will I defeat your precious Mercerian army, but I'll destroy the Warriors Throne as well. There'll be no one left to sing your praises when the empire finishes with you." He closed his eyes and took a deep breath, visibly calming himself. "We're done here, Wingate. You can escort them back."

"Back to the dungeon?" asked his aide.

"I don't think that's necessary, do you? Find them someplace nice within the fortress but keep them under constant watch."

"Yes, Your Grace."

Wingate and the guard escorted Arnim and Nikki to a room with a large bed, several cushioned chairs, and a small table.

"You will remain here until summoned," said Wingate, "but I wouldn't get too comfortable if I were you. You'll be travelling soon enough."

"How soon?" asked Nikki.

Their guide shrugged. "It all depends on who's available to escort you. In the meantime, you'll have your meals here and remain comfortable and well-fed. I'll arrange for some extra clothing to be available for your trip."

"Thank you. It's greatly appreciated."

Wingate left, though beyond the doors stood a pair of guards.

"Thank you?" said Arnim. "What happened to finding a route of escape?"

"And go where?" asked Nikki. "We don't know where we are or what direction Merceria lies. Where would we even go if we got away from here?"

"Does that mean we simply surrender to the inevitable?"

"Yes, at least until an opportunity presents itself. Look, I know this is difficult, Arnim, but we'll escape eventually. Until then, we must gather whatever information we can about this Halvarian Emperor."

"We've already learned a little."

"Such as?"

"He has an interest in Merceria or at least its subjects. Of course, that could be idle interest rather than any desire to learn something meaningful."

"Anything else you'd care to comment on?"

"As a matter of fact, yes," said Arnim, warming to the task. "The High Strategos told us the capital is called Varena. Do you think that might have something to do with the name of their empire?"

"Perhaps someone with that name founded it? Not that it will be of any help to us under our current circumstances. Anything else?"

"I propose we go one step further and cooperate with them."

"In what way?"

"We learn their customs, forgetting about escape, at least for the present."

Nikki smiled. "I see what you're saying. We lure them into a false feeling of acceptance as if we see the error of our ways."

"It can't hurt, can it?"

"I don't see how. Of course, there's no guarantee they'll fall for it. Exalor is a thorough planner, so I doubt he'd allow us too much leeway."

"Ah," said Arnim, "but he can't travel with us, can he? Not if he's overseeing an invasion."

"True, but he gave us no indication of when his campaign of conquest is to begin."

"Which tells me it's sometime soon."

"What makes you say that?"

"His tone indicated he was keen to commence. I think he's excited about going head-to-head against Gerald. Perhaps he feels the need to prove his superiority?"

"Yes," said Nikki. "I don't think I've ever seen his like before. It makes me worried, however."

"Why? He's not the first to believe he can beat our marshal."

"True, but he's made a habit of studying us. I get the feeling he understands Gerald's tactics very well, which could cost us the war."

"He can think all he likes, but we know Gerald's strength lies in his ability to improvise."

"What if Exalor does as well? We really know very little about the fellow or the army he commands. For all we know, he may outnumber us three to one."

"You make an excellent point." He moved to the window and pushed the curtains aside. "The same courtyard we saw earlier."

Nikki came up beside him. "And the same people?"

"No. The men I watched before wore mail while these are lightly armoured."

"Skirmishers?"

"Either that or archers would be my guess, although I see no signs of bows. I suspect they're practicing their close-in fighting techniques in case they find themselves in melee." He paused, staring at something. "We'll learn soon enough. Someone's about to address them."

They watched as a figure in brilliantly polished plate armour approached to address those in the courtyard. They could not hear what was being said from this distance, but after a brief speech, the men paired off and drew swords.

"Just as I expected," said Arnim. "They're using some sort of short sword."

"How short?"

"Shorter than the Mercerian blade by about half a length, assuming those warriors are average height. Such weapons are, I understand, typical of archers, along with axes."

"I would say close to a hundred men are down there. You?"

"Aye," said Arnim. "It's a curious thing to see archers practicing their swordplay."

"Do they not do that back home?"

"I've never seen them practice with anything other than their bows. Interesting."

"What is?"

"This group appears less disciplined than those we saw earlier."

"In what way?"

"The others all went through the exercises simultaneously, as if they were echoes of each other."

"And now?"

"They're each doing their own thing. My guess would be these are second-tier troops."

"Meaning?"

"Not as well-trained or equipped as their regulars. Think of them as raw recruits, and you wouldn't be far off."

"Good to know, yet of little use to us at present."

"Perhaps," said Arnim, "but it may prove useful at some point."

# TWENTY

## Ultimatum

### AUTUMN 967 MC

Aldwin held the newly repaired pauldron up to the lantern, examining his work. Viden had been nice enough to allow him to use his tools, and he had to spend the better half of the day hammering the armour back into shape, but he was finally satisfied with the result.

Beverly wouldn't be returning to the tournament. Her victory and subsequent ransom from Sir Gadron had seen to that. Now, they only waited for the repairs to his wife's armour before heading on their way.

"Nice work," came a voice. He looked up to see an unfamiliar face staring back at him. "Aldwin, isn't it?"

"Yes. And you are?"

The fellow grinned, his teeth yellow in the lantern's glare. "My name's not so important as that of my employer. I'm here at the king's behest."

Aldwin put down his tools. "What can I do for you?"

Before the man even answered, two more appeared, one coming from behind Aldwin.

"I'm afraid you're under arrest."

"For what? I've done nothing!"

The visitor moved closer, then pointed at the dagger hanging from the smith's belt. "It's against the king's law for a grey-eye to be armed."

"But it's only a dagger?"

"Is it? It looks more like a sword to me." The man nodded, and the others moved closer, seizing Aldwin by the biceps.

"Don't worry. We'll let your companions know what's happened. We wouldn't want them leaving without you, would we?"

. . .

Aubrey sat staring at the fire. Viden, Nymin, and Sir Owen watched as she ladled a thin soup into wooden bowls, passed them around, then grabbed her own bowl and filled it.

"How long have you been a smith?" she asked.

"I apprenticed when I turned twelve, but I wasn't recognized as a full smith till my twenty-first birthday. I still remember when I earned my title. It was the same day I met Nymin."

"That's right," added his wife. "It was at the Volbrook summer tournament. I was the queen of the fair."

"So you were a noble?" asked Aubrey.

"Saints, no," said Nymin. "The Queen of the Fair is a title bestowed on a young maiden from the town. Have you nothing similar where you're from?"

"We have fairs, but the idea of a tournament is something we abandoned generations ago."

"Why?"

"Our ancestors made prisoners fight to the death in an arena, but such barbaric behaviour was abolished under Queen Evermore."

"And now? Have you no place for your knights to show off their prowess?"

"We are descended from mercenaries. To us, fighting is in our blood."

"Yet you have no tournaments. How do people like Lady Beverly practice their skills?"

"Our realm has seen much bloodshed. When we're not fighting off raiders from the north, we're taking on those who would usurp the Crown. I'm afraid it's kept us in an almost continual state of war for years."

"Well," said Viden, "it certainly allowed your cousin to win us some coins." He held up his newly acquired purse and shook it. "A most profitable enterprise, if I do say so myself. So tell me, now that you have the funds you sought, will you be off to Reinwick?"

"Yes. Sir Owen here knows the way."

"Indeed," added the knight. "We are to travel east, into Zowenbruch and then up through Erlingen and Andover. Reinwick lies on the Great Northern Sea."

"That sounds like a very long trip," said Viden. "Are you sure Lady Beverly shouldn't sit through at least one more round of jousting? Travel can be an expensive proposition these days."

"I'm afraid you must make do with your share of Sir Gadron's ransom."

"Ah well. At least I tried." He was about to say more when he noticed a stranger approaching the campfire. The smith looked up, trying to place the newcomer's face. "Can I help you?"

"My name is Sir Langmar."

"You're the king's man, aren't you? The one who oversaw Lady Beverly's fight with Sir Hendrick?"

The fellow bowed. "I had that honour, yes."

"Well, what can we do for you?"

"I am seeking Lady Beverly Fitzwilliam."

"She's seeing to her horse," said Aubrey. "Perhaps I can be of assistance?"

"And you are?"

"Lady Aubrey Brandon, Baroness of Hawksburg."

"I remember her mentioning you. You are her cousin, if I recall?"

"That's right."

"I'm afraid I'm here on a delicate matter. You see, one of your entourage has gotten himself into a bit of a difficult situation."

Aubrey's gaze flicked around the campfire, but Beverly, Aldwin, and Keon were the only ones not present. Her first thought went to the former farmer. "What's Keon gotten himself into now?"

Sir Langmar locked eyes with her. "It's not Keon I'm here on behalf of. It's Aldwin."

"Why? What's happened?"

"He is under arrest for violating the king's laws."

"Which law, specifically?"

"He was caught, sword in hand. An illegal act under the king's directives concerning those descended from the Old Kingdom."

"He's not from the Old Kingdom," said Aubrey. "He's from Merceria."

"He bears the grey eyes of that ancient land. As such, he is still subject to their restrictions."

"This is outrageous!"

The knight shrugged. "I'm afraid I'm only the messenger, Lady Aubrey. If you wish to resolve this situation swiftly, I suggest you and Lady Beverly accompany me back to the Palace."

"To see the king?"

"Indeed. In his infinite wisdom, His Majesty decided he would deal with this situation in person due to Lady Beverly's outstanding performance in today's tournament."

"Wait here. I'll go fetch my cousin."

"As you will, my lady."


Beverly ran her hand over Lightning's back. The great Mercerian Charger swished his tail in delight, their bond on full display.

"We'll soon be on our way," she said. "Hopefully, it's only a few weeks of travel before Aubrey can recall us home."

"Beverly?"

She turned at the sound of her cousin's voice. "Why the long face?"

"It's Aldwin. He's been arrested."

Beverly's chest tightened. "On what charge?"

"Bearing a sword."

"Impossible. His is here with me."

"I doubt that will make much of a difference to His Majesty."

"The king? What's he got to do with this?"

"It's his law that's been broken," said Aubrey. "Sir Langmar tells me he wants to see the two of us to sort things out. Perhaps this is all a big misunderstanding?"

"It better be, or blood will be spilled."

"Wait a moment," soothed Aubrey. "Let's hear the fellow out."

"I'll not see my husband held in a dungeon."

"All the more reason for us to speak with His Majesty directly."

"Very well, but I'm taking Nature's Fury."

Her cousin offered a grim smile. "I wouldn't have it any other way."


The Palace was the largest building in all of Agran, making it easy to find. Upon their arrival, the guards escorted them directly to the great hall, where, to their surprise, it was not the king who awaited them but the queen.

"Your Majesty," said Aubrey, bowing. "We were led to understand the king wished to see us?"

"He did," replied Helisant, "but unfortunately, he is unable to meet with you. I am here in his stead."

"I came here to negotiate my husband's release," said Beverly. "What is it you want?"

"I see you wish to get to the heart of the matter, so I shall waste no more of your time. Aldwin Fitzwilliam has been charged with bearing arms in contravention of the king's law."

"He is no Therengian."

"Still, he bears the grey eyes of his race."

"He hails from Merceria, a descendant of mercenaries from almost a thousand years ago. How could he be descended from these Therengians?"

"The people who formed the Old Kingdom have existed for thousands of years, so it is not unsurprising to discover their ancestors amongst the mercenaries you speak of. However, this does not absolve him of his crime."

"I sense there is more to this than a simple arrest; else, why would you be meeting us?"

"Let's just say he's become useful to us."

"Useful?" said Aubrey.

"Why, yes. He is a guarantor of sorts. You help us, and we shall return him to your care."

"Help you, how?" asked Beverly.

"The king is ill and has been for some time. We've consulted many healers, but none possess the power of Life Magic." She looked at Aubrey. "That's what you are, isn't it? A Life Mage capable of healing flesh?"

"I am," replied Aubrey, "but you didn't need to arrest Aldwin to ask for our help."

"Ah, but that's an added incentive, don't you see? All you need to do is heal the king, and you can be on your way."

"And if I can't?"

"Then I'm afraid Aldwin's life will be forfeit. After all, we can't have people flouting the law."

"Release him, and we'll see what we can do."

"Oh no," said the queen. "I'm not about to give up my only advantage. You might decide to leave, and then where would I be?"

"What are His Majesty's symptoms," asked Aubrey.

"He's been coughing up blood and frequently finds himself weak of limb."

"Anything else?"

"Yes. His breathing can be raspy at times, and he often sneezes."

"I will help him, but I have conditions."

"I might remind you your cousin's husband is in our dungeons."

"I understand you will not release him until the king is healed, but can you hold him in more comfortable surroundings until that time?"

The queen stared back, weighing Aubrey's demand. "I can agree to that. I shall have the guards keep him in a room in the Palace. Will that suffice?"

Aubrey looked at her cousin for guidance. Beverly said nothing, merely nodded, her jaw clenched tight.

"Take me to His Majesty, and I shall see what I can do. Beverly, I suggest you come with me, if only for moral support."

"You will look at His Majesty now?" asked Helisant.

"That was the intent, wasn't it?"

"I was under the impression it would take time for you to prepare."

"Prepare?"

"Don't you need to commit the spell of healing to memory?"

"You appear to know little of magic. Our power flows from within, controlled by our understanding of the arcane language. You see..." Her voice trailed off as she realized the woman had no grasp of how things worked. "Never mind," Aubrey added. "Suffice it to say, I need no preparation. Shall we proceed?"

"Yes, of course."

The queen led them up a great set of stairs and into the east wing of the Palace. Servants scuttled around, intent on their business, ignoring the new arrival, but the guards watched with intense interest. They finally arrived at two large doors, in front of which stood two guards.

"This is the Life Mage, Aubrey Brandon," announced Queen Helisant.

The warrior dutifully opened the door, stepping aside to allow them entry. Inside, the king lay on a large, four-poster bed, covered in thick blankets, looking pale and sweaty. Around him sat three individuals. One was an old woman whose manner of dress and advanced age would suggest a relative of some sort, likely a mother or aunt. Another, with the look of a scholar, sorted through several medicinal herbs spread out on a small table before him. The third was a man of the Church who held his hands in prayer, droning on about the Afterlife being accepting of those who'd lived a good life.

The man with the herbs stood up suddenly. "What's this, Your Majesty? Another charlatan here to take your coins?"

"This," replied the queen, "is a Life Mage, come to help the king."

"Life Mage? No magic can save His Majesty. What he needs is a good bloodletting."

"I would advise against that," said Aubrey. "From what I've been told, he is in a weak state. Such a treatment would likely finish him off."

The fellow stepped towards her. "Do you not think I know the risks? I was healing the sick before you were even born!"

"If you know the risks, then why do you propose to proceed with the treatment?"

"Because all other treatments have failed. If he is to survive, we must balance his humours. I would not expect one of your age to understand."

"Ah, yes. The humours," she replied. "That would be the so-called balance between blood, phlegm, yellow, and black bile, would it not?"

His eyes narrowed. "I see you follow the teachings of Eucephalus."

"I'm afraid I'm not familiar with that name."

"Not familiar? He's the ancient Thalamite considered the father of all modern medicine! How can you know about four humours without knowing such a thing?"

"Where I'm from, we consider the practice of balancing such things archaic. We in the west have learned much from studying Life Magic."

"Bah, magic! No good will come of it, I tell you." He pleaded his case to the queen. "Please, I beg of you, Majesty. Do not let this whelp place her hands upon the king. It will only lead to his ruin."

"And what would you have me do?" replied Helisant. "Your own treatment has done no good. Am I then to sit back and watch my husband die? Move aside, Master Garrig, and allow her to use her magic."

He shifted to one side, recoiling as the new visitor approached the patient. "This is madness," he added.

Aubrey moved to the bedside, looking down at the king, who sweated profusely. Small wonder, considering how many blankets lay atop him. "Open the window," she said. "He needs some fresh air."

"No!" shouted Garrig. "That will only feed the contagion."

She placed her hand on the king's forehead. "He's feverish. How long has he been like this?"

The older woman answered. "The servants found my nephew like this when they came to wake him."

"And is this common?"

She shrugged. "He has bouts occasionally, most typically at night."

Aubrey looked at the queen. "With your permission, Majesty, I will cast a spell of heal flesh. It may not cure him, but it could serve to undo the damage caused by whatever this affliction is."

At the queen's nod, she closed her eyes and dug deep, calling on her power within. Arcane words came to her lips, and then she felt the familiar buzz of the magic building, making the air hum as if a swarm of bees had been let loose in the room.

Aubrey opened her eyes to see the familiar white light illuminating her hands, and as she placed them on the king, the colour bled into his body.

"Interesting," she said, watching the result. "This is no ordinary illness."

"Why would you say that?" asked the queen.

"When I cast this spell, it flows to the area most affected. In this case, it rushed to His Majesty's head, yet I detected no sign of damage there."

"See?" said Garrig. "Her spell is useless. What did I tell you?"

"Silence!" snapped Aubrey. "This is but the first stage of treatment. Would you so readily diagnose a patient when you have only checked their temperature? There is much to consider here before I make a diagnosis."

"Have you another spell?" asked the queen.

"There are several, but I need a better idea of what this affliction is if I am to cure him. When did this illness begin? Did he suffer from it in his youth?"

"No. He first fell ill a few months ago. At the time, we believed he'd caught a cold. He recovered, but then the symptoms returned."

"And had anything changed at that time?"

"Such as?"

"A different kind of food? Or contact with someone who'd travelled to distant lands?"

"What has that got to do with anything?" asked Garrig. "This woman knows nothing about the arts of healing, Your Majesty. I grant you she can put on a good show with glowing hands and all, but she's out of her depth!"

"Enough!" shouted Helisant. "Guards! Keep Master Garrig from interrupting. I shall deal with his impertinence later."

Aubrey watched as the guards took up positions on either side of the Royal Healer.

"I'm sorry," the queen said to Aubrey. "You shouldn't have to put up with this sort of thing." A great sorrow came over her features as she looked down at her husband. "What else can you do?" she asked, her voice harsh with emotion.

"There is a chance some sort of poison brought this malady on. Has he enemies?"

"No more so than any other ruler of a Petty Kingdom. In any case, there are food tasters for such things."

"And none of them fell sick?"

"None whatsoever."

"I should still like to attempt to neutralize toxins, just to rule it out."

"You may proceed as you feel best."

Once more, Aubrey called on her inner magic. This time she dug deeper, calling up a blue light, but when the aura flooded into him, it quickly dissipated. She shook her head. "It's not poison."

"Then what is it?"

"Something far more sinister."

# TWENTY-ONE

# Patrol

## AUTUMN 967 MC

C aptain Hugh Gardner pulled the cloak around him, for it was much colder this far north in the gap. He reminded himself it was, by all accounts, almost winter. True, there was no snow on the ground yet, but the cold winds blew with more frequency of late, and he knew it wouldn't be long before the entire area was blanketed in white.

He looked at the men riding on either side of him. Many had served with him in Wincaster. Back then, the company was little more than couriers, travelling all over Merceria bearing letters from the king, then Dame Beverly changed all that. No, he corrected himself, that would be Lady Beverly, for she was now Baroness of Bodden.

"Are you with us?"

He glanced to his left at his new sergeant, Bickerstaff, who was grinning like an idiot. He'd come a long way since the early days when he could barely stay in the saddle.

"I'm fine," replied Gardner. "Keep on the lookout, or we risk being surprised."

"You mean like that?" The sergeant pointed eastward.

The captain looked to see a small cluster of… Well, to be honest, he didn't really know what they were. They looked to be children from this range, but that couldn't be right. He ordered the company to increase its pace. Beyond this group was another, larger contingent mounted on horses charging towards them.

"Spread out," he said, "and prepare to engage."

"Surely not?" said Bickerstaff. "They have no weapons!"

"Not the ones running towards us on foot—those horsemen over there."

As they drew closer, he realized those in front weren't children but thin, short individuals with pointed ears.

"Elves?" said Bickerstaff. "Aren't the woodland folk taller?"

"These are the Wood Elves the vard spoke of," replied Gardner. "Take six men and escort them back to Ironcliff."

"Sir? What about the enemy?"

"Let the rest of us worry about them."

Gardner led his men to the left, riding past the refugees while Bicker-staff and his small group slowed. Knowing they would be safe with the sergeant, he concentrated on the enemy to his front.

Whomever it was, had formed their horsemen into two lines and were doing a grand job of keeping those lines straight, which boded ill for Captain Gardner, for it meant they were disciplined troops.

He spared a glance at his men. Were they up to the task? Even now, some insisted his promotion had been premature. Yes, he'd seen battle in the last war and was recently promoted to captain, but did that qualify him to lead the entire company?

Gardner shook his head, trying to dismiss his worries, concentrating instead on the task ahead.

To his surprise, the enemy halted. Fearing a trap, he ordered his men to do the same, coming to rest some two hundred paces from contact. Mimicking the enemy captain's actions, he urged his horse forward.

They met in the middle, neither with their weapons drawn. The entire thing felt like a joke as if hordes of cavalrymen were about to unleash their fury on an unsuspecting foe, but then Gardner's opposite raised his hand in salute.

"Greetings. I am Captain Ferran Nygard, First Provincial Cohort, Seventh Legion."

"Captain Hugh Gardner, Wincaster Light Horse."

"Are you from Ironcliff?"

"My men and I are Mercerians."

"Of course," said Nygard. "I would expect nothing else." He leaned forward, resting his palms on his pommel. "I don't suppose I could convince you to give up this little act and surrender, could I? It's been a long day."

"Men of Merceria do not surrender."

The Halvarian offered a wry smile. "I expected you might say that. In that case, we should each withdraw to our respective lines, yes?"

Gardner was growing impatient. "I don't suppose I could ask YOU to surrender?"

"I'm afraid my commander-general would flay me alive if I did that." He noted the look of shock on Gardner's face. "Not literally, though. We're not barbarians."

"Yet you cross the borders of a Dwarven stronghold."

"Do we? I don't see any flags flying hereabouts, or any Dwarves asking us to leave."

"What do you call the Wincaster Light?"

"Little more than a diversion. If you were to be on your way, we could avoid bloodshed this day."

Gardner looked over his shoulder, but his own men blocked his view of the refugees. He turned back to the interloper. "You are pursuing common folk, hardly the type who pose a threat to your army."

"Look," said Nygard. "I'm only a captain and a provincial one at that. I care little about politics, but I must follow orders."

"As must I."

"Then it seems we are at an impasse."

"Is it worth all this effort just to track down a few Elves?" Gardner spotted a flicker of annoyance. Had he hit a sore spot with the fellow? He decided to press his luck. "You could always return to your commander with the news you lost them, and who would be any the wiser?"

Nygard grinned. "That is a most excellent suggestion. I'll do just that, and with a bit of luck, my superiors will be more interested in my coming across you instead of those berry munchers."

"Berry munchers?"

"Yes, the Elves. I'm led to believe they don't eat meat."

"How is that of any relevance?"

"My dear fellow, it proves they are an inferior race. Have you learned nothing in that tiny kingdom of yours?"

"We judge people by their actions, not their diet."

"To each his own, I suppose." Nygard glanced over his shoulder. "My men are tired; I'd best get them on their way. Good day to you, Captain... Gardner, wasn't it? Of the Wincaster Light Cavalry?"

"Horse, actually, but yes."

"Isn't all cavalry horse?"

Gardner grinned. "Perhaps." His statement appeared to confuse his counterpart, but the fellow didn't bite.

"Good day to you, Captain. Perhaps we'll meet again?" Nygard turned around, riding back to his men.

Gardner returned to the Wincaster Light, then waited. True to his word, the Halvarian ordered his riders to turn around and ride eastward, presumably to return to his camp, wherever that was.

"Did you and the gentleman have a nice chat?" asked Bickerstaff.

"I'm not completely sure. I convinced him to leave the Elves alone, but I can't help but feel we'll be seeing him again." He suddenly realized with whom he was speaking. "Didn't I tell you to escort the Elves back to Ironcliff?"

"Aye. I sent six men to look after them, but I couldn't leave you here all alone, now, could I? Not when you're about to come to blows with the enemy."

"Tell me again why I made you sergeant?"

"It's all on account of my natural leadership qualities. Well, that and the fact I can still drink you under the table."

"That's it," said Gardner. "I knew there was a reason."

"What do we do now?"

"We remain here until the enemy is out of sight, then return to Ironcliff."

"What if there are other refugees?"

Gardner looked skyward. "Night will come soon, and we're in unfamiliar territory. Don't worry, we'll resume searching tomorrow, but I need to send word back to Wincaster about this strange situation we find ourselves in."

Thalgrun leaned forward on his throne. "And where did you say this was?"

"To the east, Majesty," replied Captain Gardner. "About half a day's ride from these very gates."

"Was there any sign of footmen?"

"No. We saw only horse. Their captain identified them as provincial cavalry, if that means anything."

"I have not heard of such a thing before," said Thalgrun, "but if I were to guess, I would say it's likely recruited from their conquered territories, hence the name. How were they equipped?"

"Much as my own men, Majesty. They appeared well-disciplined, far more so than the Norlanders we fought in the last war."

"What would be your assessment of this encounter?"

"Majesty?"

"What do you think it portends?"

"I suspect they're getting ready to march their army. Their lighter horsemen are presumably scouting to identify areas that might prove troublesome. There are doubtlessly more out there somewhere, probing for weaknesses."

"They're likely to find a great deal of them. We Dwarves have no cavalry, and your company alone can't be everywhere."

"They don't need to be!"

They both turned to see a Kurathian entering.

"Lord Lanaka, I presume?" said Thalgrun. "We've been expecting you."

"My apologies, Majesty. I was needed to help sort out the transport of my command."

"How much of our conversation did you hear?"

"Only that you have one company, but Agramath briefed me about recent events as soon as I arrived."

"And what news do you bring from Wincaster?"

"The situation in Stonecastle hasn't changed, though we have a better idea about their numbers. It's our considered opinion they won't make their move until spring, but we're keeping the army ready to march in case they move earlier."

"And what of us, here in Ironcliff?"

"The marshal authorized two of our Kurathian companies to join the Wincaster Light Horse and named me their commander. The first company is in the process of being brought here even as we speak, but it will be three days before they're ready to head out on patrol."

"That soon?"

"Additional trips will be required for fodder before the second company is sent, as the land hereabouts cannot feed our mounts."

"We are pleased to see you amongst us, Commander. It clearly demonstrates the friendship between our two peoples, despite its relatively young age."

"Our queen is determined to do all she can to ensure your safety, Majesty."

"And I appreciate her support, but I fear war will soon be upon us. If the enemy is sending scouts into the gap, how long before they are at our doors?"

"Perhaps a prisoner or two would shed some light on their plans. I'm curious why they would begin now when winter is at hand. Surely not the best time to start a campaign?"

"That," said Thalgrun, "is something I can answer. It is only a short march from their city to our gates. I think they mean to surround us, then spend the winter trying to starve us out, but they don't realize their actions only work to our advantage. Our crops are in, our granaries full, and we have the magic circle, allowing us to evacuate the wounded and bring reinforcements when needed. Ironcliff will not fall."

"I have no doubt of that, yet their presence here presents a bigger problem. To the west lies a large section of empty space through which to march. Once they seal you up, they can use a relatively small force to keep you in place while the rest head into Norland, making it difficult for us to pin them down."

"How so?"

"The Army of Merceria is not large, Majesty, and once the Halvarians are rampaging across Norland, we will need to spread out to locate them, thus weakening us even further. If we are to stop their advance, it must be in the gap."

"You speak of Norland. Will they send aid?"

"Queen Anna is making overtures, but even if Bronwyn agreed, she'd still have to move men here. I shouldn't have to remind you it's a long march from Galburn's Ridge."

"So we are on our own, present company excepted, of course."

"Yes. At least for the foreseeable future."

Captain Gardner cleared his throat. "My pardon, Majesty, but did we learn anything new from the Wood Elves we rescued?"

"Very little," grumbled the king. "The Aralani are not a warrior race, and though they saw many Halvarian troops, they could not provide us with anything useful. Your own report, however, was exemplary, at least as far as the enemy horsemen were concerned. If only we knew more about their footmen or siege engines."

"Could Lord Agramath not use his magic to spy out the enemy?"

"He is a master of rock and stone, not a Druid."

"Then perhaps Melethandil could be coaxed into helping?"

"And how do you propose we find her? She is a dragon and, as such, has flown deep into the Thunder Mountains to make her new home. Even if we knew where to look, it would take months for an expedition to pass through that terrain, and there's no guarantee she would agree to help!"

Thalgrun shifted in his seat before continuing. "Look, I know I'm painting a grim picture here, but I'm trying to be realistic. Our defences will hold out, but this siege will bring hardship to my people, not to mention the threat to Norland and Merceria. I'd feel better if we could strike back somehow."

"Have you considered meeting them in the gap?" asked Lanaka.

"I have, but we mountain folk are short of stride, and they would quickly outmanoeuvre us. If we could force them to battle, I have no doubt we'd be victorious, but this will be a campaign of movement, something we are sadly lacking."

"And if we overcame that weakness?"

"Then I would fight beneath the sky rather than within our halls of stone. What is it you're proposing?"

"With Agramath's help, I shall send word to Wincaster."

"To what end?"

"The Orcs of Ravensguard could be here within a week and in sufficient enough numbers that we could force a confrontation. It might not win us the war, but it would certainly blunt their advance."

"Their home is close to two hundred miles away, isn't it?"

"It is," said Lanaka, "but Orcs can cover thirty miles a day without breaking a sweat."

"But wouldn't they require supplies?"

"They carry what food they need for the trip, and we'll use magic to bring further supplies here to Ironcliff. It would be a difficult task, but having seen them in action in the last war, I can say they're up to it."

"Very well," said Thalgrun, "but I need assurances they are coming before I commit to marching my Dwarves out into the open. What think you, Captain Gardner? You've seen the enemy. Do we have time?"

"We've seen only light horsemen, Majesty, but we'll range farther east with your permission. Perhaps, with some clever tactics, we might convince the Halvarians we possess more horsemen than they think."

"Don't overextend yourself. The last thing we need is to lose a company of scouts."

"Understood, Majesty."

"And as for you, Lord Lanaka, I would have you take word directly to your queen once Agramath is ready. The sooner we put this plan of yours into action, the better."

"Understood, Majesty."

Thalgrun clasped his hands together. "It feels good to finally be doing something rather than just sitting here."

He waited until the Mercerians left before turning to one of his servants. "Fetch me Lord Garnik. I would have words."

"Yes, Majesty." The fellow ran off, his feet echoing on the stone floors.

The Vard of Ironcliff closed his eyes, trying to imagine the army they were about to assemble. He'd seen the Orcs in action during the recent war and knew they were reliable, and Lanaka's reputation was that of a distinguished commander, but what of their enemy? Were the Halvarians as capable as his allies? Taking a stand against them was a bold step, especially when there was no firm indication of the enemy's numbers.

His thoughts turned to Kasri, and he wished she were here. He valued her opinion, not only as his daughter but as an experienced, battle-hardened leader. Would she agree he was making the right decision?

It suddenly dawned on him that he must lead this expedition himself. Yes, there was a chance he might perish, but if such were the case, he had no doubt Kasri was capable of taking over.

The door opened, revealing the grave countenance of none other than Lord Garnik Hardhand, Guild Master of the Warriors Guild.

"You called for me, Majesty?"

"I did. How many stonecakes have we available?"

"Why? Surely you don't mean to march?"

"I do, though not for some days yet."

"How many companies do you intend to take?"

"Likely six, but I might change my mind."

"Six?" replied the guild master. "But that would strip our defences!"

"We are marching to war, Garnik. We can't afford to send a dribble."

"I urge caution, Majesty. Such an expedition can only lead to disaster."

"Our allies will support us."

"Which allies?"

"The Mercerian cavalry and an undisclosed number of Orcs."

"How many horse?"

"Three companies."

"I would hardly call that an expedition, Majesty."

"Still, we must do something, if only to blunt the enemy."

"Then let us reinforce our defensive works."

"You know as well as I there is little to improve upon. The time is fast approaching when the enemy will be on the march. If we don't take the opportunity to damage them now, they will flood into Norland and cause havoc for our allies."

Garnik shook his head. "We should fight for the survival of our own people, Majesty, not to safeguard the Human realms."

"Nonetheless, I have made up my mind. Fire up the furnaces if you must, but I want stonecakes aplenty when the time comes to move out."

# TWENTY-TWO

# Reports

AUTUMN 967 MC

E xalor steadied himself against the wall, causing a look of alarm on the face of his aide, Wingate.

"Are you all right, Your Grace?"

"I am merely tired. I've been teleporting a lot lately, and it's taken its toll on me."

"Then it's good we're back here in the capital, so you can rest."

"Rest? I can't rest. I must address the Inner Council. They are expecting detailed reports of our preparations."

"Surely that can wait?"

The High Strategos spared a glance for his aide. "My dear fellow, while I admire your dedication to my service, I would have thought that by now you understood the demands of my office. This campaign will not run itself. Without the council's continued support, it would quickly fail."

"What can I do to help?"

"I am going to my office to collect my thoughts. See if you can find me something to eat, will you? I'm absolutely ravenous."

"Of course, Your Grace." Wingate ran off, eager to do his master's bidding.

Exalor made his way to his office, but as soon as he fell into his chair, Kelson opened the door.

"What do you want?" he snapped.

"I bring good tidings."

"That being?"

"The Marshal of the North will no longer be available to continue his duties. Is that something to do with you?"

"I'm not sure what you're suggesting. Why? What's happened?"

"I'm told he suffered a fatal fall while out riding. Something about his horse being frightened?"

"Why am I only hearing about this now?"

"Calm down," said Kelson. "I only just learned about it myself. In any case, you were off gallivanting across the empire. Perhaps if you informed others of your travel arrangements, we could update you?"

"It couldn't be helped. Things cropped up that needed to be dealt with in person. It's hardly my fault the idiot decided to fall."

"Ah. Idiot, is it? I think you give away too much." He chuckled. "Not that I'm complaining, mind you, but he was a Sartellian, and you know what that means."

"Yes. They shall have to convene an assembly to select his replacement."

"But that could take months! Won't that upset your plans?"

Exalor merely smiled.

"Ah. I understand now. Who do you have in mind for his temporary replacement?"

"I'd rather not say."

"We're from the same line," said Kelson. "How can you not trust me?"

"It's not a matter of trust, but discretion. Were anyone to overhear, they might attempt to thwart my plans."

"Yes, but they're about to become public knowledge, aren't they? At least as far as the council is concerned."

"The subjugation of Merceria is not my only plan," said Exalor. "You, of all people, should understand that."

"Am I to infer you seek more influence over the empire's affairs?"

"You can infer what you like, but I shall deny it if you even so much as utter a whisper of such things."

"So there is a plan! Congratulations, and I must say, it's about time we got rid of those useless council members."

"Careful," warned the High Strategos. "I doubt the others would see it our way, especially the High Purifier."

"She still thinks the three lines hold each other in check. I see no reason to convince her otherwise."

"And what is your position on this new development? Are you for or against it?"

"I assume," said Kelson, "you refer to the marshal's loss, or do you mean your own plans for the position?"

"Why not both?"

"It's a bold plan, but I would step carefully. The Stormwinds and Sartellians carry a lot of influence."

"Is that a threat?"

"No, merely an observation. For my part, I'll do what I can to keep word of this from leaking out, but sooner or later, I suspect the council members will figure out something is happening."

"Hopefully by then, it'll be too late."

"What can I do to assist?"

"I'm not sure that would be a good idea. It would only serve to make yourself a target. Better to lie low and gather information regarding our opponents."

"What if my sentinels spread the word about your trustworthiness?"

"No. If it got back to the council, it would only worsen things. This wouldn't be the first time someone tried to take it all, nor, I suspect, will it be the last. What you can do is keep your ears open. If you hear even a hint of a whisper that they are suspicious about my loyalty, I need to know immediately."

"Most assuredly," said Kelson. "Now, are you ready to face the dragons?"

Exalor laughed. "They are people, just like you and I, not dragons, although I sometimes wonder if a comparison to snakes might be more appropriate. You're correct in one sense, though. We need to gird ourselves for the fight of a lifetime."

When the High Strategos last visited the Inner Council, it held only six of its twelve members, but today, all seats were filled. Exalor sat, his eyes closed, gathering his thoughts. Kestia Stormwind, the eldest council member, struck the bell, indicating the meeting should come to order.

"We are here," she began, "to decide whether to implement Lord Exalor's campaign strategy." All eyes turned to the High Strategos. "You will, as always, answer any and all questions this council has for you. Do you understand?"

Part of him wanted to rebel at the absurdity of it all, but he held himself in check. "Yes. Who wants to begin?"

Unsurprisingly, Murias spoke first. "What are our expected losses?"

"Light," he replied. "The attack in the northwest is more of holding action. Once we lock the Dwarves inside Ironcliff, we need only raid the surrounding areas. Doubtless, such actions will draw the Mercerians north in support of their allies."

"And then?"

"Then phase two commences with the attack on Stonecastle."

"You still haven't told us what to expect regarding casualties. When you say light, do you mean hundreds? Thousands? Or only dozens?"

"Nothing is guaranteed when it comes to war, but I'm expecting somewhere in the range of three hundred dead and twice that in injuries."

"You seem confident," said Murias.

"And why wouldn't I be? As I've said before, I've spent years examining the Mercerians' successes and failures. Their marshal's tactics are well-known to me, as is his strategy.

"Then why wait so long?" asked Edora. "Surely the time to strike would have been in the summer rather than now, as winter approaches."

"Winter is both a blessing and a curse," replied Exalor. "True, it can hamper our march, but it can also conceal us, making it difficult to observe our strength."

"Don't we possess the advantage already in terms of numbers?"

"We do, and by a considerable margin, but I prefer to keep it that way. This might seem like a gamble to many of you, but I have been working on this for years."

"Yes," said Agalix Sartellian, "you've pointed that out to us numerous times, yet I still harbour reservations."

"Are you saying you won't support it?"

"I haven't made up my mind. I had thought to throw my considerable weight behind this endeavour, but my cousin's untimely death has me wondering if it's the best time for such things. Surely we should wait until we choose his successor?" He looked at his fellow council members, but only the Sartellians seemed interested in his remarks.

Freya Stormwind raised her hand. She was the newest council member and the youngest, but she more than made up for that with her insight.

"Yes?" said Kestia. "You have something to ask?"

"My pardon, High Strategos, if someone has raised this issue before, but have you an actual estimate as to how long it will take for the complete destruction of the mercenaries?"

"Mercenaries?" said Exalor. "I assume by that you mean the Mercerians. Yes, by my estimation, the war will be over before the end of next year."

"You must excuse my ignorance, but doesn't that seem optimistic, considering their resiliency?"

"Not at all. My strategy is to overwhelm their defences by attacking in succession. You would know that if you'd been present at the last meeting."

"You are not here to lecture," warned Kestia. "If you want to proceed with this campaign, you need the approval of all on this council. You might also consider it is within the council's right to remove you from the position of High Strategos if we deem it necessary."

"My apologies," said Exalor. "I have been rather busy of late making the final arrangements."

"Then perhaps we should replace you with someone more capable?" said Freya.

"Hold on," replied Kelson. "We are here to ask questions about the planned campaign, not make accusations. Can we please get back to the business at hand?"

"Though I hate to admit it," said Fadra, "he's right. Now is not the time for politics. Rather, it is a time to stand together for the betterment of all."

"Easy for you to say," said Agalix. "Your line didn't lose its marshal."

"That is only a temporary setback. Such things happen from time to time. What I'm more interested in is what's going on in Weldwyn. You hinted efforts were underway to prevent them from interfering. Can you now tell us more?"

"Certainly," said Exalor. "As you are no doubt aware, Vadym Stormwind has spread our influence throughout the Clanholdings. However, you may not know that a second agent, Ryfar Shozarin, is fomenting unrest amongst the Goblins."

"Goblins?" said Fadra. "Surely you jest? Those creatures are barely capable of speech, let alone posing a serious threat to the Clans."

"And if I were talking of only a village or two, I would agree, but his efforts have been much grander in scale."

"Meaning?"

"To use his own words, he has formed a confederacy of villages, uniting them in a quest to rid the area of Human interference."

"Yet he himself is a Human. How does that work?"

"They are an impoverished and backward people, surviving only by what they can grow and hunt themselves. Ryfar has showered them with gifts, filling their heads with tales of great wealth amongst the Human settlements."

"And you mean to cause a war?"

"That's certainly the intention," said Exalor. "In fact, it's already begun. Even as we speak, they are sending raiding parties up and down the edge of the mountains, harassing the Clans."

"Do you feel that will be enough to force Weldwyn's hand?"

"Most definitely," said Exalor. "You see, the king's sister wed a Clan Chief—all part of an arranged marriage to secure peace. If they ignore the Clans' pleas for help, the marriage becomes a sham."

"Fascinating," noted Edora. "But you haven't considered all the possible ramifications. What if the Clans don't ask for help?"

"They'll have to. They took a beating when they invaded Weldwyn, and as a result, their numbers were depleted. There's no way they can carry the war to the Goblins without leaving their own towns undefended."

"How many Goblins are there?"

"Enough to infest the Sunset Peaks all the way to the coast."

"Sunset Peaks?"

"Yes," said Exalor. "That's a rough translation of the Goblin name, though the literal translation would be 'peaks behind which the sun sets'. They form the western border of the Clanholdings."

"And out of curiosity, what lies beyond them?"

"The area is unexplored, although there are scattered reports it's no more than a rocky coast sitting on the edge of the Sea of Storms."

"I have a question concerning this element of the campaign," said Agalix. "How do you know this trouble to the west will be enough to deprive Merceria of help from Weldwyn? Couldn't they do both?"

"If you'd bothered to read my reports, you wouldn't need to ask. Weldwyn took tremendous losses during the recent invasion and barely has enough men to keep the streets safe, let alone provide an army to help their allies."

"If that's the case, why send your agents into the mountains in the first place?"

"I prefer to think of it as a safeguard against unexpected events. These things take years of planning to organize, and even the best of seers is seldom accurate when predicting the future."

"I'll accept your explanation, but why send a Shozarin? Surely a Sartellian would be a better projection of power?"

Exalor stared back, biting his tongue as he tried not to sound condescending. "While your line is most accomplished regarding Fire Magic, I doubt any can speak the Goblins' language."

"And yours do?"

"You forget, we are Enchanters. As such, we can use our magic to speak in different languages."

Agalix nodded. "I concede the point. You appear to have given this much thought."

"As I've said before, this campaign has been years in the making."

"If I may," offered Edora. "I have one last question."

"By all means."

"If you could identify any weakness in this plan of yours, no matter how small, what would it be?"

"We did our best to consider all the races inhabiting the lands west of the Sullen Peaks, but there are still some doubts about which ones are willing to march against us."

"Are you suggesting the Orcs won't fight, or the Dwarves?"

"No. There can be no doubt about their commitment to the Mercerian Alliance. Rather, the Elves are the biggest unknown factor."

"And if they choose to fight?"

"It might change our battle tactics a little, but our overall strategy will remain intact."

"But are they a threat?"

"A minor one, at best. Yes, their bows are more powerful than ours, but they are not a numerous people. It's reported they only fielded a few hundred warriors at the Siege of Summersgate last year."

"Elves," Murias said, shivering. "Just the thought of them makes my skin crawl."

"They are a dying race," said Kelson. "Our scholars estimate there are only half a dozen Elvish enclaves left across the entire Continent. Their day in the sun has come to an end."

Kestia Stormwind struck the bell, calling for silence. "Are there any more questions for His Grace, Lord Exalor?" She looked around the room, but everyone shook their head. "Then I call for a vote. All in favour of supporting this campaign?"

All hands went up.

"Then it's settled. Lord Exalor, you may begin the campaign at your leisure."

"Thank you, Your Grace." The High Strategos stood, bowing to his companions. "It is an honour to serve this august council."


Exalor breathed in the cool night air, savouring the experience. A light rain fell, but he looked skyward instead of covering himself, letting the droplets fall across his face. He was exhausted, yet at the same time, exhilarated. Years of planning were finally coming to fruition. He would conquer Merceria, then return the triumphant hero, a victorious army at his beck and call.

A sudden, agonizing pain erupted from his back as a knife scraped along his backbone. His legs gave way, and he fell forward, landing face down on the steps. Blood ran out from beneath him, the rain diluting it as it spread. A rush of feet approached, and then someone grabbed his arm, flipping him over.

"Exalor? Are you alive?"

He tried to focus on the fellow's face that hovered over him, but his name would not come. The man's hands glowed, and then a warmth spread over the High Strategos, knitting flesh, and stemming the flow of blood.

"Kelson, is that you?"

"It is. Who attacked you?"

"I don't know. They came from behind, so I didn't see their face."

"You're lucky I happened along. Guards!"

More footfalls, and then soldiers lifted him up.

"This way," said Kelson. "And not a word about this to anyone!"

Exalor opened his eyes to find himself lying in a bed. A candle lit the room, the flickering light dancing along the wall. Two men stood nearby, fully armed and armoured.

"I know you," he said. "You're line warriors."

"Yes, Your Grace. We're Shozarins."

"Where is Lord Kelson?"

"Nearby, Your Grace. He's interrogating the council's guards."

"Please inform him I am awake. I would have words with him."

The older guard crossed the room and opened the door, conversing with his counterpart in the next room. Exalor sat up when his ally finally arrived.

"You're looking better," said Kelson.

"No doubt thanks to your healing."

"Hmmm. Years ago, I recall you saying I was a fool for learning a second school of magic."

"I take it all back. It was an outstanding choice."

Kelson chuckled. "Well, better late than never, I suppose."

"What did you learn about the attack?"

"Very little. There are reports of a council guardsman in the vicinity, but I've yet to identify him."

"Perhaps he only dressed as one?"

"My thought as well. It's a pity he didn't see fit to leave the murder weapon behind."

"Hardly murder. I'm still alive."

"Well, attempted murder, then. Still, it could have told us much about whoever was responsible. Have you any suspicions?"

"You don't get to be High Strategos without making a few enemies on the way up."

"Agreed, but someone willing to kill you? And on the eve of this campaign? I find the coincidence a little too incredulous."

"It is likely connected to the accident that befell Stalgrun Sartellian."

"The Marshal of the North? But that was made to look like an accident. Do you think someone suspects otherwise?"

"You tell me; you're the High Sentinel. I suggest your truthseekers talk to the other council members."

"You know I can't do that. Such a move would be considered political."

"Then you must employ other means."

"I'll find out who is responsible for this attack. I promise. In the meantime, you need to rest. You've lost a fair amount of blood."

"Rest? I have a campaign to oversee."

"Will it really make that much difference if it starts a few days late?"

"Ah, but that's just it. It's already begun."

# TWENTY-THREE

# Search

B everly stared back. "What is it?"

"Do you recall Revi's illness?" asked Aubrey.

"Of course, but that was due to the influence of the Saurian gates, wasn't it? Are you suggesting the king has been exposed to them?"

"No, but it's definitely similar."

Helisant held no patience for their conversation. "What in the name of the Saints are you two talking about? Can you heal the king or not?"

"I can," replied Aubrey, "but I'll need help."

"The Royal Court's full resources are at your disposal."

"That's not the sort of help I need."

"Then tell us what it is you require."

"Another Life Mage."

The queen fell silent.

"I've seen this type of thing before," continued Aubrey, "back in Merceria. There, we treated it with the assistance of a shaman."

"A shaman?"

"Yes, an Orc Life Mage."

"This is preposterous," said Master Garrig. "The woman is obviously a charlatan."

"She tells the truth," offered Beverly. "I saw it first-hand, but the technique she developed requires two spellcasters."

"There is not another so-called Life Mage to be found in all of Deisenbach."

"I assure you, Life Magic is real. I've benefited from it on multiple occasions, including today."

"Still, by your own admission, it's useless without another. What next, I wonder? Will you insist gold is required to cast your magic? Or are diamonds more to your taste?"

"I thought I told you to be quiet?" said the queen, turning back to the Life Mage. "Ignore him. You say you used an Orc shaman to assist you back in your land?"

"I did," said Aubrey. "A master healer named Kraloch. Why? Is there a tribe nearby that might be able to assist?"

The queen looked over at her unconscious husband, then gave her a slight nod. "There are said to be some close to our border with Zowenbruch."

"And have they shamans?"

"I wouldn't know. Our relations with the green folk are contentious, to say the least."

Beverly switched to the Orcish tongue. *"They've obviously had troubles with the Orcs. I doubt they'd be willing to assist the king."*

*"Still,"* replied Aubrey, *"we must seek them out, if only for Aldwin's sake."*

"That's enough of that," insisted Helisant. "If you are going to talk in our presence, I must insist you use a civilized tongue."

Beverly started to speak but then bit back her retort. "We shall go seek out these Orcs on your behalf."

"We? Do you take me for a fool? Your cousin remains here, as does your grey-eyed husband. Their lives are now in your hands, Lady Beverly. Fail me in this, and they both will pay with their lives."

"Go," insisted Aubrey. "We'll be fine."

Beverly had no choice. One false move, and they might all find themselves under the sentence of death. "Where do I find these Orcs?"

"I shall arrange for someone to provide you with what little information we possess on their location."

"I thought you said you knew where they were?"

"No," replied the queen. "We only have rumours. Still, we shall pass on what we know in the hope it may assist you in your endeavours." She turned to her guards. "See that Lady Beverly is provisioned as needed. She will set out first thing tomorrow morning."

"And what of my cousin?"

"She remains here, where she can monitor His Majesty."

"And my husband?"

"As I said earlier, he will be brought into the Palace, where he remains our guest. Cross me, however, and I shall return him to the dungeons."

"I will not forget this."

"I'm pleased to hear that. It should keep you motivated while searching for those greenskins."

Beverly stared back, trying to rein in her fury.

"Oh," added the queen. "One more thing. Their fates are now tied to that of the king. Should he die, your cousin and husband will quickly follow, so it's in your best interest to act with haste."

"I shall leave this very day!"


"You shouldn't go alone," said Sir Owen. "The land hereabouts can be a dangerous place for travellers."

"I'm a Knight of the Hound," replied Beverly. "I'm more than capable of taking care of myself."

"Still, I am bound to your service. I'm also familiar with the roads hereabouts, and another set of eyes wouldn't go amiss."

"You've made your point. I accept your offer."

"Any idea where we'll be travelling?"

She produced a sheaf of papers. "The queen has given these to me, not that there's much to them. All they contain are rumours and speculation."

"What about the bounty?"

"Bounty?" said Beverly. "What bounty?"

"I've heard the Crown offers a bounty for every Orc head."

"The queen made no mention of this."

"Hardly surprising," said Owen. "Are you not familiar with Orcs?"

"On the contrary. I've spent plenty of time amongst them. Back in Merceria, they are considered stalwart allies."

"Allies? But they're savages!"

"If that's your belief, you'd best stay here."

Sir Owen held his hands up in front of himself. "Wait. I've never met one; I'm only repeating what I heard, but I'm willing to put aside such beliefs with your reassurances. What can you tell me about them?"

"They are, for the most part, hunters. They live in remote locations, far from Human eyes, although there are exceptions: Hawksburg being one."

"Hawksburg?"

"Yes. Lady Aubrey's home. They helped her rebuild it after the war. Are there any hills near here?"

"To the east, though they're a bit difficult to get to."

"All the more reason to go there. If there is an Orc tribe in these parts, it's likely to be hidden away in some remote region of the kingdom. What's the best way to get there?"

"That largely depends on where you want to look," replied Owen. "The

Grey Hills lie along the banks of the Rasfeld River, from Trivoli to Santrem."

"Trivoli?" said Beverly. "We were near there when we crossed into Deisenbach. No one there spoke of Orcs, not that we were asking."

"Not surprising. That region sees a lot of traffic. The more remote portions are farther north. I suggest we take the road to Santrem. It would, however, require us to cross the Wildwood to get into those hills."

"The forest holds no fear for me."

"With all due respect," said Owen, "that entire region is filled with all manner of dangerous beasts."

"Such as?"

"Bears, wolves, and even rumours of dragons."

"Have you ever seen a dragon?"

"No, of course not."

"Well, I have, and I assure you, if one was in these parts, there would be no doubt about it."

"You've seen a dragon?"

"I have, or, to be more precise, three. They were present at the Siege of Summersgate."

Owen laughed. "You had me going there for a moment. Do I really look that gullible?"

Beverly shrugged. "It matters little whether or not you believe me, but aside from the dragon, you're describing nothing more than the normal animals one would find in a forest. However, you've convinced me we must start in Santrem. How long will it take us to get there?"

"It is close to one hundred miles, my lady."

"And is the road well-travelled?"

"Perhaps not as busy at that which leads through Trivoli, but enough that there are travellers inns along the way."

"Good. Then we shall start out at once. Gather your things, Owen. We've a hard ride ahead of us."


They set out within the hour. She offered Keon the chance to accompany them, but he declined, his fear of danger far greater than his loyalty.

"I'm curious," said Owen. "Do Orcs speak our language?"

"Some do," replied Beverly, "though likely not those who live around here. That would require interaction with Humans."

"Then how do we communicate with them?"

"I speak their language."

"You do? Where did you learn it?"

"Many Orcs serve in our army back in Merceria. We've even adapted their language for all our written orders."

"Adapted?"

"Yes. They have no written language."

"That's understandable. They're uncivilized."

"Uncivilized? Quite the reverse; they've developed a rich and full culture. Do not mistake their different approach for weakness."

Owen shook his head. "You Mercerians have experienced so much. Is your realm always at war?"

"It does seem like it."

"It must be glorious."

"Glorious? It's terrifying."

"You surprise me. I would think your training as a knight would have you seeing the honour inherent in battle?"

"Honour is not won on the battlefield, Owen. That only leads to death and destruction. War is not to be embraced; it is to be avoided."

"You cannot avoid war forever."

"No," said Beverly. "You can't, but don't be in such a rush to experience it. Even the greatest of victories comes with a high cost."

"A sobering thought. I'm sorry if I offended you, but I was raised on stories of gallant knights and great battles."

"No doubt those accounts were written by those far removed from the field of slaughter, as is often the way of those who do not risk life and limb." She looked at her travelling companion, meeting his gaze. "I have seen more than my fair share of battle, and it's not something I willingly seek to do again."

"But you would still fight if needed, wouldn't you?"

"Of course."

Ludmilla stared into the bowl as the single lantern lighting her study sent shadows dancing across the room. She closed her eyes and called on her inner power to summon her magic. The water rippled as if a pebble had been dropped into it, then the face of an older woman with greying hair materialized within.

"You have more news regarding the visitors?" the image asked.

"The Fitzwilliam woman has left Agran, heading north."

"And you have men following them?"

"I do," replied Ludmilla. "The plan is to strike when they least expect it."

"Do not underestimate the woman. She's dangerous."

"Might I ask why this stranger poses a threat to us? My understanding is she is from a far-distant land."

"Your place is not to question orders but to obey them." The face silently stared back before continuing. "Suffice it to say, her actions represent a direct threat to the family."

"And the others? Lady Aubrey and the grey-eye?"

"They are of little consequence in the grand scheme of things. If, however, Fitzwilliam finds the Orcs, it could well upset the balance of power in the region."

"Surely not?" said Ludmilla. "How can such a primitive people threaten our plans?"

"They troubled us in the east. We do not need them causing even more mayhem in Deisenbach."

"And if she should succeed in her mission?"

The older woman smiled, though it was far from comforting. "You'd best ensure she doesn't, or it will go badly for you. I trust I made myself clear?"

"Yes, Mistress. My apologies."

"You have done well up to this point, Ludmilla, but events are in motion, the likes of which you could never hope to comprehend. Now, return to court and do your best to ingratiate yourself with Aubrey Brandon."

"But she is of little consequence?"

"As I said earlier, that's true in the grand scheme of things, but she is a Life Mage. Do I need to remind you about the consequences should she find a way to cure the king?"

"Are we in that much of a hurry to put his nephew on the Throne?"

"The events in Hadenfeld have caused some concern of late. A strong army in Deisenbach, sympathetic to our cause, will help counter that threat."

"I understand, Mistress," said Ludmilla. "Rest assured. I will not fail."

"Good. Now be about your business. I have much to attend to."

The face vanished, leaving only the bottom of the bowl staring back at her. Ludmilla pushed it aside and absently looked around the room as her mind tried to sort out her conflicting emotions.

Her superior had always been secretive, yet she'd grown even more so in the last few months. It hadn't been that long since Hadenfeld had been embroiled in a second civil war. Could they have truly recovered to such an extent they were now a threat to the balance of power? And what are these events that were supposed to be in motion?

She shook her head. It was never wise to question one's superior, particularly where politics were concerned. The Stormwinds used their influence to weaken the Petty Kingdoms, but Ludmilla had never understood why. Surely it would be better to unite them than to keep them divided.

Like all members of the family, she'd been taught obedience, which had served her well, but she now wondered if she'd reached the pinnacle of her career.

She had arrived in Deisenbach five years ago, replacing an existing court mage who'd failed to gain any influence. Instead of concentrating on winning the king's approval, Ludmilla took a different approach, making herself indispensable to the queen.

The tactic proved so successful she was now considered the most influential advisor to both king and queen, an accomplishment that should have been lauded back in Karslev. Instead, her reports had been met with mild indifference until Lady Beverly arrived, then everything changed.

Ludmilla had done her duty and informed her superior about the knight's arrival, but she could never have predicted the interest the otherwise mundane visit provoked.

She rose, seeking her books. It took only a moment to find the right one, then she cracked it open, skimming through the pages.

Lady Beverly claimed to hail from a place called Merceria, yet try as she might, Ludmilla found no mention of it. She thought back to her days at the Volstrum but could recollect nothing about such a realm. Could the woman have simply lied? After her performance in the tournament, no one could deny she was a capable warrior, yet who amongst the Petty Kingdoms allowed women to serve in such a capacity? Only the Temple Knights of Saint Agnes armed themselves thus, but she wore no scarlet tabard.

Her mind drifted back to the tournament. In both jousts, the Fitzwilliam woman bore a shield embossed with a coat of arms. Perhaps that held the secret to her real identity? Ludmilla pulled a book of heraldry from the shelf and flipped through its pages, but the answer she sought was not held within.

In frustration, she tossed the book back onto the shelf. What did she know about this woman? She claimed to be the Baroness of Bodden, but even the name was strange. Then there was also the matter of her grey-eyed husband. Who in their right mind would marry a descendant of the Old Kingdom, particularly a noble?

That's when she realized this so-called Lady Beverly was not a baroness but a person of common birth. True, her manner of speech indicated someone educated and refined, but that alone did not discount her theory. Perhaps she was from the merchant class?

Ludmilla finally made up her mind. If she couldn't get the answers she sought from her superior, she must look elsewhere. The question was, where?


Edan Thackery looked down at the parchment, a sense of pride flowing through him. Illuminating manuscripts was a time-intensive endeavour that seldom garnered praise, yet it pleased him no end to know this particular piece would live on long after he turned to dust. A knock on the door drew his attention.

"Yes?" he called out.

"Master Thackery, is that you?"

He recognized the voice. "It is, Mistress Ludmilla. Come in, won't you?" He waited for the door to open. "I've just completed my latest work."

She moved to stand beside him, placing her hand on his shoulder as she looked down at the manuscript. "Most impressive!"

He smiled, sitting up straighter. "Thank you. I thought the border was particularly well done."

"Indeed."

He glanced up at her. "My pardon, Mistress. You must be here on important business. What can I help you with?"

"I am seeking information."

"Of what nature?"

"A land called Merceria. Are you familiar with it?"

"I can't say that I am. Do you know where it lies?"

"Somewhere to the west, or so I've been told."

"West? You mean beyond Halvaria?"

"I suppose it would have to be, yes. What do we know about the area?"

"Very little. The name Merceria reminds me of mercenaries; could they be related? There is an old tale of mercenaries who fled the Continent centuries ago."

"How many centuries ago?"

"Perhaps as many as ten, although such records are scarce." He wandered over to a dusty collection of scrolls, books, and folded papers and began digging through them. "I have an account here, or rather, an account of an account. It's so hard to find reliable first-hand memoirs of such things. Ah, here it is." He withdrew a scroll case stained with age and carefully unscrewed its top.

"It's very old if I recall correctly. Written some nine hundred years ago, but it makes mention of an event that might be of interest." He withdrew a yellowed paper, laying it down on his desk. "It tells of a man returning home after serving as a mercenary for many years. When asked about the fate of his fellow warriors, he relates how they fled across the sea. Could that be the origin of these Mercerians?"

"I'm not so sure," said Ludmilla. "If the mercenaries went across the sea, how did this fellow get home?"

"According to this, he was enslaved by those who pursued the mercenaries but escaped years later. Of course, there's no way to verify the accuracy of this."

"And you just happen to remember this?"

He smiled. "Not at all, but I've heard the rumours floating around the Palace of late. It was only a matter of time before someone came looking for more information."

"Thank you," said Ludmilla. "You've been a great help to me."

# TWENTY-FOUR

# Galburn's Ridge

WINTER 967 MC

Gerald entered the room to find Anna sitting before the fire, poring over an ancient tome. He wanted to surprise her, but the thump of Storm's tail put an end to such games.

"Ah," said Anna. "There you are. Your timing is fortuitous."

"It is?"

"Yes. I was about to travel to Galburn's Ridge. I thought you might like to accompany me."

"To what end?"

"We have to talk to Bronwyn." She saw his frown. "I know she's not your favourite person, but we need her help."

"I'm still not entirely convinced we can trust her," insisted Gerald. "Did you forget she betrayed us?"

"Of course not, but the realm is in danger. We have little choice if we are to come out on the winning side. Now, are you coming with me or not?"

"Of course. When have I ever refused a Royal Command?"

"It's not a command, Gerald. It's an invitation to a friend."

"Well, I certainly can't refuse that, now, can I? When do we leave?"

"As soon as Kraloch gets here. I just sent for him."

"How long will we be there?"

"A few hours, but it mostly depends on Bronwyn."

"And my role?"

"I need your assessment of her army."

"I can tell you that right now. Heward has kept me fully apprised of recent developments."

"Then you'd best tell me, for it will save us some time."

"As you know, her plan called for ten companies, but she's still only scraped together six: three foot, two archers, and one company of horse."

"Are any of those her old warriors?"

"Yes, one of foot. The rest provided a core for the other companies to be built on."

"And their quality?"

"That's where things get complicated. As I said, only one company has any real experience, but even then, I'd hardly call them seasoned. She also lacks any veteran officers above the rank of captain."

"In other words, they're useless?"

"Not useless," said Gerald. "There's a good core there, but they need more training. Are you hoping to convince Bronwyn to send them north, to Ironcliff?"

"That was my intention. What do you think? Would they be of any benefit?"

"Yes, as long as we placed them under someone with some battle experience."

"She's already familiar with Lord Heward," said Anna. "Can we spare him?"

"You tell me; you're the one who assigned him to Bronwyn's court. Can you spare him from his diplomatic post?"

"I can, though I'd have to replace him if we send him north."

"You can't have Preston; I need him to help defend our own lands. How about Hayley?"

"Won't you need her to organize the rangers?"

"She can do that just as easily from Galburn's Ridge, can't she?"

"I suppose she can, now I think of it. I'll send orders for her to meet us in Galburn's Ridge as soon as she's able."

The door opened to Lady Sophie. "Your pardon, Majesty, but Master Kraloch is here."

"Thank you. Please send him in."

The Orc shaman stepped through the door. "Good afternoon, Majesty. I was told you wanted to travel to Galburn's Ridge?"

"I do. When can you be ready to take us?"

"That largely depends on how many are going."

"Just Gerald and I."

"Should you not bring guards with you, Majesty?"

"Lord Heward has a Mercerian garrison in Galburn's Ridge. I think that sufficient."

"In that case, we can leave whenever you wish."

"We can't leave yet," insisted Gerald. "You need to send a letter to Hayley, remember?"

"Good point," said Anna. "We shall meet you in the casting room, Master Kraloch."

The Orc shaman bowed. "As you wish, Majesty."


"I'd feel better if Beverly were here," said Gerald as they gathered in the casting room.

"As would I," replied Anna, "but we must adapt to ever-changing circumstances."

"Yes, but now you have no bodyguard."

"Are you not the finest warrior in all of Merceria?"

Gerald laughed. "I'm little more than an old man, bending with age."

"Hardly that. You are Lord Gerald Matheson, Duke of Wincaster, Marshal of Merceria, and more importantly, grandfather to Prince Braedon. Let's have no more of this maudlin talk."

He grinned. "Well, I suppose it doesn't sound so bad when you put it that way."

"Shall I proceed?" asked Kraloch.

"If you would be so kind," replied the queen.

The Orc shaman closed his eyes, concentrating on their destination. Gerald felt the air buzz as the words of power tumbled from Kraloch's lips, and then the runes in the floor began to glow.

He braced himself, the hairs on the back of his neck standing on end as a cylinder of light surrounded them, blocking all view of the room. Gerald closed his eyes, and then the air changed, filling his nostrils with fresh northern air. When he opened his eyes, a trio of guards stood watching, each bearing the coat of arms of the Royal House of Merceria.

The oldest, a sergeant, bowed. "Welcome to Galburn's Ridge, Majesty."

"Is Lord Heward available?" asked the queen.

The sergeant looked at one of his men, nodded, and then the fellow hurriedly left the room.

"We were not expecting you, Majesty. I trust all is well?"

"It is, at least for now, but whether that continues to be the case is an entirely different matter."

Gerald cleared his throat. "Perhaps that is best not discussed with the sergeant, Your Majesty. I'm sure his duties here keep him busy enough without adding to his burden."

"Yes. My apologies, Sergeant."

Kraloch stepped closer to the fellow. "I have travelled here many times since the construction of this circle, but I do not remember seeing you before."

The man stared back, his eyes defiant. "Do not blame me for the faulty memory of an Orc."

"That's enough of that," snapped Gerald, moving to stand before the sergeant. "It is not your place to disrespect the queen's representative. What is your name?"

"Sergeant Efram Cookson, Your Grace."

"I shall be sure to mention your name to Lord Heward. I doubt he'll take kindly to your disrespect."

The door opened before anything more could be said.

"Majesty." Lord Heward bowed. "This is unexpected."

"So I gathered from your sergeant here," replied Anna. "Is there something you want to tell us?"

Heward's gaze wandered to his guards. "I shall endeavour to give you all the details of recent developments, but here is not the best place to discuss such things."

"Then let us find somewhere more private."

"Of course, Majesty."

They followed Heward as he made his way through the castle, finally coming to a halt as they entered a well-appointed drawing room.

"Can I offer you a drink?"

"No, thank you," replied the queen. "I'm more interested in what you have to tell us."

"Yes," added Gerald. "I'd particularly like to know why your sergeant showed such disdain for Master Kraloch."

"That," replied Heward, "is something that's been troubling me. I'm afraid sentiment against the Orcs is growing. I've done my best to stop it, but the men are spending their off-duty time in the company of Norlanders, and they're still upset at losing Ravensguard."

"But the Orcs are our allies. We can't allow that sentiment to trickle through our ranks, especially now. The danger has never been greater."

"I agree, but there is a limit to what we can do. I've tried reasoning with them, but you know how it works. They all nod but then ignore what you say."

"We must find a way to win them over. Such division could well be the death of us."

"That's likely the objective," said Anna.

"I agree," added Kraloch. "We have known for some time that someone has been stirring up passions on this very subject. It is more than mere coincidence that it coincides with threats to our allies."

"Have we heard anything from Arnim and Nikki?" asked Gerald.

The queen shook her head. "I'm afraid not. Hayley tracked them as far as Kingsford, but then they disappeared."

"You think them dead?"

"We must certainly consider it a possibility, in which case whoever is behind this likely knows we're onto them, making them that much harder to unmask."

"Their reach must be long indeed if the sentiment travelled all the way up here."

"Not necessarily," said Anna. "Lord Heward might have the right of it. Norland was forced to give up Ravensguard, essentially losing a large part of their kingdom."

"But that would work to the remaining earls' advantage, would it not? Essentially, giving them more influence over the Crown."

"Old prejudices die hard. Heward, do you know where Bronwyn sits regarding this issue?"

The Baron of Redridge took his time to respond. "While I haven't spoken of that specific issue, she sees the Orcs as an advantage."

"How so?"

"Their presence to the east is the one thing that all the remaining earls can agree is a threat, acting as a unifying force."

"And she considers that good?"

"Well," said Heward, "it diverts their attention away from controlling the queen. In fact, she's used their presence to justify the buildup of her own forces."

"And would she be willing to commit those forces to helping Ironcliff?"

"That's difficult to say. She's eager to give them some battle experience, but it leaves Galburn's Ridge dangerously exposed if she sends them north. The last thing we want is another civil war in Norland."

"But you think she might be open to the idea?"

"Possibly, but it wouldn't be without cost. Bronwyn's not the type to help without expecting something in return."

"The problem," said Gerald, "is that we don't know if we can trust her, not after she betrayed us during the war."

"We may have no choice," replied Anna. "Halvaria is moving on Ironcliff even as we speak, and if they get as far as Norland, they'll be nearly impossible to stop."

"Then that's how we present it to her. She'll have no choice but to help if she wants to keep her Throne."

"She won't like that," said Heward. "She hates the idea of being forced into a decision. You'd be better off outlining the present circumstances and letting her come to her own conclusions."

"Then that's precisely what we'll do," said the queen.

"With your permission, Your Majesty, I'll go and inform her of your arrival."

"By all means."

Gerald waited until Heward left. "Are you sure this is a good idea? What if she sides with the Halvarians?"

"I doubt even Bronwyn would stoop so low. She wants to remain queen. I can't see Halvaria going to all the trouble of invading to then allow her to continue in place, can you?"

"You make a convincing argument, but will she see it that way?"

"We need to ensure she does."


The afternoon dragged on while the earls argued about the treasury as they were wont to do, and Bronwyn began to wonder if she wasn't trapped in some sort of endless prison.

The arrival of Heward garnered her interest, and she held up her hand, interrupting Lord Calder, the Earl of Riverhurst.

"Lord Heward," said the Norland queen. "To what do we owe the pleasure of your presence?"

The Baron of Redridge bowed deeply. "Your Majesty, Queen Anna of Merceria has arrived here in Galburn's Ridge and wishes to speak with you on a matter of great importance."

"Important to her or to me?"

"Both, Majesty, but such things are best talked of privately."

"Then I shall dismiss my court. She can meet me here, in my throne room. I trust that would be acceptable?"

"Indeed, Majesty. I will relay your invitation to her."

Bronwyn watched the Mercerian noble leave the room, then turned to Captain Naran, who commanded one of her companies. "What do you know of this?"

"Nothing, Majesty."

"Yet you helped their High Ranger when she was here, did you not?"

"I did so only at your command, but she gave no indication anything was amiss in Merceria, other than a title claim."

"Keep an eye on them, particularly Lord Heward."

"You suspect treachery?"

"No, diplomacy, but my counterpart to the south likely has her own agenda, and we must strive to discover what that is."

"I shall be ever watchful, Majesty."

Bronwyn raised her voice. "As for the rest of you, leave us. We will resume discussing the realm's business on the morrow."

The room quickly emptied, save for Bronwyn, the captain, and six guards.

"Give the word, Majesty," offered Naran, "and I shall place the Mercerians under arrest."

"While I admire your bravery, Captain, such an act would see us descend once more into war, one we can ill afford at present. No, let us hear them out. I'm curious to learn what they want."

The young queen waited for the visitors to arrive, her mind in turmoil. Would the Queen of Merceria make demands or offer the hand of friendship? Her preference would be the latter, but Bronwyn had made a grave miscalculation during the recent war, an act of treachery that had very nearly cost her life. She would likely have been executed had it not been for the insistence of her earls, a development for which she was extremely thankful.

Since her instalment as Queen of Norland, she had strived to do her best for the realm, but old rivalries had quickly resurfaced, making her court as contentious as ever. Now, instead of fighting to gain the Crown, she struggled to hold on to it.

The announcement of the Mercerians' arrival snapped Bronwyn out of her reverie. She stood, befitting the greeting of an equal.

"Queen Anna," she proclaimed. "It's good to see you again."

"And you," replied Anna. "I trust we find you in fine health?"

"Indeed. And yourself?"

"I am well, thank you."

Bronwyn stepped away from her throne, and they clasped hands, their eyes meeting in a test of wills. She wanted to keep her eyes locked on those of Queen Anna, but something about the Mercerian ruler's manner threatened the Queen of Norland, and she shifted her gaze to Gerald.

"Marshal Matheson," Bronwyn said, "or should I say, Your Grace? I'm never quite sure of the proper form of address for one as distinguished as yourself."

"Marshal will do fine," he replied.

"And Master Kraloch. You honour us with your presence."

The Orc simply bowed.

"You all came here to Galburn's Ridge," continued Bronwyn, "so I assume this is not a social call."

"It is not," replied Queen Anna. "We bring dire news from the north."

"The north, you say? This is the first I'm hearing of it."

"Our recent reports reveal a large army is preparing to march through the gap."

"Are you suggesting the Dwarves of Ironcliff come seeking war?"

"No, the Halvarians."

"Oh yes? I've heard Lord Heward mention them once or twice."

"And?"

Bronwyn shrugged. "If Halvaria wants to march against the Dwarves of Ironcliff, it's of little consequence to me."

"We fear they have a grander scheme."

"Which is?"

"To conquer all the western lands."

"Aren't you being a little overdramatic? A campaign against the Dwarves I can well understand, but what has Norland ever done to them?"

"Your kingdom has the misfortune of lying between Halvaria and Merceria. Thus, you are an impediment."

"You make us sound inconsequential."

"In their minds, I suspect you are," said Queen Anna. "But you can prove them wrong."

Bronwyn smiled. "At last, we get to the crux of the matter. You want me to send warriors north to fight your battle for you."

"It's as much your fight as it is ours."

"If that's the case, why aren't you sending your own men?"

"We are," said Gerald. "We've already sent several companies using magic, but it exhausts our mages. You, however, can march overland. Act quickly, and your troops can be there before the enemy is at the gates of Ironcliff."

"You forget yourself, Marshal. Thanks to your High Ranger's little trip up here, we now have a defensive alliance. If Halvaria attacked us, you would be bound by treaty to come to our aid."

"As you would us," said Anna. "Like it or not, Halvaria threatens the existence of both our realms."

Bronwyn nodded. "I understand that, but I have few troops to spare. Whom can I send?"

"Could not the earls contribute to the campaign?"

"It would take months to collect them, and even then, their numbers are greatly reduced. It's what comes of fighting a civil war." She snickered. "Not that the war was civil by any stretch of the imagination."

"So you won't help?" asked Anna.

"I shall do what I can. I owe you that much, at least, but I need something from you in return."

"Name it."

"Funds. If I am to send men north, I must hire more to keep the capital under my control."

"How much are we talking about?"

"Enough to raise two companies."

"Foot, bow, or horse?"

"Footmen would be my first choice, I should think, although possibly an additional company of archers might prove useful."

"Agreed," said Anna. "How soon can your men march?"

"Within the week. I shall send them north to Holdcross and see if I can't convince the Earl of Greendale to assist. Those are his lands after all."

"And who will command?"

"Now, that," said Bronwyn, "is an interesting question. As you are no doubt aware, I have no experienced commanders amongst my companies."

"Might I suggest Lord Heward?"

"That would be acceptable." Bronwyn paused, her mind running through possible outcomes. "If this expedition is defeated somehow, the treaty's terms would still require you to send aid."

"We would honour that. I promise."

# TWENTY-FIVE

# At Sea

WINTER 967 MC

K ozarsky Stormwind, Admiral of the Storm Fleet, stood on the aft deck, surveying the ships in port. "Magnificent, aren't they?"

His aide had not been paying attention. "Your Grace?"

"This fleet is the largest collection of ships ever assembled. Hundreds of vessels ready to land an entire legion and supply them for six months."

"Not quite the largest, Your Grace. It is said in ancient times, the Elves created an even larger fleet to crush the Orcs."

"Little good it did. The land is still crawling with the brutes. In any case, that's not so much history as myth. They could just as easily have had only a hundred ships. However, I shall amend my statement to soothe your sense of correctness. This is the largest collection of Human ships ever assembled!"

"Indeed, Your Grace."

"Of course, it will take more than just numbers to conquer Merceria. Did you know our enemy descended from mercenaries?"

"Yes. You've mentioned it several times, Lord. Any idea when we'll be setting sail?"

"Soon, Adrik, but we must be patient. This campaign has many moving parts, and we must ensure we arrive precisely at the right time." The admiral leaned on the railing. "Do you see that flag over there, atop the fortress?"

"The red one?"

"Yes. That is our signal. When the timing is right, they will replace that flag with a blue one, signifying we are to put to sea."

"And our destination?"

"Merceria, where else?"

"That I understand, Your Grace, but I'm led to believe their coastline is expansive."

"Yes," said Kozarsky, "but the vast majority of it is nothing but swamp. We are to strike for the mouth of the river forming their western border."

"Will the river not impede our progress? We can't possibly sail hundreds of ships all the way inland?"

"No, of course not. We'll land the bulk of our troops on the coast to attack a village called Trollden. I'm told it holds little in terms of opposition, so they'll march along the riverbank to Colbridge, where our supply ships will join them."

"A brilliant plan, Your Grace."

"Yes, I thought so too. I'd like to congratulate myself, but I'm sorry to say this is all the doing of the High Strategos."

"Are we then merely merchant ships, dropping off a cargo of men?"

"Don't look so glum," said the admiral. "There'll be plunder aplenty once our people get ashore." He noticed the *Resplendent's* captain coming out of his cabin. "Captain Kersey," he called out. "Might I have a word?"

"By all means." The man came up the steps to stand on the aft deck beside his admiral and look out over the fleet. "Marvellous sight, isn't it."

"We are men of a similar mind," replied Kozarsky.

"If I'm not being too impertinent, what do you wish to see me about?"

"We will set out to sea in the next few days. I need assurances that every ship of the fleet is suitably prepared?"

"All ships report they are ready, save for the *Alantra*, Your Grace. She is still undergoing repairs."

"Enemy action?"

"No. Storms out at sea, Your Grace. Not to speak ill of the plan, Admiral, but this expedition has us sailing at the worst possible time of year. They don't call it the Sea of Storms for nothing."

"Don't worry. Even if we arrive with only half the fleet, we'd have more than enough to overwhelm their defences."

"I would feel much better about this if I knew what to expect, Your Grace."

"As I was just telling my aide, we will put men ashore near a village called Trollden."

"And what do we know of the place?"

"It is little more than a village populated by Trolls."

"Trolls?" said Captain Kersey. "No one told me anything about Trolls."

"The legion's commander knows all about them."

"Then why don't I?"

"Only the ships that put men ashore will be anywhere near them. The *Resplendent* will remain safely offshore, well out of range."

"They have ranged weapons?"

"Trolls can throw rocks," replied the admiral. "Some say as far as small siege engines, but that's mere hearsay. Even if you were in range, they'd be much more likely to attack the boats landing the men."

"What about the Mercerian fleet?"

"They have none as far as we're aware, although I suppose they might force a merchant or two into their service, not that it'll do much for them. The only real seaborne threat is the Royal Navy of Weldwyn, but I doubt they'd risk a battle with a fleet of this size."

"Still, they might pose a threat."

"Perhaps, but I'm told their new king will be much too busy dealing with events in the west."

"What does that entail?"

"I'm not at liberty to discuss it. Suffice it to say, we're not expecting them to put in an appearance." He noted a look of uncertainty on the captain's face. "Are you having doubts?"

"I don't mean to sound pessimistic, Admiral, but the fleet's accomplishments have been less than stellar of late."

"You refer to the Northern Fleet's destruction?"

"That, and our defeat at Alantra, Your Grace. We are, in essence, the last fleet of any consequence within the empire. If we fail, it could prove disastrous."

"On the contrary. Halvaria is, first and foremost, a land power. Even if we lost all our ships, our legions still dominate and outnumber our enemies. You should have more faith in our High Strategos. Do you not believe in the great dream?"

"Of course I do," replied Captain Kersey, "but that refers to liberating the Continent to the east, not this motley collection of isolated kingdoms we're facing."

The admiral straightened. "The empire has stood for more than a thousand years. Have you so little trust in its leaders?"

"It is not our own leaders who cause me concern, Your Grace, but the enemy's. Yes, the empire has won war after war for centuries, but we've seen defeat in recent years. You cannot so easily dismiss such fears."

"I grant you the defeat at Alantra was unexpected, but that of Arnsfeld was merely a miscalculation, an aberration if you will. I must also remind you, the fleet you see before you this day is larger than either of the other two, and there is no Holy Fleet here to threaten us. We will win this war, Captain. I'm certain of it."

"Yes. Of course, Your Grace. My apologies for doubting you."

"I'm glad to see you've come to your senses, Captain. You may return to your duties."

"Yes, Your Grace."

Admiral Kozarsky waved over his aide but waited until Kersey returned to the main deck before speaking. "The captain has doubts. See that he is replaced."

"Yes, Your Grace. Any particular manner in which you wish that carried out?"

"You heard the conversation?"

"I did, Lord."

"Good. Pass on the captain's doubts to the fleet's purifier. We'll let her people handle the details. That way, we avoid any potential retribution."

"Yes, Your Grace. Anything else?"

"That will do for now, Adrik."


The captain's arrest was carried out overnight, and his replacement was eager to prove himself up to the task. Admiral Kozarsky considered talking with the fellow but decided it easier to avoid discussing any campaign details at this time. Instead, he would wait until they were underway and the burden of command left no time to worry about rumours.

The *Alantra* finally sailed out to join the fleet, its damage repaired. The sight of her reminded him of the battle after which she was named. In any other realm, a navy would refrain from naming a ship after a loss, but the empire never accepted defeat, at least not publicly. As far as the general populace was concerned, Halvaria was one big happy family, and what better way to illustrate that success than by naming a ship after one of their greatest victories?

The admiral looked away from the window and dipped his quill, preparing to write in his journal, but a knock came at his door as tip touched paper.

"Yes?" he called out.

"It's Adrik, Admiral. I have news."

"Well, don't just stand there. Come in."

The aide opened the door, a large grin spread from ear to ear.

Kozarsky sat back in his chair. "Let me guess. There's a blue flag?"

"There is, Your Grace."

"Excellent! I shall be up on deck shortly. Please inform the captain to signal the rest of the fleet." He paused a moment. "And wipe that grin off your face, Adrik. We're trying to look professional here. There'll be plenty of time for celebration later."

His aide sobered. "Yes, Your Grace." He left his superior to his thoughts.

Admiral Kozarsky set aside his quill and rummaged through his collection of charts. Finding the one he searched for, he laid it on the table, using a tankard to anchor one side.

The chart outlined the coast of what was once called Terengaria, the land comprised of Merceria, Weldwyn, and the Clanholdings. The map was old, easily predating the empire's founding, and he briefly wondered what brave soul dared the Sea of Storms in ancient times to discover such a place.

It depicted the Great Swamp the High Strategos warned him about, along with the mouths of the main rivers that divided the area into separate realms. Of course, no cities were marked, for in that day and age, the land was unsettled, save for the Elder Races, and they could scarcely be called civilized.

He pulled forth another map and compared the two. His own scout ships had been busy of late, and this newer, far more accurate chart noted water depths, prevailing winds, and even currents, more than enough to guarantee a successful landing.

Initially, he'd scoffed at the idea of attacking in the cold of winter, but a frozen swamp was far easier to navigate than a thawed one. The landing itself would prove more treacherous, for ice would play havoc with the hulls of his ships, but it's not as if he himself had to land. His flagship, the *Resplendent*, would remain offshore, away from the danger of such things.

The ship vibrated slightly as the sails filled, and then, as they picked up speed, a feeling of pride flowed through him as he imagined his return from a successful expedition. Kozarsky wanted to leave his stuffy cabin and revel in the wind, but his sense of duty wouldn't permit it.

Instead, he dug through his papers one more time, extracting a carefully compiled document written in his aide's hand, listing the Army of Merceria's known companies and their last reported positions. He'd read over it dozens of times in the past few weeks but felt compelled to do so again.

The last time the Mercerians assembled was at the Siege of Summersgate, where their army numbered almost three thousand souls, but Elves and Dwarves comprised a notable portion of that.

With their allies now returned to their homelands, the High Strategos estimated the Mercerian's current strength at just over sixteen hundred. Their spies also reported that several hundred had been sent to Ironcliff and Stonecastle, further reducing their numbers. Even if they mustered all their remaining warriors to oppose his landing, he would still hold a two-to-one advantage, perhaps more.

He chuckled to himself. Exalor had done an excellent job of drawing away their already meagre forces. It only remained for him, Kozarsky Stormwind, to finish what the High Strategos had begun, the complete and utter defeat of Merceria.


The fleet drifted offshore, the end of the Sullen Peaks crumbling into the sea north of their position. They'd followed the coast of Halvaria, keeping land in sight to avoid the high winds and vicious waves of the Sea of Storms, but the time fast approached when they must turn west to enter Mercerian waters.

Admiral Kozarsky waited as the *Covenant* pulled alongside and dropped anchor. Like his other smaller vessels, it had sailed up and down the planned invasion route, collecting critical information about the enemy's movements. Now, its captain would board the *Resplendent* and report his findings, answering the admiral's last few questions before the fleet proceeded.

He noted the lowering of the ship's boat and fought to control his excitement. Part of him wanted to yell out rather than wait, but he knew discipline was all important.

The boat seemed to take forever to come alongside, and then Captain Halmar climbed onto the flagship's deck. He immediately noted the admiral's presence and marched over, a scroll case in hand.

"My report, Your Grace."

"I should like to hear the assessment from your own lips, Captain. Did you have a chance to examine Trollden?"

"Our mage did. She used her familiar to get in close. The village itself consists of many large dwellings built on stilts. Of course, they'd have to be that big to house the Trolls."

"Is there a palisade?"

"No, but there is a series of wooden spikes to ward off larger creatures. There's also a thick iron chain stretched across the river anchored on the eastern side by a large turnstile they use to raise and lower it."

"Is it something we can operate?"

"Not by hand. It's too big, although a team of horses might be able to manage it."

"They'd only have to drop the chain."

"True, but even then, there's a large lever that needs to be released, and it's quite high up, most likely to keep it from the rot of the swamp."

"What do you estimate their numbers to be?"

"That's difficult to say."

"I gave specific instructions for your mage to count them, did I not?"

"You did," said Captain Halmar, "but her familiar was brought down when it flew too close. Its loss almost killed her."

"Unfortunate," said Admiral Kozarsky. "Still, she must have an estimate of some sort?"

"Our last estimate sat at two hundred and fifty, but the bulk of those are smaller, likely children."

"And females?"

"I'm afraid it's almost impossible to distinguish gender from the air, Your Grace. We assume that roughly half the adults are female, but we cannot know if they would fight like their male counterparts, or seek shelter in the darker recesses of the swamp."

"So your final tally is?"

"One hundred adults, fifty of which are males, and one hundred and fifty children of various ages. Unfortunately, we have no idea how fast they grow, which could throw off our estimate. I don't suppose you have any information in that regard?"

"No," replied the admiral, "but it matters little. Even if we assume a hundred and fifty adults, we still vastly outnumber them. Unless the Mercerians have reinforced them?"

"If they have, we saw no sign of it or boats of any kind."

"That makes things convenient for us."

"Might I ask, Admiral, how we are to attack them? Do we land within sight of the village or head farther east and cross the swamp to begin the assault?"

"A combination of the two, I should think. We certainly have enough men for it. You're sure the mage wasn't spotted?"

"As I mentioned, they killed her familiar, but I doubt they recognized it as a mage's tool."

"Tell me more about this creature?"

"It was a hawk, Your Grace. It circled the village several times before swooping in for a closer look."

"What took it down?"

"A stone about the size of a fist."

"They have a siege engine?"

"No. A Troll tossed it, a one-handed throw that proved extremely accurate."

"I wasn't aware they could throw with such accuracy. Then again, we don't have such creatures in the empire, so that's hardly surprising." He cast his gaze towards the distant shoreline, but all he saw from his present location was where the mountains met the sea, nothing of the Great Swamp that formed Merceria's shoreline.

"Thank you, Captain. You've been of great service. Have you anything you'd like to add or a question of your own?"

"Yes, actually. I wondered if Trolls employ magic?"

"There is no indication they do, but then again, our knowledge of those creatures amounts to little more than hearsay and fairy tales."

"Could they have allies in the swamp?"

"Doubtful. What creatures could survive in such a place?"

Captain Halmar visibly relaxed. "Glad to hear it, Admiral."

Kozarsky forced a smile. "Your report, though incomplete, is encouraging. I shall return to my cabin and read over your notes." The admiral took the scroll case.

"Any idea when we might proceed?"

Kozarsky looked up at the sky before answering. "Likely first thing tomorrow morning. In the meantime, you will return to your ship and take up position behind the *Resplendent* in case I have need of you."

"Yes, Admiral."

He watched Captain Halmar climb back down to the boat and then returned to his cabin to comb through his notes.

# TWENTY-SIX

# On the Road

WINTER 967 MC

They'd travelled for days, stopping at roadside inns along the way. So far, there'd been no rumours of Orcs or stories of any strange goings-on, and Beverly was beginning to fear the entire trip was a colossal waste of time.

The chilly afternoon sky was filled with clouds that looked like they might bring rain or possibly even snow. Lightning was more than equal to the trip, but Sir Owen's mount was lagging, so she waited while he caught up.

"How much farther, do you think?" she asked.

"Somewhere along here, there's a roadside inn called the Badger. I've not stayed there myself but have ridden past it once or twice."

"And?"

He shrugged. "I'm told the ale's not too bad."

"Hardly a ringing endorsement."

"True, but it can't get much worse than that last place we tried. Just the thought of it makes my skin crawl."

Beverly laughed. "I told you we should have camped on the road. A knight like yourself should be used to such things."

"Hardly. We prefer the finer things in life."

"Says the knight who couldn't afford his ransom."

"Are the knights back in Merceria all wealthy?"

"They used to be, but that all changed when we formed the Knights of the Hound."

"Does that mean you have other orders?" asked Owen. "Your realm must be large indeed. Most Petty Kingdoms have but one."

"And so did we for a very long time. The Order of the Sword served kings for generations."

"And the Hounds?"

"We were originally sworn to Princess Anna, but when she was crowned, we became the senior order."

"Have all your Hounds seen battle?"

"They have, though not in the traditional sense. These days, the Knights of the Hound are more often used as leaders rather than riding into battle in formation."

"How many in your order?"

"Far fewer than you might think. Why? Are you interested in joining?"

"Would they even accept me?"

"I don't see why not. You need a sponsor, not to mention you'd have to pledge your loyalty to the Queen of Merceria."

"Then I shall strive to prove myself to you."

"Let's not rush things," replied Beverly. "Our main objective right now is to find those Orcs."

The road curved slightly, temporarily blocking their view. As it straightened out, three men stood there, their horses preventing any further progress.

"Halt," called out the closest one, attired in a mail coat, his hand resting on the hilt of his sword.

Beverly slowed, with Owen doing the same. "What is your business?" she shouted back.

"Is your name Beverly Fitzwilliam?"

"It is," she replied. "Who wants to know?"

"You are to turn back."

"And why would I do that?"

"Continuing down this road will only lead to your ruin."

"I'm flattered you're so concerned for my welfare. Unfortunately for you, I must insist on doing just that."

"Then you shall pay with your life." He drew his sword and held it on high. "Are you sure you won't change your mind?"

Beverly reacted quickly, galloping into the surrounding trees and underbrush. Owen stared in disbelief as crossbow bolts flew from the other side of the road and clattered against the trees, ignoring the inexperienced knight's presence in favour of his red-headed companion. He drew his sword and charged ahead, knowing it would take time for the crossbowmen to reload.

The enemy spokesman let his two companions ride forward to intercept the advancing knight. The surly-looking one with wild, unkempt hair and a long-handled axe was the first to strike. Owen easily parried the blow and then stuck the tip of his sword into the fellow's side. It didn't penetrate his foe's armour, but it was enough to cause him to shy away.

The second swung out with his mace, careening off Owen's vambrace. The knight lost his grip on the reins, but that was no inconvenience, for he used his legs to guide his horse, swinging his sword as he did so, nicking the fellow's neck. Blood burst forth, and he clutched his throat in a vain attempt to stop the tide.

Owen ignored him, turning to his first opponent, who was still coming at him. As the man raised his axe, the knight struck out, skewering the fellow's armpit, the blade sinking deep. The axe fell from the man's hand as his limb went limp, almost knocking the sword from Owen's grip.

Hearing shouts behind him, he glanced up to where a pair of crossbowmen had emerged from the side of the road, their weapons loaded. They'd spotted Beverly, but as they took aim, vines sprang from the opposite side of the road, demanding their attention.

Owen stared in fascination, but then something thudded against his back. He cursed, having forgotten the third rider's presence, who sat atop his horse, crossbow in hand.

"Is that the best you can do?" demanded Owen. He dug in his spurs and closed the range, but his opponent rode off, dropping his crossbow in his haste to depart.

The knight let him go, turning to see Beverly emerge from the woods on foot, stopping at what looked like a mass of roots in the middle of the road.

Owen moved closer, then realized he was looking at the crushed remains of the two crossbowmen he'd seen earlier. He half expected more bolts to be loosed from the woods, but then he heard their attackers fleeing through the dense undergrowth.

"Should we pursue?" he asked.

"There's little point," replied Beverly. "The chance of catching up to them in such terrain is slim."

"Who were they? They're certainly not bandits. Do you know them?"

"No, but they knew me and that I was coming this way."

"But how?"

"The most logical explanation is they came from Agran. They must have passed us in the night while we stayed at that inn."

"Are you unhurt?"

"I am. Yourself?"

"Some bruising, nothing more." He pointed at the crushed and mangled bodies. "You did that?"

"I did, or rather Nature's Fury did." She held up her hammer. "It's imbued with the power of the earth."

"A magic weapon? How did you come by such a prize?"

"Aldwin forged it, then Albreda, the greatest of all the mages of Merceria, empowered it."

"You must be important indeed to have a weapon of such power made for you."

"I… don't know what to say. I am not one to seek fame. Rather, I am a warrior content to do her duty."

"There will likely be more danger ahead."

"Agreed, but look on the bright side. The fact they tried to stop us indicates we're heading in the right direction!"


Clouds rolled in late in the afternoon, and by dusk, an ice-cold rain pelted down on them. Thankfully, up ahead lay the Badger, a roadside inn consisting of two buildings with a high wall surrounding it to keep any wild creatures at bay.

Beverly and Owen were met in the courtyard by a young man who took their mounts to the stable while the two knights went inside, seeking warmth.

She counted eight people sitting around the room, drinks in hand. The conversation halted as they entered but quickly picked back up once they were seated and clearly meant no harm.

An older woman came over, eyeing the armour of the two newcomers. "Travelled far, have you?"

"All the way from Agran," said Beverly.

"Will you be wanting something to eat?"

"Yes, and some ale, if you please."

The woman left them and headed into the kitchen. Without any warning, Beverly stood up.

"Problem?" said Owen.

"I want to check on Lightning."

"The stable hand is more than capable of looking after the horses."

"Perhaps, but he and I have been through a lot. I want to ensure he settles."

Beverly paused in the doorway, taking a quick look outside. The rain still came down in droves, but rather than accumulating in the courtyard, it poured into what looked like a grate.

The stables sat opposite the tavern, so she stepped outside and had only gone a few steps when lightning flashed. In that instance, she saw movement coming from beneath the grate.

She moved closer as the thunder rumbled through the sky, then looked down, trying to make out what she'd seen. Two eyes stared back, startling her.

"Who are you?" she asked, but they said nothing in reply. Another flash of lightning revealed a face, and there was no denying the green skin.

"*Who are you?*" she asked again, this time in Orcish.

"*I am Ugrug,*" came the reply. "*A hunter of the Sky Singers. How is it you speak our tongue, Human?*"

"*My Human name is Beverly Fitzwilliam, but I'm known as Redblade to your people. We count Orcs as our allies where I'm from.*"

"*Then you are indeed very far from home.*"

"*How did you come to find yourself here?*"

"*I was captured by bounty hunters.*"

"*Can you describe the men who captured you?*"

"*I can, though it will do you no good. They are well-armed and wear fine mail links. One has a recent scar on his cheek, put there by my hunting knife.*"

"*And he has accomplices?*"

"*He has two. One favours a thick club, while the other has a short sword.*"

Beverly looked over the grate, noting the padlock keeping it in place. They obviously used this pit for prisoners, but the thought of imprisoning an innocent Orc was too much for her to bear. "*I shall get you out, Ugrug, and escort you to safety, but first, I must find these men you spoke of. I assume they're inside?*"

"*They are likely so, yes.*"

"*Then hold tight, my friend. I shall return shortly with the key.*"

"*And if they do not surrender it?*"

"*My hammer would make short work of that lock, but I don't want to destroy it unless absolutely necessary. I'm sure the rangers hereabouts would have need of it.*"

"*Rangers?*"

"*Men and women who patrol the roads and keep the peace. I assume they have a similar position here, but they might call them something else.*" Beverly drew her dagger and handed it through the grate. "*Here, take this. If I fail, it will give you something to fight back with.*"

"*Thank you, Redblade. I shall await your return.*"

She stood, ignoring the hair that the rain had plastered onto her face. Inside were the three men, likely skilled warriors if they were anything like rangers. The question facing her now was how to proceed. Going back inside and declaring her intentions seemed foolhardy, especially since she had no idea how the other patrons viewed such things. Would they fight alongside the bounty hunters or mind their own business? Beverly resolved to find out.

The inn beckoned, and she stepped in, feeling the warmth of the fire. She scanned the room, finding the scarred face she sought at a table with his two accomplices, tipping back a tankard of ale, then thumping it down to join the others he'd already emptied.

Beverly moved over to Owen and sat down, keeping her voice low. "I need you to gather the horses," she said.

"We're leaving?" he replied. "But we only just got here!"

"Events are moving fast, and if we are to find the Orcs, we must move now."

The knight nodded. "I'll fetch them immediately and meet you in the courtyard."

"Good. Watch your back. We're not necessarily amongst friends." She watched him leave, counting to thirty to ensure he was well out of hearing range. The last thing she needed was for Sir Owen to hear the sounds of battle and come racing in to help.

"You, there," she called out. "Is that your prisoner out in the pit?"

"It is," the scarred fellow replied. "What of it?"

"I'm curious how much one gets for finding an Orc?"

He laughed. "More than enough to pay for my lodging. I can get five crowns a head, double if I bring him in alive."

"Alive? To what end?"

"You're obviously not from these parts. The king needs slaves for his soldiers to practice against."

"Where I come from, slavery is illegal."

"A pity. You can make a decent living hunting Orcs in these parts."

Beverly stood. "Not anymore, you can't."

"Says who?"

"Beverly Fitzwilliam, Knight of the Hound."

"Oh look," said the club wielder. "She must think she's a Temple Knight."

"There is no need for violence," replied Beverly. "Release your prisoner to me, and you may be on your way."

"And if we don't?"

"Then I shall be forced to make you."

The three men stood, their chairs scraping across the floor. The inn's other patrons abandoned their seats, fleeing the confines of the room as the bounty hunters drew their weapons.

"Spread out, boys," shouted the scarred one. "She has no idea what she's up against."

Beverly drew Nature's Fury and backed away from her table, giving her space to manoeuvre. She easily parried a clumsy blow from the one with the club, then used the head of her hammer to push him back.

"Is that the best you can do?" she taunted. He came at her again, using both hands to swing his club overhead.

Beverly blocked it with her arm, trusting her armour to keep her safe, then hit him in the chest with Nature's Fury, knocking him to the floor where he lay, gasping for breath as his two companions moved to either side of her, hoping to outflank her.

Instead of waiting, she feinted left, her hammer smashing into the swordsman's arm. He fell back, screaming in agony and clutching his limp arm.

The group's leader advanced, then lunged, his blade scraping along her breastplate, leaving nothing but a scratch. Beverly turned, her hammer held on high, and the man threw up his sword, confident the blade could withstand the blow, but he hadn't counted on the sky metal head of Nature's Fury. The sword snapped in two as if it were a twig. He backed up, his hands up to show he no longer wished to fight.

"I surrender." His voice wavered in fear.

"Give me the key," demanded Beverly.

"The innkeeper has it."

"Then tell your man to go and fetch it."

The scarred one nodded at his club-wielding companion.

"No tricks, now," said Beverly. She waited as the key was retrieved, moving to keep the two men in her field of view.

The club wielder returned, still out of breath from her earlier hit. He tossed the keys to her and then backed up, eager to be out of reach of her hammer.

She nodded towards the wall. "Move over there, by the fire, and don't try anything."

They did as instructed, then she backed up until she was at the door. Pushing it open, she glanced out to see Owen leading the horses into the courtyard and waved him over.

"I took the liberty of opening the gate," he said.

"Stand here," she said, "and watch those three. I'll only be a moment." She ran over to the grate, unlocked the padlock, flipped it open, and offered her hand to the Orc.

Ugrug accepted her help and climbed out of the pit. "*I thank you, Redblade.*"

"We're not done quite yet. There's a good chance those men will follow us."

"*Then I will lead you through the forest to the land of my people. There, you will find safety.*"

"*Have you ever been on a horse?*"

"*No,*" said Ugrug. "*Though I have spent several days following behind one with my hands tied.*"

"*Understood.*" She sought out her companion. "Sir Owen, it's time to leave."

He backed out of the doorway, then turned and climbed into the saddle. Beverly followed suit, holding her hand out to help the Orc climb up behind her. Owen, having never seen an Orc before, simply stared.

"Follow me," said Beverly, urging Lightning forward. They rode through the inn's gate and out onto the road.

Ugrug pointed. "*Farther down, you will come across a pair of birch trees on the right. Pass between them, and we will be well on our way to the home of my people.*"

# TWENTY-SEVEN

# The Gorge

WINTER 967 MC

Herdwin stretched, snow falling from his shoulders. "It's getting colder," he said. "It won't be long before the passes become inaccessible."

"Agreed," replied Kasri. "Yet it appears they're still clear enough to allow a messenger through."

He followed her gaze to see a Dwarf approaching, wrapped in thick furs instead of the armour more typically seen of warriors.

"Lord Herdwin?" the fellow called out.

"Aye. That's me."

"I have a dispatch for you, my lord."

"From the vard?"

"No, from Wincaster." The Dwarf halted, removed his backpack, and dug through it. He produced a folded letter, the seal of the Mercerian Crown still intact and easy to identify. Herdwin took the missive and broke it open to read over its contents, then looked up at Kasri, the colour draining from his face.

"What is it?" she asked.

"The enemy is moving on Ironcliff."

"Does it mention anything about me?"

"It doesn't explicitly name you"—their eyes met—"but I would understand if you wanted to be there."

The messenger fidgeted. "There's another letter here for Lady Kasri, my lord." He held it out, his hand shaking.

She took it, ripping it open to peruse it quickly. "It's from my father. He outlines the recent events, so I know what to expect should I need to assume the Crown."

"Are you suggesting he's going to die?"

"I can't dismiss the possibility. If I know my father, he'll choose to make a stand outside the gates rather than retreat behind its walls."

"That would be ill-advised."

"Agreed, yet he can be stubborn when it comes to things of this nature."

"You make it sound like he's done this before," said Herdwin. "I didn't know Ironcliff had ever been attacked?"

"It hasn't, but my father has fought duels over slights to his bravery. Of course, that was before he was vard. These days, he's more likely to argue the point with words rather than steel, but I know what he can be like when he feels backed against a wall. It's against his nature to back down."

"You really think he'd march out and battle the Halvarians?"

"Not out on the plain, but perhaps on the walls of the outer city. My main concern is he'd prefer death in battle to surrendering Ironcliff."

"All the more reason for you to return home."

"No," said Kasri. "I would be of better use here. If I returned to Ironcliff, I would only get in my father's way. I just wish there were more we could do here."

"Perhaps there is. I've been meaning to go down into that gorge."

"To what end?"

"To look for any signs that the enemy has been down there. Of course, it means being lowered in the dark to avoid arrows, but we've plenty of Dwarves to work the ropes." He grinned. "After all, it's not like it would be my first time down there."

"Don't joke about such things," said Kasri. "The last time you fell, my heart almost stopped."

"As did mine, I assure you. I would have died if you hadn't been waiting for me up here. I'm not eager to repeat the process."

"If you feel you must go, then we'll be lowered down together, but if we're going to do this, we need to be smart about it. That means starting just before dawn. Else, we'll see nothing but darkness."

"Agreed."

"It also means we won't be able to come back up until nightfall to avoid being riddled with arrows."

"Then we can spend the entire day exploring."

"What do you remember from the last time you were down there?"

"Not much. When the bridge collapsed, I fell into a river. Thankfully, I managed to pull myself free of it, or I would have drowned."

"Was it wide?"

"Not particularly, but it washed me downstream a good half mile."

"Any idea what's upstream?"

"None whatsoever," said Herdwin. "Why? You think they're more likely to have gone up there?"

"I do," she replied. "It makes sense that if they crossed somewhere, it would be above us, the better to view our positions."

"You make a good argument. Until then, we best get some rest. It's likely to be a very tiring day."


Someone shook Herdwin as he slept. He opened his eyes to see Kasri, bedecked in her gold armour, looking down at him with a smile.

"Wake up," she said. "It's almost dawn."

He sat up, absently scratching his beard. "Already?"

"You've been asleep for most of the night."

"Have I? It doesn't feel like it."

"I warned you drinking all that ale wasn't a good idea."

"I had no choice! It was going to spoil!"

She held out her hand. "Here. Eat this stonecake, and then don your armour. We haven't much time."

He popped it in his mouth, waiting while his saliva dissolved the outer coating. The familiar flavour soon followed, then he chewed it.

With his meal complete, he retrieved his mail coat from beside his pallet. Years of experience taught him to don armour without a second thought, and before long, he'd placed his helmet firmly atop his head. He took one look at Kasri and then grinned. "Ready when you are."

"I don't understand why you haven't made yourself a set of plate armour. You have the skill for it."

"True," he replied, "but I consider myself more a smith than a warrior."

"Yet here you are, getting ready to fight once more."

"Aye. I'll not deny it, but I look forward to the day when we can settle down and live peacefully."

"As do I, but I fear that won't be for some time."

Herdwin sighed. "Then we'd best be about today's business."

The lanterns along the wall guided them to the mouth of the cave where Gelion called them over. Their eyes quickly grew accustomed to the darkness.

"The ropes are ready," the captain announced.

A pair of warriors stepped forward to cinch belts around the two of them. Next, came ropes secured with metal rings.

"We'll lower you down slowly," said Gelion, "but be careful. The cliff face is very uneven, and the last thing we want is for you two to injure yourselves."

"You mean like I did last time?" asked Herdwin. "Don't worry. I'll be careful."

"Now, remember, it'll be pitch black, so mind your elbows."

Herdwin looked at his betrothed and nodded. As one, they moved to the edge of the gorge, then turned to face Gelion.

"You may begin when ready," said Kasri.

Over the edge they went, the Dwarves holding the ropes, playing them out slowly. Herdwin pushed away from the rock, then bent his knees as his feet hit the cliff face when he swung back in.

Beside him, Kasri's feet hit the rock in a regular rhythm, matching their speed of descent. He looked down but only saw an infinite blackness. Time slowed as if they were being lowered into an endless tunnel of darkness.

He stumbled as his feet touched the bottom of the gorge. "That was unexpected!" he grumbled.

Kasri untied her rope and drew a glowing Stormhammer, revealing their surroundings. The stream stood at their backs, the rushing water drowning out all other sounds.

Herdwin moved closer, leaning in, and raising his voice to be heard. "Noisy, isn't it?"

She nodded in reply, then looked up, but the ropes disappeared into the darkness. "I'm surprised you climbed this after the bridge fell."

He shrugged. "Good thing I'd hit my head, or I never would have tried it otherwise." His gaze wandered to the stream. The rubble from the collapsed bridge was still in evidence, the water bubbling over it, forming rapids. Fear threatened to engulf him as he remembered the events of the night the bridge fell. His legs weakened, and he reached out to steady himself against the rock wall.

Kasri moved closer, clutching his arm. "It's all right," she soothed. "It can't harm you now."

He nodded, then swept his arm to the side, smiling bravely. "Ready?"

"Most certainly, but how about we give the sun a chance to make an appearance. I don't fancy the idea of stumbling around in the dark."

They sat, their backs to the cliff, watching as the morning light banished the shadows.

"What a beautiful sight," said Herdwin.

Kasri nodded her agreement, then looked over to see Herdwin staring at her.

She smiled. "Time to get going, but I suggest you draw your weapon in case the enemy is around."

He pulled the shield off his back, took his axe in hand, and walked parallel to the stream, Kasri following. They proceeded slowly, for the footing here was uneven and slippery, thanks to the fine mist from the rushing water.

Herdwin's beard was soon drenched, as was the rest of him. He paused at a particularly treacherous collection of rocks to confirm Kasri was still nearby, only to see her laughing. "What's so funny?"

"Your beard," she replied. "It's frosted over!"

He grinned, closing one eye and imitating the vard's voice. "Aye. I'm Khazad One-Eye, Ruler of Stonecliff!"

"It suits you, but let's not lose our focus. How far upstream are we going?"

"As far as we can," he replied. "That is until we find evidence the enemy has crossed." He turned back to the task at hand and was about to take another step when something caught his eye. Instead of continuing upstream, he moved to the cliff on his left, where he found a metal spike driven into the rock, likely to form a toehold.

Kasri came up beside him. "That looks like recent work."

"I would agree. It appears they abandoned the attempt, likely because it proved difficult to drive it into the stone in the first place. We were right to fear they've been down here."

"Listen. Do you hear that?"

Herdwin struggled to make out anything above the noise of the stream pushing its way through the rock. "What is it?"

"Unless I'm mistaken, a waterfall. I don't think we'll be able to go much farther."

"Still, we must look. It might have proven an easier climb for our foes."

They hugged the stone wall as they pushed upstream. The roar of the waterfall finally greeted Herdwin's ears, and then, through the mist, he saw an unending cascade of water flowing over the edge of a cliff face, dropping at least a hundred feet into a deep pool. He stared at it, then turned to Kasri. "How in the name of Gundar did they get across? We've seen no sign of a ford."

"Perhaps behind the falls?"

"I suppose that means we'll have to climb up there, doesn't it?"

"I'll take the lead. After riding a dragon, I've no fear of heights."

"Be careful. In this weather, it'll be icy."

He waited for her to start climbing before he joined her, allowing for space between them. Kasri proved remarkably agile, though she'd been forced to sling her weapon.

Herdwin followed at a more sedate pace, constantly searching for any sign of enemy activity. He wished they'd brought more Dwarves, the better to cover their ascent with arbalests, but he quickly dismissed the thought, for the freezing mist would play havoc with the gears that operated them.

Looking up, he noticed Kasri had found a ledge halfway up, which she was leaning over, staring down at him with a look of pure exaltation. He grunted out a response, then realized the sound of the waterfall drowned him out, so he continued climbing.

The freezing mist made the slippery rocks even more so, and his fingers ached. Eventually, he threw his arm over the ledge, and Kasri pulled him up.

"That was exhausting," he said. "Let me catch my breath."

She shook her head, then pointed. From their current position, he spotted movement on the other side of the river, where a group of Humans approached the waterfall. There could be no doubt where they were heading, for the very ledge the Dwarves sat on ran behind the falling water.

Herdwin jumped to his feet and unslung his shield. Kasri tapped him on the arm to get his attention, then pointed to the uneven rock wall behind the waterfall. He tried to answer, but the roar of the water drowned him out.

They advanced in single file, and then Herdwin spotted where a part of the cliff face had fallen away, leaving an indentation. He pressed his back into it, pulling Kasri in beside him. Before them, chunks of stone littered the ledge, making the footing even more treacherous. They waited with weapons in hand for the enemy to get closer.

They saw nothing of the Halvarians from their place of concealment until two Humans passed directly in front of them. Herdwin rushed out, smashing his shield into the one that followed. So sudden was the attack that his victim had no chance to react, and he stumbled back until the waterfall tore him from the ledge.

Even above the noise of the water, Herdwin heard a crack as Stormhammer let loose with a bolt of lightning that struck the fourth Halvarian. The man fell onto the ledge, sliding on the icy surface. The only thing that saved him from going over the edge was when he grabbed hold of a rock. Beyond him, two more Halvarians advanced.

Herdwin turned to face the first pair of warriors who'd drawn their weapons. He drove the head of his axe into a forearm, the man's vambrace splitting with the force of the blow. Blood welled up, forcing him to back away. His comrade charged forward, but in his haste to attack, he tripped on a rock, twisting his ankle painfully. The Human went down, his knee crashing onto the cold stone, but before he could even cry out, Herdwin's axe silenced him.

Kasri, meanwhile, turned to face the Halvarians who brought up the rear. One waved his arms around, indicating he was casting a spell. She charged forward, hitting him hard enough to break his concentration and almost knock him over, but failed to penetrate the man's armour. She quickly followed up with another blow to his knee. Stormhammer struck true, and the fellow's leg crumpled beneath him, his screams failing to rise above the roar of the water.

The last one turned to flee, but Kasri raised Stormhammer above her, and a bolt of lightning reached out, striking the Human in the middle of his back. It wasn't enough to kill him, but it didn't have to, for the footing was so slick with water and ice, he crashed to his knees before sliding over the lip of the pathway into the mist.

Herdwin, distracted by Kasri's fight, felt a blow on his back. He whipped around, annoyed he'd forgotten his last opponent. The fellow tried stabbing him but hadn't counted on the durability of Dwarven mail.

The smith swung his axe overhead, smashing it down onto the man's helmet hard enough to penetrate the armour but not sufficiently to kill him outright. The Halvarian stepped back as blood ran down his face, blinding him. He staggered around until his foot went over the edge, and then the falls claimed him.

Herdwin turned to check on Kasri, pride at their success surging through him, but then he stumbled, and his right leg came out from under him, a victim of an icy patch. He flailed his arms around as he slid, trying to find something to stop him, then he managed to latch on to a sizeable chunk of stone that had fallen from the wall.

He let out a sigh of relief, but the rock broke off from the floor, and he slid towards the ledge, the roar of the falls smothering his screams for help. Suddenly, Kasri was there, grabbing his wrist and hauling him back from the brink. They sat there amongst the stones, catching their breath.

Herdwin looked around, worried more Humans might be coming, but those remaining lay still. He slowly got to his feet and picked his way through the rocks to where the spellcaster lay.

He knelt by the body and, with a quick hammer blow to the head, finished the mage off. Herdwin then rolled him over, searching for anything of note. Of particular interest was the gold ring on the fellow's finger. Looking closer, the Dwarf could make out the runes etched into the band, along with a strange gem set into it. Even as he watched, the gem changed from a golden hue to almost transparent. He pulled it from the mage's finger, unsure of its use but convinced it could prove useful in the right hands.

# TWENTY-EIGHT

# Wyburn

## WINTER 967 MC

E xalor Shozarin, High Strategos of Halvaria, watched as the Seventh Legion marched past. The men were ready for battle, eager despite the light covering of snow on the ground. The accepted rules of war said attacking in winter was a mistake, but he knew he must do the unexpected for his strategy to succeed.

He smiled at the thought. The Mercerian marshal was, no doubt, expecting a spring campaign. This unexpected offensive would take him completely by surprise!

The provincial cavalry set out at dawn, screening the advance. Not that there was much to oppose them. By all accounts, the Wood Elves offered no resistance, and the Dwarves, or rather, their Mercerian allies, had only scraped together a company of light horse to oppose them.

Exalor watched the provincial troops leave, heading west. They would march straight for Ironcliff, tying down any opposition until the Imperial cavalry outflanked them. Part of him wanted the Mercerians to stand and fight, but he knew Marshal Matheson would never allow it for the odds were against them.

"A fine body of men," said Idraxa. "It won't take them long to reach the Dwarven stronghold at this speed. Then the fun begins." She glanced eastward, searching for the massive siege engines that would follow in the legion's wake.

Exalor followed her gaze. "Are you sure you have enough of them?"

"Don't worry. I've studied the Dun-Galdrim campaign with great interest. The attack against Ironcliff won't produce the losses we suffered there, at least not on our side."

"You're confident. I like that. I only hope your skill matches your enthusiasm."

"It does," said Idraxa. "Although my appointment was sudden, I took it upon myself to learn all I could about our adversary in the short time I've had to prepare."

"What conclusions have you drawn from your research?"

"The Dwarves are likely to hole up in their fortress like they did in Dun-Galdrim."

"What about the Mercerians?"

"I doubt they'll offer much in the way of resistance, at least not in the early stages of the campaign. Attacking now, rather than waiting for spring, upsets their plans to reinforce their ally."

"And what do you think their reaction will be?"

"I suspect they'll organize an army to march north, but the weather will work against them."

"As it will us," said Exalor.

"True, but we'll be settled in for a siege and are relatively close to our supplies in Wyburn. On the other hand, they must transport their supplies over five hundred miles of open countryside."

"You would be wise to take precautions. The Mercerians have proven themselves capable of adapting to hardships."

"It matters little. Once Ironcliff is sealed up, we'll send our cavalry marauding through Norland. They'll have no choice but to split their pathetic army into even smaller groups to chase us down."

"You've grasped the nature of this early phase of the campaign quite well, Idraxa. Now tell me, were you commanding their side, what would be your reaction?"

"I would send troops north as quickly as possible. We've already seen some of their light cavalry, but there has yet to be any skirmishing."

"And there won't be until they're ready to engage."

"You believe they have more men to reinforce the mountain folk?"

"I expect they'll convince the Queen of Norland to aid Ironcliff, although the exact composition of her army remains to be seen."

"They're no match for an Imperial Legion."

"Even a legion has its weaknesses."

She looked at him in shock. "I'm surprised to hear you say that, Your Grace. Your words carry the smell of defeatism."

"A wise leader understands both the strengths and weaknesses of their command. In that way, they anticipate how an enemy might attack."

"I see," replied Idraxa. "My apologies for the insult."

"You have a bright future ahead of you," said Exalor, "but don't let your devotion blind you."

"What would you have me do, Your Grace?"

"You already indicated that if you were Mercerian, you would send men north with all haste. My question to you is, what would the composition of your army be for such a task?"

"That depends on what they know about our legions. Their army would need to number in the thousands to be a threat to us."

"I know our vaunted legions are said to be unbeatable, but let's be more realistic, shall we? Let's assume the Mercerians are, man for man, just as competent as our own."

"In that case, I would field an army of at least two thousand."

"And how did you arrive at that number?"

"Our legion numbers twenty-four hundred, but a portion of those will be involved in conducting the siege."

Exalor nodded. "A reasonable assumption, but you have yet to tell the composition of this proposed expedition."

"I've read your assessment of the Mercerians' capabilities."

"And?"

"I expect the greater portion of their army will be foot, perhaps as much as eighty percent."

"Why so high?"

"I suspect they'll hold back the bulk of their archers for use in their own lands."

"And their cavalry?"

"Moving horsemen requires a substantial amount of forage, and from your accounts, the land hereabouts is not horse friendly."

"Yet we're fielding a lot of cavalry."

Idraxa smiled. "Yes, but we took great pains to stock up on fodder beforehand. The Mercerians had no chance to prepare, unless there's something you're not telling me?"

"No. Your assessment is fair, although we cannot dismiss the possibility they might have anticipated our strategy."

"Then why would they bother sending reinforcements to Ironcliff?"

"They have little choice," said Exalor. "Were they to refuse, they would soon be bereft of allies."

"Surely that would be better for us. It would mean less to face in our war with the Dwarves."

"You appear to be under the mistaken impression Ironcliff is a major objective. It is merely a tool to split the Mercerian army."

"You ordered us to build siege engines?"

"How else do we convince them we mean business? Don't worry. They'll be put to use eventually, but there's no rush."

"And if they march out to face us?"

"Then so much the better. With all the cavalry we have, you should make short work of them."

"I look forward to just that opportunity," said Idraxa. "Out of curiosity, did we hear anything regarding their mages?"

"Ironcliff has an Earth Mage, but I doubt they'd risk him in open battle. He'd be better employed once we start trying to dig them out of their mountain."

"And the Mercerians?"

"They have several mages at their beck and call, but my overall strategy should prevent them from being employed in any large concentrations. Their most influential are Life Mages, so expect many of their wounded to return to battle. To counter this, you must hold the field once the battle ends. As for others, they have few of any real consequence. No Water, Fire, or Air Mages, as far as we're aware."

"I noticed you didn't mention Druids."

"You are correct. They have at least two, one quite powerful, but I doubt they'd risk her in the north. It's far more likely she'll be employed in Merceria itself."

"And will the Mercerian marshal show his face in the gap?"

"Likely not," said Exalor. "If by some chance he does, I would very much like to be made aware, but I expect one of his commanders will show up, either Lord Preston or Heward, although we cannot discount the possibility he might send one of his non-Human commanders." He smiled. "No need to worry, though. Aside from their marshal, very few of them can rival the capabilities of a trained battle mage."

"It's not my training I'm worried about; it's this terrain. The gap is completely flat, eliminating the element of surprise."

"That only works to our advantage. Should the fools decide to stand and fight, we will flood into their lands that much sooner."

He watched the companies as they continued marching past. The empire's soldiers were in a good mood, their steps lively, but he wondered how many would live to see the end of the year. Battlefield losses were usually of little concern to him, yet this campaign could last months if not years. If he lost too many men early on, it would seriously undermine his ability to gain the upper hand. He didn't fancy returning to the Inner Council and begging for another legion.

His back twinged, reminding him he'd recently been the target of an attempt on his life. Had it not been for Kelson's quick thinking, he might have died.

"Is something wrong?" asked Idraxa.

"No. Why do you ask?"

"You looked as though you were in pain."

"Merely the result of overtaxing my magic in the recent days. You'll understand better once you're older." He looked at her, ignoring the men. "I'm entrusting this legion to you, Idraxa. Don't let me down."

"Of course not, Your Grace."

He backed away, then called on his magic to teleport him to the capital. The power built within him, and then everything distorted as the spell took effect. The world spun, and he felt stretched to the point of breaking as he was pulled through the vortex. It was over in a snap, and then he staggered forward a step, now in one of the casting circles in Varena, the very heart of the empire.

The guards stepped towards him, then, realizing who he was, returned to their duty stations outside the circle. Exhaustion overcame him as if all his energy had been drained. Kelson had warned him a full recovery would take time, yet the campaign was starting; what else could he do?

Exalor looked up to see the guards watching him with concern. He straightened his back and left the room with a firm stride. Only when he was out of their sight did he lean against the wall. Was he still up to the task of leading this campaign? He briefly thought of passing command to someone else, but the thought of surrendering all his work to another galled him. Instead, he found the energy to carry on, at least to his rooms. There, he would rest before continuing with the next part of his scheme.


A grunt greeted Wingate's knock. Taking it for a reply, he opened the door to see Exalor sitting at his desk, his head resting on his arms.

"Are you quite all right, Your Grace?"

The High Strategos sat up. "I'm fine, merely tired."

"Shall I get you some food?"

"I haven't the time for it. There's too much to do."

His aide stood there waiting, knowing his master would soon reveal his intentions.

"We must go to the map room," continued Exalor. "There is something I wish to confirm."

"You are weak, Your Grace. Should you not rest?"

"I shall rest once all my plans are in motion. Have we any news from the gorge?"

"There was a report that one of our scouting parties was lost, but nothing else of any consequence. Why? Are you expecting something?"

"Nothing I can put my finger on, merely a feeling I've missed something."

"That is only to be expected, Your Grace. The coming campaign is complex and requires many to play their parts. I doubt anyone would expect it to go precisely according to plan. That's why you developed contingencies, or at least that's what you told me. Has something gone amiss?"

"I'm sorry," said Exalor. "The attack on me has shaken my confidence. I'm concerned someone is actively working against me."

"But you are the High Strategos, Your Grace. Who would dare?"

"Who indeed? If I had any idea who was behind it, they would already have been taken care of."

"What can I do to help set your mind at ease?"

"You can start by replacing my guards."

"I took the liberty of doing that while you were up in Wyburn, Your Grace. You may rest assured. Another attack of that nature is impossible now."

"That's a bold claim, considering we still don't know who's responsible." He paused, taking a deep breath. "I'm sorry, Wingate. I'm not myself today."

"Understandable, considering the circumstances. I still believe you'd feel better if you took some time to recover."

"As I've already told you, I have too much to do."

"You said everything was in readiness. What else is there, specifically, that requires your attention?"

"We have received recent reports from Merceria, so I must ensure the map room is updated appropriately."

"I am more than capable of taking care of that, Your Grace."

"There is also the matter of choosing the new Marshal of the North. The Sartellians will be expecting me to start the official process."

"I'm sure, given the circumstances, a few more days won't make much difference. In any case, you wanted to slow it down, not speed it up."

"Did we organize additional mules for the attack on Stonecastle?"

"Yes."

"And what about extra weapons for the Third Legion?"

"I initiated the process before you left for the north, Your Grace."

Exalor forced a smile. "Whatever would I do without you, Wingate?"

"I'm sure I don't know, Your Grace. Now, will you rest, or must I call on a Life Mage to put you to sleep?"

The High Strategos held up his hands. "I surrender to your pleas. Have the servants prepare my bed."

"And a meal, perhaps? You know you need it to regain your strength?"

"If you insist." Exalor stood, though he wobbled slightly. "It appears I'm more fatigued than I thought."

"Fatigued? I should think exhausted is a better word."

"This presents a bit of a problem," said Exalor. "I wanted to use my magic to revisit the Third."

"I'm sure the commander-general is more than capable of doing his duty without you peering over his shoulder. You need to restrain from over-taxing yourself, which includes the casting of teleportation. You could consider taking a carriage if you're too stubborn to rest."

"That would take weeks."

Wingate smiled. "So it would. I suppose you'll have to wait until you fully recover."

"So it would seem, but make sure you tell me if anything out of the ordinary develops!"

"Of course, Your Grace."


That evening, Wingate sat alone in Exalor's office, which was not unusual, for the High Stategos's aide was often employed in work on behalf of his master. Had someone been there to see him, however, they most certainly would have noticed how he copied information from document after document, jotting down important details into a separate book.

He paused to take a sip of wine, smiling as he thought of the coins such information would inevitably bring him. It had shocked him when he'd first been approached, but then he had come to realize it was common for aides of the family's senior members to make a little bit on the side.

It had been made plain on more than one occasion that there was no promotion in his future, so he'd been content to serve the empire and live a modest life, until the ready flow of coins quickly changed his mind. True, there was always the danger of discovery, but he had assurances that should that occur, he would be well taken care of.

Everything in the empire seemed to come down to the clash between the three lines: Shozarins, Stormwinds, and Sartellians, each striving to be the one in charge, yet, at the same time, fighting to prevent the others from doing precisely the same thing. It had lasted for centuries and would likely continue well past the end of Wingate's life. Why not take advantage of the turmoil to fill his own coffers? After all, he couldn't serve the High Strategos forever. Sooner or later, his master would succumb to the ravages of old age, and then where would he be?

A knock at the door gave him a start, but he recovered quickly, calling out, "Who's there?"

"And old friend," came the reply.

"One moment." Wingate carefully placed the documents back where they belonged before he tucked the journal into his belt. He then rose, making his way to the door and opening it to Kelson, the High Sentinel.

"Is there something I can do for you, Your Grace?"

"I happened to be passing by and saw the light underneath the door. Working late, are we?"

"Merely seeing to some administrative details."

"And the High Strategos?"

"In bed, resting, Your Grace. I'm afraid his travels of late leave him exhausted. He has always had a light constitution, and the recent injury has exacerbated it. I fear if he doesn't seek a more permanent treatment soon, he may be unable to keep up with his duties."

Kelson stared back. "And the book?"

"It is here," replied Wingate, pulling forth his journal. "Just as promised."

# TWENTY-NINE

# The Sky Singers

## WINTER 967 MC

The Grey Hills were aptly named, for wind erosion had bared the rock in numerous places. Ugrug, despite being on foot, kept up a swift pace, and after two days of travel, they topped a rise to see an Orc village off in the distance.

"*There it is,*" said Ugrug. "*Ag-Dular, the home of the Sky Singers.*"

It appeared similar to the Black Arrow's village in the Artisan Hills, with a large central building surrounded by lesser dwellings. However, a wooden palisade encircled this entire village, with a walkway atop it.

"Fascinating," said Owen. "I never would have thought it possible."

"That the Orcs would live in a village?" she asked.

"No. That they would have the wherewithal to build a palisade."

"You underestimate them. They are a resourceful people. If you were to spend some time amongst them, you would come to appreciate their gifts."

"Gifts? You make them sound so civilized."

"They are, though not in what you would consider the 'traditional' sense. If you put aside your preconceptions and give them a chance, Owen, they will surprise you."

"*Come,*" said Ugrug. "*I shall introduce you to the rest of my tribe.*"

They descended the hill, drawing interest from the Orcs patrolling the walkway. When they drew closer, those hunters nocked arrows as a group of five others came out from the palisade to greet them.

"*I have returned,*" called out Ugrug.

A huge Orc holding a spear stepped closer. "*You dare to bring Humans here?*"

"*We are friends,*" said Beverly, using the language of the Orcs. "*I am Beverly Fitzwilliam, better known to your people as Redblade.*"

"*The name means nothing to us.*"

"*I was led to believe all Orcs were allied to Merceria.*"

"*Who told you that?*"

"*Chief Urgon of the Black Arrows.*"

"*That is a name I am not familiar with.*"

"*Bloodrig might know more,*" offered one of his companions.

"*Is she your shaman?*" asked Beverly.

"*One of them,*" the Orc replied. "*Not that it is any of your concern.*"

"*These Humans helped me,*" said Ugrug. "*They are not typical of the ones from these parts.*"

"*Still, you should have known better than to bring them here. By your actions, you put the entire tribe in danger.*"

"*We are no threat to you,*" said Beverly. "*In fact, quite the reverse. Our presence here may herald a new era in which you can live in peace with the Humans of this land.*"

"*Why should we trust the word of a Human?*"

"*Is it not the custom of your people to let the tribe decide such matters?*"

Ugrug grinned. "*It is indeed.*" He turned to his counterpart. "*It appears Redblade knows our customs better than you, Tarig.*"

Tarig bared his teeth. "*I was not the one who allowed Humans to capture me.*"

A younger Orc moved up to stand beside Tarig. "*Enough! All of you! These outsiders freed Ugrug from his captors. Instead of berating those of our tribe, we should be welcoming their help.*" She stepped closer, standing before Lightning. "*I am Krazuhk, daughter of Lurzak, Chieftain of the Sky Singers. Welcome to Ag-Dular. Climb down from your horses, and we will show you inside the village.*"

Beverly dismounted, and Owen, unable to understand what they had said, simply copied her movements.

"What's happening?" he whispered.

"We are going inside the palisade to visit their chieftain."

"Are you sure they won't kill us in there?"

"Don't be ridiculous. If they wanted us dead, we'd already be so."

"That hardly fills me with confidence."

The village gates consisted of two thick doors made of logs tied to a frame with hinges of rope. Three hunters controlled access by manually lifting the doors and swinging them to either side, providing ample room for the horses to enter.

Lightning was calm, having been around Orcs before, but Owen's horse was uneasy in such surroundings, requiring the young knight to continually reassure it. Once past the gate, the doors were closed.

"So much for any hope of escape," said Owen.

"Hush now," replied Beverly. "We are amongst friends."

"With all due respect, these Orcs are a long way from those back in your homeland. How do you know we can trust them?"

"The same could be said from their point of view. To gain trust, you must first give it."

They were led past the small huts towards the larger structure in the middle of the village. Word of their arrival garnered considerable interest, and by the time they halted before the great hall, almost all the Orcs were there, eager to discover what all the fuss was about.

Krazuhk disappeared inside, then reappeared with an older Orc bearing a scar across his forehead.

"*I am Lurzak,*" he announced. "*Chieftain of the Sky Singers.*"

Beverly bowed. "*Greetings, Lurzak. I bring you greetings from the Queen of Merceria. I am Beverly Fitzwilliam, but to your people, I am known as Redblade.*"

"*And who is your companion?*"

"*Sir Owen, a knight of the Petty Kingdoms.*"

"*My daughter tells me you returned Ugrug to us. Why would a Human do such a thing?*"

"*I only did what I would do for any ally. There is a great friendship between my people and the Black Arrows, as well as the Black Ravens. Perhaps you've heard of these tribes?*"

"*No doubt our shaman, Bloodrig, would be more familiar with such things, but I must confess such names are unfamiliar to my ears.*"

"It matters little," said Beverly. "*My oath and my duty to an ally are still unwavering.*"

"*You speak our language well. Were I unable to see you with my own eyes, I might mistake you for an Orc.*"

"*You honour me, Lurzak.*"

"*Krazuhk tells me you bring an offer of peace from the Humans.*"

"*It is a little more complicated than that, but that is certainly my intention.*"

"*Then come. We shall partake of the milk of life, and you can tell me all about this offer of yours.*"

Beverly looked across the fire at Owen, who'd been the last to drink the milk of life. She knew those unused to such things could often feel disoriented, and was about to say something to him, but Lurzak chose that moment to speak.

"*I am curious to hear what you are proposing,*" said the chieftain. "*I can think of nothing that would bring everlasting peace between our people and yours.*"

"They are not my people," replied Beverly, "but their king is in poor health. Were you to agree for your shaman to heal him, I am sure he would recognize your lands."

"What assurances would we have that our shaman would be safe?"

"I give you my word, as a friend of the Orcs, to protect them."

"Words come easy to your lips, but deeds are what demonstrate commitment."

"Then set me a task, and I shall prove myself to you."

Lurzak stared into the fire before meeting her gaze once more. "There is a way in which you might prove your worth, but it would mean fighting other Humans."

"What is it you would have me do?"

"The men who took Ugrug built a camp on the edge of the forest we call the Wildwood. They prey on our people, making it difficult for us to hunt."

"You wish to attack them?"

"We tried several times," said Lurzak, "but it is not a task easily done. Much like our village, their camp is surrounded by a palisade with a well-defended gate. We attempted to breach their walls thrice, and each time our assaults ended in failure."

"You want me to get you inside," said Beverly.

"I do. Have you any idea how such a thing might be accomplished?"

"Several, in fact. I assume the gates were closed each time they spotted you?"

"They were."

"Then I suspect a ruse would be the most likely way to succeed."

"What is it you are suggesting?"

"Here's what I propose we do..."


Owen crouched in the darkness, staring at the distant lights of the bounty hunter's base. "Are you sure about this? The last thing I want to see is a massacre."

"Lurzak gave me his word the defenders will be spared, providing they surrender," replied Beverly.

"I admire the sentiment, but what's the likelihood of that? To most men in these parts, the Orcs are nothing more than savage beasts. I doubt they'd willingly throw down their arms."

"They won't surrender to Orcs, but they'll surrender to me."

"And you honestly believe they would accept that?"

"They have no choice if they want to live."

"I wish I had your confidence."

"It's a sound plan," said Beverly. "We just need to ensure we do a good job convincing them we're in danger."

Owen looked around at the Orcs crouched nearby. "I don't think that will be a problem." He closed his eyes and muttered a prayer to Saint Mathew.

"Nervous?" she asked.

"I'd feel better if I had my horse."

"If we rode up to the gates, there wouldn't be enough time for the Orcs to catch up."

"And you don't think those mercenaries will suspect a trap?"

"They're bounty hunters, not mercenaries. Most have probably seen very little actual battle."

"Nor have I," said Owen, "which worries me."

"Your armour will protect you and identify you as a knight. That alone should be more than sufficient to confuse them."

"Confuse? I thought we wanted to defeat them?"

"We do," said Beverly, "but the more confused they are, the more time the Orcs will have to get inside."

He took a deep breath, then nodded. "I'm ready. We may begin whenever you like."

She turned to Krazuhk, switching to the language of the Orcs. *"We are ready to begin. Are your hunters in position?"*

*"They are."*

Beverly stood, then motioned for Owen to join her. She'd fought in countless battles, yet the thought of the coming fight worried her. It was not that she doubted her abilities, but a stray arrow could still do fearful damage, and she'd left her helmet behind, the better to look as if she were in a panic.

Both knights walked towards the distant palisade, keeping their gaze on those atop the walls. They were halfway to their target when the woods behind them erupted into deafening yells as Orcs poured from the trees.

The two Humans burst into a run, shouting for help as they went. Beverly heard Owen cry out as he lost his balance on the uneven ground and fell. She cursed her luck and went back, hauling him to his feet as an Orc arrow landed nearby.

Shouts came from within the palisade, and then lanterns flooded the wall. Moments later, a yell came for the gate to be opened. With Owen by her side, she raced towards the entrance to the palisade, spotting someone peering back at her, waving them forward.

Owen threw himself through the open doorway, but Beverly, rather than rushing in, barrelled into the one holding the door, knocking him to the ground. She quickly followed that up by seizing the door and hauling it open even farther.

A man ran up to her, his voice high-pitched with fear. "Are you mad? We must close it, not open it!"

Beverly smashed him in the face with her gauntlet. Blood poured from the fellow's nose, and he fell back with a cry.

Owen seized the opportunity to draw his weapon and moved to stand in the open entrance as the bounty hunters massed. He screamed out a challenge, then rushed headlong into them, but they panicked, trying to get out of the reach of his sword, which he wildly flailed about.

Beverly heard the Orcs approaching, and then the first pair were through. An arrow took the lead hunter in the arm, but he kept running, his terrifying war cry echoing off the palisade walls.

Someone struck her from behind, and as she turned to meet her assailant, he swung his axe overhead, but she kicked out, her heel connecting with his knee to send him sprawling. She ignored his cries of agony, pulling Nature's Fury from her belt.

Orcs streamed into the palisade, then a lightning bolt came out of nowhere, striking a man on the walkway and pitching him over the wall. The sudden flash temporarily blinded everyone, leading to a lull in the fight.

"Surrender!" Beverly shouted in the Human tongue. "Lay down your arms, and you'll be spared!"

Some did as she bid while others, in fear for their lives, climbed onto the walkway and jumped over the palisade, seeking the safety of the woods.

On the other side of the camp, a bounty hunter rallied a group of men for a counterattack. Beverly watched as Krazuhk sent a lightning bolt into the fellow's chest. He stiffened, then fell to the ground, twitching. Those he'd gathered quickly divested themselves of their weapons, raising their hands in surrender.

Beverly walked over to her, switching to the tongue of the Orcs. "*You didn't tell me you were a master of air?*"

"*You never asked,*" replied Krazuhk. "*We are, after all, called the Sky Singers. Did you think we only lifted our voices in song?*"

"*I suppose I hadn't given it much thought.*"

"*What do you wish us to do with all these prisoners?*"

"*Bind them,*" said Beverly, "*then secure them within one of the buildings.*"

"*To what end?*"

"*They might prove useful if we have to bargain with the king. Have you enough hunters to occupy this place?*"

"*We thought to burn it to the ground following my father's wishes.*"

"*I would advise against that,*" said Beverly. "*If you destroy this, another will simply take its place. However, use it as your own, and it becomes a permanent reminder that you control the area."*

"We shall not burn it for now," said Krazuhk, *"but its ultimate fate will be at my father's discretion."*

*"Then I suggest we return to Ag-Dular with all haste and discuss the matter before your hunters get their own ideas of what to do."*


The coming of dawn found Beverly and Owen once more in the village of the Sky Singers. Lurzak, having heard of their success, heaped praise on them, insisting on proclaiming a feast. For her part, Beverly tried to bring up the idea of sending a healer to Agran, but the chieftain was having none of it. Such things, he said, were to be discussed after the festivities, when the passion of the hunt was well and truly satiated.

Thus, the two Humans found themselves sitting around a huge firepit running the length of the great hut, with almost the whole tribe in attendance.

An older Orc sitting across from Beverly met her gaze. *"I am Bloodrig,"* she said. *"Shaman of this tribe."*

*"May the blessings of the Ancestors be upon you."*

*"You are familiar with our ways. Tell me, Redblade, how did your people come to be allied with ours?"*

*"There was a war back home, and the Black Arrows came to our aid in our time of need."*

*"And what did they get in return?"*

*"Recognition of their lands and a lasting friendship. Many of that tribe now live in peace amongst Humans."*

*"I sense you are not revealing the entire story."*

*"It's true. I'll not deny it. Some still seek to drive a wedge between our peoples, but our queen is dedicated to resolving the issue."*

*"And what will happen when your queen eventually dies?"*

*"She has already enshrined their rights in the law of the land for future generations to follow."*

*"I am impressed. Admittedly, I am not an expert in Human kingdoms, but the last thing I expected to hear was that Orcs and Humans could live together peacefully. This queen of yours must be exceptional."*

"She is," said Beverly, *"and were she here herself, she would extend her hand in friendship. Merceria considers all Orcs their allies, regardless of the tribe."*

*"And you have proven that by your deeds. But tell me, will this attack on your fellow Humans not cause some animosity with the king of this land?"*

"*Most likely, but he is ill, and his health rests in the hands of my cousin, Aubrey. I'm hoping his wish to live outweighs any thoughts of revenge.*"

"*Your cousin is a healer?*"

"Yes," said Beverly. "*A Life Mage. What you would refer to as a shaman.*"

"*And is she like you?*"

"*Only in terms of her beliefs. Physically, she's a little shorter, with dark hair. She's also several years younger, although quite gifted in healing.*"

"*I should very much like to meet her one day.*"

"*You could if you accompanied me back to Agran. Were you to help heal King Justinian, you could name your price.*"

"*The Human lands are not a place for one such as me.*"

"*So you won't help the king?*"

"No," said Bloodrig. "*Then again, I am not the only healer in Ag-Dular.*"

# THIRTY

# Aid

## WINTER 967 MC

L ord Heward moved his horse to the side, allowing the companies to
pass. They'd set out from Galburn's Ridge two days ago, marching for
Anvil. He'd allowed three and a half days to reach the place, but he was
beginning to wonder if he'd been overly optimistic.

He noted Lord Calder bringing up the rear and rode to join him. The
Earl of Greendale nodded his head in greeting.

"It's a fine day," said Heward.

"I would have preferred a little more warmth, but we shall make do." He
gazed south to the hills. "I'm surprised you're not using the road, not that I
can blame you. This time of year, they're more a hindrance than a help."

"By my reckoning, we should shave off a day by staying close to the edge
of these hills."

"Yes, and they continue to Anvil, so it'll be easy to find." He looked at
Heward. "You don't like me being here, do you?"

"Not particularly. You fought against us during the war."

"I did, though that has more to do with politics than anything personal."
Heward laughed. "Politics is personal."

"So it is, but I might remind you, I was pardoned by the Crown."

"By Bronwyn, yes, but I serve the Queen of Merceria."

"Yet here you are, commanding the Army of Norland. Not that it's much
of an army."

"We must do what we can to help our allies."

"Precisely," said Calder. "That's why I've sent word ahead for what's left
of my men to assemble in Chandley. It's not much, I grant you, but adding
my four companies to the queen's gives us an effective fighting strength of

over four hundred, not an inconsequential number. Will it be enough, do you think?"

"You're forgetting the Ravens."

"Ah, yes. The Orcs. I'm not happy about working alongside them. They did, after all, usurp the rule of the Earl of Ravensguard."

"They didn't usurp anything," replied Heward. "That was their ancestral land. We merely returned what was rightfully theirs."

"And in the process, reduced the number of Norland earls by one."

"You should be happy. That means there are five earls instead of six, which makes it much easier to rule."

"Does it?" said Calder. "I fail to see how."

"It's quite simple. An odd number of earls eliminates the possibility of a stagnant vote."

"You've learned a lot about our politics."

"Enough to know you're still a contentious bunch. You argue about everything."

"It can't be helped. It's the natural order of things. Remember, our founders fled Merceria more than four hundred years ago, and our own system developed out of that distrust of royalty."

"You've had kings ever since."

"True," said Calder, "but Norland kings are weak, with most of their power given to the earls. Completely the opposite to what happened in Merceria."

"Until now," corrected Heward.

"Admittedly, our system could be better."

"But you support Bronwyn's rule now, don't you?"

"I do, and it's not just because she pardoned me. I've come to believe our power structure was flawed, with each earl ruling their lands according to their own wishes. The truth is, we were barely a kingdom at all. Rather, we were a loose amalgamation of independent states. We became so divided, we descended into civil war!"

"The same could be said of Merceria."

"I hadn't considered that," replied Calder. "Which means we have more in common than I thought."

They rode on silently for a while, each in their own thoughts. The columns kept their pace as the afternoon sun crept across the sky, and then they spotted Captain Naran waiting to one side.

"It appears," said Heward, "it's time for us to set up camp. You must excuse me, my lord. I need to see to the men."

"Of course. I understand completely."

Heward rode over to the Norland captain. "You've found a suitable spot?"

"We have, Lord. There's a stream nearby and some trees to cut the wind a little."

"You appear to have things well in hand, Captain, yet I sense you have questions."

"I do, though not concerning the camp."

"Then speak freely."

"There's a certain feeling amongst the men."

"You'll have to be much more descriptive than that," said Heward. "Do you mean fear?"

"I wouldn't say fear so much as uncertainty?"

"That's only natural. We're marching to battle. Admittedly, it's still some distance off, but it weighs heavily on a man's mind."

"What about you, Lord? Does the thought of an impending battle still frighten you?"

"It does, though only when it's closer. Fear is good; it keeps your wits about you amidst all that carnage."

Naran paled.

"Don't worry," said Heward. "You get used to it."

"Will we get used to the Orcs as well?"

"Undoubtedly. I understand you Norlanders had trouble with Orcs in the past, but they're our allies now, which makes them your friends as well. You'll see that once we reach Chandley."

"Whatever do you mean?"

"Didn't I mention it? The Black Ravens are marching there to meet up with us."

"I thought only the earl's men were assembling in Chandley? Weren't the Orcs supposed to march directly to Ironcliff?"

"They were, but I convinced them to change their minds."

"But you never left Galburn's Ridge?"

"True, I didn't, but I sent word to Wincaster, and they contacted the Black Ravens."

"Through magic?"

"Yes. How else would we get word to Ravensguard on such short notice?"

"But why assemble them in Chandley? Surely they'd be more useful marching to help the Dwarves directly."

"I felt it better to assemble a large relief force. Having us arrive piecemeal will do little good, whereas concentrating our forces may give us the advantage."

"And if we arrive too late?" asked Naran.

"That depends on your definition of 'too late'."

"What if the siege has already begun?"

"Then so much the better. It will tie down the enemy while we still have the advantage of movement." Heward watched the men setting up the camp. "We may be a small force, but the earl's men will bolster our numbers. Add the Orcs, and we stand a good chance of inflicting some serious casualties."

"But not winning?"

"Our first encounter with these Halvarians is not about winning. It's about wearing them down and learning their tactics. Right now, we have little information about how many men they have or the composition of their army. That may change once we get to Ironcliff, but we must be prepared."

"And how do we do that?"

"My plan is to rest in Chandley for a few days, giving the men a chance to recover from the march, but it also allows me to assess how best to deploy our forces in battle."

"There's a lot to planning a campaign of this nature."

"There is," said Heward, "particularly when we have such diverse troops."

"Diverse?"

"Yes. The queen's men have never served in battle alongside the earl's, nor have either of you fought beside Orcs. It'll be interesting to see how everyone works together."

"Are you not worried about the Orcs?"

Heward laughed. "I've seen them fight in battle. Why would I be worried?"

"They are undisciplined, surely?"

"Why would you think that?"

Naran stared down at his feet. "Being the primitives they are, I assumed they'd revert to their natural ways."

Heward shook his head. "It's thinking like that which prevents you from seeing the benefits. In Merceria, we embrace Dwarves, Elves, Orcs, and even Trolls. Their very difference makes them so effective on the battlefield."

"But how do you organize all that? Did they teach you how when you became a general?"

"Me? A general? Where did you get that idea?"

"Since you were in charge of this expedition, I assumed you'd carry the appropriate rank."

"I'm a Mercerian commander," said Heward, "though I've been named a brigade-commander for the duration of this campaign."

"What's a brigade?"

"A term created by Richard Fitzwilliam, the old Baron of Bodden, referring to a collection of companies held in an independent command."

"So, an army, then?"

"Well, a small army. Our marshal has this idea to divide the army into more manageable groups."

"So we're going north with only part of an army?"

"There," said Heward, grinning. "You understand perfectly."

"But if that's true, where are the rest?"

"As I mentioned, we'll be meeting them in Chandley."

"No, I mean, where is the rest of the army?"

"Merceria transported men to Ironcliff using magic. We'll join them, along with the Dwarves, when we arrive."

"And how large will that make our army?"

"That's difficult to say," said Heward. "I only have approximations for the Orcs and no details of which men are in Ironcliff. As for the Dwarves, I believe their army sits at around four hundred."

"Is that all?"

"That estimate is based on the number that marched with us during the war. If they're besieged, that will double or even triple; though, in that eventuality, I can't speak to the quality of the defenders."

"Aren't the mountain folk mighty warriors?"

"They are," said Heward. "At least their army is. In a siege, however, they'll be forced to arm everyone who can carry a weapon, and those are the folks I'm worried about. Not everyone is well-suited to the life of a warrior."

"But they'll be defending their homes. Surely that accounts for something?"

"Aye, it does, but passion will only get you so far. Simply holding a sword doesn't mean you're ready to leap into battle."

"Yet that's what they'll be forced to do, isn't it? I wish there were something we could do to help."

"We already are," replied Heward, "by marching to their aid."

"But you said we can't defeat them."

"No. I said our first encounter wasn't about winning. Our ultimate objective is still the destruction of the Halvarian army, but we must take our time and wear them down. Don't get me wrong, if I see a chance to defeat them on the field of battle, I'll take it, but I'd prefer to conserve our strength until we can do something useful with it."

Naran nodded. "There's so much to learn."

"You're still a captain. You've got plenty of time."

"Her Majesty means to make me a commander—she told me herself."

"She never informed me."

"And why would she? With all due respect, you're a Mercerian, and she wants a Norlander leading her army. That said, she's more than happy to leave you in command this time."


The fireplace crackled, throwing a spark out onto the floor. Lord Preston, the closest, stomped it out with his boot, which brought a look of disapproval from his wife, Lady Sophie.

"It's so nice to have you here," said Anna. "It feels like ages since you and Sophie were married."

"Nonsense," replied Gerald. "That was only last spring."

"No, it wasn't," corrected Lady Jane. "It was back in ninety-six before we recaptured Summersgate."

"So it was. My goodness, how quickly time passes. Still, it's good to see you here, Preston. I've been meaning to have a chat with you."

"Not now," said the queen. "We are here to socialize, not carry on with the affairs of state."

"Can't we do both?" Gerald shifted in his chair, and Storm stirred, raising his head to see what Gerald was up to, then thumped his tail.

Jane chuckled. "Someone is enjoying himself. Tell me, Majesty, why is it he lays at Gerald's feet and not yours?"

"It's the wolf inside him," replied the queen.

"I'm afraid you'll have to explain that."

"Have you not heard the story of the grey wolf?"

"No. I thought it was a term of endearment."

"It's a long tale, I'm afraid. Gerald will have to tell you the full story, but suffice it to say, he has a way with dogs."

"You mean he likes them?"

"It's far more than that. The Kurathian Mastiffs all bow down before him."

"Now you're pulling my leg," said Jane.

"No," added Gerald. "It's true; though, for the life of me, I have no idea why. Perhaps it has something to do with what happened in the Greatwood?"

"Possibly," replied Anna. "The first mention of wolves occurred when you drank the milk of life. Do you remember?"

"I can hardly forget. I thought I was going to die."

"You know full well the Orcs wouldn't have permitted that."

"You say that now, but that wasn't my belief then."

"So this wolf," prodded Jane, "it's inside you?"

"I prefer to think of it more as a guiding spirit."

"The grey wolf, a fitting name for the Marshal of Merceria. What did they call you in your youth, the brown wolf?"

"Very funny."

She smiled back. "I try."

"Well, it's better than some names I've been called. Then again, I was a sergeant once, so I used that sort of language myself."

"And now you're pleasant and refined," said Jane. "I like this version of you."

He looked down, brushing dog hair from his leg.

"Lord Preston," said Anna. "Is something worrying you? You look troubled."

"I am merely concerned, Majesty. We are facing the prospect of war with an enemy we know very little about."

"Not quite true," said Gerald. "We know their land is large enough to attack Ironcliff and Stonecastle simultaneously. That alone indicates it's much bigger than Merceria. We also have Albreda's estimation of how many men are massing near Stonecastle."

"Have they similar numbers up in the north?"

"That remains to be seen. I've asked Revi to go and look, but we've yet to hear back from him."

"You must give him a chance," said the queen. "He only just arrived and still needs to get close enough to the enemy to scout out their army."

"How many of our men are up there now?"

"Two companies of horse," said Gerald, "with another standing by here for transport. We would have sent them sooner, but the mages had other, more pressing matters."

"That's largely my fault," explained Anna. "There's been so much traffic between Wincaster and Summersgate of late."

"Trouble?"

"Not as yet, only rumours, but they bear monitoring."

"What type of rumours?" asked the marshal.

"There's been some trouble in the Clanholdings. Alric has people looking into it, but you know how isolated the Clans are. It could be months before we receive any details."

"That could prove troublesome," said Preston. "If there are issues farther west, it could tie up the army of Weldwyn."

"Yes," added Gerald, "and then they'd be unable to send us aid. This sounds a little too inconvenient to be mere coincidence."

"Can we stand against Halvaria without Weldwyn's aid?"

"Only if we prevent them from gaining a foothold in our territory, which includes Norland. The key to the coming campaign will be our efforts to tie them down in Ironcliff and Stonecastle, freeing up companies to withstand their real attack."

"Real attack?" said Preston. "You suspect a third assault?"

"Yes. Is that so surprising? If you were going to invade Merceria, would you really choose to attack two Dwarven strongholds?"

"What other alternatives have they?"

"This trouble in the Clanholdings is one possibility, but that doesn't represent much of a direct threat to us other than tying down an ally. I've suspected the real assault will come from the sea for some time now."

"Have we taken precautions?"

"Actually," replied the queen, "that's one of the reasons we asked you here."

"I thought you said we were here to socialize, not discuss matters of state?"

"I did, didn't I? I must admit that was a bit of a fib. We can still socialize, but I am the queen. By my very nature, whatever I discuss is an affair of state."

Sophie smiled. "Well played, Majesty."

"Thank you. I have my moments. Now, where was I?"

"Precautions," offered her maid.

"Yes. That's right, but I'd best leave that to Gerald."

Everyone looked at the marshal.

"As you know," he began, "we've sent warriors to Stonecastle and Ironcliff. Unfortunately, that doesn't leave us much to defend Merceria. In Beverly's absence, I've put Herdwin in charge to the east, and naturally, King Thalgrun will command the allied army in the north, ably assisted by Lords Heward and Lanaka."

"And the rest of the kingdom?" asked Preston.

"That's where you come in. I've decided to send you to Colbridge. There, you'll assume command of the garrison. Your job will be to reinforce Tog in Trollden if it proves necessary."

"Why not move them directly there?"

"Until the enemy strikes, we won't know their plans. If they somehow bypass Trollden, your men will be needed to prevent them from spreading out."

"What forces are presently there?"

"The city garrison has been reinforced, and I've sent some of our heavy horsemen to help, along with the Guard Cavalry. You'll be acting as brigade-commander until further notice, but Tog has overall command of the area, as he's more familiar with it. Any questions?"

"When do I leave?"

"Whenever you're ready, but I prefer it to be soon. There's no telling when the enemy might act."

# THIRTY-ONE

# Deceit

WINTER 967 MC

K elson Shozarin walked across the Palace grounds on a chilly afternoon, although snow had yet to appear in the capital. Several workers were covering the shrubs with burlap sacks, evidence frigid days would soon be upon them.

He ignored everyone, giving them no more than a cursory glance, his attention focused on the matter at hand. He slowed as he approached the Victory Fountain, searching for the person he was to meet.

"About time you showed up."

Her voice caught him off guard, for somehow, despite his precautions, she'd slipped in behind him. He turned, trying to maintain his calm demeanour. "Ah, Edora. I wondered when you'd show up."

"Liar. You knew I'd be waiting."

He forced a smile. "I did. You are the most punctual person I've ever met."

"Well?" she said. "Have you any information for me?"

Kelson looked around, but no one else was within earshot. "I have. Our suspicions have been confirmed."

"Do you have proof of this?"

"Only what I've heard with my own ears, but I recently came into possession of several documents which might reveal more. Unfortunately, it will take me some time to get through them."

"Perhaps I could lend a hand?" said Edora. "After all, your duties as High Sentinel must take a considerable amount of your time?"

"I am more than capable of the task," he snapped back.

"Yes, I suppose you are, but then again, if he's planning something nefarious, would it not be better to counter him now rather than later?"

"Let's not rush into this. Yes, I confirmed he has another agenda, but I've yet to hear him say precisely what that might be."

"You know as well as I that he covets the position of emperor. He wants to displace the Stormwinds and Sartellians and take the Gilded Throne as the sole ruler."

"Can you claim your line has never considered their own version of that?"

"There's one big difference," said Edora. "While we've discussed the matter, we have never acted on it. Can we now trust Exalor to do the same? You and I both know he's greedy for power, and this so-called accident removed the Marshal of the North from the picture. If he's going to act, it's likely to be soon."

"I don't think so," said Kelson. "At the moment, his attention is firmly fixed on the destruction of Merceria. Once that's complete, he'll have three legions at his beck and call. More than enough to take the Gilded Throne for himself."

"With only three legions?"

"Ah, but they wouldn't be the only ones involved. The Marshal of the Empire is a fellow Shozarin. He'd likely support Exalor's claim."

Edora looked him straight in the eye. "As are you. How do I know your duplicity isn't part of a well-conceived plot to throw us off the scent?"

"The truth is, you don't."

"And you still want me to believe you. What possible reason could you have for betraying your line?"

"Look," said Kelson. "You and I both know the system in Halvaria isn't perfect, but it's worked for centuries. If we try to replace it with anything else, we're courting disaster."

"Yet if a Shozarin was made emperor, you would be the one most likely to benefit."

"I don't think you grasp the extent of Exalor's ego. It's one thing to have a puppet emperor, quite another to have one who actually rules!"

"I'm still not convinced you're being honest with me. Not that it matters. We still need to act, whether you're sincere or not. It won't go well for you, however, if this entire thing turns out to be a trick."

"I assure you it's nothing of the sort. Rather, it is an attempt to remove a possible impediment to the smooth running of the Shozarin line."

"So that's it, is it? A power play to elevate yourself within your own line?"

Kelson kept his expression neutral. "I said nothing of the sort."

"You didn't need to; your manner reveals your true intent. I am curious, though. If you wished to see Exalor removed, why did you save him after the attack on his life?"

"There are others who feel as he does, and killing him would only perpetuate his beliefs. I must see him thoroughly discredited to raise my status within the Shozarin line."

"And you expect us to do that for you?"

"Better for my line to suspect outside interference than someone from inside."

"Clever," said Edora. "But if this goes awry, it could start a war between our lines."

"And you don't think Exalor will do that with his unbridled quest for power? How long does the Inner Council last if he makes himself emperor?"

"Longer than you, I suspect. I'm afraid you'll need to offer something more than mere speculation if you want us to act."

Kelson looked around to ensure no one else had entered the area. "What if I offered you an opportunity?"

"I'm interested, but only if you get straight to the point."

"You need evidence to move against Exalor, yes?"

"Agreed," said Edora, "but it needs to be more than idle gossip."

"What if I could provide witnesses to his plans? People who could testify he was working against the emperor's interests?"

"Surely you're not suggesting that you yourself would speak out?"

"No, of course not. I'm much too careful for that. The last thing I want is to make myself a target. No. I have something else in mind, but you'd have to move quickly. Still interested?"

"You've intrigued me, but that's a far cry from us taking action. Who are these people?"

"Prisoners. Mercerians captured by our agents, who were then taken to Zefara."

"Why? Wouldn't it be more expedient to kill them?"

"That was what I thought," said Kelson. "But Exalor is of the mind they might prove more useful."

"More useful, how?"

"That's just it. I don't know."

"Perhaps they have information about Merceria that might help the campaign?"

"If that is the case, why has he taken no steps to interrogate them? My informants tell me he only met them once for a brief visit, and they've been kept in relative comfort ever since."

Edora considered the story. "Could he be secretly plotting an alliance with them? Perhaps he intends for Merceria to support his campaign to seize the Gilded Throne?"

"I would agree, had he sent them back home. Instead, he's kept them in Zefara. It's all quite mystifying."

"Where is Exalor now?"

"Here, in the capital, but I understand he will soon return north to keep a close eye on the early stages of the campaign. And that would provide the perfect opportunity for someone to snatch those prisoners."

"It would," said Edora. "The question is, how do we use them? The other problem is time. It won't take long for word to reach him that we've stolen them away, which means whatever we do must be done before he reacts. Are you sure they know his plans?"

"Does it matter? You know as well as I, prisoners can present whatever message you want. I can always have a truthseeker present to confirm the story you come up with."

"I shall consult with my peers; this is not a decision I can make alone."

"Understood," said Kelson, "but I would caution against delay. There is a very limited window of opportunity here. If you don't act soon, he may move the prisoners, and then the entire thing falls apart."

"Where are they being held?"

"I shall reveal all the details once you agree to take action."

"And if we don't?"

Kelson shrugged. "Then we'll say no more about the entire affair."


Evening found Edora making her way to the room of Agalix Sartellian. As usual, he was awake and perusing an old tome when she opened the door.

"Busy?" she asked.

He looked up from his book, squinting slightly to focus his eyes. Age was starting to take its toll on him physically, but his mind remained sharp.

"Edora? What brings you here at this time of night?"

"An opportunity," she replied. "Whether or not we should take advantage of it is another thing entirely."

He waved her to a seat. "You must tell me more."

"It has come to my attention that Exalor Shozarin seeks greater power, perhaps even the Gilded Throne itself."

"Many have tried over the centuries, but our way works the best. If you recall, the family infiltrated the ruling class of Halvaria almost five hundred years ago, and look at us now?"

"True, but if we are to remain in control, we must be vigilant."

"You make a good point," said Agalix. "Tell me, is this information about Exalor reliable?"

"I still haven't decided. It certainly fits his personality, yet I can't help but feel there's more to these accusations."

"Then perhaps you should trust your instincts. Tell me what you fear?"

"My information comes from a Shozarin," said Edora, "thus making it suspect. He could be telling the truth, but then that means the Shozarin line is struggling with internal divisions."

"Not an entirely unexpected development. Our own line had similar troubles in the past, as have the Stormwinds. That isn't the only possible explanation, though, is it?"

"No," she replied. "There's also the chance this leak is part of an elaborate plan to discredit us. I just can't figure out how that would work."

"I can," said Agalix, "and I don't even know the nature of this information you speak of. If we acted, and this opportunity proved false, what would happen?"

"We would likely be accused of treason, which would damage the influence of all Sartellians and foment unrest in the council."

He nodded sagely. "That is a possibility. Of course, it would be much easier to analyze this situation if you gave me the details."

"I have news that a pair of Mercerians are being held in Zefara, brought there by Exalor's agents."

"Mercerians, you say? How interesting. Have we any idea why he's taken an interest in them?"

"No, but there are rumours he told them his plans to seize the Gilded Throne."

"That seems highly unlikely to me. If he were plotting such a thing, he would keep it as secret as possible. Why tell a prisoner?"

"That's what I thought, but then it was suggested we need only use them to plant a seed of doubt concerning Exalor's loyalty."

"And who came up with that?"

"Kelson, the High Sentinel. He suggested his truthseekers would help validate the prisoners' claims, true or not."

"That would certainly make things more convenient," said Agalix, "but that knife could just as easily disembowel us."

"How?"

"Imagine this scenario, if you will. The prisoners are brought before the emperor or the High Council and give their story only to have the truthseekers reveal they are, in fact, lying. Instead of confirming the treachery of Exalor, it would make us look like we're the ones doing all the plotting!"

"You and I both know the truthseekers lie."

"We do, but it still plays into the theatre of politics, don't you see? Our very presence here, our shadow government running the empire, is one of deception and intrigue. The system works because we distrust the other lines yet are willing to perpetuate the myth that we all get along. If that breaks down, the empire, as we know it, would be shattered."

"So you're saying we all know they're lying, yet we still play along? Doesn't that give the Shozarins all the power?"

"In the sense Kelson is the High Sentinel, yes, but we've worked with him on multiple occasions, and it's always come out in our favour."

"So we trust him?"

"No," said Agalix, "not in the least. My general rule of thumb is we don't do anything that can be turned against us."

"What if these prisoners actually know something?"

"I suppose that's a legitimate concern, but if we did act here, we'd need to minimize the danger to ourselves."

"What do you suggest?" asked Edora.

"The first step would be securing these so-called prisoners. For all we know, they may not even be Mercerians."

"You suspect they are agents of Exalor?"

"What better way to spread false lies?"

"Are you suggesting they would throw their lives away to damage our reputation?"

"Yes," said Agalix. "Is that so hard to believe? Our history is full of people sacrificing themselves for the greater good of our own line. Why would the Shozarins be any different?"

"You see much more in this than I do."

"Of course. I'm older. In time, your own experiences will shed light on such things."

"I suppose this means I should leave these prisoners where they are?"

"No. If I were you, I'd retrieve them. Better to have them under our control and not use them than for them to tell their story to another, more sympathetic line."

Edora chuckled. "A more sympathetic line? The only one left is the Stormwinds, yet you refrain from naming them out loud. Do they truly hold that much fear for you?"

"Not at all. I am merely being diplomatic. You yourself are usually quiet at meetings of the Inner Council, yet when we meet privately, you talk my ear off. You must learn to be more circumspect in your choice of words both publicly and in private."

"Then I shall arrange to bring the prisoners here to Varena at the first opportunity. What do I do with them once we have them?"

"The first step," said Agalix, "will be to sit down and have a little chat with them."

"Don't you mean interrogation?"

"If you're suggesting torture, then no. Such methods seldom yield any information of value. I prefer a more delicate touch."

"Meaning?"

"To my mind, it's far easier to establish the truth of a matter through simple conversation. Those who lie will often be tripped up by inconsistencies in their story."

"And if there is nothing to their story?"

"Then we make them disappear, permanently. These Mercerians are useless to us if they won't support our narrative."

"And if they agree to help?"

"Well," said Agalix, "that largely depends on what they're willing to reveal. It's one thing to say Exalor is plotting, but what are his exact plans? Has he a timetable? Do we know which legions might be involved? There are too many variables to make definite long-term plans. You agree to fetch them; let's deal with that first. Once they're in our custody, we'll meet again to discuss options."

That evening found Kelson sitting by the fire. Recent reports from his truthseekers indicated a rising discontent within the empire, fueled by the loss in Arnsfeld. Six years ago, one of the empire's legions marched to defeat in the north.

Militarily, it was only a minor setback, but the loss had spurred hope in the territories under Halvaria's control. The campaign against Merceria needed to succeed if only to quash any thoughts of overthrowing the empire's rule. With their dominance reasserted, they could continue building towards the great dream.

A knock on the door startled him. "Who is it?"

"A friend," came the reply.

He recognized the voice. "Come in, Murias." He waited for her to open the door. "Care for a drink?"

She took a seat as he poured her some wine. "You wanted to see me?" she asked.

"Not you, specifically, but definitely a Stormwind, yes."

"Are we going to start a tedious conversation, or can you get directly to the point?"

"Now you've upset me," replied Kelson. "Can two colleagues not share their experiences of the day?"

"I'm a busy woman," said Murias, "and I'm sure your duties as High Sentinel give you plenty to do. Must we continue with this charade?"

"No. I suppose not." He put down his drink, steepling his fingers as he pondered how to begin. "No doubt you are familiar with what goes on behind the Palace walls."

"That goes without saying. Why?"

He ignored her question. "As High Sentinel, a great many things come across my desk. Most are trivial matters, but every now and then, a tidbit of information appears that cannot be ignored. It just so happens I discovered something of that nature this very day."

"It must be strange indeed if you feel it necessary to bring it to a Stormwind. I would have thought your own line more suitable to hear such things."

"And ordinarily, I would have agreed, but in this case, it concerns something of interest to all of us."

"Which is?"

"It appears there has been some plotting of late."

"That's nothing out of the ordinary. The empire is rife with it. What makes this instance any different?"

"This is the kind of thing that leads to problems for all of us."

"Now you've piqued my interest."

Kelson smiled, knowing the trap was complete. "What if I said an opportunity has presented itself?"

# THIRTY-TWO

## Intercession

WINTER 967 MC

B everly stared down at Sir Owen, but all he could do was shield his eyes against the sun and squint up at her.

"Are you recovered?" she asked.

"From?"

"Last night's celebrations. You drank more than your fill of the Orc brew."

He strained to sit up, then placed his hand on his forehead. "My head hurts. How is it you aren't in a similar state?"

"Unlike you, I drink in moderation."

The knight got to his feet, wobbling slightly. "What time is it?"

"Well past noon."

"I slept that long?"

"Look for yourself," said Beverly, pointing at the afternoon sun. "You'd best get some water into you."

"Can't I go back to sleep?"

"No. We have work to do. Lest you forget, we came here seeking a shaman."

"It's not my fault the Orcs wanted to celebrate."

"I didn't mean to infer it was, but the time for such things is now at an end. I was going to suggest we speak with the chieftain, Lurzak, but you'd be useless to me in your current state."

"All the more reason I should stay here. In any case, I don't know their language, so my help would have been of questionable value anyway."

"I suppose I can't argue with logic like that."

"Good luck," said Sir Owen. "And feel free to let me know how you've made out after I've slept some more."

Beverly shook her head, then set off for the great hut. She was only halfway there when she spotted Krazuhk heading for an intercept course.

"*Redblade*," the Orc called out. "*I would have words.*"

"*Most certainly*," replied Beverly, effortlessly switching to the Orcish language. "*What can I do for you?*"

"*I wanted to talk to you before you met with my father.*"

"*Concerning?*"

"*Your request for aid. You indicated the Human king in these parts is ill. I wondered if you might provide me with more information regarding his illness.*"

"*I wasn't aware you were a shaman.*"

Krazuhk chuckled, a deep-throated sound reminding her of Kraloch. "*I am a master of air, not a healer, but your tale interests me. You said your cousin was a... What did you call her?*"

"*A Life Mage, and an accomplished one at that.*"

"*Yet she was unable to heal this king. My question to you is, why did you come to us? Do you think our shamans can succeed where your own failed?*"

"*My cousin Aubrey has worked closely with a shaman called Kraloch. Between them, they developed a method of healing which is much more effective in treating ailments of an arcane nature.*"

"*Are you suggesting this illness is magical?*"

"*Yes. A corruption of the mind caused by exposure to the energy of ley lines. Are you familiar with them?*"

"*The lines of force? Most definitely. According to the Ancestors, the stone gates that pepper the entire Continent were built upon them.*"

"*Have you one here?*"

"*I am afraid not*," said Krazuhk. "*But our original village far to the west had one. Unfortunately, the Humans destroyed it when they drove us from our ancestral home.*"

"*I'm sorry to hear that.*"

"*There is nothing you could have done to prevent it, but we are getting off-topic. You were speaking of the ley lines?*"

"*Yes, that's right*," said Beverly. "*One of our mages, Revi Bloom, tried to study them and spent too much time in their proximity. Aubrey discovered a complex ritual that eventually cured him, but it required the participation of a second mage.*"

"*The healer, Kraloch, which you mentioned earlier?*"

"*Yes.*"

"*And you are certain she could reproduce this ritual with a shaman helping her?*"

"She wouldn't have suggested it if she couldn't. Do you think Bloodrig changed her mind about helping us?"

"I doubt it," said Krazuhk. "But, as she is so fond of saying, she is not the only shaman within the tribe."

"If not her, then who?"

"I suspect the most logical candidate would be Garok. Although he is not yet considered a fully trained shaman, he has shown remarkable progress. He is also far more likely to agree to travel."

"Why is that?"

"Like me, he has an adventurous soul."

"You appear to know him well."

"He and I are of a similar age. We underwent our ordeals within the same season. Are you familiar with our customs in this regard?"

"It's your coming-of-age ceremony, isn't it? If I recall, you must survive in the wilderness for a ten-day."

"You are correct."

"Should I approach him directly?"

"No. That would be seen as an insult. If you wish to offer Garok the chance to accompany you back to the Human king, you must seek our chieftain's permission."

"You mean your father?" said Beverly. "Couldn't you ask on our behalf?"

"That would make you appear weak. I am surprised you are unaware of that, considering how much time you say you spent in the company of Orcs."

"The Black Arrows are less strict about such things, likely due to their familiarity with Humans. Any advice on how best to deal with your father?"

"With patience. He likes to weigh his options carefully. He will also wish to be fully informed about the situation before he deigns to make a decision."

"As we all should. Thank you. I shall bear that in mind."

"Good," said Krazuhk. "Now, let us go and enter the great hut to discuss this with the Chieftain of the Sky Singers." She took a step, then paused. "On second thought, I have another piece of advice for you."

"Which is?"

"Speak in a soft tone and refrain from raising your voice."

"To avoid conflict?"

"No, to avoid irritating him when he is suffering."

"Suffering? Is he ill?"

"Only from imbibing too much last evening."

Lurzak stared back, unblinking. Beverly had laid out her idea but, so far, had seen nothing to indicate the chieftain's opinion on the matter.

"*It is a well-thought-out plan,*" added Krazuhk, "*and is of little risk to us. The benefits, however, have the potential to be life-changing.*"

"*I am aware of that,*" replied her father, "*but I must weigh not only the danger to the tribe but to Garok himself. What if this Human king refuses to honour the agreement?*"

"*I doubt he would dare do such a thing,*" replied Beverly. "*Kings who betray agreements soon find themselves isolated and alone. He'll likely be glad to be away from death's door. There's also the spectre that his illness might return one day, in which case he would again need your help.*"

Lurzak turned to his shaman. "*What do you think, Bloodrig?*"

"*It is worth pursuing, providing Garok is willing to undertake the journey. He should not, however, travel alone.*"

"*I will be with him,*" said Beverly, "*as will Sir Owen.*"

"*This I understand,*" replied Bloodrig, "*but we must consider what could happen once you leave this land.*"

Lurzak grunted. "*You are always stirring up trouble, Bloodrig. What is it you are suggesting?*"

"*Merely that we send hunters to accompany Garok.*"

"*How many?*"

"*I would think ten is a suitable number. Would you not agree?*"

"*Ten, it is, but I will only send those who volunteer.*"

"*Agreed.*"

Lurzak stared at his shaman. "*I am glad you remember that I, the chieftain, will make the final decision. Now, may we proceed?*"

"*By all means.*"

Lurzak turned back to Beverly. "*It seems you have our answer. Krazuhk, it will be your duty to speak with Garok and determine if he is willing to undertake this journey. While you do that, I shall look for ten hunters to escort him.*"

"*You need only nine, Father. I am going.*"

"*You are a master of air, not a hunter.*"

"*Yes, one of five, which means I can be spared.*"

"*This is not a game, Krazuhk. There is real danger out there.*"

"*It has been some years since I passed my ordeal, Father, yet still you treat me as a youngling. I mastered the magic of air; what else must I do to prove myself to you?*"

Lurzak wanted to say more, but the presence of Beverly seemed to hold him in check. "*It is true,*" he finally admitted. "*You are grown and a full member of the tribe, capable of making your own decisions, but you will always be my daughter. I will not apologize for voicing my concern. If you wish to accompany Garok to Agran, that is your decision. I rescind my objection.*"

"*Thank you, Father.*"

The chieftain looked at Beverly, his face flushing a deeper shade of green. *"I apologize. This was neither the time nor the place to talk of such things."*

*"Do not apologize,"* she replied. *"It is not so different amongst Humans."*

*"Have you children?"*

*"No. At least not yet."*

*"And your parents?"*

*"My father joined the Ancestors only last year."*

*"And your mother?"*

*"I never knew her; she died the night I was born."*

The chieftain nodded. *"It was so with Krazuhk, but I see my bondmate's spirit behind those eyes."*

*"I will keep her safe,"* said Beverly. *"I promise you."*

*"I shall hold you to that promise, Redblade. Now, I suggest you gather that knight of yours. You have a long journey ahead of you."*

*"Have we your permission to leave today?"*

*"Tomorrow would be better,"* said Lurzak. *"That gives us time to gather the others and prepare food for your journey."*

*"Then tomorrow it shall be."*


They set out at dawn, heading west into the early morning mist. The two knights led the way lest they encounter Humans on their journey. Owen was in fine spirits, and as the mist cleared, Beverly found him chuckling.

"Something you want to share?" she asked.

He grinned back. "I was imagining the look on the Palace guards when we show up with a dozen Orcs."

"There's eleven, not twelve."

"Close enough by my count."

"You should learn to be more precise. It's an important trait in a Knight of the Hound."

"Isn't martial prowess more important?"

"Don't get me wrong," said Beverly. "The ability to fight is important, but more often than not, we're in positions of authority. Accurately assessing an opponent's strength can mean the difference between victory and defeat."

Owen sobered. "Sorry. I meant no offence."

"Nor did I. I mention it to bring it to your attention. Your traditions here in the Petty Kingdoms are different from those of Merceria. It's important we make note of them."

"I shall bear that in mind in future." He glanced once more at the Orcs before turning back to Beverly. "Are the greenskins back in Merceria armed the same as these?"

"We don't call them that."

"Then what do you call them?"

"Orcs," said Beverly. "That is their name after all."

"Still, you haven't answered my question."

"The Sky Singers are armed much as the Orc hunters back in Merceria."

"Are there Orcs who aren't hunters?"

"Technically, they all consider themselves hunters, but we've trained some in close-order formations and armed them with long spears. They've proven effective in battle."

"I wonder if the Orcs here are so inclined?"

"I suspect it depends more on how they were trained than any particular inclination."

"You speak like a true warrior. Just exactly how many battles have you seen?"

"Too many. I know you've read battle is honourable or glorious, but the truth is, it's neither."

"All the knightly orders of the Continent would say otherwise."

"If they told the truth, no one would wish to join their ranks."

"Perhaps that's only your perspective. You are a woman after all." He paused as he realized what he'd said. "Sorry. I meant no offence. It's just that battle is not something we men of the Petty Kingdoms associate with women."

"I'm from a warrior culture," said Beverly, "and while few women rise to become famous warriors, it's not unknown. I would also point out I am not the only one with such beliefs. Our marshal is of a similar mind, and he's been a warrior far longer than I."

"You speak of a warrior culture, yet I was always taught the Petty King-doms were in a state of perpetual war."

"But you said you've never seen battle. How is that possible?"

"I fought off bandits, but I suppose you might consider that more of a skirmish. The truth is, very few knights will ever witness more than one war, perhaps two in their lifetime."

"I'm confused," said Beverly. "You just said the Petty Kingdoms were constantly at war."

"I did give that impression, and for that, I apologize. I meant to say there's always a war somewhere in the Petty Kingdoms, but not the same kingdom."

"Just how many Petty Kingdoms are there?"

"You know, I'm not exactly sure. I've heard estimates of fifty, all the way to almost a hundred. It would depend to a large extent on how you define a Petty Kingdom."

"What do you mean?"

"Well, take Therengia, for example; by that, I mean the new one, not the old one. I'm told it sits far to the east, but I doubt many would consider it a Petty Kingdom. There's also the city-state of Corassus, which isn't really a kingdom at all."

"I get the idea," said Beverly. "It's complicated."

"Far more so than it needs to be, in my opinion."

"And who are the major powers?"

"I'm not sure what you are asking?"

"Let me put it another way. Which kingdoms have the strongest armies?"

"That's difficult to say. I would have said Hadenfeld in this region, but they've had troubles of their own these last few years. If you go far to the east, they say Therengia has a great army, although I've heard nothing of their numbers. All pale in comparison to Halvaria, however."

"Halvaria?" said Beverly. "We've had problems with them back home. What can you tell me about them?"

"They are an empire lying west of the great mountains. They've existed for over a thousand years and are intent on claiming the entire Continent for their own."

"Anything else you can tell me?"

"Why? Are they threatening you?"

"Not so much us as our allies."

"Then you should prepare for the inevitable invasion. They won't stop until all your lands are under their thumb."

"Do they not threaten the Petty Kingdoms?"

"They do, but they seem content to only absorb us at the rate of one kingdom every ten years or so."

"How generous of them. Do you not come to each other's aid?"

"The Petty Kingdoms are a mess of alliances and enemies. Getting everyone to agree to work together would take a miracle."

"But if what you say is true, why hasn't this empire defeated all of you?"

Owen smiled. "That's simple. They fear the Church."

"That would be the Church of the Saints?"

"Well, not so much the Church itself as the fighting orders. Have you no Temple Knights where you're from?"

"We most certainly do not," said Beverly, "though I met some back in Agran. How many orders of Temple Knights are there?"

"Only three of any consequence," said Owen. "The rest are primarily confined to the Antonine, or so I'm led to believe."

"What's the Antonine?"

"That's where the Church is based, a sort of city within a city, if you will."

"I'm not sure I understand what you mean."

"It's Church property," said Owen. "An independent state in the middle of the Kingdom of Regensbach. There's no other place quite like it."

"You've been there?"

"Me? Saints, no. That's hundreds of miles away. Still, I'd like to see it one day."

"You said there are three orders of consequence. I assume one of those is the Temple Knights of Saint Agnes?"

"Yes, and the other two are Saint Mathew and Saint Cunar, the last being the backbone of the Holy Army. It's the one thing that's historically held off the Halvarians."

"So they've fought the empire?"

"Not to my knowledge."

"Then how did they hold them off?"

"Through the threat of their involvement."

"By your own admission," said Beverly, "they haven't stopped the empire's growth. You said earlier they absorb another kingdom every ten years."

"I did, didn't I? I'm afraid the politics of the Petty Kingdoms have never been my area of expertise."

"You know a remarkable amount about Halvaria, though."

"Of course," said Owen. "It's the biggest threat to us. Every knight on the Continent knows about them."

"What do you know of their army?" asked Beverly.

"You mean armies," he corrected. "They have many, although they prefer to use the term legions. Each is a balance of horse, foot, and bow. Just one of them outnumbers any army fielded by a Petty Kingdom."

"What kind of numbers are we talking about here?"

Owen shrugged. "No one seems to know for certain, but estimates range from two to three thousand. Does that give you a better idea of what your own kingdom is up against?"

"It does, although I was more comfortable when I didn't know. Our allies are facing not one, but likely two of these legions unless they would spread them out over large areas?"

"I doubt they'd do that," said Owen. "They like to keep their legions concentrated when they attack."

"That's what I was afraid you were going to say."

## THIRTY-THREE

# Allies

WINTER 967 MC

H eward led his men towards Chandley, and the biting winds blowing in from the north made the long march seem even more so. They were exhausted, yet the sight of their allies emboldened them. Lord Calder's men waited by the side of the road, lifting spirits, but the presence of the Orcs caused the most interest, for the Black Ravens had arrived with three hundred Orcs and cavalry amongst their numbers.

Lord Heward spotted Ghodrug, their chieftain, and rode towards her. "*Greetings,*" he called out, using the language of the Orcs.

"Well met," she replied, in the Human tongue.

"You surprise me, Ghodrug. I didn't know you spoke our language."

"Many Humans elected to stay in Ravensguard since we were given control of it. I took it upon myself to learn their language to better rule over them."

"And how has that gone?"

"Surprisingly well. There are a small minority who still object to our presence, but the vast majority settled down now that they realize we mean them no harm."

"I imagine a lot of them expected reprisals. After all, they treated your people terribly."

"That is not our way."

"Sorry," said Heward. "I didn't mean to imply it was, merely that most Humans expected it."

"If there is one thing I learned in the last few years, it is that Humans are far more complicated than I expected."

"Did you run into any trouble on the way here?"

"Not at all, but it was mostly wilderness. What manner of creature would take an interest in so many Orcs?"

"You make an excellent point."

"Now we are all here in Chandley, what are your plans?"

"I'd like to rest my men for a day before we move up the road towards Holdcross."

"I am not familiar with the area. How far of a trip is that?"

"Just shy of a hundred miles. Once we're there, we'll be within striking distance of the enemy, so we must take care."

"My Orc cavalry is at your disposal." She looked around at the men as they filed into the camp. "I expected you to have more horses of your own."

"Queen Bronwyn was lucky to raise one company," replied Heward, "but I'm told there are at least two Mercerian companies up at Ironcliff."

"That still leaves us weak."

"It does. And those we have are all lightly armoured."

"There was little we could do about it," replied Ghodrug. "We Orcs are new to riding horses, and up until now, very few of our hunters wore armour. Since retaking Ravensguard, we have had the armourers working day and night, yet we could not equip more than three companies of spearmen with mail. Had we more time…"

"I shan't complain. Your spear carriers will doubtless prove their worth. Did you bring archers?"

She smiled. "I did. One hundred, to be exact, and they are armed with warbows."

"You have been busy," said Heward. "Even the Orcs of the Black Arrows haven't been able to field those numbers."

"True, but they are not under threat of attack. We Black Ravens must remain strong to dissuade the Norlanders from retaking the city."

"That's fair."

"I also saw fit to bring Kharzug, our master of earth, along with one of our younger shamans, Rulahk."

"I'm sure their presence will be most appreciated. If you're available, I'd like to meet with you and Lord Calder this evening to discuss tactics." He glanced over at the town's buildings. "Now, where should we go?"

"Have you no tent?"

"I do," replied Heward, "but the night grows cold, and the last thing I want is for us to be shivering while we're trying to make plans. It would be far too distracting."

"There is an inn called the Green Pony which might prove suitable. I am told the men of Lord Calder's army frequent it. Shall I make enquiries on your behalf?"

"If you would be so kind. Now, I'd best hunt down the earl. The last thing I need is to lose him in the streets of this town."

"How does one lose an earl?" asked Ghodrug. "The town is not so large that he could simply disappear amongst its people."

"It's not so much that he'd disappear, but that he would soon be incapacitated."

"I am afraid I do not understand."

"The earl," said Heward, "likes his drink and often does so excessively. He'll be completely useless if I don't nip it in the bud."

"Ah, yes. The Human proclivity for imbibing alcohol. I have seen much of it since retaking Ravensguard."

"Then you understand what we're up against."

"On the contrary. While I understand the effects of too much drink, I do not grasp why Humans insist on carrying it to extremes."

"In some cases, it serves to help us forget the horrors of war."

"And Lord Calder?"

"I think for him, it's the fact he ended up on the losing side. You could call it shame, although humiliation might be a better name. Had his side won the civil war, he'd be one of the rulers of Norland."

"Is he not still an earl?"

"He is," said Heward, "but his words don't carry the same weight as they used to."

"Is that why he is here with us?"

"I believe it is. He wants to make amends by showing his support for the queen."

"So he is now loyal to the very regime he opposed?"

Heward chuckled. "It seems you have become knowledgeable regarding the politics of Norland."

"Only out of necessity. The recent war is still very much on people's minds, both Orc and Human. If we are to live in peace, it serves us well to learn more about each other."

"It does."

"I have detained you long enough," said Ghodrug. "As you said earlier, you must hunt down Lord Calder before he is... What is the Human expression?"

"Drunk?"

"Yes. That is the one."

They met that evening in the back room of the Green Pony. Heward, Ghodrug, and Lord Calder stared down at a map spread out on the table.

"We are here," said the earl, "while Holdcross lies some ninety miles distant. If we wished, we could ride cross-country, thus avoiding the hills to our north, but I'd say the better choice would be to follow the road. At least we won't lose our way."

"Are you suggesting we are unable to navigate in the wilds?" asked the Orc.

"Not at all, but there are supply wagons to consider, and they're not the most manoeuvrable of things."

Heward leaned lower, examining the scrawls. "Not the most detailed of maps, is it?"

"There's little we can do to improve it," said Calder. "There are but three towns in the area, with roads to connect them. What else does one need in a map?"

"A sense of scale?"

"Yes, I suppose that would be nice. Then again, up until now, there has been no need. This part of Norland has seen little in the way of battle."

"Was there not a battle at Holdcross during the war?"

Calder looked away for a moment. "Yes. I was afraid you'd bring that up."

"Please explain," said Ghodrug.

"If I must," replied the earl. "During the war, the Dwarves of Ironcliff marched on us at the behest of the Mercerians. They met outside of Holdcross and won themselves a victory."

"I think there's a little more to the story," said Heward. "My understanding is it was a crushing defeat for Norland. So complete was the victory, the Dwarves of Ironcliff marched south, assisting in the latter stages of the war."

"Yes. Well, I suppose that's one way of looking at it."

"I might also point out the presence of those Dwarves let us defeat the spirit army of Kythelia, something which benefited both our realms."

"All true," said Calder, "yet here we are, two and a half years later, working together, Norlander and Mercerian. Even stranger, we count Orcs as our allies!"

"And a good thing too," said Heward, "else we'd lack the numbers to do much of anything." He stabbed his finger down. "Have you any additional troops here at Holdcross?"

"Only a small garrison, and most are little more than peasants."

"Peasants?" said Ghodrug. "I do not believe I am familiar with the term."

"They are mostly farmers," replied Calder, "lacking any proper weapons training."

Heward sighed. "What he means is he sees them as his social inferiors."

"I do not understand," said the Orc. "Are they not needed to supply the food vital to his survival?"

"They are indeed, but it is common amongst the nobility to denigrate those who perform manual labour. Not that I agree with it. I merely offer it as an observation."

"You're a baron yourself, Heward," said Calder. "Have you no servants of your own?"

"Of course, but unlike you, I value their contributions."

"Such bickering will get us nowhere," said Ghodrug. "We would be better served to concentrate on tactics."

"Yes, quite right," said Calder.

"If we encounter the enemy, what will be our response?"

"That largely depends on their numbers," said Heward. "If we found ourselves with a temporary numerical superiority, we would be well-advised to make a stand, but I'll not risk the lives of our troops needlessly."

"And if we are to make a stand, how would we form up for battle?"

"Foot to the front, archers behind, and horse on the flanks."

"Surely not," said Calder. "Wouldn't it be better if we deployed the archers on the flanks, with the horses in reserve?"

"That would expose our archers. They are better employed loosing arrows over the heads of our own troops. We also need horses placed to counter any threat from enemy cavalry."

"And if they outnumber us, do we still make a stand?"

"That largely depends on the composition of their forces," replied Heward. "If they're weak in cavalry, then we can make a stand knowing they can't outflank us."

"Footmen can still flank a line if they come in sufficient numbers."

"They can, but they'll pay heavily for it."

"So," said Calder, "you're saying we can't win?"

"Our objective isn't to win. It's to wear down their numbers and give them a reason to move more cautiously."

"I agree," said Ghodrug. "Slowing down their advance works to our advantage."

"I don't see how," replied the earl. "No additional men are coming our way. If we can't stop them with what we have, they'll flood into Norland."

"You forget. They still need to attack Ironcliff. That assault will tie up many of their warriors."

"But none of their cavalry, and that's the real danger." Calder looked at Heward. "Do we know how many horses are in the enemy army?"

"I'm afraid not. Early reports from Lanaka's men would indicate they use a screening force of light cavalry, but beyond that, we have no real numbers."

"Then we are doomed!"

"Not quite," said Ghodrug. "You forget. We have a master of earth along with a shaman, which allows us to prepare our defences should it prove necessary, as well as heal our wounded."

"Does the enemy employ magic wielders?"

"That's difficult to say," said Heward. "One of our commanders, Herdwin Steelarm, sent reports of something called truthseekers, but we have no idea what type of magic they wield."

"I suspect they are shamans," said Ghodrug. "Amongst the Ancestors, there are tales of shamans using their magic to tell if a person were lying, but such a spell has not proved necessary for generations."

"Because it was forgotten?" said Calder.

"No, because it was unnecessary. Orcs, by our very nature, do not lie. There are exceptions, but such things seldom require magic to determine the truth."

"Have you no courts? How do you enforce the rule of law?"

"We have few laws, as you call them. If one of our people misbehaves, they are brought before the entire tribe for judgement."

"The entire tribe? How in the name of the Gods does that work?"

"By the counting of stones," replied Ghodrug. "Each side in a dispute is given time to explain their position, and then the tribe votes on the outcome, with shamans acting as neutral third parties."

Calder shook his head. "No wonder your people haven't progressed as a civilization."

"That's enough of that kind of talk," said Heward. "I might remind you we are allies here, not enemies."

"Yes, of course. I apologize. I'm not used to being in the presence of such a different culture."

"We, too, have had to adapt," replied Ghodrug. "I sense that if the future is to be prosperous, we must learn to work together."

Calder fell silent, staring at the map. "What about the order of march?" he finally said.

"The queen's cavalry will take the lead," replied Heward. "The footmen next, followed by your men, Lord Calder."

"And the Orcs?"

"I should like the Orc cavalry on either side, acting as a screening force, with the rest of their troops bringing up the rear behind the supply wagons."

"Why is that?"

"An Orc's gait is longer, allowing them to march faster should the situation demand it. If we encounter hostile warriors, they could move up to support our line faster than any Human troops."

"I concur," said Ghodrug.

"I'm curious," said Calder. "Your Orc cavalry is mounted on larger horses than those employed by the queen, yet they are unarmoured. How are we to use them in battle?"

"They will be employed in whatever manner Lord Heward sees fit."

"Have you no thoughts on the matter?"

"Mounted warriors are new to us," said Ghodrug. "Thus, I leave it to Lord Heward, an experienced warrior, to know best how to use them. Did I not make myself clear?"

"Now, listen here. There's no need to be rude."

The Orc ignored him. "In the interest of cooperation, I suggest we allow him to assume complete command of all our forces."

"Preposterous!"

"Our army is relatively small, so it makes little sense for three people to issue orders, particularly when such orders might prove contradictory. There is also the matter of Lord Heward's experience to consider. Have you won any battles, Lord Calder?"

"I can't claim I have."

"Nor can I, thus it makes sense for Lord Heward to take overall command, does it not?"

"Yes. I suppose it would."

"Thank you for that," said Heward.

"What about the Orc mages?" asked Calder.

"The shaman is easy to place," replied Heward, "but I suspect most of his work will be after the battle. As to their master of earth, I have little experience in how to best employ him. Have you any suggestions, Ghodrug?"

"There are many spells that might benefit us, but most require preparation."

"Such as?"

"They can shape the ground, creating small hills on which our warriors can claim a height advantage. The magic of the earth could also be used to create a wall of thorns, or an earth wall, providing us with some protection from arrows."

"Anything else?"

"Yes. Kharzug is capable of bringing forth a mist to obscure us if needed, as well as summoning wolves, assuming they exist in these parts."

"I fail to see how a few wolves would help," said Calder.

"It would be more than just a few, and their presence might upset enemy horses, their natural prey. You should be aware, however, there are limits to how many spells a master of earth can cast in a day."

"I shall bear that in mind," said Heward. "Thank you, both of you. You've been a great help to me today, not only by bringing your troops but with your advice and suggestions."

"Is that it?" said Calder. "Are we to now simply resume the march?"

"Not right away. We shall refrain from marching tomorrow, but I want to practice a few manoeuvres. If we are to fight together in the coming weeks, then it's vital our respective troops learn to work side by side for the betterment of all."

"You seem remarkably calm for someone in your position."

"Do I?" replied Heward. "I certainly don't feel calm. In fact, I would say I'm quite nervous."

"I was led to believe you were one of the most experienced warriors in all of Merceria."

"I am," said Heward, "but that doesn't mean I don't have doubts from time to time."

"Doubts? You don't show it."

"Over the years, I've developed a philosophy to guide me when it comes to battle."

"Perhaps you'd care to share it?"

"By all means. It all comes down to a simple question I ask myself. If I know the answer, I can work out how to get there."

"And this question is?" asked Lord Calder.

He smiled. "What would Beverly do?"

# THIRTY-FOUR

# Preparation

Alitor Verathras slowed his horse. Behind him rode his fellow mages, although one could hardly tell who they were from the thick fur wraps keeping the chill at bay. They drew up beside him, and he pointed at the camp ahead.

"There it is," he announced. "The Third Legion." His gaze drifted to the peaks off in the distance. "We'll camp here tonight and head to the tower first thing in the morning."

"Shouldn't we make ourselves known to the marshal?" asked Rhedra. "It would be rude to ignore him."

"You have a point, though I'm not looking forward to spending time in his company."

"Why? Is there bad blood between you?"

"None whatsoever, but the fellow is exceedingly dull, despite his so-called prowess as a mage, and I'm not sure how much of his company I can take."

"I heard he covets the position of High Strategos."

"Hardly surprising," replied Alitor. "All the marshals want that."

"Remind me again what line he's from?"

"Shozarin, the same as Exalor."

"Does that mean we can trust him?"

"What has trust to do with anything? He's the marshal. Ultimately, he's commanding the legion in these parts."

"That doesn't answer my question," said Rhedra.

Alitor swore under his breath. She could be contrary sometimes, and he believed she did it just to get on his nerves. He closed his eyes and took a deep breath to calm his temper.

"Well?" she pressed. "Have you an answer for me?"

"In the absence of the High Strategos, you take your orders from the marshal."

"I thought we took our orders from you?"

"You do, but I, in turn, must do what the marshal tells me."

"And why should that be of any interest to me?"

"Because if something happened to me, you would be expected to carry on in my stead. Do I make myself clear?"

"Most assuredly," said Rhedra.

"Good. Let us proceed to the camp." Alitor urged his horse forward, putting her from his mind, at least for the moment.

They'd only travelled a short distance when a pair of guards challenged them. After the mages announced themselves, they were escorted into the encampment of the Third Imperial Legion.

Rhedra noted the perfect lines of tents. "Impressive. I wonder how long it took them to learn to do that?"

"The normal training period of a new warrior is half a year," replied Alitor. "I'm surprised you didn't know that."

"My studies concentrated on the magic of the earth, not military matters."

"They trained you for the battlefield, did they not?"

"Naturally, but only in terms of how our magic might best serve the empire."

"Then tell me how we are to cross the gorge."

"That's easy," said Rhedra. "We grow those spikes like we've been practicing for months on end."

"I think you'll find there's much more to it than that."

"Perhaps you know a better way to cross the gap?"

Alitor grimaced. "We've gone over this before. There is no better way."

"Then why are you arguing?"

"I'm not arguing, merely pointing out the spikes alone won't work."

"Why not?"

"For the simple reason our warriors must cross the gap. How do you expect them to climb across spikes of rock?"

"Why couldn't they?"

"Well, for one thing, they'd lose their footing."

"So, what's your solution?"

"We use the spell of shaping stone to smooth the spikes out, thus creating a bridge. In that way, they'll be able to cross without putting themselves in danger."

"But they'll still be in danger while crossing."

"Nothing is guaranteed in any type of assault, particularly when the enemy expects you." He looked over his shoulder. "And that's where Graffard comes in."

"I'm not sure we should trust him—he's a Sartellian."

"He is, but it can't be helped. We need someone capable of forcing the defenders to keep their heads down while we cross, and Fire Magic is the best option."

"I note you didn't say ONLY option."

"I considered others," said Alitor, "but this approach requires fewer people to manage."

Rhedra met his gaze. "I… suppose that makes sense."

"You have a question. I see it in your eyes."

"I understand the need for Earth Mages here. My question is whether or not you think we have enough to complete the task at hand?"

"Of course, else I wouldn't be here."

She laughed. "You make it sound like you had a choice."

"We all serve the empire in our different ways, Rhedra. Mine happens to include obedience to the hierarchy. Is that so bad?"

"Don't you ever tire of the family taking all the top spots?"

"Be careful what you say," said Alitor. "The family rules over everything."

"Yet here we are, providing the very magic they don't possess. Sometimes, I think we should ask for equal status."

"Equal status? Are you mad? That would upset the delicate balance of power."

"What good is power if we are unable to attain it?"

"I would watch my words if I were you. You never know who's listening."

Rhedra looked over her shoulder at the five mages following them. "I will heed your warning."

They came to a halt, and Alitor dismounted, handing his reins to one of the legion's soldiers. Moments later, a man displaying the purple sash of a captain arrived to greet them.

"My lord. I am Captain Cardosa. I hope you're the mages we're expecting?"

"Indeed we are," replied Alitor. "Have you prepared tents for our use?"

"We have, Lord. If you follow me, I'll take you to them. My men will look after your horses."

"Thank you, Captain. Is the marshal available?"

"I'm afraid not. He's gone up to the gorge to take another look."

"Interesting. I'm eager to see it for myself. I've read all about it, but seeing it with one's own eyes is another thing. Have you seen it?"

"I have."

"And your impressions?"

The captain thought it over as the other mages dismounted. "The distance we need to cross is substantial."

"We are more than capable of providing that service," replied Alitor.

"Might I ask how?"

"Why, through magic, of course."

"I understand that, my lord. I hoped you could give us some idea of what spells you will employ."

"I would, but I'm afraid you'd find the explanation of how they work tiresome. In the past, I've often found those lacking in magic themselves cannot understand the intricacies of manipulating rock and stone. I assure you the situation is well in hand."

"Then I shall take your word for it, Lord." Having noted that all his guests were now on foot, the captain led them towards a group of tents sitting off by themselves. "We thought it best to give you some privacy," he explained, "but the guards will still patrol the area on foot to keep you safe. If you need anything, you have only to call out for them."

"Thank you. That's most thoughtful. Are you in command here?"

"No," said Cardosa. "I am but one of many captains serving in the Third. I am, however, the guard captain tonight. We take turns, you see—"

"An explanation is unnecessary," said Alitor.

"Yes, of course. My apologies, my lord." He stopped in front of the tents. "Shall I arrange for some food?"

"Most certainly."

"Then I bid you good afternoon."

The Earth Mage waited until the captain was out of earshot. "The sooner we can get out of here, the better."

"Why?" asked Rhedra. "Are you suggesting you don't like the idea of camping in the middle of a legion?"

"I find soldiers to be tiresome to the extreme. All they think about is fighting, whoring, and drinking."

"Your point being?"

"They are vulgar."

"They are Human, which is more than I can say for our enemy here."

"You speak of the mountain folk?"

She laughed. "Mountain folk? You make them sound like some wise old hermits who happen to live in the hills."

"I would take them seriously if I were you. It won't be long before we're within range of their bows."

"Bolts don't scare me."

"Well, they should," said Alitor. "I've heard they've already picked off more than a dozen of our archers with those crossbows of theirs."

"Arbalests," corrected Grafford, drawn in by their conversation.

"What would you know of such things?" asked Rhedra.

"I've made a study of them."

"Since when?"

"Since I heard we'd be coming here."

"Go on," urged Alitor. "I'm eager to hear what you've learned."

"They are stubborn folk, used to fighting in the mountains. They favour axes and hammers and typically protect themselves with links of mail."

"I could have told you that."

"Perhaps," continued Grafford, "but are you aware those arbalests of theirs can pierce our strongest mail at up to a hundred paces? I would take great care while up at the gorge; the empire has invested a lot in your training."

"Coins well spent," offered Rhedra. "What of yourself? Have you any magic that might benefit us during the assault?"

"I'm a Fire Mage. What do you think?"

"I'm sure you're more than capable, but I was hoping for some examples of spells you might use to keep the enemy at bay while we work."

Grafford placed his finger on his chin, tapping it. "I considered several, but I have yet to see where the assault will occur. I'm also led to believe the Dwarves took it upon themselves to fortify their side of the gorge."

"In other words, you're in the same situation as the rest of us."

"That is an accurate assessment, yes."

"Then it appears we are all in this together."

"Enough of this useless discussion," said Alitor. "There is much to do tomorrow, so I suggest you all get a good meal inside of you and then grab some sleep."

They dispersed into their tents, save for Grafford and Alitor.

"Can I trust you?" asked the Fire Mage.

"What a curious question. Are you expecting some sort of trouble?"

"I am a Sartellian, operating in a military campaign overseen by a Shozarin. What do you think?"

"I am neither Sartellian nor Shozarin nor, for that matter, a Stormwind. Such petty politics are none of my concern."

"Still, the success of this operation is of paramount importance to the empire, is it not?"

"Admittedly, it is," said Alitor. "But the legions of the empire always win in the end."

"Except in a place called Arnsfeld, it would appear."

"A minor setback."

"On the contrary," said Grafford. "It portends a troubling future for our legions."

"Would you care to explain that?"

"The might of Halvaria has never before been questioned. Our legions have expanded our borders for centuries, crushing whoever stood against us."

"And?"

"Our unquestionable success was what brought fear to our enemies."

"And you're afraid our recent defeat gives them hope?"

"Is it so unreasonable to make that assumption?"

Alitor glanced around, but no one else was within earshot. Still, he lowered his voice. "This is a dangerous discussion to have out in the open."

"Quite the opposite, in fact. Only out in the open like this can we be sure there are no eavesdroppers."

"Are you suggesting this campaign is doomed?"

"I am merely pointing out that our internal strife brought about a defeat that may lead to lasting ramifications. How do we know this assault in the mountains isn't another misstep by those in charge?"

"I cannot speak to the competency of those in the upper echelons of the empire, but I assure you that I, along with my fellow mages, are more than capable of getting this legion across that gorge. After that, it is up to the soldiers."

They rose early the following day and headed into the mountains well before sunrise. Alitor sat in the carriage with Rhedra and Grafford, while the other four followed in a second carriage.

The ride was quiet, save for the rattle of the wheels and the snorting of horses. As the morning wore on, Alitor's companions fell asleep, leaving him time to ponder his future. He was, he told himself, one of the most powerful Earth Mages in the empire, yet there was no prospect of advancement beyond his current role, for the trio of lines calling themselves 'the family' controlled everything.

Grafford's remarks stuck in his mind. The Fire Mage had suggested the empire's recent loss in Arnsfeld gave the Petty Kingdoms hope, and he wondered if this might be the beginning of the end for Halvaria. After all, empires don't last forever. He tried to imagine what the Continent would look like in a post-Halvarian world, but it was difficult.

Perhaps it wasn't so much about the empire falling as evolving. The great dream was of a Continent united under one rule, but what would that look like? What would hold Halvaria together without enemies to conquer? Would it fall into civil war as various factions vied for power? At that point, he wondered if it hadn't already started.

The Marshal of the North had recently died in an accident, and they would eventually choose another Sartellian to replace him, but the bureaucracy of the family was notoriously slow to act. Rumour was a Shozarin had been appointed as a temporary replacement. Did that mean the High Strategos was making a bid for the Gilded Throne?

"Something wrong?"

He looked up to see Rhedra staring at him.

"No," he replied a little too loudly. "I was merely going over some of the finer points of the coming campaign."

"Then why do you look so guilty?"

"I assure you I am nothing of the sort."

"It matters little to me." She glanced at Grafford. "It appears our Fire Mage is a heavy sleeper."

"It's common amongst Pyromancers, or so I'm told. I suspect it comes from dealing with such a destructive element. It can wear a person down."

"Careful now," replied Rhedra. "Earth Magic is just as powerful."

"I didn't say powerful; I said destructive. The magic of the earth deals with nature and, as such, is restorative. Fire only consumes."

"That's fair." She glanced out the window. "We're slowing down. We must have arrived at our destination."

The carriage rolled to a stop, and then a soldier opened the door. "Welcome to the frontier, my lords." He glanced at Rhedra but refused to change his greeting on her behalf. "If you come with me, I'll conduct you to the captured Dwarf tower."

"That won't be necessary," said Alitor. "I'm here to see the tower we built, not the one from the mountain folk."

"Of course, Lord. Whatever you wish."

A frigid blast of air met Alitor as he stepped from the carriage, invigorating him. He was about to say as much when he caught sight of the wooden tower. His previous thoughts were forgotten as he strode towards it.

"Magnificent," he said. "It's just as I envisioned it."

The warrior struggled to keep up with him. "It was made to very exacting standards, my lord."

"And it hangs over the gorge a little?"

"It does, though I've never understood why."

"That, my man, is so we mages can see the cliff face on our side of the gorge."

"If you don't mind me asking, Lord, why might you need to do that?"

Ordinarily, he would have balked at an underling daring to speak to him in such a familiar tone, but nothing could dampen his spirits. "It's simple. To cross this gorge, we will reshape the cliff face, but we can't do that if we can't see it."

"Reshape the cliff? You intend to make a new bridge using magic?"

"That is the idea, yes."

"Does that mean the attack is about to begin?"

"It won't be today if that's what you're asking, but the time will soon be upon us when you will be called to do your duty."

They arrived at the tower and halted, Alitor looking over every detail of its construction. "You've done a marvellous job here."

"It wasn't me, Lord."

He waved away the remark like a fly. "I didn't mean you personally. Is it safe to enter?"

"Yes, but you should keep your head down when you reach the top. The enemy archers like to loose bolts at tempting targets."

Alitor chuckled. "I imagine they do, but I will heed your advice. There shall be little chance of them hitting me today."

He entered the structure, which was basically just a large wooden tower. The back, facing their own side, was open, while the other three sides were blocked off with waist-high walls and hanging skins on each level, allowing archers or mages to take up positions when the time came.

The warrior followed him as he climbed to the top. Alitor looked back at the carriage where Rhedra and Grafford waited nearby, content to watch him do all the climbing. He wondered if they would have the courage to do their part when the time came.

He turned and peeked through a gap in the hanging skin, looking down on the far side of the gorge. The Dwarves had constructed a stone wall to conceal their arbalesters, but he doubted that would impact his role in the coming attack. He smiled at the thought. This was going to be easier than he'd anticipated!

# THIRTY-FIVE

# Aid

### WINTER 967 MC

The King of Deisenbach tossed and turned, the sheets damp from sweat. He'd made no improvement, his health only worsening, leading Aubrey to wonder if these might be his final days.

"Hand me that cloth," she said.

Aldwin wrung out the water and passed it to her. "Beverly will return soon."

"I hope so. Our time is quickly running out."

"Is there nothing more you can do for him?"

"I'm afraid not," replied Aubrey. "I've tried every spell I know, and it's made no difference. If his mental capacity is reduced any further, he'll be unable to speak."

"And if he dies?"

She met his gaze. "Let's hope it doesn't come to that, or both our fates are sealed. I wish I knew what was taking them so long."

"Well, it's not as if the Orcs are walking out in the open."

"We must also face the possibility she failed to find them."

"No," said Aldwin. "I refuse to believe that. Beverly is resourceful, and if there are Orcs out there, she'll find them. I'm sure of it."

"But that's just it, don't you see? The Orcs may have moved on years ago. All she's got to go on is rumours."

"She's faced worse and come through in the end."

"I admire your faith, Aldwin. If anyone could find them, it would be Beverly, but it's been weeks now, and we still haven't heard anything."

"Assuming she does find the Orcs, what happens then?"

"If she found a shaman, I'll need to teach them how to assist me in casting the spell."

"Are you certain there are no other choices?"

"I'm open to suggestions."

"Would sleep help?"

"I've already considered that. Whatever is raging within him has infected his mind. If I put him to sleep, there's no guarantee I'd be able to wake him."

"At least he'd be more comfortable."

"He would," said Aubrey, "but then he would be uncommunicative, and I doubt the queen would be happy about that."

"So, while we wait for Beverly's return, we just pretend we know what we're doing?"

"Hey, at least I got you out of that dungeon."

"And for that, I'm thankful. I just hoped my release from imprisonment would be a little more permanent." He took the cloth from Aubrey, rinsed it, and handed it back. "Any word from Kraloch?"

"I contacted him last night," said Aubrey. "Things are heating up back home."

"In what way?"

"The Halvarians are marching on Ironcliff, and Gerald expects another attack near Stonecastle."

"In winter? That's a little hard to believe, isn't it?"

"It's not as if the Mercerian army has never marched in winter."

"If I recall, pulling that off took a lot of organizing."

"Yes," replied Aubrey, "and that worries me. It speaks to the enemy's competency."

"Meaning they're disciplined?"

"They would have to be if they're attacking in the winter, which also means they have a weakness."

"They do?"

"Their supply lines."

"Then that's where the marshal should strike," said Aldwin.

"Easier said than done. Getting Mercerian troops to Ironcliff is the first step; attacking their baggage train will likely be next to impossible. In any case, it's not our concern at the moment. There are more pressing issues to consider."

"Like Beverly's return?"

Aubrey nodded. "There's a very real possibility that, even if we cure the king, they might see fit to execute us."

"Why would they do that?"

"Because we know the true nature of the king's illness. Were word to get out he was poisoned, it might make him appear weak. I could be wrong, but something about Helisant's manner tells me the queen is not the sort to let secrets like that slip out."

Footsteps approached, and then the door opened, revealing Ludmilla. "I hope I'm not interrupting."

"Not at all," replied Aubrey.

"How fares His Majesty?"

"He's no worse than yesterday."

"But no better?"

"As I've said before," replied Aubrey, "I can't heal that kind of damage without help."

Ludmilla stared down at Justinian. "I'm not surprised to see the king so weak after all he's been through."

"What do you mean?" asked Aldwin.

"Simply that the politics of the Petty Kingdoms have severely strained King Justinian. How much longer do you think he has?"

"A few days at most," replied Aubrey. "Why?"

"Merely professional curiosity. I know his nephew is waiting for news. Would it not be more humane to end the king's misery?"

"Misery? He's half out of his mind. I doubt he's even aware of what's happening around him."

"All the more reason to let him die with dignity."

"I will not surrender the life of a patient under my care!" said Aubrey. "Not while there's still a chance."

"Chance? I assume you refer to Lady Beverly. To my mind, you put far too much faith in your cousin."

"Why? Have you heard something?"

Ludmilla hesitated. "I hate to dash your hopes, but we received reports bandits attacked her on the road to Santrem."

"Why wasn't I told?"

"I only just heard of it myself," replied Ludmilla.

"Was her body recovered?"

"Not that I know of. As I said, these are only reports."

"Then she's not dead," insisted Aldwin.

"You don't know bandits."

"True, I don't, but Beverly does. It wouldn't be the first time they've tried to bring her down, and I daresay it won't be the last."

Ludmilla tilted her head. "What in the name of the Saints are you talking about?"

"The Bandit King," said Aubrey. "I've heard the tale before. When

Beverly was only a knight, she was sent to bring a notorious bandit to justice."

"And did she succeed?"

"She did. Not only did she rid the world of the fellow, she also broke up his band."

"By killing all of them?"

"No," said Aldwin, "by redeeming them. They would have been hanged if she had left them to face the earl's justice. Instead, they became productive subjects of the queen." He paused. "Well, in those days, I suppose it would be the king, but the point is still made."

"Well then," said Ludmilla, "it appears Lady Beverly is more resourceful than I suspected. Perhaps she will return after all."


Sir Owen exited the treeline and halted, gazing off at the distant capital. They'd paralleled the road for days, keeping to the occasional clusters of trees to mask their presence. There'd been no sign of soldiers or bandits intent on attacking them, but Beverly remained adamant such precautions should be taken.

He looked around before waving the others forward. Ugrug led the Orcs, keeping his bow handy in case danger threatened. Garok came next with Krazuhk at his side, her eyes skyward as she watched the hawk circling overhead. Behind them walked the other Orc hunters, with Beverly bringing up the rear.

Krazuhk suddenly halted, throwing up her left arm as a sign for the others to do likewise.

"*Trouble?*" asked Beverly in the Orcish tongue.

The master of air closed her eyes, letting her magically see through the hawk's eyes. "*There are men to the west, beyond that copse of trees.*"

"*More merchants to avoid?*"

"*I am afraid this time they are warriors, and by the look of it, they are searching the area.*"

"*How many?*"

"*Two groups of ten, at least, although they are spread out.*" She tilted her head. "*I stand corrected. They are not searching so much as sealing off the approach to the city. I suspect they are on the lookout for something.*"

"*Likely us,*" said Beverly. "*They are probably working with the same folks who attacked us on our way to Ag-Dular.*"

"Is something wrong?" called out Owen.

"Soldiers," replied Beverly, "or possibly bandits. I'm not entirely sure of the difference in these parts. They appear to be looking for someone."

"You think it's us?"

"Who else?"

"But how did they know we were coming?"

"They must have found the bodies we left behind, which means they know we survived."

"How does that tell them we're returning?"

"It stands to reason, doesn't it?" said Beverly. "There's only so many ways back from the Orc lands."

"Yes, but how do they know we're here? We could have travelled farther south or even west."

"I imagine they've sent other groups out to look for us. The question I have is, who do they work for?"

"Perhaps we should ask them," said Owen.

Beverly laughed. "You're suggesting we ride up and speak with whoever's in charge?"

"No, not you. Your red hair gives you too distinctive a look. On the other hand, I could pass for a typical knight of the Petty Kingdoms. Don't worry. I'll be sure not to use my real name."

"I'm not certain I like the sound of this. Do you intend to ride up to them, have words, then come back? That will only alert them you're up to something."

"That wasn't precisely what I had in mind."

"Oh? So you have an actual plan, then?"

"I do," said Owen. "As you indicated, I shall talk to them, hopefully tricking them into revealing who they work for. Then, I'll say something to anger them so they'll come after me. Once I reach that group of trees there" —he pointed—"the rest of you can take out my pursuers. It shouldn't be too difficult with all these Orcs and their bows."

"I suppose it's as good an idea as any."

"Thank you. I'll ride ahead while you explain everything to our friends here." He rode off, leaving the others behind.

He angled slightly to his right, circling to the north as the last knot of trees grew closer. The soldiers were spread out in a single line, every fifth or sixth man on a horse. The rest wore padded armour, although as far as he could tell, none wore surcoats identifying their lord.

They called out for him to identify himself. He slowed his horse, adopting a casual air of interest. "Sir Galdrick," Owen yelled back. "A knight of Erlingen. I'm on my way to Agran to visit a friend. Is something wrong?" He stopped in front of a mounted man with a patchy beard and long, black hair.

"We're on the lookout for criminals," replied the soldier. "We have reliable information they'll pass through this way sometime in the next few days."

"Can you describe these fiends?"

"Aye. Sir Owen, a knight, travelling in the company of a red-headed woman wearing armour."

"Wearing armour, you say? Is she a Temple Knight?"

"Do you honestly believe we'd try to arrest a Temple Knight?"

"My pardon. Are you in service to the king?"

"No, we're bounty hunters. Now, have you seen anyone matching those descriptions?"

Owen twisted in his saddle, looking back from whence he came. "Come to think of it, I did see someone in amongst those trees." He turned back to the fellow. "You don't suppose that was them, do you?"

The bounty hunter suddenly yelled out to his men, and they advanced in a ragged line, heading towards the trees.

Sir Owen turned his horse around and fell in behind them, drawing his sword. They spared him only a cursory glance, believing him intent on helping them, and why not? He was doing what they expected of a law-abiding knight, helping bring a criminal to justice.

"Who put up the bounty?" he asked, raising his voice.

"One of the queen's people, a mage by the name of Ludmilla Stormwind."

"Stormwind, you say?"

"Which makes it all the more important we kill these people."

"Kill? I thought you wanted to catch them. You can hardly collect a bounty if they're dead."

The fellow laughed. "They've got a price on their heads. Why in the name of the Saints would we want to go to the bother of capturing them alive?"

"A valid point." Owen glanced around surreptitiously, trying to ascertain the quality of these men.

As they neared the trees, an arrow flew forth, striking a man in the neck. He fell forward, gurgling as blood welled up into his throat. As one, the others charged, eager to come to grips with their attackers.

More arrows came from the trees, followed by a bolt of lightning that struck a rider. The poor fool went rigid before falling lifeless from the saddle.

Seizing the opportunity to act, Owen spurred on his mount, sinking the tip of his blade into a rider's back. The padded jacket stopped it, so the knight thrust harder, driving it through the armour. The rider slumped forward, his horse no longer under control.

Beverly burst from the trees, Lightning in full gallop. She rode down two men, then smashed her hammer against the last rider's chest. Owen heard the sickening crunch as the head of Nature's Fury penetrated the armour, and then the body fell from the saddle. The Orcs rushed out, axes in hand, but the men had no fight left. They ran off in fear, scattering in all directions.

"Well, that was fun," said Owen. "What do we do now?"

"We make for Agran," replied Beverly, "before word of their defeat reaches whoever was in charge. Did you get a name?"

"I did, and you'll find it most interesting."

"Let's have it, then."

"Ludmilla Stormwind. I don't know if you are aware of this but—"

"Did you say Stormwind?"

"I did. Why? Don't tell me you're familiar with the Stormwinds? I thought you said you were from the far west?"

"I am, but I've heard that name before."

"They're an influential family, with members in most of the courts of the Petty Kingdoms."

"No. That's not it. There's something else, but I can't quite remember what. We must ask Aubrey once we return." She watched as the Orcs retrieved their arrows, then shifted to their language. *"Did you receive any injuries?"*

*"None at all,"* replied Ugrug. *"That encounter was brief and bloody, just not for us."*

*"What do we do with their bodies?"* asked Krazuhk. *"I am not familiar with the customs of Humans."*

*"Ordinarily,"* replied Beverly, *"I'd say bury them, but we haven't the time. We must get to Agran before news of our presence here reaches the people behind this."* She swept her arm to indicate the area. *"Might I ask you to contact the hawk again? I would hate to be surprised by more men."*

*"I shall do as you request."*

Beverly turned back to Sir Owen. "I'd like you to ride ahead a good hundred paces or so. The closer we get to the city, the more likely we will encounter trouble."

"You think they'd try again?"

"I do, at least until we reach the Palace."

"And how do we do that, exactly? We're travelling with nearly a dozen Orcs. That's bound to raise the ire of the locals."

"Do you honestly believe they'd try anything with two knights escorting them?"

"No. I suppose I hadn't considered that, but didn't you tell me to ride ahead?"

"Only until we're in amongst the city streets. At that point, let us catch up."

"And if they attack us?"

"Then we form a ring around the shaman, Garok. His survival is of paramount importance."

"Maybe we should leave the rest of the Orcs here and ride on to the Palace?"

"No. They'd be seen as hostiles without us to speak on their behalf."

"True," said Owen. "What about after all this is over?"

"Once we're done healing the king, we'll be heading north, but I won't leave Garok here without making certain he'll be safe."

"You think ten Orcs can do that?"

"I'm hoping the king will be thankful we saved his life," said Beverly. "That's assuming he hasn't died while we were away."

"And if that should prove to be the case?"

"That largely depends on his replacement. One thing's for certain, though. I'm not leaving without Aldwin and Aubrey. If that means spilling blood, then so be it."

"And the Orc shaman?"

"We'll take him as well, along with his escort."

"That might prove difficult."

"Let's not worry over something that hasn't happened," said Beverly. "We must trust Aubrey has kept His Majesty alive long enough for us to return. That being the case, all she has to do is tutor Garok on combining his magic with hers, and the king should fully recover."

"This would be a lot easier if there weren't bounties on Orc heads."

"Something I intend to address once the king is healed."

"How do you know he won't revert to his old ways once you leave?"

"I don't for certain, but I suspect he'll see the wisdom in it. Just to make sure, I'll point out the benefits Merceria has realized from their friendship with the Orcs."

"And if that doesn't work?"

"Then we'll escort the Orcs back to Ag-Dular and be on our way."

# THIRTY-SIX

## Assault

WINTER 967 MC

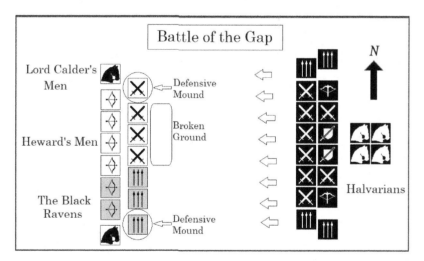

H eward surveyed his lines. Thanks to the magic of Kharzug, they'd spotted the Halvarians early, giving them plenty of time to take up a defensive position. Unfortunately, the flat terrain in the gap offered little cover or concealment. To counter this lack, the master of earth used his magic to create two defensive mounds, essentially small hills upon which a company would find some advantage. These anchored either flank.

His plan was simple—footmen forming a straight line, north to south, anchored by these hills, with his archers arrayed behind. Calder's men would take the northernmost position, with the Black Ravens taking the south. Heward placed himself in the middle of Bronwyn's men to bolster their confidence.

The Norland light horse was on his northern flank, the Orc cavalry in the south, ready to counter any cavalry charge the enemy might offer.

The Halvarians had broken off only a portion of their army to deal with this new threat, but they still outnumbered the alliance. Estimates placed the enemy at nearly one thousand men, while Heward's force was closer to seven hundred and fifty. He would have been content if they were Mercerian companies he was leading, but the untested nature of these Norlanders concerned him. Would they stand?

Calder rode over. "The enemy is forming up opposite us. They've decided to fight."

"And why wouldn't they?" asked Heward. "They outnumber us and likely see this as a golden opportunity."

"Are you certain this is wise? Surely it would be better to withdraw?"

"To do that this close to the enemy would be a disaster. Their cavalry would ruin us."

"They might still; they have more horses than we do."

"You must have faith, my lord. Our men will stand because they have no other option."

"And the Orcs?" said Calder. "Will they hold their portion of the line?"

"I have no doubts where they are concerned," replied Heward. "I'm more worried about your Norlanders. Not that your men aren't brave, you understand, but they lack battle experience."

"So you choose to stand with inexperienced warriors against a numerically superior enemy?"

"They have the numbers on us, but if you look closely, you'll see we have one big advantage."

"That being?"

"Archers make up almost half our forces, while the enemy has nearly none."

The earl shifted his gaze to the distant lines. "By the Gods, you're right. Do you believe that will be enough to give us victory?"

"We shall soon see."

The Halvarians elected to advance all at once, moving slowly to maintain their formation. It spoke of a disciplined army, and Heward realized this enemy was far more capable than he assumed. He'd spent his career fighting Norlanders and, later on, the Twelve Clans and their Kurathian allies. Merceria had won due to its superior training and discipline, but he now found himself on the opposite end of just such an army.

He waved over Kharzug, the master of earth. The Orc was soon at his side, peering over the men to see the enemy.

"*Have you any spells to break up their advance?*" asked Heward, using the Orcish tongue.

"*I have several, but I am unable to use some of them, for creating the defensive mounds has expended a lot of my energy.*"

"*I'm open to suggestions?*"

"*What is your greatest area of concern?*"

"*In front of our Humans. Unlike your people, these Norlanders are inexperienced and likely to panic.*"

"*Then let me see what I can do.*" The master of earth moved to stand in front of the Norland line. He raised his arms as a stream of arcane words poured from his mouth, then threw his hands down. All around him, fist-sized, pointed stones sprang up. The Orc then proceeded north, stones popping up in his wake.

"By the Gods," said Calder. "What strange magic is this?"

"The magic of the earth," replied Heward.

"And those spikes will injure the enemy?"

"No, but they will slow them down and break up their formation. Now they must concentrate on their feet rather than their weapons, giving us a temporary advantage."

"And will that be enough?"

"Yes, providing your men carry out their instructions."

"And that's all there is to it?"

"What else did you expect?"

"Why, to kill more of them than they do of us! I fail to see how we'll do that standing here and waiting."

"Winning a battle isn't about inflicting losses. It's about breaking their will to fight."

"Understood, but killing them is the best way to do that."

"That's certainly one way, yes. An army is a complex entity, my lord. A collection of men held together through discipline, camaraderie, and valour. Break any of those, and it will collapse."

"And how does one break an enemy's discipline?"

"By presenting them with a situation not within their experience."

Calder smiled. "Ah, the stones. Now I see."

The enemy advanced, still out of bowshot, even for the warbows of the Orcs, but it was now possible to make out details.

"Their armour is much like ours," noted Calder.

"For their footmen, yes, but if you look at the horsemen coming up behind, you'll note their plate armour is similar to that employed by the Dwarves of Ironcliff."

"That doesn't bode well."

"Thankfully, they are in small numbers. In any case, it won't be the horse that decides this battle; it'll be the footmen. Break them, and the enemy cavalry will be forced to cover their retreat."

"You sound confident."

Inside, Heward was a bundle of nerves, the contents of his stomach threatening to overwhelm him; hardly the image he wanted to portray to Lord Calder, so he forced a smile. "I am, and why wouldn't I be? We finally have the advantage."

"We do?"

Heward simply nodded.

Kharzug returned to stand once more beside his brigade-commander. *"I have done all I can for now."*

*"Have you any energy left?"* asked Heward.

*"A little, but I must save it in case it is needed later."*

*"Thank you, Master Kharzug. Your efforts today may well turn defeat into victory."*

Captain-General Stivern Lindman, commander of the second cohort of the Seventh Legion, watched the advance. The enemy had made their stand on a flat stretch of land southwest of Ironcliff. With the rest of the Seventh readying to siege the Dwarven stronghold, the duty of ridding the gap of this nuisance fell to him.

Ordinarily, he would've used magic to break up the enemy lines before making contact, but with the legion's mages preparing for the siege, he must do without. Not that it mattered. He would brush aside this makeshift army of miscreants and charge into Norland, where his cavalry would have free rein.

One of his captains rode over, halting with a bow.

"What is it?" snapped Lindman. "Can't you see I'm busy?"

"The Mercerians have Orcs, my lord."

"What of it?"

"One is parading in front of the enemy line."

"And?"

The captain hesitated.

"Out with it, man!"

"He appears to be casting, my lord."

"It is of little consequence. You see those two hills anchoring either flank? They're called defensive mounds, created by Earth Magic. They are a nuisance, but creating them would have required a lot of energy. I'd wager that caster of theirs has almost exhausted his reserves."

"Reserves?"

"Yes, of energy. Have you no concept of how magic works?"

"No, Lord. I am but a simple warrior."

Lindman wanted to bite back but held his tongue. The captain was no fool, else he wouldn't be in charge of a company, yet his lack of knowledge was frustrating. "Mages draw power from within themselves, but there is only so much they can call on before they must rest."

"So his efforts are in vain?"

"No doubt a minor inconvenience awaits us, but consider the source."

"What do you mean by that?"

"He's an Orc. Such creatures possess only crude magic. They can't possibly rival the power of one of our mages."

"But there are no mages with us, Lord."

"Then we shall rely on the valour of our warriors. Return to your post, Captain. The fighting is about to begin."

"Yes, my lord." The captain wheeled his horse around and galloped off.

The captain-general looked over the forces arrayed against him. Rumour had it the empire was once again expanding, which meant more legions were needed. A victory here could propel him to the vaulted rank of commander-general, the highest honour he could hope to achieve under the emperor's rule. All he needed to guarantee such a promotion was a victory, and this ragtag bunch of miscreants had provided him with the perfect opportunity.

Lindman held his breath as the men of Halvaria advanced on their target. He forced himself to relax lest he give his command the idea he was nervous. They were moments away from making contact, and then it would come down to a duel of steel as both sides struggled to crush their enemy, but he harboured no doubt of the outcome. The legions of Halvaria had conquered their enemies for a thousand years. The mightiest kingdoms of the Continent had fallen under the swords of the empire. What hope did this pitiful collection of fools have against that?

～

Heward watched the enemy march straight into the area where Kharzug had cast his spells. The spikes of stone disrupted their formation, and the warriors of the empire were suddenly faced with the unexpected difficulty of navigating the hazard.

He raised his axe on high, then swept it down, signalling the archers to commence their volleys. Three hundred archers aimed their bows above the heads of their allies, their arrows flying through the sky to rain down on an enemy in disarray. Arrowheads dug into exposed arms and bounced off helmets, the clatter sounding like hail.

The men of the empire began to waver, and then another volley landed, felling even more. They halted short of their target and raised their shields to protect themselves from the arrows.

Heward looked to the south, where the Orcs of the Black Raven had wreaked terrible damage with their powerful warbows. He was at a loss as to why their volleys were so much more effective, then he realized the Orcs in front of their archers had opened their ranks, allowing the hunters to pour arrows directly into the enemy.

To the south, a group of Halvarians tried storming the defensive mound only to be pushed back by the Orcs. Heward sought out the enemy cavalry, fearing they might try to outflank his small army, but they were still uncommitted.

He gripped the handle of his axe as he watched, ready to launch himself into the fight. More than anything, he wanted to wade through the enemy, slicing away as he had done in countless battles before, but he knew it was not to be. As commander, his responsibility was to remain here, directing the battle.

The empire was weakening, their losses making maintaining a full line of battle challenging. Heward raised his axe, circling it in the air.

The Norlanders advanced, their weapons reaching out to attack the enemy while their shields were raised in defence of the onslaught of arrows. Some got their shields down in time, but most were taken by surprise.

Opposite Bronwyn's footmen, a gap appeared. At first, Heward feared the empire's horsemen might seek to take advantage of the flaw, but it only widened as the legion's warriors sought safety from the Norlander's onslaught. They pulled back, rushing into the tightly packed cavalry and disrupting their formation.

Then, above the din of battle, he heard a howling echoing off the distant mountain. He raised himself in the stirrups, eager to see over his own soldiers, but all he could make out was a press of men and Orcs struggling for dominance.

The battle dragged on. His own footmen tried to push forward, to widen the break in the enemy line, but the empire struck back with a vengeance. Halvarian casualties were replaced with men in plate armour, and he realized the enemy commander had ordered heavy footmen to plug the openings.

The battle was now at a precarious stage. His archers could no longer let loose their arrows lest they hit their own men, and the enemy's superior training was taking its toll. The allied line was mere moments away from catastrophe.

～

Kharzug stood atop the mound, his eyes closed, words of power tumbling from his lips. The wolves he'd already summoned poured across the gap, rushing towards the battle, yet he continued casting, tasting blood as he used up the last of his reserves. He opened his eyes to witness the results of his magic.

Dozens of his wolves tore into the Halvarian army's southern flank. These men, mostly provincials, were ill-equipped to face such a foe and dropped back, their formations destroyed.

Sensing the moment was at hand, Ghodrug released the Orc cavalry, and they raced forward to join the fray, their horses accustomed to the presence of wolves. They came from behind the mound, smashing into what little resistance remained. In only moments, the Halvarians were fleeing in panic, desperate for safety.

Kharzug felt weak. That last spell had taken more power than he could spare. Even now, his breath came in rasps, and he struggled to stay upright, then an arm gripped him, and he turned to see the shaman, Rulahk, his hands already glowing with magic. As Kharzug felt the wash of healing enter his body, the taste of blood left.

"*I am spent,*" he said, falling to his knees.

"*You must rest,*" replied Rulahk. "*I will see to the others.*"

～

Heward watched as the enemy's southern flank disintegrated. The empire's horsemen moved to prevent an absolute disaster, forming a line to halt the wolves' advance, but the battle was over as far as he was concerned.

"Hold your ground," he called out, eager to keep his small command intact.

"Surely now is the time to advance!" shouted Calder. "We have them on the run!"

"No. Pursuit would only bring the attention of the rest of their army."

"But they're at Ironcliff!"

"Our purpose here was to blunt the enemy's advance, and we've done that. To proceed any further would throw away our accomplishment."

"By the Gods, I never took you for a coward."

Heward gritted his teeth. "You may call me what you like, but my duty is to preserve this army to fight another day. We shall let the enemy withdraw and then march back to Holdcross."

"And throw away the chance to utterly defeat them?"

"Do you honestly believe this was their whole army? They brought enough men to assault Ironcliff, which would take an army three times larger than this. Would you have us advance only to face their entire force?"

Calder sobered. "No. Still, what will retreat gain us? We'll be giving up ground."

"The enemy has learned we can fight. They'll hesitate before moving to engage again."

"You mean until they have even greater numbers."

"I do, but that means they'd have fewer men to assault Ironcliff. It forces them to either move to destroy us or continue their attempts to take Ironcliff. I doubt they have the resources to do both."

"How can you be so sure?"

"If more men were available, why didn't they send them against us? They could have easily outflanked us if they had a few more horsemen."

"Then we must thank the Gods they did not."

"We also learned an important lesson: several, in fact."

"Did we?" said Calder. "And what might they be?"

"First, the men of Norland can fight."

"And second?"

"That we have far more archers than they do," replied Heward, "although I suspect that was only luck on our part."

"Why would you say that?"

"Likely, most of their archers are employed at the siege. I doubt we'll be so lucky next time."

"You think there'll be a next time?"

"Most certainly. I only hope the reinforcements from Merceria arrive by then."

"Not just from Merceria," said Calder. "I shall write to the other earls, imploring them to send additional men. This is not some petty squabble amongst nobles but a fight for the very survival of our kingdom." He scanned the battlefield. The enemy was still withdrawing, leaving wounded and dead in their wake. Following their officers' orders, the Norlanders refrained from advancing any farther and were dealing with their own casualties. Ghodrug made her way over to their position.

"*You must thank Master Kharzug,*" said Heward, quickly switching to Orc. "*Those wolves of his proved most decisive.*"

"*You can thank him yourself once he has recovered. He almost died summoning them. He will be fine in time, but it will be some days before he can cast again.*"

# THIRTY-SEVEN

# Audience

Arnim looked up as a guard unlocked the door. "What's happening?" he asked.

"You two are being moved."

"To where?"

"That's not for me to say." He looked around the room. "Gather your things. You won't be returning."

"Things?" said Nikki. "You make it sound like we're travelling in style."

"You were given a change of clothes, were you not?"

"Yes, several."

"Then I suggest you gather them, unless you'd prefer to wear the same clothes from this day forth."

"And how are we to carry them?"

"I shall have someone bring a chest."

"Just out of curiosity," said Arnim, "when are we leaving?"

"This afternoon."

"By carriage?"

The guard laughed. "A carriage? Don't be absurd; that would take weeks." He turned to leave, then paused. "I'll send someone to help you pack, but don't waste their time. We're on a tight schedule."

"Why is that?"

The guard shrugged. "It's not for the likes of me to understand the habits of mages." With that, he left, closing the door behind him.

"Well," said Nikki. "That was interesting. What do you suppose it means?"

"That the mages of Halvaria can use the spell of recall?"

"And here I was thinking only Mercerian mages knew that spell. Where do you think they're taking us?"

"I have no idea."

"Why move us in the first place? Do you think they want to parade us before their nobles?"

"Like some sort of prize of war?" said Arnim. "I suppose it's possible, but why keep us in relative comfort if that were the case? Surely a display like that would be more entertaining if we looked like prisoners."

"I can't argue with your reasoning, but there's not much we can do about it unless you think the time is right to attempt an escape?"

"And go where? We're in a city called Zefara, but we have no idea where that is in relation to Merceria."

"We know we came here by ship," offered Nikki.

"We do, but even if we did steal a boat, what direction would we head? North? South? West? And besides, neither one of us knows a thing about sailing. I'm afraid our only choice is to go along with whatever they're proposing." He lowered his voice. "Who knows? We might get close enough to someone important to kill him?"

"Or her. We really have no idea how their empire is run."

"All the more reason to bide our time and learn what we can."

The door opened, and two women bearing a chest between them entered. "We were told you'll be travelling?" said the older one.

"Yes," said Nikki. "That's right, though we have no idea where we're going."

"I wouldn't know anything about that. We were told to pack your clothes."

Nikki stepped aside, allowing them access to their belongings, meagre as they were.

"This must be so exciting for you," gushed the younger woman.

"Exciting?" said Arnim. "Whatever gave you that idea?"

"It's not every day a person gets to travel through a ring of fire."

"Ring of fire? Is that even safe?"

"Of course it is. That's how all the Sartellians travel. Are you not familiar with such things?"

"No," said Nikki. "Am I to understand all Sartellians are Fire Mages?"

"They are, although some prefer the term Pyromancer."

"And this ring of fire is, I assume, a spell?"

The young woman nodded. "I've only seen it once, but I'll never forget it. The mage utters these strange words, and then fire encircles them, the flames reaching up to the ceiling, blocking all sight of them, and then— poof, it disappears, along with the mage and anyone else with them."

"And you've never travelled that way yourself?"

"Of course not. That's only for important people."

"You hear that, Arnim? We're considered important now."

"Well," he replied, "at least they realize we have worth."

"All packed," said the older woman. She motioned for her companion to help her lift the chest, and they carried it from the room.

"What now?" said Arnim.

"I assume we follow," replied Nikki.

They stepped outside the door, and the guards there waved at them to follow the servants, then fell in behind. Not long afterwards, they descended a set of circular stairs.

"Down below here is the casting chamber," the older servant announced. "Whoever's taking you will meet you there."

Nikki adopted a relaxed manner. "Any advice for a first-time magic traveller?"

"Always refer to mages as Your Grace, and only speak when spoken to."

Nikki looked at her husband. "It appears some things are universal."

The stairs ended in a large chamber where two more guards stood watch over a pair of doors decorated with strange symbols. The opposite wall featured a second, less ornate door.

The servants set the chest down, then wiped their hands on their skirts. "This is as far as we go," said the elder one. They both curtsied before quickly disappearing up the stairs.

Arnim looked at their escort. "What now?"

"We wait," the guard replied.

It didn't take long for the mage to arrive, a woman wearing a flowing dress decorated with embroidered flames.

"Greetings," she began. "My name is Edora Sartellian. I'll be taking you to Varena."

"Isn't that the capital?" asked Nikki.

"Yes, that's right. Why? Were you not informed?"

"We've been kept in the dark ever since our capture. Might I ask the purpose of this trip?"

"Several people have expressed an interest in meeting you. Chief amongst them are... Well, let's call them people of power and influence."

Nikki stiffened. "We have no intention of helping you conquer Merceria."

"And I wouldn't expect you to, nor do I believe my colleagues will. This has more to do with your recent experiences here, in Zefara."

"I'm not sure I understand."

"Nor do I," said Arnim. "Are you suggesting we were witness to something?"

Edora looked sidelong at the guards. "This is not the time or place to speak of such things. If you come with me, we'll enter the casting circle." She nodded at the door guards, who opened the rune-covered doors.

Beyond lay a round chamber, similar to the casting circle in Wincaster. Inlaid in the floor was an elaborate circle with magic runes cast in gold, strands of silver, and the occasional jewel.

"Come," said Edora, looking at their escorts. "You may place their chest beside me. Now, you two"—she looked back at Arnim and Nikki—"stand on the other side."

The guards placed the chest where she indicated, then left the room, closing the doors behind them.

"I will be casting a spell called ring of fire, but don't worry, it's harmless. However, if you wander beyond its perimeter while I'm casting, we might end up in the wrong location." She chuckled. "I'm only teasing, but you may find the experience disorienting. All set?" She waited for them to nod before beginning her casting, the words of power flowing from her lips as she raised her hands.

Arnim and Nikki had both travelled using the spell of recall, but this was their first experience with a Fire Mage. A blast of heat overwhelmed them as flames leapt up, forming a circle, and then all sight of the walls was lost, hidden behind the fire. For a moment, they felt as though they were flying through the air, then they smelled something like roses instead of the sea air of Zefara.

The flames dissipated, revealing a room quite different from their origin. The circle was similar, but this chamber was a large rectangle instead of being round. There were also ten guards standing watch, their weapons drawn, though they sheathed them at the sight of Edora.

Nikki looked around the room. "You have two casting circles."

"Yes," said the mage. "That far one is for Water Mages, for they suffer a disadvantage when using a circle of fire."

"Opposite schools of magic," said Arnim.

"You know about that?"

"Only in the broadest sense. We're not complete novices to the idea of magic."

"So I've been told. It's a pity neither of you is a mage. It would have been interesting to compare notes."

"Why not call off the invasion? Then you could come and visit us in peace?"

Edora laughed. "It is not for me alone to make such decisions."

"But you are a decision-maker?"

"Let's just say I have significant influence amongst the ruling class of the empire."

"And these friends of yours that you want us to meet?"

"I could take you to a couple of them now if you like?"

"By all means," said Nikki.

"Then follow me."

They left the room, entering a long corridor with marble floors and a high ceiling. Arnim noted the gilded decorations and wondered at the extravagance. Was the empire truly so prosperous that they would throw away coins in such a manner?

"Here we are," announced Edora as she led them through a door into a room that wasn't overly large. Though it didn't match the hallway's luxury, it was well-appointed, with seating for six. Two individuals sat there, an older man with a wrinkled countenance and a middle-aged woman dressed in elegant clothes.

"This is Agalix Sartellian," said Edora. The mage bowed his head in acknowledgement.

"And this is Olynia Sartellian. She's come to us all the way from Korascajan."

"Greetings," said Nikki.

"Please, sit," said Olynia. "I assure you we mean you no harm."

The woman waited for them to take a seat before continuing. "No doubt you're wondering why we brought you here?"

"That thought had crossed my mind," said Nikki.

"You and your husband are in a rather unique position."

"We are nothing more than prisoners."

"Oh, you are so much more than that," replied Olynia.

"How?"

"Your arrival in the empire has presented us with an opportunity."

"We're listening," said Arnim.

"We've learned much of Merceria's history and know you've had troubles of your own. I speak not of war but of politics."

"And?"

"Like your realm, we in Halvaria have our own... Well, let's just call them factions."

"How is that of any interest to us?"

"There is a constant struggle for dominance here, a fight involving three different lines."

"Lines?"

"You might think of them as families, but they're so much more than that. As I said, there are three: the Shozarins, the Stormwinds, and us, the Sartellians."

"It matters little to us who rules."

"Ah, but it should; don't you see?"

Agalix cleared his throat. "They do not understand the situation, Olynia." He leaned forward in his chair. "If the Sartellians gained dominance, we could halt this war of yours."

"This war was not of our making," said Arnim. "Your empire is massed on OUR borders."

"It's a little more complicated than you might believe."

"Then why don't you explain it to us?"

"The High Strategos controls our army. His plan put those legions on your border, and his quest for power inevitably led to the current situation. You see, he wants to claim the empire as his own."

"Why invade our land?"

"The empire loves a hero," replied Agalix. "With your realm subjugated, the legions would worship him."

"Making it easy for him to lead a revolt. Is that what you're suggesting?"

"It is."

"Interesting," said Nikki, "yet I don't see how we fit into all of this."

"You were prisoners of the High Strategos. A few words from you, and we could have the man arrested for treason."

"But we didn't hear anything."

"Does that really matter?" added Edora.

"It's simple," said Agalix. "We're talking about political expediency. You do this for us, and in return, we send you back to your homeland."

"You make it sound so simple."

"It is when you think about it. We're not saying you must prove any of these allegations; merely raise suspicion. Our allies will do the rest."

"What I don't understand," said Arnim, "is how you managed all this? If this High Strategos is planning a revolt, why would he let us out of his custody?"

"That was my doing," offered Edora. "I waited until he travelled north and swept in. No one refuses a command from a council member."

"And what council might that be?"

She looked at Agalix, who merely nodded. "The true ruling power in Halvaria is the Inner Council."

"I thought you had an emperor?" said Arnim.

"We do, but he's largely a figurehead. He still has his uses, one of which is the illusion he is a god. It serves us well in controlling the populace but requires some finesse in dealing with him."

"I assume he believes he rules?"

"He does," replied Olynia, "and we'd like to keep it that way."

"But if that's true," said Nikki, "then why does it matter if this High Strategos makes himself emperor? Wouldn't he just be a figurehead as well?"

"Not when he has the legions backing him. He'll disband the council and declare martial law."

"Surely that would be better for us. If a civil war consumes your empire, they can hardly spare resources to conquer Merceria."

"I don't think you quite grasp the situation," said Edora. "Exalor won't move on the capital until after he's finished off Merceria. Act now, and you can prevent the legions from overrunning your tiny little kingdom."

"What is it you want us to say?" asked Arnim.

"When you are taken before the emperor, tell him you've heard rumours Exalor seeks the Gilded Throne for himself."

"Without proof?"

"You need only plant the seed of doubt. His Eminence will take it from there."

"How can you be so certain?"

"We have others who will feed that doubt, building on it until the emperor pushes the council to do something. At that point, we will have little choice but to act."

"And in the meantime, the war against our allies continues?"

"Of course. To act precipitously would only serve to tip our hand."

"This is a dangerous game you're playing," said Arnim. "How do you know we wouldn't tell him of your own plot?"

"Because," replied Olynia, "if you don't do as we say, we'll have you killed."

"I hoped it wouldn't come to this," said Edora. "We are reasonable people, as are you. Surely you can see the sense in our approach. Succeed in this, and we both get what we want. You mentioned that it matters little to you who's in charge here, but I disagree. If Exalor takes the Gilded Throne, he'll have absolute power over the largest army on the Continent. How long before he turns it to subjugating your people?"

"Ah," said Nikki, "but you said he would move on Merceria BEFORE seizing the Throne."

"Admittedly, I did, but our plan is to discredit him before his campaign in the west is complete."

"What you ask is a lot. Might Arnim and I discuss this in private?"

"Of course." Edora stood, followed by her colleagues. "We'll leave a guard outside; you can alert them once you've made a decision."

"Thank you."

They waited until the Halvarians left.

"Well?" whispered Arnim. "What are you thinking?"

"That they're going to kill us as soon as we've done their bidding."

"That was my thought as well. This whole thing about planting doubt seems a little strange too."

"There is another alternative."

"Which is?"

"They're trying to make it look like Merceria is plotting to overthrow the emperor. The problem is, we don't know this emperor of theirs or how he'll react when we meet him."

"You mean IF we meet him. We still haven't agreed to any of this."

"It's beginning to sound like we have little choice in the matter," said Nikki. "If we don't agree, we'll be of no use to them."

"In which case, they'll kill us; we're dead either way."

"Not necessarily. Perhaps there's a third option?"

"I'm listening."

"The emperor obviously isn't in control, yet he must wield significant influence, else why send us there in the first place?"

"I don't see how that helps us," replied Arnim.

"What if we appeal to him for help?"

"You mean help, as in revealing the plot, or not killing us?"

"Both, or neither. I can't get a feeling for the man until we meet him."

"So you suggest we improvise? You're starting to sound a lot like Gerald."

"I'll take that as a compliment," said Nikki. "In the meantime, if we are to survive, we must play along with these people to ensure an audience."

"I hope you know what you're doing."

"So do I, but there are no guarantees here. This could just as easily turn against us."

Arnim smiled. "True, but we're dead anyway. If we accept that, then there's nothing left to lose."

"Are you trying to cheer me up? Because if you are, you're doing a terrible job of it."

"All I'm saying is we'll be going in with our eyes wide open. If that gets us killed, then so be it."

# THIRTY-EIGHT

# The Cure

WINTER 967 MC

The Queen of Deisenbach entered the room. "Your cousin has returned."

"Did she find the Orcs?" asked Aubrey.

"So it would appear. There are a few of the savages downstairs."

"Hardly a fitting way of addressing someone here to help the king."

"You dare lecture a queen?"

"If she's acting the fool, then yes. Shall we greet these people, or would you prefer your husband not to receive treatment?"

"Follow me," snapped Helisant. "I'll take you to them." She strode from the room, leaving Aubrey and Aldwin to catch up. They descended the stairs to see Beverly, Owen, and a collection of Orcs. Beverly wasted no time, embracing her husband before he even hit the bottom step.

"I see you've been busy," said Aubrey, then switched to Orc. "*Greetings. I am Aubrey Brandon, Life Mage.*"

A female Orc stepped forward. "*I am Krazuhk, master of air and daughter of Lurzak, Chieftain of the Sky Singers.*"

"*Honour to you, Krazuhk.*"

"*And to you. We brought Garok, a shaman of our tribe, to assist you in healing your king. These other hunters are here to assure his safety.*"

"*What do you require of me?*" asked Garok.

"*I assume you've performed healing before?*" replied Aubrey.

"*Yes.*"

"*Then I need only teach you how to enhance your magic and combine it with mine.*" She switched to the Human tongue. "We shall need a room with some privacy."

"Why?" asked the queen.

"I must link my magic with Garok's to heal the king, and that is something which takes practice."

The queen had opened her mouth to speak when her mage entered the room, interrupting the conversation.

"Your Majesty," said Ludmilla. "It appears I arrived just in time to stop you."

"Stop me?" replied the queen. "Why?"

"These people plot to kill the king, Majesty."

"What's this, now?" Helisant stepped back. "Guards!" Royal guards flooded into the room. "Thank the Saints you came when you did, Ludmilla. You have a gift for timing."

"Ludmilla?" shouted Sir Owen. "As in, Ludmilla Stormwind?"

"Stormwind?" said Aubrey. "I know that name. Your family has been linked to the empire."

"What nonsense is this?" replied the Water Mage. "I'll have you know the Stormwinds are the most sought-after mages in the Petty Kingdoms!"

Owen turned to the queen. "Your Majesty, this woman did everything she could to stop us from finding the Orcs. First, she had us attacked on the road north, then when that failed, she tried to prevent us from returning to Agran."

Aubrey took a step closer. "Your Majesty, your husband, the king, is at death's door. Surely you can see that?"

"I... I can," said the queen. "Yet how do I know you're not attempting to finish him off?"

"I know this is a tough decision for you, but to do nothing will only result in his death. You have nothing to lose if we try to help him, and everything to gain."

"Don't listen to them," insisted Ludmilla. "They're lying to you in an attempt to gain influence."

"Influence?" said Aubrey. "Of what use is that to us? Once the king is healed, we are leaving Deisenbach, never to return. How would such influence benefit us?"

"Ask yourself this," added Beverly. "Who would benefit from the king's death?"

"Caldon, his nephew," replied the queen, her gaze shifting to Ludmilla. "Who happens to be on good terms with my court mage."

"This is all a misunderstanding," said Ludmilla. "I am on good terms with everyone here at the Palace."

"Yet you advise me to leave my husband untreated, despite knowing he's on his deathbed. Seize her!" The guards moved in, taking the Water Mage by the arms. "See that she's detained in the dungeon."

"You'll regret this!" shouted Ludmilla. "Treating a Stormwind in such a manner will not be easily forgiven."

"I can live with that, providing my husband survives." The queen turned pleading eyes on Aubrey. "Tell me you can save him."

"I shall do all I can, Majesty. You have my word."

"Then show your Orc friend what he needs to know. All within the Palace are at your disposal."

"Not so fast," said Beverly. "There are a few things we need to discuss first."

"Such as?"

"Your treatment of the Orcs."

"This is not the time for such things."

"On the contrary, this is precisely the time."

The queen bit back a response. "What are your demands?"

"First, you will remove the bounty on Orcs."

"Done."

"You will also guarantee the safety of Master Garok and these other Orcs, both now and in the future."

"You are asking for a great sacrifice."

"Sacrifice? How?" said Beverly. "I'm asking you to grant these people the same dignity and respect as the rest of your subjects. I think you'll find that doing so will benefit you."

"How so?"

"Garok is a shaman, a Life Mage in Human terms. How many courts in the Petty Kingdoms have magical healers at their disposal?"

"Very few."

"Think of the status that would give you amongst your peers?"

"And he would agree to remain here at court once the king recovered?"

"I think it safe to say arrangements could be made, providing they were treated with respect."

"Lady Aubrey, please teach this shaman what he needs to heal my husband. While you're doing that, I shall work with Lady Beverly to compose Royal Edicts to accomplish what she has asked for. Will that suffice?"

"It will," said Beverly. "And thank you, Your Majesty, for your willingness to change."

. . .

Aubrey and Garok stood over the sleeping form of King Justinian. The queen's healer, Garrig, waited nearby, though he lacked the scowl this time.

Beverly held Aldwin's hand as the pair of mages cast their spell. They'd seen Aubrey heal before, but this was something else. She and Garok worked as one, speaking the words of power in harmony as if singing a hymn to Saxnor.

A calm settled over the room, and everyone visibly relaxed. The mages' hands glowed with a pale-green light as they leaned over the king, gently cradling his head between them. The light flowed from their fingers into him, yet the spell continued.

A profound weariness overwhelmed Beverly as if all her strength had been drained. Aldwin squeezed her hand, waking her mind once more, and she met his gaze, losing herself in his grey eyes.

"We are done," announced Aubrey, her voice betraying her fatigue.

"Is he healed?" asked the queen.

"Partially. The spell was successful but requires repeated castings to ensure a full recovery."

"Then cast again."

"I cannot, for his body needs time to process the magic. Garok and I will repeat the procedure tomorrow and possibly the day after."

"Thank the Saints. This illness was almost the death of him."

"This was no ordinary illness," insisted Aubrey. "It was more akin to poison."

"Was it something he ate? I shall have the servants interrogated."

"It was not ingested. Rather, it was magical in nature. I've seen this before in Merceria. There, the energy of ley lines caused it. I fear it was something similar here."

"Whatever do you mean?"

"Merely that he came into close proximity with a material which affected his mind. I would guess a vial containing a glowing, green energy similar to that found in the ley lines. By its very nature, it is magic in its purest form, but it corrupts the mind."

"I shall order these quarters searched. Would it be dangerous to handle?"

"Only after prolonged exposure, and even then, you'd have to be very close to it. I would start by searching his mattress. That's the most likely place to conceal it."

"Do you mean to suggest moving him to another bed would have allowed him to recover?"

"No," said Aubrey. "The infection, once present, will not end on its own."

"And if it should return once you've left?"

"I've taught Garok how to work with others, so he can pass the skill on to another shaman if needed."

"How can I ever thank you?"

"You might consider having some of your people learn the language of the Orcs so you can communicate with them."

"Certainly."

"Now, having healed him, how about we transfer him to another room, then you can search this one?"

"I shall see to it at once."


The hour was late. Beverly sat at a table, picking away at a plate of food while Aldwin sipped an ale. Aubrey snoozed in a nearby chair while Sir Owen read from a book.

"What have you got there?" asked Beverly.

"It is the Book of Mathew," the knight replied. "A written account of his teachings. I find it gives me solace when my mind is troubled."

"Troubled?" said Aldwin. "Everything turned out for the best. You should be happy."

"I'm glad the king is showing signs of recovery, but the implication that a Stormwind was somehow involved gives me the shivers. Have you any idea how influential that family is?"

"Not as much as they used to be after all this, I imagine."

Beverly couldn't help but laugh. "Aldwin has a point. These Stormwinds are clearly trouble."

"Indeed," said Owen, "but I wish you'd told me what you knew, earlier."

"Don't look at me," said Beverly. "Aubrey's the one who's been in contact with Shaluhk, not me. I wouldn't know a Stormwind from a... Well, whatever the opposite of a Stormwind would be."

"That would be a Sartellian. They are the Fire Mages."

"I believe Aubrey's mentioned that name before too. If I recall, they're also involved with the empire."

Owen paled. "This is getting worse and worse. Have you any idea the influence they wield?"

"Until now, they've been a distant threat, but if we are to travel north, we must be wary of further interference. You're more knowledgeable about the politics of this region. Can you take a guess as to what Ludmilla was up to?"

"It's pretty clear she wanted the nephew to be crowned king."

"Yes, but why? What was the reason behind that?"

"We won't know until she's been properly interrogated."

Aubrey suddenly sat up with a start. She looked around the room, unfocused.

"Are you all right, Cousin?"

"I'm fine," the mage replied. "What are you talking about?"

"Ludmilla," said Beverly. "We were speculating about why she wanted to replace the king."

"And what did you come up with?"

"Nothing yet."

One of the queen's guards entered the room. "My pardon, Lady Aubrey, but we found something in the king's mattress, just as you speculated. A small crystal vial with a glowing green liquid inside. Her Majesty wants to know what to do with it."

"Bury it as deep as you can and hope it never again sees the light of day."

"Where does one acquire such a thing?"

"That's an excellent question for which I have no easy answer."

The guard chuckled. "Have you a difficult answer?"

"I do, as a matter of fact. I imagine someone found a way to tap into the ley lines, using magic, then cast some sort of containment spell to put it into that vial."

"Is such a thing even possible?" asked Beverly.

"Theoretically," said Aubrey. "I know Kiren-Jool has a spell of preservation. The Kurathians use it to prevent food from spoiling on long voyages. I'll admit it's not quite the same thing, but I see how something similar could be used."

"But that would make it an enchantment, wouldn't it? I was under the impression Ludmilla's a Water Mage?"

"She is," replied the guard.

"This mystery only deepens," said Beverly. "Perhaps we'd best have a word with her?"

"I can take you to her cell if you like."

"Thank you. And while you're at it, you might wish to inform the queen. She'll likely want someone she trusts there for the interrogation."

"Of course. I'll make the necessary arrangements." He left them, calling out for others as he went.

Sir Owen rubbed his hands together. "A mystery. How exciting. You Mercerians certainly know how to keep things interesting."

Aubrey sighed. "All we wanted to do was head to Reinwick, and now we're getting caught up in regional politics. Is there no end to this?"

"Hush," said Beverly. "We'll soon see this all behind us."

It wasn't long before the queen arrived, looking at them expectantly. "You wanted to talk to Ludmilla?"

"If that's permissible," said Beverly.

"I shall accompany you. The better to judge the truthfulness of her answers. The dungeons are this way."

They followed her through the Palace, eventually descending into the cellars. Aubrey shivered, for the air was noticeably cooler. "Something's wrong."

"Yes," added the queen. "It's far too cold down here." They came upon a guard standing before a door. "Open it up. We would have words with the prisoner."

The guard grabbed the ring of keys from his belt, then fumbled with the lock. A moment later, the latch clicked, and the door swung open with a groan. The room beyond was small, but more worrying was that it was empty, save for a smattering of chunks of ice.

"What's this?" said the queen.

"Magic," replied Aubrey.

Beverly paced the room, looking for anything that might indicate what had happened. "She must have used a spell of recall. We should have anticipated that."

"Not recall," replied her cousin, picking up a small cube that melted in her hands. "This was Water Magic."

"Unfortunate," said the queen. "It appears we shall get no answers this day."

"She may not have been working alone," suggested Aubrey. "Something of this magnitude required inside help. You might wish to interrogate the servants."

"You think they betrayed their king?"

"It's more likely someone fooled them into thinking they were helping. Either that, or they were coerced. Still, it bears investigating."

"And I shall. I promise you."


Three days later, the group prepared to depart. Beverly, Aubrey, and Aldwin would travel north, to Reinwick, with Sir Owen guiding them. Keon had proven useful to Viden and accepted an offer to become an apprentice smith.

True to her word, the queen convinced King Justinian to grant an amnesty to all Orcs, rescinding the bounty and ordering the release of those currently under lock and key.

Garok would remain in the capital for a few weeks to keep an eye on the king, as would his protectors, but in a surprising move, Krazuhk refused.

Instead, she announced she would return to Ag-Dular to tell her father of the change in their fortunes.

Since they were going in that direction anyway, Beverly suggested they accompany her, if only to ensure she arrived home safely. They travelled the road to Santrem for two days before circling around the edge of the Wildwood, heading east. Several days later, the Orc village came into sight.

Their return was cause for celebration, and Lurzak ordered a feast in their honour. They served the milk of life, and the Humans were made honorary members of the Sky Singers.

Later that night, they sat around a dying fire. Sir Owen had once again passed out due to an overabundance of drink, but the other three, more used to Orc celebrations, were wide awake.

"I'm glad this is all over," said Aldwin.

"As am I," agreed Aubrey. "Let's hope the rest of this trip is a little less exciting."

"I'll second that."

"One thing's for certain," said Beverly. "We're not splitting up again."

"Agreed," chimed in the other two.

"Still," said Aubrey, "it was very educational, but I don't want to cross paths with any more Stormwinds."

"Or Sartellians," added Aldwin. "Don't forget them."

"I tell you what," said Beverly. "If we run across any more mages, we'll turn around and ride in the other direction." They all laughed.

An Orc emerged from the shadows, the fire's light revealing it was Krazuhk.

"*I hope I am not interrupting,*" she said.

"*Not at all,*" replied Beverly, speaking in the Orcish tongue. "*It's nice to see you again, although I can't help but feel something's troubling you.*"

"*I am surprised you can read the facial expressions of an Orc. Then again, I suppose it is not unexpected. By your own admission, you have spent much time amongst our people.*"

"*Feel free to speak your mind, Krazuhk. Perhaps we can help?*"

The Orc nodded. "*I discussed the matter with my father, and while he is not in agreement, he will honour my decision.*"

"*And what decision would that be?*"

"*I wish to travel with you.*"

"*North? To Reinwick?*"

"*No. All the way back to your home in Merceria.*"

"*That could take months,*" said Aubrey. "*And once we're there, we have no way of returning here to Ag-Dular.*"

"*I am aware of that, yet I find myself filled with a yearning to travel. You say Orcs are accepted in your lands. Would they welcome one such as me?*"

"*Most definitely. In fact, your presence there would be particularly advantageous.*"

"*Why is that?*"

"*You're a master of air, and our academy has an Air Mage who needs to be trained.*"

The Orc grinned. "*Then our meeting is most fortuitous.*"

# THIRTY-NINE

# Retreat

WINTER 967 MC

L anaka reined in his horse. Before him, wagons sat broken, evidence his raids had found the enemy's weakness, but he knew it wouldn't last. They would soon escort their supplies with cavalry, something they seemed to have in abundance, and raids like this would become a thing of the past.

Captain Gardner rode towards him. "The Wincaster Light Horse performed well today. I trust your men didn't suffer?"

"Only light casualties," replied Gardner. "Nothing serious, but we discovered something." He slowed to a stop beside his commander. "The Halvarians suffered a loss a few days ago."

"Loss? Was there a battle?"

"Yes, though from the sounds of it, they're describing it more as a skirmish."

"That must be Heward's group," said Lanaka. "They were due in the region some time ago. Did they speak of anything specific?"

"They mentioned Orcs, but that was about it. Then again, these people aren't warriors, they're wagon drivers."

"Still useful sources of information."

"We've taken some of their stores for our own use. I assume we'll burn the rest?"

"Yes," replied Lanaka. "Along with the remaining wagons, but let's leave the people out of this, shall we? As you said, they're not warriors."

"There is one more thing," added Gardner. "They've ordered more siege engines to Ironcliff. I'd suggest attacking them before they arrive, but they're apparently heavily guarded."

"It's tempting, but we must preserve what forces we have. If Ironcliff is now under siege, we cannot get replacements." He looked westward. "Somewhere over there, is Lord Heward's army. The problem we face is that between us and them sits a large number of Halvarians, many of them mounted. What we need is a way of getting past them."

Gardner smiled. "I have just the thing." He shifted to one side and pointed at a nearby pile of crates. "Do you see those?"

Lanaka nodded. "What are they?"

"Replacement standards, if you can believe it. I thought we might use them to hide our true allegiance."

His commander smiled. "You're suggesting we masquerade as our enemy? What an excellent idea."

"It won't work if we get too close as our armour is too different from theirs, not to mention your Kurathian saddles, but at long range, we should be able to pull it off."

"Have your men distribute them amongst our companies."

"What do we do with the prisoners?"

"Confiscate their weapons, then send them eastward on foot. We can't afford to take them into custody."

"They might know more about this legion of theirs."

"Undoubtedly, but we can spare neither the men nor the time to interrogate them. If we are to make it to Holdcross, we must move quickly." Gardner rode off to issue the orders.

Lanaka had three companies under his command, all light cavalry, yet it wasn't enough. True, they had gotten behind the enemy army and done significant damage, but the gap was not an area that favoured mobility. The mountains blocked them both north and south, leaving only a flat plain with little to hide their presence. Even now, he wondered how long it would be before the Halvarians responded to the sight of their wagons burning. He must ensure his men were well out of the area before that came to pass.


The smoke trails were high as they rode out, their course taking them south. Lanaka decided to ride close to the edge of the mountains, thus putting as much distance between themselves and the enemy's main objective of Ironcliff.

The day wore on, and with it came a cold northern wind. As a Kurathian, he was more accustomed to warmer climes, but years in Merceria had hardened him to the realities of life in his new home.

His men maintained their formation despite the bitter winds. Two-thirds were Kurathians like him, who'd come to serve the Queen of Merceria, while the rest were the Wincaster Light Horse, a company Beverly had reorganized some years ago. They'd proved the equal of his Kurathian comrades, and he was proud to have them under his command.

On and on, they rode, the miles slipping away behind them. It was easy to lose one's sense of distance here, for the scenery changed little—flat plains to the north and rugged mountains to the south.

The sun grew lower in the west, and then he spotted a thin line on the horizon, indicating someone was marching. He sent Captain Caluman forward with six men, keen eyes all, and it didn't take long for them to return.

"Cavalry," he reported. "Their horses are small, and their armour light. I suspect they are similar to those Captain Gardner encountered before our arrival."

"Numbers?" asked Lanaka.

"Two hundred or so."

"Any sign they saw you?"

"None, Commander. They're riding west, much as we are, but at a much slower pace."

"No doubt to conserve their strength. From what I've seen so far, our mounts are superior."

"What do you want us to do?"

Lanaka raised his hand, signalling the column to halt. "Captains to me," he called out. "I have an idea, but it will require some explanation."

He waited, going over the plan in his mind. It was risky, but then again, what battle wasn't? If he succeeded, he would not only see his men to safety but strike a blow that would further hurt their enemy.

Caluman was soon joined by Captains Ruzak and Gardner. Lanaka looked at each in turn but saw only determination. These were good men, all experienced in battle, and although Gardner was new to the position of captain, he'd already distinguished himself.

"Night is almost upon us," Lanaka started, "but the enemy blocks our way. Thanks to our recent raid, we have Halvarian standards to carry. I propose we ride into their camp and return them."

He paused as smiles broke out on the faces of his captains. "In the dark, we look much the same as them. We will carry on this ruse until we are amongst them, then we'll strike. Our objective is to sow fear and panic, but don't linger. Inflict your damage and ride on before they organize a defence. If you find the opportunity to capture or drive off their horses, then do so, but not at risk to yourselves. Understood?"

They all nodded.

"Any questions?"

Ruzak spoke first: "What can we expect when we strike?"

"They are highly disciplined, so they will set up their fires in nice, neat rows, making it that much easier to navigate our way through. As to their horses, you can expect them to be nearby, likely each company having their own area. We've fought them before, so we know what to anticipate regarding fighting spirit. What we don't know is how many guards they'll have or whether they'll be mounted or not."

"Their captains are competent," he continued, "but past experience tells us they lack initiative. They have no sergeants we know of, and their companies are twice the size of ours, meaning their officers are stretched very thin. By the way, if you see one of their captains, feel free to take it upon yourself to kill him, not that they'll be easy to identify at night."

"Above all, keep an eye on your men. The last thing we want is people getting lost in the dark and left behind."

"Have we a rendezvous point, just in case?" asked Gardner.

"Head west, along the edge of the mountains, but make sure you're well out of range of the enemy."

Caluman grinned. "When do we start?"

Lanaka looked west to where the top of the sun still peeked over the horizon. "Once that disappears, return to your companies, my friends. Battle will soon be joined."

They rode in darkness, their horses moving slowly to maintain the cohesion of the companies. Lanaka led Caluman's company, while Gardner's brought up the rear. He had complete faith in his captains, but even so, there were a lot of variables in an attack like this. Uneven ground, or an alert sentry, could easily ruin what little advantage they possessed.

The campfires grew brighter, providing a convenient aiming point for the column. A guard standing beside a fire noted their approach, and Lanaka casually waved back, hoping to convince him they were all one big, happy legion, his riders returning from a long patrol.

Once he was close enough to see the guard's face, Lanaka urged his horse into a canter and drew his sword. He steered directly for the guard, saying a silent prayer to Saint Mathew.

Moments later, his weapon descended, striking the fellow in the head, cleaving his helmet in two. Lanaka's blade nearly ripped out of his hand as the body fell, but he pulled it free in time.

Unlike most other cavalrymen, Kurathians didn't scream in battle. Instead, they came silently, bringing death to their enemies in the dark. He jumped the fire and then rode beside a row of tents, slicing through ropes, creating as much confusion as possible. In his wake, his command spread out to cover a larger area.

Despite his fears, there were no mounted Halvarians to greet him or armed guards in sufficient quantity to put up any sort of resistance.

It felt surreal as if he were riding along in a dream, his sword rising and falling with precision, collapsing tents, and occasionally striking down one of the empire's warriors. He reached the other side of the camp and slowed, twisting around to see how his men fared.

Torches lit the camp, both from the enemy, now awakened to the danger, and from some of Lanaka's men eager to set fire to tents. The sound of hoofbeats off to his right drew his attention, and he turned to see a group of enemy horsemen riding straight for him, their weapons bared, many unarmoured due to their rush to respond to the threat.

Rather than stand and fight, he urged his horse onward, leading them away from the camp. They took the bait, galloping after him with wild abandon.

Caluman's company, having followed Lanaka through the camp, kept riding, their Kurathian mounts faster than the enemy's. They caught up with the group pursuing their commander and made short work of them.

Lanaka, glancing over his shoulder, noted the lack of pursuit and circled around to rendezvous with Caluman. The second Kurathian company soon joined them, but there was no sign of the Wincaster Light Horse.

Caluman looked towards the enemy camp. "Do we go back for them?"

"No," said Lanaka. "We stick to the plan and ride west. Saints willing, Captain Gardner will rendezvous with us there."


The night was bitter, but the Kurathians refrained from building fires lest it alert the enemy. Still, the horses needed to rest and the men to eat, so they set up a makeshift camp at the foot of the mountains. Pickets were set and the men ordered to sleep in their armour in case of attack, but the enemy didn't show itself.

The sun was peeking over the horizon when riders were spotted off in the distance. At first, they were taken for Halvarians, so the alarm was given, but when they continued trotting instead of charging in, they realized it was only Gardner's company. However, they had a surprise of their own—captured horses.

Lanaka sat in his saddle, waiting as they entered the camp. Captain Gardner, wearing an enormous grin, rode right up to him.

"Sorry for the delay, Commander. We got a little mixed up in the dark.

We were halfway back to our starting position when we realized our mistake."

"I see," replied Lanaka. "And so you rode through the camp once more to retrieve those horses?"

"Not quite. We captured these on our first visit. The second time, we rode around the north end to avoid them. Admittedly, they were a little preoccupied at the time."

"Doing what?"

"Putting out fires and repairing tents, I assume. Any idea of losses?"

"We lost three," said Lanaka, "and only killed a dozen or so, but we left at least as many wounded, if accounts are to be believed. Those horses you liberated constitute a greater loss as far as they're concerned." He paused as he saw the state of Gardner's men. "They must be exhausted."

"The joy of battle is still raging, so I doubt any would be able to sleep just yet."

"In that case, we'll head out without delay. We might be past the Halvarians, but we've still got a good day's ride, possibly two, before we reach Holdcross." He forced a smile. "What I wouldn't give to have a decent map. You lead, Captain. You've earned that right."


Lord Heward looked out from atop the roof of the Singing Crow. It wasn't much of an inn, but the building was one of the tallest structures in Holdcross and gave him a superb view of the area. His army was secure for the moment, and he'd taken pains to fortify the town. There was no wall, but they'd used barrels and wagons to block off the streets while spikes were erected to keep enemy horsemen at bay.

His own cavalry continued to scout the area but had yet to report any significant activity on the part of the empire. They appeared content to focus their attention elsewhere, likely towards the siege of Ironcliff.

The thought made him wonder how the Dwarves fared. They'd been preparing for some time now, and Saxnor knew a Dwarven stronghold was not an easy nut to crack, yet he worried nonetheless. The warrior in him wanted to march east to relieve the siege, but such a move would be pure recklessness. He must content himself to remain here, where he could work to contain any attempt to push into Norland.

He felt a presence beside him and turned to see the master of earth, Kharzug.

"*Greetings,*" said the Orc. "*I hope I am not disturbing you?*"

"*Not at all,*" replied Heward, easily slipping into the Orc's native tongue. "*I came up here for some fresh air.*"

"Let me guess. Too many people offering their advice?"

"You know me well."

"I must admit, it is strange to be here amongst so many Norland warriors, particularly since we fought them in the recent war. It is a good thing, though, for it brings our two races closer to one another. If there is to be a lasting peace between our peoples, then this may be the best way to accomplish that."

"You forget," said Heward. "I'm a Mercerian. My people already accept Orcs."

"True, but those are not of my tribe. I have high hopes we can find the same camaraderie here as our cousins the Black Arrows have done in the south with you Mercerians."

"You will. It takes time."

Kharzug's gaze locked on to something. "Time is a luxury we may not have."

Far off in the distance, a large group of horsemen approached.

"Sound the alarm!" called out Heward, then switched back to Orcish. "Can you make out who they are?"

"Give me a moment, and I shall cast a spell." The master of earth closed his eyes, calling on his inner magic. Strange words tumbled from his mouth, and then his eyes glazed over.

Heward looked skyward. "I see no birds."

"Why would you? I am seeing through the eyes of another creature." He pointed to the north, where a single deer ran across the plain, its antlers on full display.

"You chose a deer? I would have thought their eyesight inferior to ours?"

The Orc smiled. "Then you would not understand the way of nature. While Humans see better than deer during the day, the reverse is true in the setting sun."

"And you would know this how, exactly?"

"Through experience. This is not the first time I have seen through the eyes of one."

"Why not use a wolf?"

"For the simple reason there are none in the area. I can summon various animals, but I do not call them out of thin air. I must, therefore, call on those in the vicinity."

"And what does your deer tell you?"

"Those riders are friendly."

"And how do you know that?"

"While it is true most Humans look alike in the eyes of an Orc, a Kurathian is a far different matter. I am assuming the enemy does not employ them?"

"Not to my knowledge."

"Then I think it safe to assume they are our allies."

"That makes sense," said Heward. "I know Commander Lanaka was working *out of Ironcliff. I can only assume he avoided getting trapped inside."* He broke into a grin. *"It seems Saxnor is with us. The addition of those horsemen gives us exactly what we needed—a cavalry force capable of taking the fight to the enemy."*

# Epilogue

WINTER 967 MC

(In the tongue of the Trolls)

The sun was yet to put in an appearance when Tog awoke, rising from his bed to look out the window. All he could see by the moon's light was the mist hugging the ground as it drifted through Trollden in tiny swirls.

He breathed deeply. There was a slight chill in the air along with the humidity, not an unexpected thing, considering the swamp, but that was precisely what he liked about the place.

Turning away from the window, he picked up a pitcher to pour himself some water. He was still half asleep, yet that didn't prevent him from registering a cry of alarm. He raced back to the window, pitcher still in hand, to see a Troll with a familiar gait running towards his hut.

Tog leaned out the window. "Gral? Is that you?"

"It is," came the reply. "There is danger!"

"Where?"

Gral halted and turned seaward, extending his arm. "There."

"I see nothing."

"Look above the fog, not into it."

Tog struggled to make out what Gral was speaking about, then he noticed what looked like poles sticking out of the blanket of fog. He instantly knew what it was. "Sound the alarm," he called back. "It is time to man the defences."

Someone sounded the gong, the signal they were under attack. Tog went to his bed, grabbed his club, and returned to the window, staring into the gloom. The fog thinned, revealing dark shapes beneath the poles. Ships! A massive armada that could only mean one thing—the invasion of Merceria had begun.

<<<<>>>>

REVIEW ENEMY OF THE CROWN

~

READ PERIL OF THE CROWN NEXT

~

If you liked *Enemy of the Crown* then *Temple Knight,* the first book in the *Power Ascending* series awaits.

START TEMPLE KNIGHT

# Cast of Characters

## MAIN CHARACTERS

### MERCERIA & ALLIES
Aldwin Fitzwilliam - Master Smith, married to Beverly Fitzwilliam
Anna - Queen of Merceria, married to Alric, mother of Braedon
Arnim Caster - Viscount of Haverston, Knight of the Hound, married to Nikki
Aubrey Brandon - Baroness of Hawksburg, Life Mage
Beverly Fitzwilliam (Redblade) - Baroness of Bodden, married to Aldwin Fitzwilliam
Gerald Matheson - Duke of Wincaster, Marshal of the Army
Hayley Chambers - Baroness of Queenston, Knight of the Hound, High Ranger
Herdwin Steelarm - Dwarf, smith
Heward 'The Axe' Manton - Baron of Redridge, Knight of the Hound
Kasri Ironheart - Dwarf, Warrior, daughter of Thalgrun Stormhammer
Lanaka - Kurathian, Mercerian Commander of Cavalry
Nicole 'Nikki' Arendale - Viscountess Haverston, married to Arnim Caster
Owen - Knight of Erlingen

### HALVARIA
Edora Sartellian - Fire Mage, Inner Council
Exalor Shozarin - Enchanter, High Strategos
Kelson Shozarin - Enchanter, Life Mage, High Sentinel

## SECONDARY CHARACTERS

### MERCERIANS
Albreda - Mistress of the Whitewood, Earth Mage
Aldus Hearn - Earth Mage
Alric – King of Weldwyn, married to Queen Anna, father of Braedon
Andronicus (Deceased) – Royal Life Mage, Mentor to Revi Bloom
Arandil Greycloak - Fire Mage, Enchanter, Elven ruler of the Darkwood
Bickerstaff - Sergeant, Wincaster Light Horse
Braedon Gerald - Prince of Merceria, son of Anna and Alric

Caluman - Kurathian Captain, Light Cavalry
Carlson - Cavalry commander
Clara - Conservatory student, Life Mage in training
Efram Cookson - Sergeant, 5th Wincaster Foot
Evard Brenton - Royal Guardsman
Evermore (Deceased) - Queen of Merceria (635 - 655 MC)
Gral - Troll, Trollden
Jane Goodwin - Weldwyn noblewoman, paramour of Gerald Matheson
Kiren-Jool - Kurathian Enchanter
Lightning - Beverly's Mercerian Charger
Preston Wright - Baron of Wickfield, Knight of the Hound, married to Sophie Wright
Randolf Blackburn - Disgraced Knight of the Sword
Revi Bloom - Life Mage, Enchanter
Richard (Fitz) Fitzwilliam (Deceased) - Baron of Bodden, father of Beverly Fitzwilliam
Ruzak - Kurathian Captain, Light Cavalry
Samantha (Sam) - Queen's Ranger
Shellbreaker (Jamie) - Revi Bloom's avian familiar
Snarl - Large wolf of Albreda's pack, The Whitewood
Sophie Wright - Queen Anna's Lady-in-Waiting, married to Sir Preston
Storm - Kurathian Mastiff, Queen Anna's pet
Tog - Earl of Trollden, Leader of the Trolls

## Dwarves
Agramath - Master of Rock and Stone, Ironcliff
Galman Boldhammer - Captain, Stonecastle
Garnik Hardhand - Guildmaster, Warriors Guild, Ironcliff
Gelion Brightaxe - Captain, Stonecastle
Kharzun (Deceased) - Vard of Stonecastle, built Kharzun's Folly
Khazad - Vard of Stonecastle
Malrun Bronzefist - Master of Revels, Ironcliff
Margel - Forgemate to Gelion
Strodar Goldeye - Guildmaster, Bankers Guild, Ironcliff
Thalgrun Stormhammer - Vard of Ironcliff
Thyrim Broadaxe - Guidmaster, Warriors Guild, Stonecastle
Tindal - Warrior, Stonecastle

## Orcs
Bloodrig - Shaman, Sky Singers, Deisenbach
Garok - Shaman in training, Sky Singers, Deisenbach

Ghodrug - Chieftain, Black Ravens, Norland
Kharzug - Master of Earth, Black Ravens, Norland
Kraloch - Shaman, Black Arrows, Merceria
Krazuhk - Master of Air, chieftain's daughter, Sky Singers, Deisenbach
Lurzak - Chieftain, Sky Singers, Deisenbach
Rotuk - Master of Air, Cloud Hunters, Therengia
Rulahk - Shaman, Black Ravens, Norland
Shaluhk - Shaman, Red Hand, Therengia
Tarig - Hunter, Sky Singers, Deisenbach
Ugrug - Hunter, Sky Singer, Deisenbach
Urgon - Chieftain, Black Arrows, Merceria

## HALVARIANS

Adrik - Aide to Admiral Kozarsky Stormwind
Agalix Sartellian - Fire Mage, Inner Council
Alitor Verathras - Earth Mage
Anexil Shozarin - Enchanter
Bastien Lambert - Commander General, 7th Halvarian Legion
Enelle Sartellian - Fire Mage, High Purifier, High Council
Esteve Solinak - Commander-General 3rd Halvarian Legion
Fadra Stormwind - Water Mage, Inner Council
Ferran Nygard - Captain General, 1st Provincial Cohort, 7th Legion
Francesco Cardosa - Captain, 2nd Company, 1st Imperial Cohort, 3rd Halvarian Legion
Freya Stormwind - Water Mage, Inner Council
Grafford - Fire Mage, Halvaria
Halmar - Captain, *Covenant*, Halvarian warship
Idraxa Shozarin - Enchanter, Acting Marshal of the North
Janek - Servant at the Imperial Court
Karliss Stormwind - Water Mage, High Scholar
Karoulus - High Regent, Heir to the Crown of Halvaria
Kersey - Captain, *Resplendent*
Kestia Stormwind - Water Mage, Inner Council
Kozarsky Stormwind - Water Mage, Admiral of the Storm Fleet
Murias Stormwind - Water Mage, Inner Council
Nevarus - God Emperor of Halvaria
Olynia Sartellian - Fire Mage
Orland Sartellian - Fire Mage, High Magister
Praxar Shozarin - Enchanter, Marshal of the Empire
Rhedra - Earth Mage, Halvaria
Ryfar Shozarin - Enchanter, Halvarian Agent, Clanholdings

Stalgrun Sartellian - Fire Mage, Marshal of the North
Stivern Lindman - Captain General, 2nd Imperial Cohort, 7th Legion
Yuliya Stormwind - Water Mage, Marshal of the South
Vadym Stormwind - Water Mage, Halvarian Agent, Clanholdings
Wingate - Aide to Exalor

## OTHERS

Alfonce - Knight, Deisenbach
Athgar - High Thane of Therengia
Bronwyn - Queen of Norland
Calden - Nephew and heir to King Justinian, Deisenbach
Calder - Earl of Riverhurst, Norland
Catherine Montrose (Deceased) - Countess of Shrewesdale, Merceria
Deiter Heinrich - Duke of Erlingen, Petty Kingdoms
Edan Thackery - Keeper of Scrolls, Deisenbach
Eucephalus - Ancient Thalamite healer
Flan Delving – Aralani (Wood Elf), Wayward Wood
Gadron - Knight, king's champion, Deisenbach
Garrig - Master Healer, Deisenbach
Giselle - Temple Captain of Saint Agnes, Deisenbach
Graxion Stormwind - Water Mage, the Volstrum, Rhuzina
Gundar - God of Earth
Helisant - Queen, Deisenbach
Hendrick - Knight, Deisenbach
Jack Marlowe - Viscount of Aynsbury, Cavalier, Weldwyn
Justinian - King of Deisenbach
Kayson (Deceased) - King, Rudor
Keon - Rogue, Deisenbach
Kythelia (Deceased) - Elf, Necromancer
Langmar - Knight, Deisenbach
Leonid - Knight, Deisenbach
Ludmilla Stormwind - Water Mage, Deisenbach
Melethandil – Dragon, Thunder Mountains
Morningstar - Horse of Sir Owen
Naran - Captain, Queen Bronwyn's guards
Natalia Stormwind - Water Mage, Warmaster of Therengia
Nymin - Wife of Viden, Deisenbach
Osbourne Megantis - Fire Mage, Weldwyn
Edwina - Princess of Weldwyn, Air Mage in training
Rowan - Temple Knight of Saint Agnes, Deisenbach
Saxnor - God of Strength

Swiftwing - Cairn Eagle
Viden - Smith, Deisenbach

## PLACES

### HALVARIA
Alantra - Coastal city, Shimmering Sea
Calabria - Halvarian conquest, coast of the Shimmering Sea
Dun-Galdrim - Dwarven stronghold, fell to the Halvarians
Varena - Capital of the Empire
Wyburn – City, western border near the gap
Zefara - Coastal city, Sea of Storms

### DEISENBACH
Ag-Dular - Orc Village, Sky Singers, Deisenbach
Agran (The Pale Lady) - Capital, Deisenbach
Badger - Roadside Inn, Deisenbach
Bessin – Town, Agran-Santrem road, Deisenbach
Damenholtz - Town, southwest of Agran, Deisenbach
Freizel - Town, northern Deisenbach
Grey Hills – Hills, eastern region of Deisenbach
Herst - Town, northern Deisenbach
Rasfeld River – River, eastern border of Deisenbach
Rotmar - Town, western Deisenbach
Rusty Axe - Roadside Inn, Deisenbach
Trivoli - Town, Deisenbach
Underfeld - Town, southwest of Agran, Deisenbach
Volbruck - Town, Deisenbach
Lumly - Village between Trivoli and Volbruck, Deisenbach
Santrem - Village on border with Zowenbruch

### PETTY KINGDOMS
Andover – Kingdom, northern coast
Angvil - Kingdom, north of Zowenbruch
Arnsfeld – Kingdom, northern coast
Corassus - City state on the coast of the Shimmering Sea
Deisenbach - Kingdom north of Hadenfelf
Eidolon - Northern kingdom
Erlingen - Kingdom mid way between Hadenfeld and Reinwick
Gotfeld - Kingdom bordering Deisenbach to the northwest
Grislagen - Kingdom bordering Deisenbach to the south

Hadenfeld - Petty Kingdom bordering Deisenbach to the south east
Ilea - Kingdom on the coast of the Shimmering Sea
Novarsk - Eastern Petty Kingdom absorbed by Therengia
Reinwick - Northern kingdom on the coast of the Great Northern Sea
Rudor - Kingdom on the border with Halvaria
Talstadt - Petty Kingdom west of Deisenbach
Zowenbruch - Kingdom east of Deisenbach
Regensbach - Eastern kingdom, home to the Antonine

## MERCERIA

Bodden – Town, Barony
Colbridge – City, Dukedom
Eastwood –City, Earldom
Haverston – Town, Viscountcy
Hawksburg – Town, Barony
Redridge – Town, Barony
Shrewesdale – City, Earldom
Tewsbury – City, Earldom
Trollden – Village, Earldom
Uxley - Village
Wincaster - Capital City, Dukedom

## OTHER KINGDOMS

Ironcliff - Dwarven Stronghold
Norland – Kingdom, north of Merceria
Old Kingdom - Name for historical kingdom of Therengia
Ravensguard - Orc stronghold, east of Norland
Stonecastle - Dwarven stronghold, east of Merceria
Thalemia - Ancient Empire, Shimmering Sea
Therengia - Realm east of the Petty Kingdoms
Kurathia - Series of island principalities lying far to the south
Twelve Clans (Clanholdings) - West of Weldwyn

## CITTIES AND TOWNS

Antonine - Capital of the Church of the Saints, Regensbach
Anvil - Town, Norland
Galburn's Ridge - Capital City, Norland
Holdcross - Northern town, Norland
Karslev - City, Capital of Ruzhina, Home of the Volstrum
Summersgate - Capital City, Weldwyn
Ravensguard – Orc city, formally part of Norland

## LOCATIONS

College of Mages - School for Enchanters, Halvaria
Darkwood - Elven realm and forest, west of Stonecastle
Green Pony - Tavern, Chandley, Norland
Imperial Archives - Repository of knowledge, Varena, Halvaria
Korascajan – Magical Academy for Fire Mages
Kharzun's Folly - Collapsed bridge, east of Stonecastle
Queen's Arms - Tavern, Wincaster, Merceria
Singing Crow - Inn, Holdcross, Norland
Sullen Peaks - Mountain range, Stonecastle to Ironcliff
Sunset Peaks - Mountain range, western border of the Clanholdings
Sword and Scabbard - Inn, Agran, Deisenbach
Terengaria - Ancient name for land now taken by Merceria, Weldwyn, and the Clans
The Badger - Roadside Inn, Deisenbach
The Greatwood - Large forest, north of Weldwyn
Thunder Mountains – Mountain range, north of Norland, location of Ironcliff
Twelve Clans (Clanholdings) - West of Weldwyn
Volstrum - Magical Academy for Water Mages, Karslev, Rhuzina
Wayward Wood – Forest, east of Ironcliff, inhabited by the Aralani
Wickfield Hills – Hills, west of Wickfield, Merceria
Wildwood – Forest, northeast of Agran, Deisenbach

## ORC TRIBES

Ashwalkers - Reinwick
Orcs of the Black Arrow - Artisan Hills
Orcs of the Black Raven - Ravensguard
Red Hand - Therengia
Sky Singers - Deisenbach

## BATTLES AND SHIPS

*Alantra* - Halvarian warship
*Covenant* - Halvarian Warship
*Fantine* - Halvarian merchant ship
*Resplendent* - Halvarian Flagship
The Siege of Summersgate (966 MC) - Mercerian\Weldwyn Army retakes Summersgate

## TERMS

Aralani - Wood Elves

Cairn Eagle (Mountain Coaster) - Rare bird found in the Sullen Peaks
Cunars - Temple Knights of Saint Cunar, religious fighting order
Great Dream - Halvarian goal to conquer the entire Continent
Hearth Guard - Elite Dwarven warriors, Ironcliff
High Council - Halvarian council serving the Emperor
High Ranger - Commander of all Mercerian Rangers
Inner Council - True rulers of Halvaria
Knights of the Sceptre - Order of Chivalry, Erlingen
Mercerian Charger - Large breed of warhorse, raised in Merceria
Milk of Life - Ceremonial Orc drink
Nature's Fury - Magical hammer wielded by Beverly Fitzwilliam
Purifier - Halvarian agents, eliminate opposition to the Emperor
Quest for Knowledge - Dwarven coming-of-age ritual
Saint Agnes - Patron Saint of women
Saint Cunar - Patron Saint of warriors
Saint Mathew - Patron Saint of the poor and sick
Saurian - Ancient race predating the coming of the Elder Races
Sentinel – Halvarian Life Mages, act as judge, also called Truthseekers
Shadowbark - A type of wood that is stronger than steel
Strategos - The highest military rank in Halvaria
Temple Knights - Religious fighting order dedicated the Saintly orders
Thalamites – Ancient race of people from Thalemia
The Gilded Throne - The Throne of Halvaria
Vard - Dwarven King or Queen
Victory Fountain - Memorial in Varena

# A Few Words from Paul

This book is a departure of sorts from my regular style of writing as it delves deeply into the inner workings of the Halvarian Empire. It allowed me to get inside the minds of those who seek to conquer the world of Eiddenwerthe, as well as finally reveal several plot points lingering in the background.

The empire has had people in Merceria for years, and yes, they have been interfering in the region for most of that time. The big question, of course, is who these agents are and what positions they hold, but I'm afraid you'll have to wait for the answer to that.

This book also doesn't end with a massive battle but with a pair of relatively small-scale clashes, though it does hint at what is to come.

With Merceria now under siege, Gerald Matheson, Marshal of the Realm, will have to use all his wits to defeat an enemy that has studied his every move! The story continues in Peril of the Crown, Book 13 of Heir to the Crown.

At this time, I would like to acknowledge the hard work and dedication of my wife, Carol, who has become an integral part of preparing this tale for publication. She not only edits and promotes these tales but also assists me with handling the myriad of questions I get on social media.

I must also thank Stephanie Sandrock, Amanda Bennett, and Christie Bennett, for their encouragement, along with Brad Aitken, Stephen Brown, and the late Jeffrey Parker, whose characters live on in these tales.

Once again, My BETA team has been of great use, providing valuable feedback that has helped improve this manuscript. Thank you to Rachel Deibler, Michael Rhew, Phyllis Simpson, Don Hinckley, Charles Mohapel, Debra Reeves, Susan Young, Anna Ostberg, Mitchell Schneidkraut, Joanna Smith, James McGinnis, Jim Burke, Lisa Hanika, Lisa Hunt, and Keven Hutchinson.

Finally, I would like to acknowledge you, the reader. Your encouragement has exceeded anything I could have ever hoped for when I set out on my author journey, and you have played a key role in keeping me going. I look forward to bringing you more stories.

## About the Author

Paul J Bennett (b. 1961) emigrated from England to Canada in 1967. His father served in the British Royal Navy, and his mother worked for the BBC in London. As a young man, Paul followed in his father's footsteps, joining the Canadian Armed Forces in 1983. He is married to Carol Bennett and has three daughters who are all creative in their own right.

Paul's interest in writing started in his teen years when he discovered the roleplaying game, Dungeons & Dragons (D & D). What attracted him to this new hobby was the creativity it required; the need to create realms, worlds and adventures that pulled the gamers into his stories.

In his 30's, Paul started to dabble in designing his own roleplaying system, using the Peninsular War in Portugal as his backdrop. His regular gaming group were willing victims, er, participants in helping to playtest this new system. A few years later, he added additional settings to his game, including Science Fiction, Post-Apocalyptic, World War II, and the all-important Fantasy Realm where his stories take place.

The beginnings of his first book 'Servant to the Crown' originated over five years ago when he began running a new fantasy campaign. For the world that the Kingdom of Merceria is in, he ran his adventures like a TV show, with seasons that each had twelve episodes, and an overarching plot. When the campaign ended, he knew all the characters, what they had to accomplish, what needed to happen to move the plot along, and it was this that inspired to sit down to write his first novel.

Paul now has four series based in his fantasy world of Eiddenwerthe, and is looking forward to sharing many more books with his readers over the coming years.

# About the Author

Paul J Bennett (b. 1961) emigrated from England to Canada in 1967. His father served in the British Royal Navy, and his mother worked for the BBC in London. As a young man, Paul followed in his father's footsteps, joining the Canadian Armed Forces in 1983. He is married to Carol Bennett and has three daughters who are all creative in their own right.

Paul's interest in writing started in his teen years when he discovered the roleplaying game, Dungeons & Dragons (D & D). What attracted him to this new hobby was the creativity it required; the need to create realms, worlds and adventures that pulled the gamers into his stories.

In his 30's, Paul started to dabble in designing his own roleplaying system, using the Peninsular War in Portugal as his backdrop. His regular gaming group were willing victims, er, participants in helping to playtest this new system. A few years later, he added additional settings to his game, including Science Fiction, Post-Apocalyptic, World War II, and the all-important Fantasy Realm where his stories take place.

The beginnings of his first book 'Servant to the Crown' originated over five years ago when he began a new fantasy campaign. For the world that the Kingdom of Merceria is in, he ran his adventures like a TV show, with seasons that each had twelve episodes, and an overarching plot. When the campaign ended, he knew all the characters, what they had to accomplish, what needed to happen to move the plot along, and it was this that inspired to sit down to write his first novel.

Paul now has four series based in Eiddenwerthe, his fantasy realm and is looking forward to sharing many more books with his readers over the coming years.

.

Printed in Great Britain
by Amazon

41289121R00202